FIC   Hemingway, Amanda.
           The poison heart.

$19.45

DATE			

The
POISON
HEART

AMANDA
HEMINGWAY

SIMON AND SCHUSTER

New York   London   Toronto   Sydney   Tokyo   Singapore

FIC

Simon and Schuster
Simon & Schuster Building
Rockefeller Center
1230 Avenue of the Americas
New York, New York 10020

Copyright © 1990 by Amanda Hemingway

Originally published in Great Britain by Penguin Group

SIMON AND SCHUSTER and colophon are registered trademarks
of Simon & Schuster, Inc.

Published by arrangement with the author

Designed by Deirdre C. Amthor

Manufactured in the United States of America

1 2 3 4 5 6 7 8 9 10

Library of Congress Cataloging in Publication Data

Hemingway, Amanda.
[Viper's heart]
The poison heart / Amanda Hemingway.
p. cm.
Previously published in England as: The Viper's heart.
I. Title.
PR6058.E49188P65   1990   90-34047
823'.914—dc20   CIP

ISBN 0-671-70975-5

For Emarë

The
POISON
HEART

PROLOGUE

Rupert Van Leer, celebrated architect, knight of the realm, was buried at a church of his own design on 13th January 1987, the second day of a week that was already being called the Big Freeze. Winter in the south of England normally produces a light snow-shower, soon melted, a succession of frosty nights, and a lot of mud, but that year it had come up with blizzards and sub-zero temperatures that threatened to break all records. A handful of journalists and photographers stood outside the church, suffering. Sir Rupert's death had been covered at length in the obituary columns and the funeral promised little in the way of action. Few celebrities, they judged, would turn out in this weather. They would be reduced to resurrecting old stories: the spectre of tragedy which had dogged Sir Rupert's personal life, the youth and beauty of his grieving widow, his five-year-old confrontation with the Prince of Wales over a futuristic knitting factory in Yorkshire. The situation was not promising. They stamped their feet, turned up their collars, and refreshed themselves from hip-flasks. Everyone was miserable. No one thought to feel sad.

It was snowing again when a procession of cars began to arrive, disgorging family, colleagues and other mourners.

Among these last, an ageing Shakespearian actor, a retired union leader, a minor duchess in a sumptuous fox-fur, and an art dealer in an even more sumptuous lynx. A TV camera jammed and its operator gave vent to some very unfunereal language. The two principal mourners emerged significantly from separate Daimlers, each supported by her lawyer. Sir Rupert's widow was a diminutive figure smothered up to the ears in sable, with a small black hat shaped like a quarter-pounder affixed to one side of her head, a floss of red-gold hair on the other, and a wisp of spangled net covering her face. Little could be seen under the veil save a hint of artistic pallor and the glitter of eyes which might have been watchful. Somehow, the expensive trappings made her appear fragile and almost child-like, a faerie creature overburdened by her furs. She leaned rather too carefully on the arm of a man with a fleshy nose and a paternalistic air who proved to be Greenbaum of Schnurrer, Greenbaum and McTavish. He was the only person present who looked warm, presumably at the thought of the account he was going to render for his services. Lady Van Leer, in spite of her sable coat, seemed to be shivering.

Elsa Van Leer, the daughter of Sir Rupert's first marriage, followed them into the church. Considerably taller than her stepmother and ethereally thin, she wore her black cashmere coat and Gucci boots with the hapless elegance of someone who has never had to check a price-tag or plan a co-ordinated wardrobe. To the knowledgeable, her face was a ghostly reflection of earlier Van Leers, the nose perhaps too straight and delicate, the distinctive bone structure seemingly cast in porcelain where Sir Rupert's giant skull had been hacked unmistakably out of granite. She wore no make-up and her over-full mouth was pale, her eyes darkened with their own shadows. Her long mane of hair, the colour of dried blood, hung down her back in a luxurious tangle. Her lawyer, in marked contrast to Mr. Greenbaum, was extremely youthful, a pink-cheeked graduate with a Bourbour jacket over his city suit and the shoulders of a rugger Blue. His name was Jonathan Sterling (Jon to his friends) and he was the most recent incumbent of Langley and Mayhew, Van Leer family solicitors for more than fifty years. He walked a little way behind Elsa, watching her with covert admiration. Possibly he would have liked to offer her the support of his arm, even as the arm of the unctuous Greenbaum was offering such blatant support to her stepmother; but he could not quite summon the self-confidence to make the gesture. It was probably just as well. Elsa Van Leer did not seem to require support, or even to remember that he was there.

"Which is which?" hissed a reporter after the two women had gone into the church, evidently baffled by the similarity of age and colouring.

"The second one's the daughter," supplied a colleague with prompt comprehension. "Gets the red hair from her mother. Rupert liked redheads."

Several people wrote that down. None of them paid much attention to a couple of senior executives from the Van Leer Diamond Company or the staff of Sir Rupert's architectural practice, all of whom were devoid of news value. The man who went in last—a man of medium height in a worn sheepskin flying-jacket—attracted scarcely a glance. The fact that he did not wear black implied only a distant connection with the deceased; an acquaintance in the building trade, maybe. Nobody realized that this was the unofficial heir to the Van Leer practice, someone who had been, in the past, Sir Rupert's office boy, acolyte, apprentice, disciple. He showed neither grief nor eagerness: but then, Michael Kovacs was not given to betraying his emotions. At forty, he might have been ten years older or ten years younger. He had a pale, pock-marked, tight-featured face with the sort of ugliness that can fascinate more than any beauty. His hair was the colour of damp straw, his eyes as grey and cold as the snow-laden sky. There was a quality of secrecy in his expression, a watchfulness, a species of chill intensity which, to the observant, might have suggested some dominating passion carefully contained—ambition maybe, although his low profile did not accord with the image of an ambitious man. Inside the church he stood well to the back, on his own. During the hymns and prayers he did not speak or sing, save for one moment, close to the end, when his lips moved on the word "Amen." His gaze roamed round the building with the automatic interest of the professional. Occasionally, he looked at one or other of the Van Leer women: the widow, her head drooping like a flower on its stem, if such a fine-stemmed flower could be imagined sprouting from a collar of expensive fur, and Elsa, in her own way as solitary as he, very straight, even stiff about the neck, proud, desolate, oblivious (he thought) to those around her. It seemed to him that the widow flaunted her vulnerability while that of the daughter was desperately concealed, belied by the rigid `backbone and aloof profile. He watched for a long, still minute before returning to his dispassionate scrutiny of the architecture.

The church of St. Mary Magdalene, known locally as St. Mary-the-Whore, had been built in the mid-sixties on the site of another church of the same name which was destroyed in the Blitz. The original building had been squat, undistinguished, begrimed by the smoke of the Industrial Revolution. The new one—product of the dreams and finances of a group of municipal philanthropists—was the pride (or scandal) of the borough. Stark white walls rose to a ceiling of inverted angles; stained-glass panels of assorted shapes and sizes represented indecipherable religious concepts. Possibly Sir Rupert, an atheist at heart, saw a church in the same light as he would have seen some pseudo-classical folly in the garden of a stately manor: a frivolous, functionless monument to whimsy. Yet the building, like all religious premises, had its own solemnity. Above the altar there was a bronze of Christ on the Cross by Édouard Duny. It was neither large nor imposing, yet it seemed to dominate the church: a wasted figure, reduced by suffering or the artist's eye to the raw elements of bone and sinew and spirit, an unchristian defiance in the stretched tendons and upturned face, the straining ribs, the arch of the spine. There was nothing here of resignation or forgiveness, only the fury of despair and the mute cry of a human creature who, in his darkest hour, has lost touch with Faith. "My God, my God, why hast Thou forsaken me?" The statue created a furore when it was first shown. Yet Duny himself was a man of conventional religion, a peasant from the wine-growing valleys around Bordeaux who, after a lifetime of success, had returned there to be buried at the age of eighty-nine in the village churchyard beside his parents. The image of Christ, like all his sculpture, recalled in its tortured limbs the wind-writhen vines on the hillside where he had grown up.

Among the mourners, only Michael Kovacs thought to reflect on the significance of his surroundings. The ageing actor—who had come to the funeral in a desperate attempt to get a few seconds on TV and recall his face to public and producers—thought about his hairline and his bank balance. The retired union leader thought about his memoirs, which he rather endearingly imagined he was going to write himself. The minor duchess tried very hard to think about God and mortality but was diverted by the vaster problems of frozen water pipes and defective central heating. The art dealer thought about his boyfriend. Of these, only the art dealer achieved the expression of lofty solemnity suitable to the occasion. The building had originally been well heated but the system had been turned down due to cold-weather power shortages, and breath smoked faintly on the air. There were not enough people (or fur coats) to raise the temperature. The vicar, a conscientious man, spoke at some length. At appropriate intervals Sir Rupert's widow drooped a little more and the assiduous Greenbaum made a performance of proffering his handkerchief. Elsa Van Leer did not appear to be listening. When it was over they all rose to follow the coffin outside.

The moment came when the mourners were waiting to proceed down the aisle. Elsa and her stepmother stood face to face. Most of those present knew nothing of the two women—the dead man they had shared, loved, used, their reciprocal liking or loathing, their state of mutual grief or armed truce. Yet, though no word was spoken, everyone felt that it was a kind of confrontation. This was the first time they had actually faced each other, looked at each other. In the cold church the atmosphere grew a little colder. Elsa's abstracted mood slid from her like a cloud; her faintly slanting eyes, smoky green like dull jade, fixed the other woman with a stare worthy of a basilisk. And behind her spangled veil the widow's spangled gaze seemed to widen, though whether in fear, or shock, or anger it was impossible to tell. The air quivered with indecipherable emotions. The lawyers leapt into the breach like seconds. Elsa allowed herself to draw back, Jonathan's hand on her arm. Her profile, with its impossibly perfect nose, managed to convey a species of aristocratic contempt. The widow passed first down the aisle, but no one imagined it was a victory.

Outside, it was still snowing. The artistic front elevation of St. Mary-the-Whore was half buried under ambiguous humps and bulges of white, which might or might not bear any relation to the architect's original concept. The hardiest of the journalists waited, resigned if not patient, exchanging speculation. The contents of their hip-flasks were much depleted. "What about the will?" asked one of the tabloids. "Supposing he's left it all to the wife?" That, of course, would be a story, complete with court cases and private feud. His comrades looked wistful, if not very sanguine; Sir Rupert had the reputation of a conscientious family man. Someone wrote: "Ice Maiden Disinherited," just in case. (Elsa Van Leer, presumed heiress not only to her father's self-made fortune but also to part of a family business in diamonds, had inevitably been nicknamed the Ice Maiden.) Briefly, wishful thinking took over. Did the widow have a boyfriend? Had she ever been a stripper, or made a pornographic film? Could anything further be extracted from the dispute with Prince Charles?

The church doors opened: the coffin emerged and processed through the churchyard. Mourners filed after, the press at the rear. The waiting grave was a black hole in the whiteness of the snow. They gathered round it, the widow on one side, the daughter on the other. Lady Van Leer had recaptured her drooping-flower attitude; Elsa relapsed into her hypnotic trance. Neither of them wept. Nor, indeed, did Michael Kovacs, who owed his whole career to Sir Rupert's guidance and inspiration. Possibly it was too cold for weeping, on a day when tears would freeze on the cheek and an icy wind chilled heart and blood and bone. Maybe they would weep later, by some secret fireside where it was warm enough for the luxury of tears. Sorrow—like most obligations—is more easily fulfilled in comfort.

Nonetheless, they did not weep.

The vicar went through his final peroration with commendable speed; a handful of frozen earth and snow rattled on to the coffin lid. Across the grave, once again, the eyes of the two Van Leer women met. Elsa's lips moved, her voice—if voice it could be called—was a whisper which no journalist detected, no casual ear overheard. The fleeting vapour of her breath hung on the air a moment and was gone. Michael Kovacs looked, guessed, frowned slightly. The vicar glanced up from a posture of prayer. But the widow heard, though her ears were no sharper; in her mind she heard, and the voiceless whisper filled her hearing like a shout.

"Murderess . . ."

She hardly moved and yet her whole stance seemed to alter, as if she shrank inward upon herself, tightening every nerve, every muscle, becoming suddenly hard and wary and alert. Her lips parted: the word that escaped might have been another accusation or merely a shocked echo. *"Murderess . . ."* The press, unsuspecting, were already leaving; even the lawyers had withdrawn. Widow, daughter and heir were left alone at the edge of the grave—alone with grief, anger, suspicion, guilt, whatever it was they felt. Three isolated figures, dark against the snow.

Alone with their dead.

PART ONE

1

Rupert Van Leer was born to wealth, position, and paternal expectations.

The family fortune had originated in South Africa, where Rupert's grandfather, a red-haired, red-blooded Boer of notorious temper and eccentric habits, had discovered and excavated his own diamond mine. Bertram, the eldest son, was brought up in England by aristocratic relations of his mother and subsequently became responsible for the British end of the diamond company. He was a solid, uninspiring figure, beginning to be portly by the time he was thirty and little resembling his more exuberant ancestors: a man who thought in banknotes and dreamed in dividends, to whom the beauty of a jewel was merely a matter of carats and market value. Nonetheless, he had proved himself a true Van Leer in the First World War, when he left the business in the meek hands of an elderly subordinate and enlisted. He rose rapidly through the officer ranks, remained imperturbable under fire, and impressed his superiors if only by staying alive. The horrors of trench warfare left him cold, as did most things. In his veins, the hot blood of the Van Leers seemed to have become unaccountably chilled: if he had warmer passions no one ever discovered what they were, least of all Rupert, the belated son of his middle years. He emerged from the war with an assortment of medals and the grudging respect of those private soldiers who had survived his command. Back in civilian life, he set about growing richer and portlier. His cheeks sagged into his neck, his neck encroached on his collar, his body became a monument of expensive tailoring. A plump white slug of a man whose fat hands were a little too well manicured for respectability—but under the slug-softness, the enveloping cushion of flesh, Rupert always sensed hard strong bones, a vulcanized heart, a will of stone.

The estrangement from his father began in Rupert's early teens, but they were never close. Bertram was not a father who believed in closeness: the long-planned heir was merely another, exceptionally sensitive investment, to be nurtured by nanny and mother, by Eton and Oxford, until ready to produce the expected profits. His ambition to be an architect—an ambition which originated, according to his mother, with Rupert's first set of building bricks—was a childish fancy, unworthy of serious consideration. Rose Van Leer thought otherwise, but she was too sensible to argue before argument became really necessary, and she contented herself with quiet encouragement for her son and the avoidance of confrontation with her husband. Formerly Rose Beamish, she was a war widow who had married Bertram for convenience rather than love after his first wife died of diphtheria. It was she who had introduced the artistic strain into the Van Leer stock: Bertram, seeing art— like everything else—purely in terms of pounds and pence, thought of her as a shrewd collector; but she had a modest talent of her own, though she never exhibited her work and rarely hung it, even at home. Thanks to her tact and common sense, Rupert's childhood passed in relative tranquillity. Bertram was an aloof, awesome, omnipotent father-figure who fulfilled his duty to his offspring with the occasional cold inquisition on his school work and left his table manners to his nanny and his playtime to his mother. By the time he chose to involve himself, it was too late.

Inevitably it was Rupert who precipitated matters, long before it was necessary. At the age of fourteen it was borne upon him, first, that his father expected him to join the family business, second, that he was definitely going to be an architect,

and third—most important—that there was no way in which
these two aims could be reconciled. He flung himself into the
conflict with an energy, an enthusiasm and a violence that
might have recalled his grandfather, had Bertram been given
to such recollections. But the poetic image of his own genes
rising up against him—like most poetic images—never troubled the diamond merchant's mind. He remained chilly and
outwardly controlled, too used to issuing edicts which had always been promptly obeyed to adapt to the demands of argument. He ordained "You will do this" and "You will do that,"
met rebellion with punishment, challenge with scorn, protest
with silence. His rage was permanently bottled up, fearful in
its containment, a storm which never broke but hung over the
horizon, black and ominous, just about to rain down thunder-
bolt and lightning. Only once did Rupert remember seeing that
rage made manifest—when he was sixteen, and had refused to
attend some company function as heir apparent. Possibly by
then Bertram was beginning to realize that no matter how
many battles he might notch up, he had lost the war. That
mountain of implacable flesh shook like a blancmange in an
earth tremor, the jaws champed, fists pounded at the desk top
so that ink spilled and oak shuddered. It was, very faintly, an
echo of the battle-fury of his ancestors; but in this overweight,
elderly man it had become something both terrible and pathetic. Rupert, who feared nothing else under the sun, was,
deep down inside, just a little afraid of his father. That germ
of fear acted as the final stimulant, driving him to further extremes of fury and defiance—to outpourings of impassioned
verbiage, to stormings-out, slammed doors, sullen silences at
the dinnertable. Rose counselled patience in vain. Fortunately
for the war at home, a bigger war had started outside, and no
Van Leer ever missed a war. Rupert tried to join up, after two
of the stormings-out, at both fifteen and sixteen. At seventeen,
he succeeded. He kissed his mother, and rode off into the sunset
(metaphorically speaking) without leaving Bertram so much
as a farewell note. He never saw his father again.

Rupert was in French North Africa with the Eighth Army
when he heard of Bertram's death. Absorbed in the battle for
the Kasserine Pass, he was hardly in a position to go home. His
father, it transpired, had collapsed with a heart attack in their
country house, said to have been brought on by the imperti-

nence of a seven-year-old cockney evacuee who had escaped
from the servants' quarters. Bertram retired to his bed, attended by a couple of nurses, and succumbed to a second attack
within the week. Since he had omitted to change his will—
perhaps because he still hoped to bring Rupert to heel, perhaps
because he had lost interest in a fruitless struggle—the management of the company passed to a business partner and a
large slice of the ownership and profits to his wife and son. A
story that a deathbed demand for his solicitor (in Rose's absence) had been ignored by both the butler and the housekeeper
was never substantiated. The butler claimed age and deafness,
the housekeeper had been distracted by the evacuees and the
nurse who told the story had fallen asleep on duty. Bertram's
widow often wondered if he died of exasperation, baulked of
his last attempt to enforce a failing dictatorship.

Rupert came home in the summer of '43, now a corporal and
(unknown to the army) still some months short of nineteen. "A
fine, upstanding young man," declared the housekeeper: upstanding in fact to a height of six foot five, with his pioneering
grandfather's width of shoulder and lanky, muscular build. He
was not handsome but his face, helped by strong cheekbones,
a heavy brow and out-thrust jaw, already showed force of character. A lion's face, both feral and kingly, with a savage frown,
a ferocious laugh, and deepset eyes, intent as a hunter's. It was
scarcely surprising that the youngest evacuees dogged his footsteps, the butler produced from the depths of the cellar a bottle
so ancient that only he had known it was there, and Rose, who
was never sentimental, made unobtrusive use of a handkerchief, both proud and sorry to see that her son had so soon
become a man.

The machinery of war rolled laboriously on its way. In the
summer of 1944 came the long-awaited invasion of France.
Rupert, determined to be in the forefront of danger, had volunteered for the Paras and obtained promotion to the rank of
sub-lieutenant. He fought his way across Normandy, liberated
Belgium, Holland and anything else he found in his path, and
was eventually seconded to the American forces marching east-
ward into Germany. There were moments when he knew he
should be afraid, mostly during the periods of waiting: slow
nights before an attack, hour-long pauses in the jungle warfare
of the bocage country, dreadful pits of quiet between the thud

of shell and mortar. He would feel the familiar tingle at his nerve-endings, the exquisite knife-edge of suspense, and always the presence of Death, skulking at his shoulder, watching for that instant of false security, of dropped guard, when he would snatch his victim out of life for good. Death in the boom of the guns and the growl of the tanks, Death in the dawn and the afternoon, Death under fire, under moonlight, under the shadow of dancing leaves. Rupert lived every second with Death, played little games with him, defied him and cheated him and slipped from his grasp. His subordinates found him both terrifying and heartening: they boasted of him to their compeers, followed him in trepidation. His superiors shook their heads, raised their eyebrows, and recommended him for medals. And Rupert, relegating peacetime ambitions to some unspecified point in the future, made the most of the war while he could. He had all the family recklessness—a recklessness which had its roots, according to an unauthorized biographer, in arrogance. The Van Leers in their madness did not defy God: they scorned Him. In their hearts they believed that no fate, no doom, no mortal or immortal being would ever dare to strike them down with anything so casual as a chance bullet or stray shell. Earthquakes might rock their cradle, tidal waves might wet their feet, but Death, when he came, would come slowly, respectfully, with hooded brow and lowered sickle, waiting until his prospective victim had wrung all that his ruthless hands could possibly wring from a worn-out life.

Rupert survived the disintegration of Europe insulated against fear and vitually unscathed, protected by who knew what freak or fortune. There were many who said the Devil looked after his own.

They came to Dachau on 29th April 1945. Those who could stood up to welcome them. Others tottered, stumbled, crawled. Many lay on the ground who would never stand again. The dead were piled like garbage, naked, naked to their bones, stinking. The undead seemed like figures from some surrealist nightmare, walking skeletons grotesquely clad in striped pyjamas. They stared at their liberators like those who have lived in a darkness without God, gazing at last on a morning beyond hope or dreams. They might have wept, but their tear-ducts had long run dry. And Rupert— who had hardly flinched when his comrades fell beside him, or enemy fire singed the hair off his head—felt his stomach shrink, and his mouth dry, and his skin grow clammy. He knew he ought to feel compassion but instead there was only an overwhelming disgust. Disgust, and a sort of shame that human beings could be brought so low, deprived not simply of health and strength but of all dignity and humanity. Without having thought about it Rupert had always believed himself basically decent, civilized, a "good chap"— only now was he aware of the futility of that concept, of the true man, the beast-man, rising up inside him against all morality, half choking him with repulsion and fury. He wanted to pick up his gun, squeeze the trigger, fire and go on firing, until the last of these pariahs had fallen. And then he would bulldoze them into the ground, and bury them deep, so that the sight and the smell and the touch of them would be expunged from the earth, leaving less than a memory. The civilized part of him tried to resist, groping for the clichés of church and school, but the beast-man was too strong for him. A little way inside the camp they came upon a German guard, presumably killed by the inmates. Part of his skull was beaten in but one side of his face remained intact, a fresh, youthful face with fair curls and baby skin, the splayed body, in contrast to the prisoners, plump and rounded with health. Yet he was dead, and the corpse-creatures, unnaturally alive, hovered in his vicinity like predatory insects.

That was the moment when Rupert was actually sick.

One of his American companions lent him a handkerchief, murmured: "It's OK, Rupe" and "We all feel like that," without specifying what it was they all felt. They were men, and soldiers: it was not done to discuss their feelings. And under the circumstances, it did not seem to be necessary. They liked the big, tawny-haired, befreckled young Limey, who had seen more campaigns than any of them and who had all the reckless dash they associated with heroes and lunatics. It did not occur to them that his reactions might differ from theirs. Later, when they were able, they cursed the Nazis with those old familiar words—words that had done yeoman service on every battlefield of the war—but to Rupert, in his bitter self-awakening, they sounded automatic and insincere, a cover-up for indifference. Because he felt no compassion, compassion could not exist. Christian charity, love-thy-neighbour, and all the junk of religion and principle was an invention of dreamers, an effort to convince themselves that mankind was of a higher order than the beasts. After the war, in the general outcry over the concentration camps, Rupert heard only the bleatings of hypocrisy, self-deceivers trying to conceal their guilt because they did not really care. It seemed to him that the whole of society was bound in a conspiracy of platitudes, acting out pointless court scenes, mouthing empty protests. From that time, Rupert no longer believed in humanity, only a superior species of animal, stronger and more cunning and more terrible than all the rest. And he knew himself to be one of them.

He was sent home in 1946, after what appeared to be a bout of flu had developed into rheumatic fever. His mother drove him to the house in Surrey, the housekeeper wept over him, the butler (who was fast becoming decrepit) assisted him perilously to bed. The London house had been destroyed the previous year by a direct hit from a V-2, but fortunately Rose had moved most of her art collection into the country long before. In the sombre Victorian bedroom, with its heavy period furniture and sweeping brocade curtains, a photogram by Moholy-Nagy and an original drawing by Grosz looked dreadfully out of place, the latter bitter and cruel and all too apposite, the former full of light and space, blissfully free from any taint of humanity. One day, thought Rupert, trying to focus his mind on something pleasant, I shall build myself a house like that, all straight walls and wide windows. A sleek white modern house with no panels, no cobwebs, no stuffy brocades, very little furniture. From childhood, he had disliked his parents' Surrey home, a cheerless memorial to nineteenth-century Gothic, complete with arched windows, gables, chimneys, doors and stairways that creaked at random. It was something of a paradox that he was to live most of his life in that house.

Back in the peacetime world, Rupert reverted to the pursuit of his vocation. He studied at the Architectural Association, then joined a major practice for a year or so before setting up on his own. He was an aficionado of pure functionalism, an admirer of Le Corbusier and Mies van der Rohe, of clean lines, clear-cut angles, soaring façades of metal and concrete criss-crossed with a thousand windows—of houses without rooms, rooms without walls, walls without doors. He had learnt from

his mother to appreciate Cubist sculpture and the paintings of
Mondrian. Perhaps, in his craving for geometric outlines and
a superimposed order, he was expressing a subconscious desire
to escape or transcend his own animal nature, and all the blood-
iness, brutality and confusion of the dominion of mankind. His
waking dreams were filled with crystal skyscrapers and snow-
white caverns of virgin space. His sleeping dreams were darker
and less easy to control.

His great opportunity—that once-in-a-lifetime opportunity
that all architects dream of—arrived on the back doorstep almost by accident. He was taking a weekend in Surrey in the
autumn of 1955 when Rose informed him, by way of casual
gossip, that Josiah Stallibrass, the notorious Mean Millionaire,
had bought some land in the area and was planning to build
himself a country house. Two architects, both well established,
had already been sacked from the project for overspending.
Stallibrass had made a fortune in scrap metal before the war
and had doubled or trebled it in the property business, buying
up bomb sites, adorning them with office blocks and reselling
for staggering profits. Born in Newcastle under circumstances
of much-vaunted poverty, he had made his money too soon and
too quickly and lapsed inevitably into paranoia. Perhaps judg-
ing other people by his own standards, he believed that the
rest of the world was out to swindle him of his well-gotten
gains. He haggled with window-cleaners, under-tipped waiters,
did not tip cabbies at all and laboured under the delusion that
all professional men (such as architects) would, if allowed, take
advantage of his uneducated background by using lengthy jar-
gon and complex drawings to disguise inflated pricing and dis-
honesty. Now pushing fifty, overweight and obstinate, he had
formed the habit of making up his mind what he should pay
for a job of work (whether he understood what it entailed or
not) and refusing to go so much as a farthing higher. He had
once fired a secretary for writing a telephone message on letterhead notepaper, an example of extravagance which, he
claimed, if unchecked, would bring the company to the edge
of bankruptcy inside a month. Since the war he had been living
in an Edwardian mansion in St. John's Wood, but he had recently come to the conclusion that his prestige demanded a
country residence. Having cast an antipathic eye over worm-
eaten Tudor and draughty Victoriana, bemoaned the asking

price, the lack of facilities, the cost of installing same, and the idiocy, the latent criminality of all estate agents, his plans were unexpectedly overturned when his wife announced that she was pregnant. As she was forty-two and already had two daughters, the elder of whom was in her teens, this came as something of a shock. A sensible woman who rarely interfered with her husband's prestige, the imminent arrival of the baby stirred in her a fresh determination: for several evenings in a row she mentioned in wistful yet penetrating tones the advantage to her unborn son of modern plumbing, central heating, and the latest kitchen fittings. It was enough. Joe Stallibrass realized that his future heir could not possibly survive in some antiquated ruin: he must have a modern house. As at the same time he failed to realize why a luxury domicile designed by a fashionable architect should cost any more than a utilitarian office block which had scarcely been designed at all, this was to lead to problems.

Rupert, discussing the news with his mother, remarked casually that he would give his soul for a chance like that, and prepared to put the matter out of his mind. But the seed once sown began to germinate. Throughout dinner, Rupert's between-mouthful silences grew tense with thought, his brow furrowed, he glared fiercely at the family silver, which winked placidly back at him. In bed, he resolved to sleep on it; but he did not sleep. Over the next few weeks he prowled round the site, asked innocent questions in the local pub, worked in his own time (and some of his employer's) on preliminary drawings and estimates. Meanwhile Joe Stallibrass hired and fired two more leading lights of the architectural profession, and Mrs. Stallibrass retired to an expensive maternity clinic. On the day after she was delivered of a healthy baby boy (weight: 7 lbs. 3 oz., to be christened Anthony Charles Philip, mostly after the Royal Family), Rupert presented himself at her husband's office. Stallibrass refused to see him. The next day, Rupert came back. And the next. And the next. By this time, Stallibrass had realized that the name Van Leer was familiar to him, though he associated it with diamonds rather than architecture. Brenda Stallibrass owned a good many diamonds, mainly in very ugly settings, surrounded by excess rubies, sapphires and pearls, and worn with the emphasis on quantity rather than style. Finally, he agreed to give Rupert ten minutes.

It took Joe Stallibrass four days to study the drawings, consult his advisers, ignore them, and make a decision. "I like the lad," he told his wife, sitting in the clinic surrounded by hothouse flowers. "Tough. Determined. Got a head on his shoulders. Reminds me of myself at that age. Not one of these long-haired artistic pansies, thank God. Seems to have some idea of the value of money, too. Daresay he gets it from his father." He paused for a minute, ruminating. "Met him once, years ago. The father. Bertrand—Bertram—something posh. Cold sort of man. No *heart*." It was Joe's favourite delusion that he himself was a man of warm and generous heart, wilfully misunderstood by the rest of the world. "Rupert's all right. Ought to get married. He'll do."

He was interrupted by a yell from Anthony Charles Philip, signifying hunger. The nurse arrived on cue with a warmed bottle. "Mind you," said the proud father, jokingly, "no son of mine is going to grow up to be an architect, or any of that nonsense. If he doesn't like my company, he can build his own; that's fine by me. But I won't have him getting mixed up in Art." He sounded, had he but known it, exactly like Bertram Van Leer. However, there are worse things in life than Art. There are protest songs, and marijuana, and Socialism. A wicked fairy, bending over the cradle, smiled to herself and raised her thin black wand. Fortunately for his peace of mind, Stallibrass could not see her.

As for Rupert, he walked into Drayton Galsworthy, Architects and Surveyors, F.R.I.B.A., etc., packed his briefcase, his drawingboard, and his secretary, and left. Financed by family capital, he rented his own London office and placed the Van Leer moniker on the door in solitary splendour. And for the next year he concentrated on building for Joe Stallibrass the ultimate status symbol, managing—by a superhuman effort—to keep both his temper and his expenditure in check, counting on this one big coup to make his name. He even thanked God for the opportunity, though it was a long time since he had believed in the Deity. The house grew, and was beautiful. At least, according to some people. The avant-garde praised its pure lines, its endless windows, its *unité*. Critics condemned its crude angularity, its bleak north elevation, its elusive resemblance to an aquarium. It was a milestone in modern design, a blot on the gentle Surrey landscape. Joe Stallibrass, tutored by his architect, regarded it with a mixture of doubt and pride, while his wife surveyed the plumbing and kitchen fittings with profound satisfaction. Rupert's name was known if not made. He proceeded to build a house for himself— smaller, simpler, bare of almost everything save air and light— and in the spring of 1957 he got married.

Johanna Van Leer, née Johanna Muldoon, was the daughter of Rupert's first cousin Isobel—a relationship close enough to make matrimony questionable if not actually illegal. Rose contained her disapproval, knowing it was useless. Isobel was more vocal, but Patrick Muldoon, with an eye on the main chance, discounted his wife's objections. He had arrived from South Africa with his family in the summer of '56 to take over the management of the English branch of the Van Leer diamond business, and, finding himself caught up in company in-fighting, felt the need to consolidate his position. The marriage of his elder daughter to one of the principal shareholders could only be an asset. As for Johanna herself, she answered every question in monosyllables, listened docilely to the arguments and anxieties of her mother, and seemed (according to Isobel) to be totally under the influence of her fiancé. It was difficult to know what Johanna really thought or felt about anything, or, indeed, if she had any thoughts or feelings at all. Possibly only her sister Barbara ever tried to understand her; certainly Rupert never did. He—in common with most people—got no further than her face.

For Johanna Muldoon was beautiful, not just ordinarily beautiful but with that faultless, daunting beauty that generates its own brand of mystery—even if that mystery is merely skin-deep. She had a full, passionate mouth; classic bone structure; an arum-lily throat; a brow of marble. Her eyes, usually described as blue, changed to green with a green evening dress (such as the one she was wearing the first time Rupert saw her). Her hair was the hereditary Van Leer red—in Johanna's case a deep blood-orange colour with a golden sheen, too soft to be called metallic, too subtle for shot silk. The young men of London society found her invincible perfection a little off-putting: they admired her from a safe distance and sought instead the less rarefied company of seventeen-year-old Barbara, who had a freckled nose, a quick smile, an irregular dimple. Johanna rarely smiled. She had no wit, no conversation, no changes of expression, no expression to change. From childhood, all that had been required of her was to sit still and look beautiful. She had learned the lesson thoroughly; but it was the only lesson she had ever learned.

"I like him," she told Barbara the night she met Rupert.

Barbara stared at her. She had never heard her sister express either like or dislike for a young man before. "Why?" she asked, determined to explore the matter properly.

"He's different," said Johanna, sublimely unaware of cliché. "I know he's not handsome, but—he's *more* than handsome. He's more . . . more everything. More alive, more intense, more self-assured. When he asked me to pass him the butter, he made it sound *important*."

"Yes," said Barbara, pensively. "He did, didn't he?"

Long afterwards, remembering that conversation, Barbara concluded that it was the ultimate attraction of opposites. Johanna's personality was not so much nonexistent as unformed: Rupert, in contrast, was positive, violent, forceful. Ignorance was drawn to cynicism, compliance to aggression, tranquillity to turbulence. Possibly, somewhere beneath Johanna's immaculate façade there was even a vein of sensuality, a tiny germ of unawakened desire, which responded instinctively to Rupert's obvious physical magnetism. If so, it must have remained largely untouched. To Rupert, Johanna was the living expression of something he sought in his stark concrete fascias, his bleak visions of glass and stone: a perfection beyond humanity, form and line rather than flesh and blood, a work of art and not a woman. He treated her always with an unnatural gentleness, as though afraid that real passion might break or mar her. Yet, being human himself and therefore inconsistent, he managed at the same time to endow her with all the virtues which he had denied his fellow men: sincerity, purity, compassion, love. He would pour out his ideas to her with characteristic vehemence, taking her comprehension for granted, while Johanna, the perfect listener, agreed or prompted according to necessity. Watching her beautiful attentive face, he visualized himself spending endless evenings in such outpourings, discussing, confiding, solaced by the prospect of her wide-eyed aquamarine gaze, her immaculate symmetry of feature.

He pictured her growing older with a fading of the bright hair,
a sharpening of cheekbones, a pencil etching of lines here and
there. He had had many women, both pretty and plain, but
none with whom he had thought to contemplate the ageing
process; in most cases, he had barely registered the colour of
their eyes. Johanna, so he believed, was his first and last love.
But it never occurred to him to ask for her confidence, or seek
even a glimmering of the girl behind the face. The night she
agreed to marry him, he was filled with a sort of wonder, as if
at his own special miracle. Yet he had never seriously imagined
she might refuse.

They were married in church, surrounded by expensive floral
arrangements and a guest-list of the rich and the respectable.
Johanna wore a long train and floating veil which recalled the
wedding of Princess Elizabeth. Isobel Muldoon looked anxious,
Rose Van Leer gracious, and Patrick Muldoon openly satisfied.
Barbara flirted with the best man and drank too much champagne. Afterwards, the newly-weds departed for a honeymoon
in Venice, a location chosen largely so that Rupert could study
the surrounding architecture. In a postcard home, Johanna said
she was happy. If it was untrue no one ever found out.

Later that year, she sat for her portrait by Duny. As in his
sculpture, he tried to reduce his subject to the bare essentials
of feature and personality, using the one to illustrate the other.
It must have been a uniquely awkward approach to apply to
Johanna Van Leer. Yet, under his sweeping brush-strokes and
vehement palette knife, her face lost beauty and acquired character. The curve of the jaw became too strong, the cheekbones
too broad, the skin too white and smooth—not magnolia but
chalk. The long greenish eyes fixed themselves upon the artist
with a stare of almost animal intensity. It was the face of a
child, not wondering and innocent but raw, eager, with a child's
crudity and untutored passion. The effect (according to some
critics) was as if the artist had superimposed the qualities of
the husband on the unsuspecting image of his wife. The dress
was unimportant, a pale swirl of paint free from detail, with
a wide fifties neckline which left most of the shoulders bare;
but Van Leer diamonds were prominent, exaggerated in size
and brilliance, hanging from her ear-lobes, clasping her neck
and wrists, one huge stone dominating a slender hand like a
glittering knuckleduster. A child dressed up in the jewels of her

seniors, armoured or imprisoned, it was not clear which, in the trappings of wealth. Duny called it "La Femme aux Diamants, a Portrait of Johanna Van Leer," and was evidently satisfied with it—the satisfaction of an artist who has pulled off something that no one else will understand. Rupert hated it and the picture passed eventually to Barbara, who married an American called Richard Heydon and took it to the States with her.

By the end of '57 Johanna was pregnant. Rupert was transformed, alight with a savage happiness, a maverick lion who has unexpectedly inherited his own kingdom in the jungle. Like many people who lay claim to an indiscriminate misanthropy, he reserved a separate category for his family, directing the full force of his ardour and illusion on to an overburdened few: Johanna, whom he hardly knew, his mother Rose (when he thought about her), and now his future offspring. He did not care if it was a son or a daughter as long as it was *his* child, flesh of his flesh, the object of his violent and possessive love. Johanna herself was content to please him and appeared to accept her condition placidly enough, but Barbara thought that beneath her usual calm façade she was nervous. None of them knew that she skipped half her ante-natal classes and showed a tendency to forget medical check-ups, sitting in her new and still unfamiliar home, staring emptily out of the window, or eating rotten-ripe avocados with an unnatural voracity. The housekeeper, under orders from Rupert, spent hours combing the shops to pander to her every craving.

The accident happened only two weeks before the baby was due. They found her at the foot of the stairs, bleeding; it was never clear how she came to fall. Maybe a sudden faintness, maybe she turned her ankle, tripped, snatched in vain at the smooth and slippery banister. The stairs were open tread, after the fashion of the time; they had not yet been made illegal. An ambulance rushed her to hospital. Rupert's secretary, contacted by the housekeeper, took a little while to locate him since he was in the middle of a site inspection. It was nearly three hours before he reached Johanna's bedside.

"I'm afraid she isn't doing too well," the doctor told him, between cryptic instructions to the nurses. "We didn't realize it was twins. The tests didn't pick up two heartbeats."

Rupert said: "Twins?" without really hearing him. He could not see Johanna's face: only the heaving mound of her belly under a crumpled sheet and a spill of red hair on the pillow. It was a moment or two before he had absorbed the sight of her parted thighs and the bloodstains in between. Her limbs looked pale and ungraceful in the disorder of pain, little resembling the perfect body he had made love to so carefully. He asked the doctor: "Will she be all right?" but the doctor was busy telling him that he had a fine, healthy daughter and they would do their best to save the other baby. Rupert said: "What about my wife?" in a voice that made the doctor blanch and the nurses falter. But the mound in the bed did not listen. When he bent over her, her eyes were glazed, unseeing. Yet she was still grotesquely beautiful, though her white skin was slimed with sweat, her forehead bunched into tiny knots and creases of agony. He took her hand, but her nails were dug into her palm and her fingers would not uncurl. Time passed—a long time or a little, he did not know. Once or twice, he shouted: mostly, he was rigid and silent. Johanna made occasional moaning noises but she did not speak or seem to be aware of him. The doctors and nurses did things between her thighs which he could not see. There came a moment when her eyes opened wide—green eyes, he thought inconsequently, not blue at all but green as emeralds. She drew her breath in sharply— in the sudden hush he could hear the rasp in her throat—and then released it in a long gentle sigh. Gradually, the knots and creases in her forehead were smoothed away. The sweat evaporated from her face, leaving her skin as bland as milk. The blue-green stare grew vacant. He stood there like a figure in stone, still holding her wrist, unable to take it in.

Presently, he noticed that the doctors and nurses had not ceased their activities. He shouted at them to leave her alone but the doctor muttered something about the baby and the nurses glanced up briefly and then continued. He said again: "Leave her alone!" grasping one of the nurses by her overalls and pulling her back with such force that she stumbled. There was blood on her hands—Johanna's blood—and on her skirt and on his arm where she clutched at him. The doctor said: *"Please"* and "You *must* understand—we have to try and save the child." Rupert hit him. He fell backwards, a nurse screamed, a trolley loaded with instruments overturned with a crash. Metal rang and glass crunched. From somewhere, two men materialized—big, burly men, hospital porters. They grabbed Rupert from behind, trying to restrain him, but he was too strong for them. For a few minutes everything was chaos—bodies tangled, fists flew, feet scrabbled on the antiseptic floor. The ward sister fell against the wall with a bruised lip and an expression of outrage on her prosaic features. Rupert did not care who he hit or who he hurt. His eyes were red; spots danced in his vision. Anger without goal or meaning gnawed him, ate him, burned him up.

The bed was knocked aside in the struggle, sliding across the floor with the easy mobility of all hospital beds, but even jammed into a corner one nurse was still at work. Her cry of triumph—oblivious to all around her—stopped the fight, silenced the ward sister's flood of invective. Staring in sudden horror, Rupert saw her draw something out of the still heap of flesh which had been Johanna. Something alive and squirming and covered in blood. A monster in miniature with a huge, wobbling head and insect limbs—like a living parasite torn protesting from the corpse of its host. A repulsion deeper than thought or logic knotted Rupert's stomach. The umbilical cord was severed; the nurse turned the baby upside down and smacked its bottom. It took in its first gulp of air; hesitated; yelled. The untried voice, raw and crude and disproportionately strong, seemed to fill the world. The nurse, holding the child, negotiated the displaced furniture and came towards Rupert. She was young, with dark hair and Irish bones, and her face shone as if the posthumous birth was her own personal achievement. "See," she said smiling up at the father. "It's all right now. You have another lovely daughter."

Rupert's sickness rose in him so that he thought he would really vomit. When he finally spoke, his voice was flat and dreadfully quiet.

"Kill it," he said.

Afterwards, when assorted relations had arrived and Rupert had eventually been persuaded to take a sedative, Rose Van Leer surveyed her twin grandchildren. "They're non-identical," explained the young Irish nurse. "That one—the bigger one—she was first. What will you call them?"

Barbara Muldoon said: "Jo told me she liked Diana. If it was a girl . . ." She thought she had finished crying but now, seeing the babies, she wanted to cry all over again.

Rose said briskly: "Diana for the elder, then."

"What about the other one?" the nurse asked with false brightness, half hoping to divert Barbara from tragedy.

"I don't know," Rose murmured. And then, looking up at the nurse's earnest young face, she said: "You saved her, didn't you? That's what the doctor said. What's your name?"

"Corrigan." The girl was startled. "Elspeth Corrigan."

"Elspeth," said Rose. "That'll do."

2

Diana was a pretty baby; Elspeth wasn't. On such trifles can the course of a lifetime hang. Had Rupert, when he finally brought himself to look at the twins, seen two more or less indistinguishable cherubs, equally kitten-eyed and button-nosed, his initial repulsion for his second daughter might have dissipated. But only Diana had the requisite charms, and—unfortunately for her sister—she had them in excess. The wide-eyed kitten stare, its blue changed to green by the hospital lights or paternal fancy, the squashed rosebud mouth, curling fingers, peach-bloom bottom. There was even a tiny wisp of hair, unmistakably golden-red. In Diana Rupert saw, not a replica, but a fragment of his dead wife, a morsel of her beauty, a mystery born of her mystery, a life born of her life. In Elspeth, he saw her death. He even asked the nurses if she was deformed, so very ugly did she appear beside Diana's infantine perfection. A puckered, screwed up, scrunched up ball of flesh, with a mouth like a hole and tight-clenched fists and eyes, crying ceaselessly as though in protest at the world in which she had been abandoned. Afterwards, he dreamed of her, crawling like a worm from a widening rip in Johanna's body. One night she had grown into a monster in striped pyjamas, climbing out of her cot to go and drink her sister's blood. It took time and tact for Rose to persuade him that the babies should come home to the same nursery.

He sold the new house which he had built for Johanna almost immediately, taking the first offer. In the end, he only went back there once, leaving Rose to manage the removal of everything, even his clothes. The open-tread staircase rose up in front of him in all its bleak nudity, full of treacherous gaps, hinting at an unthinkable guilt. He never used such a stair again. Back in his mother's Surrey home, he seemed to have lost the urge to design another place for himself. He devoted his creative energies to business contracts: a controversial office block, an award-winning art gallery, a Mediterranean villa that looked like a Cubist fantasy in concrete and glass. It was at this time that he was given the commission for St. Mary-the-Whore, a commission undertaken in a spirit of repressed grief and deepening cynicism. Yet he asked to be buried there, perhaps attracted by the irony of building his own tomb, like some ancient pharaoh, and lying there at last amidst all the trappings of a religion he scorned. His home evidently meant no more to him than walls and a roof; the oppressive Victoriana which he had always hated—which he still hated, when he stopped to think about it—had become too unimportant to waste more of his time. It was left to Rose to decorate the nursery, selecting the wallpaper patterned with shamrocks, the chintz curtains, white-barred cots and Mabel Lucy Atwell prints which she considered appropriate. Rupert had assumed without asking that she would be responsible for the children's upbringing, a responsibility which she had accepted after certain stipulations. A succession of nannies came and went, no longer vintage family retainers but bright young women who knew about Spock and child psychology. Times changed. Rose knew she was no longer young, even at heart: despite the outward appearance of robust middle age she suffered increasingly from arthritis in her hands and at night she was troubled by fears which she could not ignore. She would soon be seventy; Death might be far away but he could also be perilously close, and she felt anxious for the twins when she was gone. She had tried to talk to Rupert about Elspeth, but at the mere mention of the subject something would close in his face, a shutter which she could not lift: he would hear her out without listening and turn away, indifferent. Sometimes she wondered what had become of the fearless, arrogant, ardent young man who had been her son. Now, there was a cloud upon him that was not—quite—fear, arrogance made him turn from her as from any other, his ardour was all for his work and his elder child. He would lift Diana into his arms, his eyes devouring her rumpled baby beauty, even swinging her above his head while she shrieked with glee. If Rose prompted him he would lift and swing Elspeth too, as one performing a painful duty, but there was a note in her shriek that seemed more like terror. Most of the time, it was as if he willed her not to exist. When childish misdemeanours brought her to his attention he would either be violently and disproportionately angry, or merely cold. Rose, though not naturally demonstrative, lavished both twins with her love, but the shadows of the future ended her peace of mind, and her arthritis worsened.

The cots were exchanged for beds, and Rose's own sketch of the children, executed slowly and painfully with twisted fingers, became the only one of her drawings to be framed and hung on the wall. For some reason she felt it was important to finish it, though the details were less photographic than of yore and the features of her granddaughters were partly exaggerated, partly blurred. Diana's face was round-cheeked as an apple, soft as a plum; her eyes were wide and bright; her curls all but wind-tossed. Elspeth's mouth had a droop that was meant for wistfulness, her cheeks a pallor meant for sorrow ("Sulking," said Rupert, when forced to comment). Her dark gaze was too sombre for a child, her hair a gypsy tangle. What can you do, Rose asked herself in sudden bitterness, for a girl whose father does not love her? Love cannot be commanded, cannot be compelled. It is not a domesticated plant that you can dose with fertilizer, nurture in the dark, induce into the light. Love is a wild thing which thrives or shrivels at will, regardless of the elements or the gardener's care. Rose gave of her love unstintingly, but she could not order Rupert's. The twins grew, and her heart darkened. Disillusionment set in, lines mapped her face, her nights were sleepless with a pain she would not acknowledge. By the time she knew it was cancer, it was too late.

The last thing she said, faint with exhaustion, hoarse with urgency, was "Elspeth."

"What did she say?" asked the nurse who closed her eyes.
"I don't know," said Rupert.

Elspeth's first visual memory was of the shamrocks on the
wall beside her bed. Sometimes, she thought she could remember seeing them between the bars of her cot; sometimes, in the
glow of the nightlight on the bedside table. Also on the table
was a mug of Robinson's barley water, in case she woke in the
night and felt thirsty. Barley water was good for you but
Elspeth thought it tasted horrid. Diana liked it. Diana liked
most things regardless of taste, eating or drinking whatever
was put in front of her with enthusiasm. Elspeth, said Aunty
Grizzle, was pernickety, fussy, difficult, ought to eat up her
greens, and didn't she know there were children in Africa who
were starving? Once, Elspeth had packed her leftovers in an
empty biscuit tin and had taken it to the village post office to
send away to Africa. The post lady had accepted it kindly but
Aunty Grizzle scolded. She even smacked Elspeth's arm, not
hard (she never smacked hard), but right out in the street, in
front of people, and then she insisted on telling everyone about
her stupidity, tittering contemptuously, until Elspeth thought
starvation or even torture must be preferable to public embarrassment and humiliation.

Aunty Grizzle had come to live with them after Grandma
died. The twins were nearly five: they went to nursery school
in Churston village and would be starting primary school in
September. Elspeth never remembered her grandmother except as a vague image, very small and far away, of a woman
with an upright carriage and a warm smile, her hair of that
creamy-white which, she realized years later, comes only out
of a bottle. The children knew nothing of her last illness, which
happened in hospital at a safe distance; they registered only
the cancellation of their birthday party, a brief period of absence and loss, and then—as is the way with children—change,
forgetfulness, adaptation to a new regime. Nonetheless, Elspeth
always thought it was around that time when she hid in the
cupboard. She couldn't recall why, only a faint echo of some
terrible injustice and an overwhelming misery. Not grief, but
the total, self-absorbed, self-pitying misery of childhood, when
present wretchedness seems interminable and escape incon-

ceivable. The cupboard in which she hid was under the back stairs, cramped and uncomfortable even for a very small child, and she locked herself in, by mistake or on purpose, and stayed there, according to memory, for hours and hours. She thought the whole household had forgotten her, and she would die there, unwanted, ignored, abandoned by everyone, even Smitty (the latest housekeeper) and Diana. In the end she began to scream and bang on the door, and the housekeeper let her out, and she burst into tears and was duly spanked, though spankings made little impression on Elspeth. But she always remembered being inside the cupboard: the stuffy darkness, and the thread of light around the door, and the furry black spider which shinned up her leg to keep her company. She was too young to have learnt from her timid great-aunt that nice little girls are afraid of spiders.

Aunty Grizzle (so-called at first behind her back and later to her face) was technically their great-aunt, Rose's younger sister by some fifteen years. Her proper name was Grizelda Skerritt, and she had turned up from time to time, at weddings, christenings and funerals, always in the same hat and trying rather pathetically to ingratiate herself with her grand relations. When Rose died, Rupert had suddenly noticed and found a use for her. A week later she moved in to look after the twins, wearing a new hat indistinguishable from the old one and overflowing with a gratitude that would have been tiresome had Rupert been conscious of it. He was her god, Diana her instant favourite, Elspeth obviously a "problem child," introverted, sullen, and regrettably unattractive. Grizelda herself had been a pretty, spoilt little girl and thus she believed that all little girls should be pretty and spoilt; anything else was an aberration of nature. Unfortunately, her prettiness had disappeared early, leaving behind only its attendant mannerisms. Now, she was a faded, wispy, fluttery woman, elderly before her time, alternately gushing and nitpicking, little resembling her poised and practical elder sister. An archetypal old maid, there had once—she claimed—been a Mr. Skerritt, far back in the mists of time, a clergyman of some sort who had died or disappeared bequeathing her his name and a scale of income which she thought of as undignified. In her nephew's house she liked to touch the antique silver, gloat over the Spode porcelain and Waterford crystal, pester the servants in a proprietary fashion about the care of carpets and curtains and the dusting of valuable ornaments. Rupert paid her an allowance comfortably in excess of the housekeeping and she appeared in still more new hats and, later, new dresses, each increasingly expensive as she grew more daring, and in all of which she looked exactly the same. Shortly after moving in she wrote to several friends with whom she had previously lost touch, mainly in order to flaunt the letterhead notepaper, and she gloried in secret when visitors and tradesmen called her "Mrs. Van Leer," assuming her to be some remote scion of the Family. Possibly she nourished an illicit passion for Rupert: she was the right age for such a weakness, and he was large, handsome and domineering, all the qualities she admired in a man. The twins once saw her, on being addressed as Rupert's wife (by someone who did not know Rupert, of course), blush and giggle coyly, although she made haste to deny it. Hopeless fantasy, harmless vanity—had it only been accompanied by a little humility and humour. Grizelda, however, had neither. Furthermore, it was her favourite delusion that she was fond of children. She declared she had always wanted offspring of her own, and vowed to be "like a mother" to the unhappy twins. All of which by-passed Rupert, for whom it was intended, and caused the housekeeper, Mrs. Smith, to shrug her ample shoulders. As for the twins, Diana—a resilient child who remained more or less unspoilt despite all her spoiling—learned easily to manage her; Elspeth, the "problem child," rebelled, sulked, suffered and endured.

It was an article of faith in the Van Leer household that Diana was the image of her mother. In fact, this was not true; Rupert had merely begun to superimpose the features of his daughter on the recollection of his wife, replacing a past object of passion with a present one. Grizelda, who had only seen Johanna once or twice, picked up her cue, commenting frequently on the extraordinary likeness. Actually, Diana was neither as beautiful as her mother nor as pretty as her father, great-aunt and twin sister all imagined. She had vivid red hair, clear eyes—grey with a fleck of hazel in their depths but not a hint of green— and a healthy if slightly too rosy complexion, which later on would brush through puberty and adolescence without a single spot. In temperament, Johanna had been an aloof madonna whose surface calm was the calm of innocence, hinting at depths unplumbed, emotions unaroused. Her daughter, however, was merely a child of equable humour and serene outlook, more or less happy with the world and with herself. Receiving love, she came to expect it, always sure—maybe a little too sure—that the universe was well disposed towards her, asking no awkward questions either of her conventional God or of the people around her. Perhaps she was simply too young—too young to think, too young to hurt, much too young to dispute the rules of her existence. Yet even at seven or eight years old her contentment, as much as her assurance, seemed formed, settled, the attitude of a much older child. If she had any capacity for self-doubt, for turmoil or pain, no one ever suspected, least of all Diana herself. Her trust was effortless, her courage untried, her defences non-existent. She gave love as easily as she received it: to her father, to her grandmother, to the housekeeper, to her great-aunt. But her twin came first.

In colouring, Elspeth and Diana were not unalike. Elspeth was pale, without the roses that her great-aunt considered indispensable for prettiness, her hair much darker, a rusty brown mop whose obstinate tangles and dullness of sheen resulted mainly from the fact that she screamed and even kicked or bit when Grizelda attempted to cut it or used a brush too vigorously. (Aunty Grizzle, she knew, might smack or berate her, but she would not persist.) Standing side by side, the twins looked as if one was permanently in sunlight, the other permanently in shadow. Elspeth's eyes, it was true, were green, but not the emerald green of Johanna's; hers were a dark, dark green with a core of ochre—witch's eyes (said Grizelda) that two hundred years earlier would have marked her for a changeling. Why blue-green eyes should be beautiful and yellow-green eyes wicked was a mystery which was never explained, but Elspeth accepted it and grew up with it as children do grow up believing in their first fairy-tales. Nonetheless, it was sometimes hard to live with the fact that no matter what she did, she was always bad, just as Diana was always good.

Grizelda was a great believer in the value of traditional English cooking: the meals she ordered consisted invariably of such things as roast beef and Yorkshire pudding, jam roly-poly, toad-in-the-hole. Herself as thin as a rail, she had no understanding of metabolism, blood-sugar levels, or the quirks of human biology; in her view fat people were fat because they were greedy, and fat children should be punished for their fatness, since they obviously ate too many sweets and chocolates instead of Proper Food. Accordingly, when Elspeth began putting on weight, at around the age of seven, she found that it was all her own fault, and a period of unique unfairness ensued. She liked chocolate but was no longer allowed any, since liking chocolate was an unmistakable sign of gluttony in a plump child. On family outings, when Diana, who was naturally slender, was given an ice-cream, Elspeth had to be content with an apple or a raw carrot—all of which might have done some good if at mealtimes her great-aunt had not insisted on her finishing unwanted portions of the suet, pastries and pies which she loathed, on the grounds that they were "good for you." Inevitably, Elspeth's figure grew more solid, her complexion paler. Aided by her sister, she hid bars of chocolate in her bedroom and ate them in secret, each delicious bite accompanied by an overwhelming guilt and misery which, somehow, did not deter her, but only spurred her on to further orgies of joyless greed. Once, she ate Mars bars until she was actually sick. By the age of ten, her face was as round as a dumpling and more or less the same colour, her plump mouth fixed in a habitual expression of sullenness. Diana's features mirrored every transient emotion, but Elspeth's did not seem to mirror anything very much beyond a certain stubborn blankness which Grizelda, not without reason, invariably interpreted as insolence. Overweight children often appear bland and pancake-faced, flesh masking feeling: it takes time and lines to reveal unhappiness. Elspeth's feelings were deep, but only her sister ever realized.

Born with a capacity for passion which came, no doubt, from her more red-blooded ancestors, Elspeth loved or hated with an intensity which precluded any half shades. She loved Smitty, who was sorry for her and sometimes saved her a forbidden biscuit, and Josh the gardener who helped her to hide a pet toad in a box in the shed. She hated her great-aunt, while absorbing all her teachings: convinced of her own ugliness, gluttony and innate wickedness, she gave herself up (as she thought) to total evil, hating with all the strength and fury of her suffering heart. Once, she made an effigy from a wax candle, decorating it with a paper flower from one of Aunty Grizzle's hats and a clot of hair stolen from her brush. She stuck it full of pins, plunged a darning needle into its torso, and put it in the oven, where it was found by Smitty when the wax had begun to drip on the casserole beneath. Smitty called her "wicked" too, as if she needed confirmation, and said she would have to tell her aunt unless she promised on her honour not to do it again. Elspeth promised with her fingers crossed behind her back, and Smitty did not tell.

However, it was for her two greatest loves that Elspeth endured the most. She shared with her sister that inexplicable bond which generally occurs between twins: absolute loyalty, instinctive understanding, wordless communication that borders on telepathy. But in Elspeth's case that unquestioning love was turned to torment by a seed of jealousy which she knew to be wrong but could not suppress. All those things in Diana which she loved she also envied: the brightness of her hair, the bloom in her cheeks, her popularity, her friendliness, the affection she inspired—apparently without effort—in everyone around her. And the bitterness of her envy sharpened her love, making it both a pleasure and a pain; she would watch her sister, sometimes, in an agony of confused emotion. But the worst torture was seeing her father with Diana. For Elspeth loved her father more than anything in the world, with a desperation that only unrequited love can produce, and it tore her apart to see him looking at Diana, a savage adoration in his lion's face—Diana, who took love so lightly, so carelessly— while she, Elspeth, would have given her soul for a few crumbs of his tenderness. She was like a worshipper at the altar of an indifferent god, waiting in vain for a miracle, seeing the form of her deity among the stars and praying without hope that one day he would bend down and touch the earth. She learned early that love feeds upon pain, growing strong with its own afflictions—indeed, she could not imagine a love that grew in any other way, never having known the love of normal children, love uncomplicated, love untainted, love without guilt and anguish and the savour of wormwood. All her favourite stories were of those rejected by the people they loved, yet who triumphed in adversity through the greatness of their sacrifice: the little mermaid, dancing on knives for a prince who did not care; Sydney Carton, mounting the steps to the guillotine; Iphigenia at Aulis, laying down her life for her father's war. She dreamed ceaselessly of winning Rupert's love—by some improbable act of heroism, by the revelation of a hitherto unsuspected genius, by becoming, somehow, more like Diana. But he never noticed either achievement or failure, and the fury of her longing remained a secret in her own heart.

Diana was dimly conscious of her twin's hoarded misery, but it was many years before she began to comprehend the cause. Initially she accepted a predilection for unhappiness as a part of Elspeth's characer, as natural to her as the colour of her eyes or the tangles in her hair. Occasionally she tried to help her, to put right that vaguely sensed wrongness in her childhood world; but all too often these attempts ended in disaster. The worst instance occurred at dancing classes, when the twins were nine. Elspeth hated dancing classes. Size made her self-conscious; self-consciousness made her clumsy; and the scorn of the other children, real or imagined, tormented her soul. The dancing mistress encouraged her in the hearty tones of a jockey urging on an inferior horse. "Keep that leg straight, Elspeth—*straight*. Point that toe! I know you can do it. Watch Diana."

Elspeth duly watched Diana. In fact, her twin was not particularly graceful, but she looked pretty, tried hard, and the guaranteed praise of her family had made her free from embarrassment or the spectre of failure. "You can do it," Diana would insist in a childish echo of her teacher, only with far more confidence. "Pretend—pretend you're Margot Fonteyn."

It was hopeless. Deep inside, like so many little girls, Elspeth ached to be Margot Fonteyn—to be a fairy creature in a dress like a wisp of frozen mist, with muscles of steel and feet of gossamer, floating from arabesque to arabesque like a zephyr. Her own un-zephyr-like movements were more of a torture to her than the derision of the other children.

"Of course, if you weren't such a little podge . . ." Aunty Grizzle said after watching a succession of ungainly pirouettes.

"She's not a podge!" Diana said loyally. And, to Elspeth: "Don't mind her. We'll show them—we'll show all of them! I've got an idea."

At the end of each year there was a full-costume dancing display where besotted parents were invited to watch their little darlings perform. In the past, Elspeth had always managed to hide in the crowd or at the back, her efforts limited to a few simple steps and a quick retreat. This time, the older

girls were doing an extract from *A Mid-summer Night's Dream*
and Diana, offered the part of Moth, suggested brilliantly that
her twin should dance Mustard-seed. By the time Elspeth de-
murred it was too late. Rupert Van Leer was the Great Man of
the neighbourhood, Diana the class favourite: she had her way.
"It'll be all right," she told her sister with unquenchable assurance. "I'll help you. We'll practise and practise . . ." Elspeth,
still nurturing a tiny dream of one day becoming a ballerina,
allowed herself to be persuaded. They rehearsed in secret, in
Diana's bedroom (they had had separate bedrooms since the
age of five), with the door barricaded against any invasion by
Aunty Grizzle. Diana was exuberant; Elspeth painstaking.
Diana bounced; Elspeth thumped. When they were ready, they
staged a preview in the kitchen for Smitty and Josh, and were
rewarded with applause and chocolate biscuits. Then the big
day came. Diana looked endearing, if not very lepidopterous,
with her flaming hair and spangled green wings. Elspeth's yellow tights wrinkled around her stomach. They waited by the
door, Elspeth feeling actually sick with nerves. On the make-
shift stage Titania, very grown-up in real blocked satin pumps,
balanced precariously *en pointe*. A beckoning gesture: and they
were on. Both twirled, curtsied, and paused, left leg extended,
right arm curved, ready for the next part. In the subsequent
lull Elspeth, too close to the audience, heard a whisper, a hasty
shush, a snigger.

"Looks more like a goblin than a fairy, if you ask me." Someone's father, dragged along against his will, forgetting, as adults
so often do, that children are neither deaf nor insensible.

"Like one of those hippos in *Fantasia* . . ."

"Miss Morrison would have chosen Deborah, but of course,
the Van Leer twins get whatever they want . . ."

And, worst of all: "Oh, the *poor* child . . ."

Elspeth's curved arm drooped, her left leg began to wobble.
Shame made her feel hot and cold all over. How could she ever
have dared to dream of becoming a ballerina? She was there
only on sufferance, because of Diana. Everyone was giggling,
sneering at her, feeling sorry for her. The next part of the dance
began and Diana went blithely into her routine. Elspeth just
stood there, one arm still half lifted, stuck in the sagging remnants of her pose like a puppet abandoned by the puppeteer.
Her feet seemed to be glued to the floor. "Come on!" her twin

urged in stage whisper. "Like we rehearsed. You know you can
do it." But Elspeth could not move. A tear trickled down her
tight little face, followed by another. In the audience, there was
a shifting of restless bottoms, a muttering of dissatisfied voices.
Parents of rival children looked pitying or superior, according
to temperament. The dancing mistress forgot her stock optimism and covered her eyes with her hand. Titania looked
peeved. "Please, Elspeth!" Diana hissed in anguish. *"Please
try!"* Elspeth could only shake her head. Diana finished her
dance too fast for the pianist, ran to her sister, and led her off
stage. In the back row Rupert, who had left work early especially for the performance, sat with clamped mouth and jaw
of iron. Beside him Aunty Grizzle twittered, grumbled, sought
for excuses and condemned the culprit all in one breath.

"It doesn't matter," Rupert said, briefly unclamping rigid
muscles. Obviously, it mattered. Aunty Grizzle, feeling herself
unjustly blamed for Elspeth's shortcomings, groped for her
handkerchief. Rupert did not notice. Much later, when it was
all over—Aunty Grizzle's jeremiad, Rupert's abrupt censure,
the tears, pleas, recriminations—the twins sat in Elspeth's
room, side by side on the bed. Elspeth had been sent upstairs
supperless, her taut silence an exact mirror of her father's, had
he but seen it. Diana, who had done most of the weeping and
all of the pleading, picked at her food and sneaked up later
with a couple of biscuits from Smitty. "I don't want them,"
Elspeth said. "I'm not hungry." Her stomach seemed to be full
of misery, knotted and twisted inside her into a huge lump of
confused pain. She sat with her knees bunched against her chest
and her arms locked around them in a semi-foetal position,
tense as a bundle of wire. Presently, she asked her sister: "What
time is it?"

Diana consulted her watch, a recent birthday present.
Elspeth had one too—she invariably got what Diana wanted
for Christmas and birthdays—but hers was broken.

"Twenty-three minutes past ten."

"I've made up my mind," Elspeth said. "I'm going to run
away. I can't bear it any more."

She did not ask if Diana was coming with her. Diana did not
offer. She saw Elspeth through a fog of love and doubt, vaguely
aware that "it" was not just the dancing display: "it" was
something invisible and incomprehensible, looming over them

like a cloud. The shadow of last week and the storm warning tomorrow; the nightmare that you cannot quite remember; the moon turning black.

She said: "Tonight?"

Elspeth nodded. "Very late," she added. "When everyone's in bed. After midnight."

Diana asked: "Where shall we go?"

If Elspeth noticed the "we," she did not say so. In little things—small mischiefs, conventional ploys—Diana was the leader. But in rarer, more reckless exploits, it was always Elspeth who took charge. Either way, where one led, the other followed. It was an unwritten law.

"We'll go to America," Elspeth decided. "To Aunt Barbara." She knew little of her Aunt Barbara and less about America, but it sounded sufficiently exciting and far away. Their escape acquired purpose, and with purpose, reality. They began to make plans.

"We can walk to Newhaven," Elspeth said, "and stow away on a ship."

"Ships from Newhaven don't go to America," Diana pointed out. "They only go to Dieppe."

"That's passenger ships. Merchant ships go everywhere. Don't you remember, when we went to see the harbour with Daddy, there was a ship from Sweden, and one from the Gulf?"

"Where's the Gulf?" Diana queried.

But Elspeth didn't know.

"Anyway," she said, "there'll be a ship to America. There *has* to be."

Her sister returned to her room and, without further consultation, they packed a few things into their school satchels: some chocolate, Smitty's biscuits, spare sweaters, what little pocket-money they hadn't spent. Diana took a toothbrush and her favourite doll; Elspeth a battered copy of *The Hobbit* and, by some sort of sibling intuition, a face flannel, so that between them the twins could manage a proper wash. Still dressed, they curled up in their separate beds, in case Aunty Grizzle should look in to say goodnight. Diana fell asleep but Elspeth lay wakeful until the house was quiet and the hands of her clock crept towards twelve. There was a great weight pressing on her— the consciousness of her own wrongdoing, maybe, or that intangible "it" which she could no longer bear—and for that night, that hour, she believed if only she could get away not just the weight of her sorrows but her very self would be left behind, sloughed off like a skin and left to wither in the abandonment of her old life. She woke her sister and they stole downstairs and out into the dark.

It was a fine summer night, a night of teeming stars and the many-fingered shadows of trees. At first, the twins felt excited and adventurous. They set out in what they hoped was the right direction for the coast, satchels on their backs, ducking out of sight beneath the hedge whenever they saw a car approaching. Gradually, Churston was left behind and the night-time silence of the countryside closed about them. Now and then they paused to listen, uncertain of the darkness and the waiting hush all around; but they heard only the faint sound of a slumbering wind, the footfall of a leaf astray on the road, the voiceless murmur of the grasses.

"It's awfully quiet," Diana whispered. She didn't say so, but she sounded frightened.

"It's all right," Elspeth said, answering the feeling, not the words. Her twin's fear made her bolder: for the first time she knew she was the braver and stronger of the two. For a brief instant, it was as if she had discarded the shy, awkward exterior and become instead, not someone else, but the self she had always dreamed of, the self who had hidden so long at the back of her personality. She belonged to the night, to a magical world of shadows and stars: she was in her element.

Towards morning the wind changed: dawn was a swift spill of gold under a brow of cloud. With daylight and weariness Elspeth's oppression returned; under the spell of darkness everything had seemed possible, but in the dreary morning she realized America was too far, her Aunt Barbara almost a stranger. She shrank in upon herself, becoming once again a fat little girl whose dreams were too big for her. In her heart, she knew they would have to go back.

At around nine, they sat down on a bank and ate the biscuits. "I'm so tired," Diana said. "Couldn't we—can't we go back now?"

"I'm never going back," Elspeth said doggedly.

About an hour later a police car picked them up and drove them home. Rupert hugged Diana; Aunty Grizzle cried; everyone scolded, even Smitty. And Elspeth, blamed—for once with reason—for the entire escapade, was locked in her room for a day and deprived of pocket-money for a month.

When they were eleven years old the twins were sent to separate schools. Elspeth might be less popular than Diana but she was much more academic, and it seemed only natural that she should help her sister with her homework, even do it for her on occasion, just as Diana would defend her in the playground from classmates who teased her about her weight or other juvenile shortcomings. When teachers endeavoured to convey all this to Rupert during the course of a Parents' Evening they were slightly startled by the results. Rupert could not believe that his adored Diana would "cheat," any more than he could accept her intellectual inferiority. She obviously needed "special attention"; Elspeth was a "bad influence," "holding her back"—with Grizelda's assistance he found an assortment of useful clichés to conceal his prejudice even from himself. The teachers were evidently presumptuous idiots; how could they profess to understand his daughter better than her own family? (He always thought of Diana as *his daughter*, singular, without reference to Elspeth, whom he tried never to consider in terms of their relationship at all.) Accordingly, Diana was sent to an expensive boarding school in Kent and Elspeth was left at the local comprehensive. Inevitably it was Elspeth who minded the separation the most.

Diana missed her twin, but she adjusted quickly, wrote infrequently, and soon learnt to be happy in her new school. Brayfield was a beautiful old house in the country, rambling in both size and style, mellow brick overhung with Virginia creeper, surrounded by a clutch of outbuildings and a patchwork of tennis courts and set against a backdrop of rolling downs. The younger girls were promenaded at weekends, two by two, in pinafores and panama hats, held midnight feasts in the dormitories and had violent "pashes" on the older girls. The older girls shinned up and down the Virginia creeper, played tennis on the tennis courts and truant in the village, and sunbathed naked on an area of flat roof which could just be seen (through binoculars) from the boys' school some two or three miles away. The usual amount of work got done and the usual number of exams were passed. Diana fitted in easily, as she would have fitted in anywhere. She was a little late having her first "pash," but in her second year she duly fell in love with the daughter of a South American millionaire, seen on the tennis courts with long bronzed legs and flying black hair. Diana saved her tuck for her idol, received a chaste kiss on the lips behind the gym, and spent several sleepless nights in the tremulous ecstasy of new-found emotion. It wore off in due course, to be replaced by similar passions for Robert Wagner and Clint Eastwood, but she was left with the residual belief that black hair and brown skin were the most attractive combination in the world. Her own looks she accepted, without any particular self-admiration; she knew she was pretty, but she reserved her appreciation for the cheekbones of Sophia Loren, the petite features of Audrey Hepburn, the long blond hair of Brigitte Bardot—anything, in short, that was different from herself. However, comfortable as she was with her own inadequacies, she knew nothing of the agonizing jealousies and heart-rending imperfections that tormented her sister.

On her fourteenth birthday her father gave her a pony. Several of the girls had ponies stabled at Brayfield, in addition to the dozen or so actually owned by the school; the extensive grounds contained all the facilities for pupils to learn to ride, jump, and fall in comparative safety. Diana asked for riding lessons but she did not dare to ask for a pony: she had been given, in the past, a hamster, a pair of angora rabbits, a bicycle, and grown-up leather boots with two-inch heels, but all these things seemed trivial compared with the wonder and the responsibility of a pony of her own. She hoped, but she did not ask. When the pony duly materialized, she accepted it with all the incredulous delight of a child who had never had a present in her life—or never one comparable to this. She was spoilt, it was true, but not sufficiently spoilt to have become blasé. The pony was grey, dappled like the rocking-horse she and Elspeth had shared in the nursery, with a tousled mane, a sweeping tail, and liquid eyes under curling Disney eyelashes. Diana called him Moonshadow, and loved him with the same wholehearted passion her less prudent sister reserved for unreceptive humans. The sight of his velvet muzzle and silver-strippled flanks filled her with a strange, hungry pain; the feel of his body between her thighs aroused in her vague, semi-sexual longings which she did not understand. He was the centre of her world;

only twice in her life would she be so totally in love. When she rode him she knew a sense of freedom that was entirely new to her, a feeling of power, of exhilaration, of communion with a fellow spirit which became somehow a conscious step in her teenage development, as if her soul was being daily uplifted and extended. And so very gradually she came to realize that in other respects she was not perhaps as free as she had once believed. The discipline of Brayfield did not worry her, but at home she began to be conscious of more subtle constraints. School gave her perspective: every term she was growing up in leaps and bounds, every holiday she was transformed, every homecoming she saw with new-opened eyes. Her father's preference, formerly almost unconsidered, started to trouble her a little, and the overpowering nature of his love became a burden on her heart—slight, almost imperceptible, but nonetheless a burden.

Elspeth had no such burdens to bear. When her twin was away she suffered in loneliness, without the pressures of being loved. It was something of a paradox that Rupert, in his anxiety for Diana's welfare, had sent away his favourite daughter and kept the one he did not want at home. But if Elspeth had ever dreamed of some sort of a rapport she was disappointed. In term-time, Rupert merely worked harder, returning home late or not at all and scarcely seeing either her or her great-aunt. Smitty had recently retired and Elspeth and Grizelda were thrown upon each other's company, sitting down to supper of an evening on opposite sides of a wide table, staring in uncomfortable silence across a bleak expanse of linen. If there was a war of nerves, Elspeth always won. After a few minutes Aunty Grizzle would invariably succumb to the temptation to nag, or prattle, or find fault, hardly pausing to swallow or draw breath, as though she dreaded the deathly hush that would supersede the moment she stopped her busy clucking. And Elspeth would hear her out, unresponsive, her face wearing the stony expression that only a fat child can achieve, eating little—she ate later, in her room, crisps and chocolate from a secret hoard under her bed—just sitting there, as their great-aunt said, like a lump. She looked like a lump, she felt like a lump, and she hated Aunty Grizzle and the whole world, herself most of all. And so she indulged her furtive greed, growing lumpier and more wretched every day, inflicting a futile revenge on her own body, her existence, everyone who had to put up with her. A vicious circle, and she knew it, but it didn't help.

Churston Comprehensive had none of the amenities of Brayfield. No panama hats, no midnight feats, no Virginia creeper, and the boys were in the same classroom instead of at another school a few miles away, something which inevitably made them less exciting. However, the teachers did their best, and Elspeth, fortunately for her, was bright enough not to need much in the way of instruction or application. Her art master, Mr. Scofield, was particularly interested in her. She knew she ought to have a crush on him, since it was appropriate to have a crush on the art master, but although comparatively young he was balding, bespectacled, and superficially weedy, with an intense, boiled-gooseberry stare and a nose that reminded her of a snout. Just the same, after a few words of praise and encouragement from him she tried very hard, convincing herself of his beautiful soul and the unimportance of external appearances. After all, what right had she, in all her ugliness, to expect to fall in love with a really good-looking boy—let alone to be loved in return? She even showed him some of her poetry, a privilege normally accorded only to Diana. And one day, working late, she confided in him how much she hated being fat and unattractive. He told her that looks were unimportant, and promptly launched into a long lecture on the artist's search for the perfect model: da Vinci and his Gioconda, Botticelli's Simonetta Vespucci, Andy Warhol and Marilyn Monroe. He himself would have liked to paint Helen Asher, in the Lower Sixth, but only for the line of her jaw. Elspeth went home, cried for half a minute, and expunged him without difficulty from her heart.

In her teens, the semi-sexual sensations which Diana obtained on horseback Elspeth experienced on the pillion of a motorbike. She took to wearing a tasselled leather jacket and regrettably tight jeans, seeking to conceal beneath layers of sweaters a spare tyre of Michelin-man proportions, somewhere between squeezed-in hips and unsupported bosom. Her face had lost a little of its dumpling roundness, but any improvement was disguised under purple lipstick and black eyeliner, disheveled hair and a nasal stud. Even the nasal stud failed to draw the attention of her father. She tried swearing in front of her great-aunt, who was easily shocked, but nobody made any

serious attempt to discipline her. Grizelda found it less bother
to complain about her than to do anything, and Rupert—as
ever—did not care. She rode around at night with a band of
local thugs, who terrorized law-abiding citizens by revving
their bikes too loudly in sleepy village streets, gate-crashing
barn dances, and omitting to shave. Sometimes, she came home
drunk or stoned and barely able to stand. Once, she was sick
in the living-room, and spent half the night shampooing the
carpet. No one woke up. No one ordered her to her room. No
one noticed. She made her way upstairs, clinging to the bannister for support, and lay down on her bed in the spinning
darkness. The next day, only the cleaning lady asked her if she
was feeling better.

Elspeth was thirteen when she had her first encounter with
sex. In fact, it was hardly an encounter, little more than a touch,
a brush, a flicker of awakening hormones; but it disturbed her
in a way she was to remember for a very long time. It happened
one weekend in the summer when her father and Aunty Grizzle
had gone to Brayfield for Diana's Sports Day, and a student
arrived from the London office with some papers which (he
said) Rupert required before the following week. The Van Leer
practice took students now and then, if they were exceptionally
bright, usually with a view to possible employment after they
qualified. They were supposed to be overawed by the prestige
of such a celebrated firm, to worship Rupert like a guru—and
to run errands, make tea, and perform without complaint a
succession of menial tasks that often had little to do with architecture. This particular student was in his early twenties
with a face too old for his years and an air of implacable reserve.
He said his name was Michael O'Hara, but he did not look
Irish. Elspeth thought him almost as ugly as Mr. Scofield (he
who had been recently expunged), and wondered how anyone
ever managed to fall in love when the world was so full of
unattractive men. However, in the absence of her great-aunt
she was willing to exhibit her good manners, and she invited
him in, made a pot of tea with too many teabags, and at his
request agreed to show him round the house.

"I'm surprised," he remarked thoughtfully, halfway down
the back stairs, "your father doesn't choose to build himself
something a little more . . . modern."

"He likes this place," said Elspeth erroneously. "It belonged to my grandma."

"Is she dead?"

"Yes."

"And—your mother?"

"Yes."

He had reached the foot of the stairs ahead of her; now, he turned unexpectedly to look up into her face. She found herself thinking that his ugliness was different from the ugliness of Mr. Scofield, though she could not define exactly how. The surface of his skin was pitted like rough stone, his eyes were stone-grey, his fair hair long and lustreless after the fashion of the early seventies. When he spoke, she was suddenly conscious of his voice—a voice both abrasive and caressing, coarse as sandpaper, smooth as velvet.

He said: "You must be lonely."

She wanted to move but her feet seemed to be glued to the floor. There was an unfamiliar sensation in her lower abdomen, both a yielding and a tension. She said staunchly: "I've got my twin."

He waited.

"Daddy loves me." She always told people her father loved her, as if repetition would make it true. Or maybe she felt the truth would be an act of disloyalty.

"Does he?" The aloof gaze seemed to be assessing her with a horrible intimacy, her fatness, her plainness, the latent truculence of her mouth. Maybe she imagined the faint satisfaction in his eyes. He said: "Tell me about your twin."

"She's pretty," Elspeth declared loudly. "Not like me."

"Pretty." He sounded almost amused. He came towards her, tilted her face to the light. His fingers were blunt and strong, not the tapering artistic fingers she had always associated with her father's profession. "There are bones behind that face," he said. "One day, they'll begin to show. Perhaps they'll be interesting bones. Perhaps even beautiful. One day, you'll look in the mirror, eat celery for a fortnight, and grow thin. You'll buy yourself expensive clothes—some of them may even suit you. Now, you look like plasticine, unshaped. Pretty—ugly—pretty ugly—those are just the words of the moment. They won't last. How old are you?"

"Thirteen."

"Thirteen. In ten years' time we may have some idea how

you're going to turn out. All this"— he pinched her cheek, painfully —"this is merely the chrysalis. Who knows what kind of a butterfly it may hatch?"

Elspeth just stared at him. She could find nothing to say. Neither friend nor stranger had ever spoken to her like that in all her life.

"In ten years' time," he added, "I might even want to kiss you."

He was very close to her now: she could see the gritty texture of his skin, the scant, mousy lashes fringing his wintry eyes. She could not bring herself to look at his mouth. His fingers released her chin, sought the pulse in her throat. There was an instant—a heartbeat—an intake of breath—when his lips touched hers in a kiss as soft as a whisper, his hand cupped her breast in the ghost of a caress. She stood paralysed, engulfed in a chaos of conflicting reactions: shock, disgust, terror, a humiliating urge to wet her knickers. But even before she had rediscovered movement he had let her go. He drew back to a polite distance, watching her with the trace of a smile which she promptly labelled satanic. "Don't be afraid," he said. "I can wait ten years. Or thereabouts."

Her pulse began to decelerate as though responding to his will. Fear oozed out of her, leaving behind indignation and doubt. She led the way back to the kitchen without a word, stubbornly determined to maintain control. "Daddy will be back soon," she informed him with a confidence that was founded on nothing whatsoever.

The house was empty apart from themselves, and Josh, in the garden, might not hear if she screamed; he was growing very deaf. In any case, she couldn't scream: it would be weak, childish, and cowardly—and what would she say? Already she felt like an accomplice in some unspecified crime. Still resolutely grown-up, she enquired with stiff attention to duty whether he would like a drink.

"Yes, please." She didn't know whether to be frightened or annoyed at the lingering amusement in his tone. "Whisky. If you'll join me."

"Yes," she snapped. "I will." She didn't quite say *So there.*

Her hand shook when she poured the drinks but it wasn't from fear. He sipped his, she sipped hers, trying to imitate his self-possession. It tasted incredibly nasty, even nastier than it smelt. Michael O'Hara seemed to guess, but all he said was: "Where is your twin now?"

"At school," Elspeth explained. "She's at boarding school. I'm not."

"Maybe," Michael said, "your father loves you best. Maybe . . . he couldn't bear to send you away."

She nodded, wordless.

He turned the glass in his blunt, strong fingers. Peasant fingers. "Don't grow into just another poor little rich kid," he said absently, "will you?"

By the time her father and Grizelda came home he had gone. "Looks like your father may be late," he had remarked after an interminable half-hour of whisky and silence. Elspeth was sure he was mocking her but fortunately she was not prone to blushing. Her heart thumped uncomfortably while he got to his feet, smiled down at her (the satanic smile again), murmured: "Aren't you going to show me out?" She followed him to the door and wished him an awkward goodbye. When the door was shut behind him she ran to the window and peered out, possibly to reassure herself that he had really gone. He was walking down the driveway but he stopped suddenly, turned, and stared back at the house for a long minute, as if he knew she was watching him.

She lost her virginity three years later, after the advent of motorbikes and young men in leather jackets had further bestirred her hormones. In the end, however, it was an act performed less out of lust than curiosity, rebellion, pique. She knew it would shock her great-aunt, she hoped it would shock her father, although she never seriously considered telling either of them. She told her twin, of course: she told her twin everything, except, for some unspecified reason, about Michael O'Hara. She didn't tell Diana quite how hurried it was, in a back bedroom at somebody's party with wet coats on the bed and people banging on the door every five minutes and her partner grunting and smelling of stale beer. She felt embarrassingly conscious of her spare tyre, but he was too drunk to be particular and she wasn't drunk enough. And it hurt. Nothing she had read, nothing she had learnt from her friends at school had prepared her for so much pain. She bit his shoulder to keep herself from screaming; if he noticed, he probably thought it was passion. "Relax," he murmured automatically, jabbing something that felt as hard and unfriendly as a wooden club at the entrance to her body. Somehow he forced himself in and then proceeded to batter away at her until at last he had jerked, grunted, burped and sighed his way to orgasm. The sudden gush of semen soothed her raw and bleeding flesh; she trusted he was right about her "safe" time, and wondered if she ought to go on the pill, and whether it was worth it, just for this.

"It didn't hurt for *me*," Diana said later.

Diana had lost her virginity to Moonshadow during a particularly vigorous canter when she was fifteen. Matron had dealt with her bloodstained underwear, and, being a sensible woman, had told her not to worry. She lost it all over again the following spring to a young man from the neighbouring boys' school called Nigel, with whom she was declared to be "going steady." He had blond hair, a soft chin, and a mouth—according to his admirers—like David Essex. Several of the girls were in love with him, so there was a certain cachet in ensnaring him in a stable relationship, if only for half a term. Nigel was ideally equipped for painless defloration since he had a very small prick which could slip in and out of the relevant orifice virtually unnoticed. Diana found her experience with him at first mildly titillating, later boring (secretly, she still preferred her pony), but relatively harmless and free from trauma. Traumas seemed to give Diana a wide berth, perhaps aware that she was unsuitable material.

She went out on a succession of dates with Nigel, usually via the Virginia creeper and accompanied by his friend Terry and Terry's latest, the girl from the tobacconist's. Without conscious snobbery it made Diana feel very socialist and decadent, going out in a four with the tobacconist's daughter. Her name was Nicky and she had a Reputation. The boys said she was "hot stuff" and the girls said she was tarty, all of which gave her, in Diana's eyes, a certain seedy glamour. She was not particularly pretty, having straight dust-brown hair and the unhealthy pallor of someone who does not get enough exercise, but there was a curious fascination about her huge grey eyes, set very far apart, and the small colourless mouth that could widen into an unexpectedly dazzling smile. She wore too much make-up for a "nice" girl and her skirts were very short, although the mini was going out of fashion by then, but Diana found her conversation amusing if slightly shocking and even declared to her classmates (though not to Nigel) that she liked her. This was just as well, since dates with Nigel would not otherwise have been very entertaining. The four of them usually went to a local pub much frequented by under-age drinkers, where the boys played the fruit machines and watched out for marauding schoolmasters, and the girls sat in a corner talking about the boys. Once they went to a cinema, but the film was not one Diana wished to see. Sex normally happened in the bedroom above the tobacconist's when Nicky's mother was out (she didn't have a father), taking turns on Nicky's bed or the sitting-room floor. On the last occasion Mrs. Simpson came back early when they were still upstairs, and looked at Diana afterwards in a way that made her feel dirty, and shouted at Nicky behind a closed door so the others could hear the tone but not the words. Later, Diana was surprised to see Nicky did not appear to be much upset; possibly she was used to it.

Diana's final date with Nigel ended abruptly when, daringly patronizing a pub in the next village, the boys spotted the games master in the public bar. They escaped through a side door without the formality of a farewell, and the girls were left to make their way home as best they could. The four of them had planned to share a taxi, but Nicky and Diana did not have enough money on their own and, after making enquiries, they decided to catch a bus. The bus-stop was on a quiet stretch of road some fifty yards beyond the village, set in a lay-by and equipped with a shelter that leaked when it rained. In due course, it rained. They waited over an hour for a bus that did not materialize. A man came past who looked (Diana thought) like a potential molester of unaccompanied girls; he stopped and stared at them, but when Nicky giggled he blushed and went away. Diana had been thinking mostly how angry she was with Nigel, but suddenly she was conscious of feeling close to her companion in a way she had never done before, as if the two of them were really friends, equals, instead of the rich schoolgirl and the tobacconist's daughter, thrown together by circumstances. When Nicky suggested they should hitch, Diana doubtfully agreed. Nicky stuck out her thumb and her leg with professional competence at every passing car, but traffic was sparse and another forty minutes went by before they picked up a lift. Diana was nervous about getting into the car, but

Nicky thrust her into the back seat and climbed into the front herself. The driver, a travelling salesman, merely wanted company: he launched into a rather one-sided discourse with Nicky prompting at judicious intervals and allowing him to admire her knees while Diana sat stiff and silent. However, nothing more dreadful happened to them than the conversation of the travelling salesman, which was largely about his wife, who did not understand him. They got out at Mrs. Simpson's shop, Nicky bored, Diana relieved. At least one stage in a journey which had begun to seem impossible was safely over. She was not looking forward to the walk back to school: it was dark now and she would have to find the place to climb the boundary wall without the aid of Nigel's torch. On previous occasions he had always been with her, and the darkness had been intimate with kisses and whispers. This time, although she was not—of course—afraid (Diana knew that, as a Van Leer, she must naturally be afraid of nothing), she felt infuriated with Nigel and curiously unsure of herself. "Will you be all right?" Nicky asked her.

Diana hesitated. "Could I—do you have a torch? There's a place where I can get over the wall but it's difficult to find and—"

"Wait here." Nicky fumbled with the lock and disappeared into the shop, reappearing a few minutes later empty-handed.

"Where—?"

"It's in my pocket." Once again, a key scrabbled in the lock. "I'm coming with you."

"But—you'll have to walk back *alone*."

"I don't mind." Carelessly. "Anyway, I'm coming with you."

Despite the dark, Diana could sense Nicky's nonchalant attitude to unlit roads and the phantoms of tree and hedgerow. She felt both grateful and a little ashamed. "You don't have to," she said. "Thanks just the same."

But Nicky came. No one passed them on the road and they found the low place in the wall easily enough. A strategic branch gave Diana a foothold. "I hope you don't get into trouble," Nicky said as she swung herself over.

"It doesn't matter." After her former display of nerves, Diana was determined to match the other girl's indifference to danger. She wanted to say something more—something about gratitude, and indebtedness, and how, after this night, the two of them would always be friends—but her schooling had made her too formal and British. "See you," she whispered. "Goodnight." She vanished into the gloom of the school grounds, and Nicky turned and began to walk back to the village.

In the holidays, Diana, as usual, related the whole saga to her twin: the loss of her virginity, and Nigel, and her unexpected and vaguely daring friendship with Nicky Simpson. "Is she pretty?" Elspeth asked, the inevitable gremlin of jealousy suddenly on the alert. Diana said no, she didn't think so, but she had big eyes. It was enough. Being so much alone, Elspeth read far more widely than her sister, and thus she knew only too well that meek-looking girls with big eyes (she was sure Nicky must look meek) were the worst kind. They were the Becky Sharps and Lucy Steeles, soft-voiced flatters, wide-eyed listeners, superficially plain yet somehow irresistible to men. For such a girl, being a tobacconist's daughter was only a starting-point from which to climb to Higher Things. In fact, Nicky Simpson was neither meek nor irresistible, but Diana's descriptive powers failed to convey as much. Elspeth caught only a whiff of the tawdry glamour with which her twin had endowed Nicky, but that was all her imagination needed to enable her to torment herself.

"I love you best," Diana told her before she went back to school. "You're my twin. You'll always come first." They both knew it was important for her to say it from time to time. Elspeth loved her sister equally, if not more—more deeply, more ardently, more painfully—but it was never necessary for her to say so.

At Brayfield, the summer came and went. Diana did her best to keep the unspoken promise she had made to herself to be Nicky's friend. She visited the room above the tobacconist's, and the two of them would curl up in Nicky's bedroom, smoking cigarettes, drinking Coke out of cans ("You mustn't drink out of the can," Aunty Grizzle had said. "It will give you lead poisoning."), talking about make-up, pop groups, TV stars, teachers, tampons, boys. Terry—it transpired—had been replaced by Andrew, Andrew by Jake. Jake was not from the boys' school: he was very old (about twenty-four) and had a job. "Older men are the best," said Nicky, worldly-wise. Diana had not found a replacement for Nigel but Nicky thought she might like Jake's friend, Lenny; however, she didn't. Occasionally, she found herself wondering if Nicky really did have something of the insidious charm with which Elspeth had credited her. There were moments when Diana felt she had whispered a secret which should never have been whispered, shared a thought which should never have been shared—drawn in by an inexplicable desire to please, by the glimmer of Nicky's smile, by the guilt born of her undefined sense of social superiority. Whatever the truth, it was scarcely enough to justify ending the association. The two girls continued to see each other, and Diana, disliking her own instinctive caution, continued to give a little too much of herself to the friend she did not quite trust.

No friendship between two people with little in common could last long under these circumstances. Diana's O-levels kept her confined (supposedly) to her books, though with few tangible results. Nicky, too, had O-levels, at her local state school; she was also much preoccupied by her love life. However, when Diana turned up at the tobacconist's she was always eagerly welcomed—an eagerness which gave a temporary boost to her flagging resolve and once led her to invite Nicky to the stables with her to admire Moonshadow. Mrs. Simpson disapproved: despite her careful politeness she invariably seemed to disapprove, Diana noticed, although she did not know why. But Nicky brushed her mother's feelings aside without comment, as if mothers, like spots, were annoyances which all teenagers had to endure until they grew out of them.

"Why doesn't she like me?" Diana asked on the way to Brayfield. "Is it because of that time—you know—with Nigel?"

"Oh no. She likes you really," Nicky explained coolly. "She just dislikes my seeing you."

Diana thought of enquiring further, but decided it was better not to.

At the stables, Nicky stroked Moonshadow's nose, fed him lumps of sugar, and made a fuss of him in the accepted fashion. Secretly, Diana had imagined she would find herself ill at ease with horses, and the glow in Nicky's eyes both surprised and disconcerted her. When Nicky asked "Please . . . could I sit on him? Just for a minute?" she knew it would be churlish to refuse. Impossible to explain that Moonshadow was *her* pony, that he had never been ridden by anyone but her, that Nicky might as well have asked to borrow her boyfriend or her twin. She did suggest that he might not welcome a stranger on his back, but Nicky laughed, and patted his neck, and said she would be all right. "He likes me. See!" Diana knew a sinking sensation in her stomach which would have been all too familiar to her sister—the sudden nausea of a jealousy she had not known she could feel. She helped Nicky to mount although Nicky did not appear to need much help, and led her pony with her unwanted rider for a walk round the yard. Moonshadow tossed his head and blew through his nostrils, but he made no other protest although she half hoped, half feared he might throw the interloper to the ground. I am being mean, Diana told herself sternly. Her mother could never afford to give her a pony. I ought to be ready to share. But it was no good. She realized, dismally, that she had no socialist inclinations: Moonshadow belonged to *her*, and she had invited Nicky, on a regrettable impulse, to see him, not to ride him. This act was an unwitting injury which she might forgive but would not forget. And suddenly, glancing up—for the first time—at the other girl, she was assailed by a strange idea—strange at least for Diana, whose imagination was limited. Nicky was smiling. Tanned from the summer, her limp hair lifted in an airy breeze, sitting on ponyback as if she had been born to it; and for a moment it seemed to Diana that her erstwhile friend had taken her place, slipping into her persona as easily and unthinkingly as she might slip into a new dress. All differences of class and background were meaningless—chance, hazard, the fall of the dice—somehow, Nicky had become Diana.

The vision faded, but too slowly. Nicky dismounted and seemed to sense, belatedly, that she had done something wrong. Diana spoke cheerfully enough but she knew that she could never again pretend that they were friends. The holidays were approaching; it would be a simple matter to drift apart. She said: "See you later," but she did not mean it and Nicky probably understood. Next week, or the week after, she would go into the shop, stay twenty minutes, drink half a cup of coffee. That would suffice for her conscience. By the autumn term, it would be all history.

Elspeth was relieved when her twin told her, carelessly, that she wasn't seeing much of Nicky Simpson any more. But Diana did not tell her why.

3

Elspeth had first seen Stallibrass House when she was six. Aunty Grizzle, for some reason, decided it was her duty to show the children an example of their father's work—although she herself did not really appreciate the extremes of modern architecture and would certainly not have admired the building had it been designed by anyone else. For years Elspeth retained a dim memory of a wide glass façade reflecting cloud, grey bands of wall supporting a non-existent roof, peaks and triangles of concrete rearing up ominously against the sky. When she was older she went back alone, catching the bus and then walking round to a nearby hillside where she could look down on the house. She came to the conclusion that it was not a house at all but a vast piece of geometric sculpture which people had inadvertently occupied. It helped her to understand it, thinking of it like that. It stood on rising ground, splendidly isolated, untouched by any climbing plant, unshadowed by any tree, surrounded by slabs of terrace and lozenges of lawn and the electric blue rhomboid of a swimming pool—a harsh, manmade, earth-forged creation which she began, with time, to find strangely beautiful. Somehow, it helped her to feel closer to her father, learning to appreciate this thing that he had made. She dreamed of being able to discuss it with him, of his surprise at her perception, her artistic sensitivity; but, as always, she said nothing, fearing to put her dreams to the test of reality. Once, she tried to talk to her twin about it, since she talked to her twin about most things, but Diana wasn't interested in architecture.

When she was in her teens she would go drinking sometimes in neighbouring pubs with her biker friends, and she would hear the locals refer to the house with a sort of pride in its dauntless heterodoxy. The Glass House, they called it, the Concrete Dream, the Fish-Tank, the Monstrosity. As for Miser Joe, the mean old bugger, he wouldn't give a used tea-bag to a church fête: that was a well-known fact. He had filled the place with central heating but he was too stingy to switch it on, and the huge rooms were said to be as cold and echoing as a cave. There was even a story that it was haunted, though no one was very sure why. A young workman had fallen from the roof while it was being built; an accident, according to the coroner, but he was supposed to have had Words with Joe Stallibrass the previous day, and even with Rupert, all of which opened up agreeably sinister possibilities to a sensation-starved populace. The truth, Elspeth learnt, was that the unlucky youth had stepped on a loose plank, which tipped up and threw him down, and that was that. However, fatal accidents are rare on building sites and modern houses sparsely endowed with ghosts, and so it was allowed its questionable apparitions. The story was principally perpetuated by the young man's mother, a haggard-looking woman of fifty-odd who, after suitable encouragement and several drinks, would rave about "blood and stone," and a curse on the house, or Joe Stallibrass, or somebody. One evening Elspeth was identified to her in a bar, and a hideously embarrassing scene ensued. "So you're *his* daughter," the wretched woman declared. "*His* daughter! You would be: you don't look like a nice girl. *Sir* Rupert, he calls himself now—who does he think he is? *Sir* Rupert. He'll pay—you'll all pay. You wait and see. My son didn't die in no accident. *They* did it—they threw him down and said it was a loose plank and who was to contradict them? A loose plank indeed! He wasn't stupid, my boy. He said it was a bad house built by bad men and so they did for him. But one day—one day he'll do for them. *Sir* Rupert—balls! We'll both do for them. You wait and see!"

"My father doesn't usually kill off his labourers," Elspeth

said later, in an attempt to lighten the atmosphere. "It slows
the job down." Her friends laughed, and the subject was forgotten, by them if not by her. She knew, without pausing to
think why, how common it was for people to find a scapegoat
for personal tragedy; but the woman's vehemence had upset
her. The next day, she went to see the house again: it looked
totally unhaunted, contemporary, the product of a brutal civilization which dismissed the paranormal as mere superstition
from a rustic past. A house, she thought suddenly, with no
doubts, no feelings, no heart. Its isolation, its stark angularity,
became inexplicably oppressive. It seemed to her that no birds
sang there, not an insect crawled on the seamless stone. And
then a figure emerged on to the terrace and dived into the pool.
The blue enamel water cracked and rose up in a disorderly
splash, breaking the uniformity of the picture. Elspeth felt the
tension inside her begin to relax. A young man, she thought
idly: flesh and blood, no ghost. From that distance she could
see only that he was thin and brown with dark hair. The son
of the house, maybe; she had an idea there was a son.

She went away, thinking no more about him.

Anthony Charles Philip Stallibrass had his eighteenth birthday party the following summer. The twins, now sixteen, were
invited largely because of their father. They had never met
Anthony, not even when they were children, and his sisters
were a whole generation older. But Rupert and Josiah had
retained a polite acquaintance, the families were near enough
neighbours, and the Van Leer name had both cash and cachet.
The invitation arrived: Aunty Grizzle was fluttered, Diana
pleased, Elspeth apparently contemptuous. New dresses were
to be made for the occasion by a local dressmaker; at Diana's
suggestion they would have a similar style but be in different
colours, in order to make an effective pair. Otherwise, she
feared her great-aunt might try to avoid buying Elspeth a new
dress at all. Diana chose the pattern; it was not her fault that
she had no clothes sense. The tight bodice and frills which—
mainly by chance—suited her so well did nothing whatsoever
for her sister. Elspeth, in fact, did have a burgeoning clothes
sense, but since she considered her face and figure hopeless and
was determined to despise the whole affair, it seemed scarcely

relevant. "What *would* you have liked?" Diana asked unhappily, staring in the mirror as they stood side by side on the night of the party. The mirror stared uncompromisingly back.

"Something shapeless and baggy," Elspeth said, "to hide my shapeless baggy body."

Few Cinderellas can have gone to the ball feeling more uncomfortable in their enchanted robes. Elspeth had chosen purple, solely to annoy Aunty Grizzle, who did not like it; had she been older, slimmer, and more flamboyant, the colour might have worked; as it was, she merely looked (and felt) like a large purple parcel tied up with too much ribbon, bulging awkwardly through her wrappings. Worse still (if possible) her hair, still uncut except by herself when she felt destructive, had been puffed out into a sort of cushion, then twisted into a bun on top, like a cottage loaf, and speared through with enormous hair-grips to secure it, since it was really too long for the style. The same idea on Diana (whose hair was the right length) looked regal and just a little sophisticated, rather like Princess Anne, with curly tendrils hanging down around her ears and on the nape of her neck. Furthermore, Diana had chosen blue, which toned down any excess colour in her complexion and set off her youth, her radiance, the brilliance of her lips, and the burnish of her cottage loaf. Needless to say, Diana was nervous, Elspeth terrified. But Elspeth need not have worried. No one was going to notice her.

They arrived late since Diana mislaid her favourite earrings and Aunty Grizzle had forgotten to book a taxi. (Rupert was invited but didn't go.) The house was already full of guests; Elspeth tried to absorb the internal architecture but was defeated by the crowd and the lights and the noise. A thousand voices seemed to be competing furiously with each other and with the live music, which was provided by an ageing jazz band (hired by Joe) valiantly trying to play modern tunes. At the far end of what might have been, under normal circumstances, an overgrown drawing-room, a rock group from Anthony's old school were setting up their equipment. Assorted generations stood shoulder to shoulder (and occasionally thigh to thigh), shining with sweat and party smiles, a-glitter with rhinestones and diamonds and fluorescent plastic, clad in a hotch-potch of leather and taffeta, silk and denim. Elspeth thought longingly of her nasal stud, which Aunty Grizzle and Diana had joined forces to make her remove. In the hallway, Anthony's elder sister was talking vegetable gardens with a bishop's wife; in the conservatory, a former classmate of his was rolling a joint, and his ex-girlfriend and supposed prospective girlfriend were eyeing each other in mutual loathing. The proud father, greeting his guests, looked even grumpier than usual, his wife faintly bewildered, as if it had all got out of control, which it evidently had. "Of course," she murmured. "Sir Rupert's daughters . . . You must meet my son."

In due course, they did.

Both girls had experienced, in their different ways, the emotions of Cinderella attending her first ball. Neither had been prepared for Prince Charming. Certainly not in the form of Anthony Stallibrass, of all people—Anthony Stallibrass, whom all the laws of fate and genetics should have made fat and pimply and physically repulsive. Instead, at his conception the goddess of heredity had pulled off one of her most mischievous tricks. Josiah was short and squat with a ponderous belly, laminated chins, a face like a horned toad and a broad, flabby, fungoid nose that would have looked more natural sprouting from a rotten tree-stump. His wife Brenda was also short and built for comfort, not speed; their two daughters were taller and considerably slimmer but otherwise much as Mendel would have predicted. But Anthony—by a freak, a throwback, a bizarre genetic mutation—Anthony was beautiful.

He stood just half an inch under six foot, with the physique of a Greek youth and the face of a gypsy: Mongolian cheekbones, dark wild eyes, shaggy black hair in a Corybantic disorder. Disdaining the suit his father had demanded, he wore bleached jeans and a peasant shirt, adorned here and there with tatty embroidery and laced across the chest, leaving several gaps of bare torso tanned to the colour of molten caramel. But most fatal of all, he was obviously and instantly *nice*. There was gentleness as well as wildness in his dark eyes, and his smile was not merely devastating, it was kind. Much has been written of the harm done by the beautiful and the cruel, but how much more harm is done by young men who are considerate, thoughtful, unstinting of their charm—the sort of young men who will dance with a wallflower, and chat to the quiet girl in the corner, and go on their way leaving hearts in pieces all over the floor.

Such men are mercifully rare, but by some strange juggling of parental chromosomes Anthony was one of them. His smile was for Elspeth as well as for Diana; his dark eyes seemed to be searching for the timid, sensitive, fascinating creature he knew was hiding somewhere behind her unprepossessing exterior. If only, Elspeth reflected sadly, there really *was* a timid, sensitive, fascinating creature hiding somewhere. However, there wasn't. If only she could lose weight. Perhaps if she starved herself for a week . . . She recalled, over a year ago, watching a lithe brown body plunge into a swimming pool, and her heart turned over at the carelessness of that memory. Lines like "So near, and yet so far" ran through her mind. But it was too late now. He had seen Diana—characteristically, she disregarded every other girl in the room—so it was bound to be too late.

As for Diana, all the residents of the boys' school sank without trace into the shadows of an unremembered and unmemorable past. She teetered on the brink, gasped, dived—and was lost. "Take down your hair," he told her much later, out on the terrace. "I don't like that style. It makes you look like Princess Anne." She pulled at the grips and presently it began to come down, knots and twists slowly unravelling themselves, heavy waves, still stiff with lacquer, flopping on to her shoulders. She ran her fingers through it and shook her head—a gesture very like Moonshadow tossing his mane—and suddenly pins and hairspray gave up the unequal struggle and it was all flowing free. Anthony filled his hands with it, pressed his face into it, inhaled the faint smell of apples (Diana's shampoo) that still clung despite the overtones of lacquer and cigarette smoke from the party. "Kiss me," he whispered, but she did not need to be asked. Her lips were sticky and tasted of her strawberry-flavoured lip gloss; he visualized her as a whole fruit-bowl waiting to be eaten. But he took it slowly, not wanting to rush her: a new relationship—if such it was—should never be rushed. Anyway, it was his birthday party.

After a while he went back inside, danced with a girl who had not danced, talked to Elspeth, to his godmother, to an uncle, a cousin, a family friend. Out in the garden, Diana sat gazing at the stars, feeling as she had not felt since she was fourteen years old, and her father had given her a pony of her own.

· · ·

Anthony and Diana saw each other with increasing frequency over the next two years. He was at Cambridge, she doing her A-levels, but in the holidays it was easy for them to be together and Diana was philosophical about the term-time. "I don't mind if he sees other girls when I'm not there," she would explain with a detachment that Elspeth could almost believe in. "I mean—I'd *rather* he didn't, of course, but if he feels free now and plays around a bit then it'll be easier for him to settle down in the future." She seemed to have no doubts that he *would* settle down, and with her. Her detachment was the product of much serious cogitation; she could not take him for granted but she felt it was important that she should pretend to do so, that she was never possessive, never neurotic, never overtly jealous. He was so beautiful that whenever they went out together she could sense the other girls looking at him, planning to drop their glasses, their phone numbers—or their knickers—in his vicinity, but she always managed to appear unconscious of the attention he received, behaving as if he was just an ordinary boy, ordinarily attractive or unattractive, whom she happened to like a little more than all the rest. If she was to keep him, she knew, it was not enough to be in love: she would have to learn to be sensible. Fortunately, being sensible had always come easily to Diana. Even under the influence of strong emotion and teenage hormones her temperament remained fairly unruffled—the result not so much of self-control as of habit. Occasionally, she had violent impulses—to ring him up at three o'clock in the morning, or to build a willow cabin at his gate, or to elope to Gretna Green—but they frightened her a little and she never thought of giving in to them. His ex-girlfriend took an overdose and his (rumoured) prospective girlfriend slashed her wrists, and Anthony, being both chivalrous and conscientious, rushed to their sides; but the only time he and Diana had a row she sat by the telephone with her fists clenched in stoicism and waited.

"You're so restful," he told her afterwards. "I could stay with you forever."

It was enough.

For Elspeth, this was a period of bitterness, hopelessness, dreams. Diana knew her twin liked Anthony but she must never know how much. Yet the secret did not drive them apart; in some ways it drew them closer together, since Elspeth could not have borne for her sister to be hurt, could not have borne for Anthony to hurt *her* with anyone other than Diana. And there were brief interludes of bliss, of dangerous wistfulness. One afternoon when Diana had to go out, Anthony taught Elspeth to play chess, laughing when she finally beat him. On another day, he took her for a ride in the old Morgan which he had persuaded his father he would prefer to a Mercedes (Miser Joe was never ungenerous with his only son). There were even instances of terrible treachery when Elspeth found herself wondering if he and Diana were really so well suited, or if he cared for her quite as deeply as she assumed he did. Diana—for example—had scraped through five O-levels and seemed likely to fail all her As, but Anthony, by yet another genetic mutation, was clever. His father was shrewd but uneducated and had not troubled to remedy this defect in later life; his mother was a good cook with common sense rather than intellect. But Anthony was that rare thing, a student who brought a genuine ardour to learning, who would burn the midnight oil if sufficiently engrossed and longed to give his half-formed ideals some foundation in solid fact. He moved from Classics to Philosophy, from Plato to Karl Marx. He began to talk of the sick society, of the greed and decadence of both West and East, of the desperate need for true socialism to bring justice and equality to everyone. All this (Elspeth thought) was way over Diana's head. As for love, she could see that he cared for her sister, but she sometimes suspected he might have cared for almost anyone in a similar situation, bringing the same warmth, generosity and tenderness to every relationship he had. She even imagined, on occasion, that the smile in his eyes when he looked at her was quite as special as the one he reserved for Diana.

But it was all nonsense, of course. When Anthony and Diana got engaged, in the summer of '76, she told herself that she was too inexperienced to judge them, too naive to understand. Unrequited passion, envy, wishful thinking—these things had taken hold of her mind so that, in the first shock of her sister's news, she was horrified at the realization of her secret perfidy. She did not know that it was Diana who had brought up the subject of an engagement and Anthony who had accepted the idea, seeing it more as a formal expression of "going steady" than a serious commitment to marriage. To Diana, however, it was not merely serious: it was irrevocable. She came home early from dinner with her new fiancé, bubbling over like a mountain stream in flood. She ran to her sister's room to tell her, to her great-aunt's room to tell Grizelda. And—last but not least—she went to tell her father.

If there was a shade of trepidation at the back of her joy, a twinge of doubt in her heart, she did not acknowledge it. Not till she saw his face. Even then she would not see, would not admit that there was anything more than surprise in his expression. She said: "I'm *engaged*, Daddy. I'm going to be married. Isn't it wonderful?"—willing him to say that it *was* wonderful, to wish her happy like any ordinary father.

But he was not an ordinary father. A thought that had long lain dormant in her mind woke up and whispered that perhaps nothing was as ordinary as she had hitherto supposed. He did not look as though he was going to wish her happy. There was a blankness in his eyes—not surprise: shock. He said: "Shut the door."

She obeyed. The door was solid oak, with a knob that resisted her hand. As it closed, she had a sudden feeling that she had shut herself in a prison. But it was only her father's study— tall bookshelves, dark panelling, the angled desk lamp making top-heavy shadows against the walls. All very familiar and, had Diana ever considered it, the antithesis of his art. But Diana, in common with most teenagers, rarely considered her parent objectively, seeing him solely in relation to herself.

She went on, still trying to recapture the bubbling-over mood of a few minutes earlier: "I'm going to be married. Aren't you pleased? Aren't you happy for me, Daddy?"

There was a pause that lasted a fraction too long. Then Rupert asked: "Who?"

"Anthony!" She saw him frown, knew, incredibly, that he was not quite sure which Anthony she meant. Desperately, she blundered on. "Anthony *Stallibrass*. You know, Daddy. I've been seeing him for years." And again: "I'm going to marry him."

Anthony Stallibrass. Son of Josiah. Vaguely, Rupert remembered meeting him in the house once or twice. Just another of Diana's friends—or so he had always imagined. He said, gratingly: "How well do you know him?"

"What—what do you mean?" Evidently she didn't understand. "I know him terribly well—of course I do! We've been going out together since his eighteenth birthday party. Don't worry: he hasn't got any awful secrets. He isn't a junkie or gay or anything. He's quite normal and—very, very nice. Daddy . . ."

She came towards him, holding out her hands. But a faint hesitation betrayed her; somehow, the gesture was not quite natural. Rupert had moved so that the light was almost directly behind him, leaving his features in shadow; she could only guess at a certain rigidity. His hunched shoulders loomed huge and faintly ominous in silhouette. Before him, the light shone full in her face—a child's face: rosy skin, tremulous smile, grey eyes clear as rainwater. A child hoping, doubting, wanting to trust . . .

He said: "Have you slept with him?"

"Well, I—"

"Have you slept with him?"

She had never dreamt it would be like this. "Yes, I—yes. Of course I have. Everyone does these days. I mean, I thought you would—I assumed—"

He hit her. Slowly. She saw his hand come up, slowly, felt the impact of the blow knocking her sideways in a slow-motion stumble. "Whore." He scarcely raised his voice. *"Whore."* He had never struck her, never smacked her, hardly spoken a cross word to her in her life. She could not believe it. She struggled to her feet, fighting for breath, for some way out of this madness. He hit her again. And again. She tripped in the flex of the desk lamp, jerking it on to the floor. The reeling light showed her his face suddenly contorted, his eyes bloodshot. She screamed: "Daddy! Daddy!" but he did not seem to hear, he went on hitting her, and she sank to the floor, the blows thudding through her head, through her body, until darkness rushed over her and into her and filled her up . . .

She was being lifted. There were arms round her, strong arms, her father's arms. Lifting her out of the darkness, holding her—crushing her. His face in her neck, the sound of his voice. Sobs. Her name: "Diana . . . Diana . . ." A confused moment of warmth, of sanity, of a return to love and normalcy. Bruises beginning to throb, tensed muscles hesitating on the edge of relief. But his arms were too strong; his embrace hurt her. She tried to speak, tried to breathe. The dark engulfed her again, so that she thought she was suffocating, and in the dark there was the touch of hands on her back, a caress harder than violence, his lips on her throat, her cheek, her mouth . . . She opened her eyes, but the blood was beating in her head and she could not see. She opened her mouth—to cry out, to plead with him—and his tongue came in, entering her, possessing her, violating her. A huge, rough tongue, like the tongue of an animal, that seemed to reach into every corner of her being. Nausea filled her, taking from her all resistance. The illusion of love and normalcy vanished for ever. The world changed.

In another time, another dimension, he let her go. She ran for the door, colliding with the furniture, unable to coordinate mind and limb. If he spoke, she did not listen. The brass knob was stiff, the door yielded too slowly. Then she was on the stairs, running up the stairs, plunging down the corridor, shutting herself at last into her room. Sanctuary. She slid to the floor and sat there, gasping, numb, too stunned for tears.

Presently, sickness overwhelmed her. She staggered into the connecting bathroom, threw up her dinner, her tea, her lunch—went on throwing up until the effort tore at the walls of her stomach. After the paroxysm was over she stayed there for a few minutes, clutching the rim of the lavatory, eyes and nose streaming. When she was able, she went back into her room. Footsteps on the stairs brought her heart into her mouth; at the top they hesitated, then moved away towards the other end of the house. The ebb of fear left her weak and shaking; she leaned against the door, fumbling for the lock, but there was no key—there had never been any need for a key. She rammed a chair under the handle, pushed a heavy chest of drawers until she was satisfied it would block any attempt at ingress. After that, she had to sit down again, faintness and nausea returning. She did not think; she knew it was best not to think. Thinking meant facing the future, searching for reassurance, for someone to turn to, somewhere to run—all the things she had taken for granted from home and family. *Home . . . family . . .* meaningless words. Even her own room seemed unsafe, despite the barricades. She could always share her sister's bed—when they were younger the twins had often slept together, after a nightmare, or before an exam—but Elspeth might see too far and too deep, and the thought of such telepathic comprehension terrified her. She stayed where she was, huddled on the rug, trembling like a puppy in a thunderstorm.

Later, she went back into the bathroom. She washed her mouth out at the sink, ran herself a bath, scrubbed savagely at every inch of her body, as though by doing so she could somehow cleanse herself of the memory of his touch. Afterwards, she climbed into bed, but she could not sleep and eventually she got up, ran another bath, and began the frenetic scrubbing all over again.

Next door, Elspeth heard her twin come upstairs, registered the haste and stumble of her feet. She waited for Diana to come to her. The sound of bathwater gurgling down the pipes jerked her from an uneasy doze; she frowned, turned over, wondered hazily why Diana was taking a bath at this hour. Normally, she bathed in the morning or in the early evening before going out. Elspeth dozed off again and woke once more to the gurgling of the pipes; peering at the clock, she saw it was over an hour later. Her misgivings grew; she contemplated getting up but the plumbing had lapsed into silence and the house was totally quiet. In the end, she drifted into a troubled dream in which Diana was sitting in a bath of greenish slime, holding up dripping hands and looking at her with an expression of piteous bewilderment on her face.

When Elspeth woke in the morning, around six-thirty, the first thing she heard was the noise of bathwater running away.

She got out of bed, snatched a dressing-gown and went to her sister's room. The door appeared to be stuck and she knocked. Diana called out: "Who is it?"

Elspeth said: "It's me," and there was a scraping sound as of something heavy being dragged out of the way. Then the door opened.

"Sorry," Diana said, unconvincingly. "I jammed a chair against it last night. You know how these doors rattle in the wind." She was half dressed, flushed and a little puffy-eyed, perhaps from the bath. She did not meet her twin's gaze.

Elspeth thought: There was no wind last night. Her sense of wrongness increased; she felt her twin avoiding not only her eyes but her mind. And suddenly it seemed to her that for all the sun on her hair and the colour in her cheeks there was a darkness on Diana, a thin shadow cutting her off from the daylight. The impression was so strong that for a second Elspeth actually thought a cloud had passed over the sun. But

Diana stood by the window; beyond, the sky was blue and empty; there was no visible shadow on her. Only the impression did not fade.

"Did you tell him about your engagement?" Elspeth asked, meaning Rupert. And: "What did he say?"

Diana achieved a shrug. "Oh, you know. He looked a bit taken aback. I think it was rather a shock. He'll get used to it."

Elspeth hadn't thought about it before, but it occurred to her then that her father would *not* get used to it. She said, "Yes, of course," with unaccustomed tact; she wasn't normally tactful with her twin, but there was something about that day—a sort of dreadful fragility—to which she reacted by instinct.

Later, Diana went out riding. Moonshadow, kept at home since she finished at Brayfield, was unexpectedly fretful, sidling and fidgeting under his mistress's hand. Elspeth watched them go through that same imperceptible darkness, stricken by a sudden fear that there would be an accident, that they would not return, or worse still, that Moonshadow would come galloping home alone, wild-eyed and trailing an empty rein. Yet when pony and rider got back unharmed, she was not relieved. The roses in Diana's cheeks seemed to her too vivid, her voice too quick and unsteady, her gaze always shifting as though to avoid something she did not wish to see. Elspeth longed to say: "Please—tell me what is wrong," yet she knew intuitively she must not ask: the very question would destroy Diana's tenuous self-command. All she could do for her twin was to be there if she was needed, and be patient. She realized the problem must have something to do with Anthony, and the engagement, and her father; but what it was she did not know and could not begin to guess.

In the afternoon, Diana shut herself in the bathroom and ran another bath. Elspeth, listening from next door, thought the sound of water running down the pipes the most ominous she had ever heard.

Although it was a Saturday Rupert had gone to work—he often did—and was not back in time for dinner. Anthony was at a family wedding with his parents, presumably taking advantage of the opportunity to tell them about his fiancée, so Diana was left at a loose end. Nonetheless, Elspeth was surprised when her twin asked—rather diffidently—to come out with her. Diana didn't criticize her but she had shown little enthusiasm for motorbikes and young toughs in leather jackets. "We could stay in," Elspeth offered. "There's a party but it probably won't be much good."

But Diana didn't want to stay in.

Rupert, returning home around ten, was slightly relieved to find his favourite daughter absent. As usual, he did not give a thought to Elspeth. He had stayed late at the office, poring over drawings he did not see, his mind going round in circles while his spirit was torn between remorse and other shades of anguish which he would not attempt to define. Somehow, he would have to explain, to apologize, to make her understand. He told himself it was Johanna he had seen, bursting into his study, recklessly avowing her betrayal—Johanna on whom he had turned, after his long and lonely fidelity—Johanna whom he had struck, and wept over, and kissed. After all, Diana was the image of her mother. Diana in a green dress which matched the colour of her eyes, with the same red-gold hair and rose-leaf skin—no, Diana's eyes were grey, and Johanna's complexion, surely, had emulated the magnolia and not the rose; but dreams played strange tricks and he had not kept even a photograph. In essence, however, the daughter was endowed with her mother's unforgettable loveliness—or so he believed, bedazzled by her bright youth and his own adoration. Past tragedy, overwork, exhaustion—these things had confused his brain, throwing him temporarily into chaos. Diana would understand. She *must* understand. All would be well between them. Of course, she could not be allowed to marry that young man. Diana was little more than a child; it was far too soon for her to think of marriage. And Anthony Stallibrass, in his dim recollection, was a long-haired hippy with the face of a girl who must already be giving Josiah sleepless nights. It was all nonsense, puppy love, a fantasy that would vanish like a will-o'-the-wisp in cold daylight and common sense. He did not remember—or did not wish to remember—that Johanna had been very little older when he had married her.

Something made him glance up; he realized with a shock that he was still in his office, that it was growing late, that one of his assistants was leaning against a desk, watching him. There was no one else about. The young man—twenty-eight or so—wore a neutral expression too careful for his years. Michael Kovacs. Talented. He had been there as a student, calling himself O'Hara. Rupert had no idea why he had changed his name.

He asked: "What time is it?," mainly for something to say.

"Eight-thirty. Sir."

Rupert ran a hand through his hair, scowling with weariness as much as displeasure. "I'm off," he said. "Lock up for me."

It was a long drive home, with a scene ahead which he anticipated with both eagerness and dread. When he found Diana had gone out, he decided she was merely being prudent. Confrontation would come more easily after a brief respite.

The party, as Elspeth had expected, was not much good. Too many people in one small room, joints passed up and down the stairs, spilt beer, nameless activity in the loo. In common with most teenage parties, the music was too loud for conversation, probably to conceal the fact that nobody had anything to say. Diana got drunk; Elspeth didn't. The world, she felt, was upside down. She had seen her twin grow giggly over champagne, but she had never seen the giggles turn to wild laughter, to sudden silences, to dropped head, parted lips, the glazed look of unresponsive stupidity. When they left, Diana seemed to come to herself. She glanced round in unreasoning terror, cried that she wouldn't go home. Her terror infected Elspeth: she had a sensation of being in a nightmare where there was no visible threat, only a vast underlying fear which transformed the most normal objects into symbols of doom. There was something waiting for her, in the future, in the shadows, in her sister's eyes, something huge and unspeakable which she must avoid or avert; but she could not see it and did not know what it was. They took Diana into the kitchen and dosed her with coffee. "I won't go home," she reiterated, when she was calmer. "I don't *want* to go home. I'm going to stay with Anthony."

"Anthony's away," Elspeth said patiently. "You told me they were all away for the night." She had a sudden feeling her twin had begun to sober up but was using drunkenness to cover her irrationality. The thought disturbed her even more than Diana's former hysteria.

"I don't care," Diana said. "I'm going to stay with Anthony. He won't mind. He loves me."

"He's *away*. The house is empty. There's no one there."

"I'll climb in the window."

"You'll be arrested."

But Diana insisted, sticking to her point with an obstinacy that might or might not have had its origin in alcohol. In the end, they drove round to Stallibrass House in a van belonging to someone's brother. The brother was a window-cleaner and there was a ladder in the back which Diana appropriated to scale the estate wall. Elspeth followed her, bringing the ladder. The driver of the van, one of her leather-jacketed friends, waited outside. In the grounds of Stallibrass House it was dark and very silent. Part of a moon, yellow as stale cheese, shone down between the trees, making bewildering shadows. Elspeth, hampered by the ladder, had trouble keeping up. Presently she came to an open stretch of grass. Beyond, the house reared up suddenly, jagged roof-shapes half seen against the stars, sheer blank windows reflecting night. There were no lights anywhere, no servants. Mister Joe did not believe in live-in staff or unnecessary electricity bills. Off to the left, a fragment of the rotten moon blinked back from what must have been the swimming pool. Elspeth hissed: "Diana!" and was thankful to hear her sister's voice.

"Here."

They played the ladder against a wall somewhere in the vicinity of Anthony's bedroom. Elspeth wondered belatedly where it would all end, and if there was anything she could do to discourage her twin; but in this new, strange mood Diana was beyond all influence. She climbed up quickly—too quickly, reckless with drink. Elspeth steadied the ladder with shaking hands and followed. There was a horror on her deeper than any darkness.

At the top, she found herself scrambling onto a roof which sloped down towards what she thought might be an internal courtyard. She inched cautiously along it, clinging to the edge of the wall; ahead, she could see her sister's silhouette, teetering perilously. The cheating moonlight made distances and dangers unreal. She called out, softly and sharply: "Diana—Diana . . ." but the silhouette was moving too fast for her. As in a dream, she struggled forward with feet that dragged like lead, the figure in front of her always just out of reach. She saw it wobble—saw the flailing arms, the irresistible swing off balance, the slow tilt into a fall . . . There was a millisecond of time when all the night-magic blew out of her head, leaving it horribly clear. Danger came into focus. She lurched along the roof, heedless of her own safety, one hand gripping the wall's edge, the other reaching for her twin—

"Diana!"

Fingers closed on her wrist, her muscles tore, the moonlight spiralled around her. She could not scream: breath was pummelled from her lungs. She heard Diana's feet scrabbling for purchase; one shoe came off and fell clattering down the roof. Somewhere below, it struck concrete. She tried to say: "Hang on," but her voice made no sound and the grip on her wrist seemed to rend her very sinews. And now, there was only a moment left. A moment in which—at last—she saw into Diana's mind, knew her thought. She sensed the pinpoint clarity of sudden shock, the reflex of fear, the urge to live. And then— an inexplicable hesitation. Something that felt almost like relief. Surrender . . .

No! Elspeth's scream was gagged, a cry of the heart. *No! No!*

Diana's hold loosened; her hand slipped from her sister's grasp. Briefly, Elspeth saw her upturned face, with the moon in her eyes. Then she slid down the roof into the dark.

There was a thud as her body hit the ground.

Then a great silence.

4

The months following Diana's death always remained mercifully dim in Elspeth's recollection. The events of that last day—the growing fear, the shadow on her twin, the feeling of something inexplicably wrong—became a part of one terrible event, and Elspeth, stupefied with grief, ceased to speculate on unknown causes; although, long after, the sound of bathwater running away still gave her a chill around the heart. She drifted into a succession of days that grew ever darker as the realization of her loss intensified: if she had thought herself lonely before, she knew that with her twin life had been full of light and colour, whereas now it was bleak and empty for ever. Diana had been her companion, her friend, her soul-mate, the one person who had understood her by instinct, loved her beyond criticism. Who would ever love her or understand her again, unwanted Elspeth, ugly of body, ugly of mind, alone for eternity?

The formalities came and went: the funeral, the inquest (verdict: death by misadventure), flowers, condolences. The coroner absolved Elspeth of any guilt but her father did not: he merely stared through her, stony-faced, as if she too had died with Diana and only her ghost endured, haunting Churston

Grange almost unnoticed. The last of the servants left, presumably driven away by the prevailing atmosphere of tragedy, and nobody bothered to employ any new ones. The three of them lived on in their separate cells, Rupert for the most part in his study, shut up with his grief and other emotions too terrible to reveal, Aunty Grizzle in her sitting-room, whispering to herself and cultivating hypochrondia, Elspeth in her bedroom, forgotten by everyone. They no longer met even at the dinner table: there was no proper "dinner" now. Outside in the stables, Moonshadow grew fat and fretful for want of exercise, but Rupert could not bear to sell him. One day he collapsed and died, probably from overfeeding; but local gossip credited him with a broken heart. Sometimes, Elspeth remembered the supposed phantom of Stallibrass House, and the woman who had cursed her family. She thought: They killed Diana. If I met that woman now, I would kill *her*. I would kill her *myself*. Sometimes—not often—she remembered Anthony. He had been at the funeral, sallow under his tan from shock or sorrow, wearing the right kind of dark suit even if he couldn't manage a tie. He had hugged Elspeth and said something kind, but she hadn't felt grateful, hadn't really cared. Anthony and all her hopeless fancies belonged to the past: he meant nothing to her now. Whatever his feelings, he could not have loved as she had loved, nor understood her loss. She could not bring herself to visit it, but she dreamed of the grave, and Diana stifling under the lilies, which Rupert had ordered should be renewed every week. And more than once, in dream or nightmare, she felt a hand on her wrist, and clutching fingers which could not keep their hold. She would think, uselessly: I could have stopped her. Yet she knew there was nothing more she could have done, and now all remorse, all self-condemnation, was futile.

The hottest summer for many years withered slowly, with brown grass and water shortages. Elspeth stayed in her room, no longer eating chocolate. She had scarcely touched food for several days after Diana's death, and she noticed at the funeral that her clothes hung loose. Never in all her life had her clothes hung loose. She ate less, and the space between waist and waistband on her skirt widened, her jeans slouched around hip and thigh, bones appeared where she had not known she had bones. She told herself she was pining away, and one day even her father would realize, and cleave to her with penitence and new-found love; but in truth the act of not eating had become an object in itself, a focus for her unfocused mind, gradually driving out all other purpose. With school over, she was supposed to be taking a year off before going to college, but she made no attempt to get a job or apply for the planned secretarial course. Instead, she took to standing on the scales daily, watching the pounds and ounces creep away. She drank only black coffee, and the smell of chocolate made her sick. One afternoon, half famished, she bought a packet of peanuts, something she had rarely enjoyed before. She ate them slowly, and found them ambrosial. Using a calorie chart and kitchen scales, she worked out that if she had just two packets of peanuts a day she would go on losing weight. After that she lived off peanuts, her world revolving around the ritual indulgence. She bought smaller jeans, but soon they too sagged from her jutting pelvis. Her periods stopped, her breasts shriveled, the newly discovered space between her thighs began to gape. There came an evening when she looked in the mirror and saw no stomach, no bust, only a profile of sculpted bone. Her face, without its excess flesh, had shrunk from the cheekbones of Garbo to those of Yorick; her nose, always verging on the aquiline, had become a beak. She was starving but she could not eat; the sight and smell of food filled her with a mouth-watering terror. Her diet was now nothing but peanuts and black coffee: she increased her intake from two packets to three, managed somehow to put on an ounce or two, and lay awake all night tormented with guilt.

"You've lost weight," Aunty Grizzle told her, encountering her one day on the landing. "You look dreadful."

For the next few evenings, Aunty Grizzle actually cooked, if not very well, calling Elspeth to the table around eight o'clock (Rupert would not come). But Elspeth looked at the meal, and looked at her great-aunt, and went back to her peanuts.

Two weeks later she fainted on the stairs.

Aunty Grizzle called the doctor. By the time he arrived Elspeth had recovered and was sitting on the bottom stair pressing a handkerchief to her temple, bright blood dripping down her bloodless cheek. A medical examination followed; the doctor was severe. Aunty Grizzle took refuge in weeping and wringing of hands. In due course there were discussions with Rupert and much talk of adolescent psychology. Permission was given, bags packed, and a hired car arrived to transport Elspeth to a suitably expensive and prestigious clinic. She went without comment, without complaint. It was, after all, something to do, something to fill up her empty life. Aunty Grizzle, as one in duty bound, waved a limp farewell.

In his office, Rupert made out the necessary cheque. Without comment, without complaint. He would have paid double, treble the amount, paid willingly, hoping in his heart that he would never have to see his remaining daughter again. He did not wish her well or ill, he merely wanted her away, out of his home and his existence for good. She it was who had led Diana to her death, or so he told himself, fearing to glimpse in her face the shadow of a sisterly confidence, or the remotest echo of Diana's smile.

It was many months and the loss of another stone in weight before Elspeth realized that she might die. She had reached the stage where food had become a drug which she craved beyond hunger and beyond sense; she would steal down to the kitchen in the night and eat everything she could find, stale bread, tinned treacle, even raw meat. The kitchen was supposed to be kept locked, but Elspeth learned quickly how to pick the lock or climb in through the window. Afterwards, her stomach bulging with the obscene feast, she would stick two fingers down her throat and throw it all up again, in terror of an imaginary obesity and revolted by the pressure of food in her belly. Then she would fall into a sleep of exhaustion and dreams, waking once again to the same famine, the same terrors, and a dulled capacity for self-disgust.

It was in the small hours that the realization came to her. She had been dreaming that she was living in a cloister, shut up in a room like a nun's cell with walls of mellow stone, a hard, narrow bed, sunlight falling through a slender Gothic window. She was sitting on the floor cross-legged, meditating or praying; she felt calm and peaceful and remote from the outside world. And then suddenly she heard the Food. It was piling up against the door behind her, clamouring to get in. She set her back to the door but it was shaking perilously from the battering of tins and the thud of manic vegetables and flying hunks of meat. Peanuts drummed against it like rifle fire. And then, somehow—she didn't know how—a single peach found its way in. It rolled slowly across the floor and landed in a patch of sunlight, looking innocent and beautiful, gold and rose and edible velvet. In happier days Elspeth had been very fond of peaches. Involuntarily she took a step towards it, bent down with outstretched hand . . . Instantly, the door behind her burst open, and the Food, unchecked, came tumbling into the room to smother her . . .

She woke abruptly, trembling all over. Presently, she got up, went to the window and opened it wide. The night air was cold, so cold it cut her to the bone; but then it had not far to cut. In the light of the new moon she seemed a spindly figure like a child's drawing, with hollowed eyes in a skull-face. The winter stars glittered like spangles of frost in a black sky. "Stars are wishes," her grandmother used to say when she was too young to remember. The words came back to her though she could not think from where. "Stars are wishes that have come true." And for the first time she knew that if she could not find a way to live she would surely die.

She did not want to die.

The cure was long and slow, with many setbacks. "She needs motivation," declared the psychiatrists. "Something to live for," said her favourite nurse. When asked what she wanted to do, Elspeth said she did not know. She had not been particularly excited by the prospect of a degree in English (her teacher's choice), but she could not think of any alternative. Long sessions supposedly exploring her subconscious produced the staggering conclusion that she had a father complex and was missing her sister. According to the psychiatrists these factors were the principal causes of her bulimia; not her former fatness. They tried to persuade Rupert to visit her, but he refused, merely writing a cheque for a few more sessions. In the course of one of these, they elicited the information that she was interested in art, and thence in architecture. Reassured by genetic precedents, they dismissed the theory that this might be another attempt to gain the support and affection of her father. This, they declared, was the solution. Elspeth must learn to be an architect. The possibility that a gruelling seven-year course might be too much for her both physically and (in her present state) mentally did not occur to them. She needed Motivation. They had given her Motivation. She would be an architect.

Elspeth, duly motivated, allowed herself to think they were right. Very slowly, ounce by ounce, millimetre by millimetre, she began to put on weight. Regularly, she would have fits of panic, believing she was getting fat again. She would bang on the wall and scream and accuse everyone of being in a plot to make her ugly. Her favourite nurse, who had been both kind and resourceful, obtained several posters of bikini-clad beauties—Monroe, Bardot, Raquel Welch—and pinned them up around her room, and although Elspeth tore them down from time to time in one of her frenzies, gradually they helped her to retrieve her sense of proportion. She ate carefully regulated meals and kept them down; she exercised; she even began to study. The thought of that seven-year course was daunting but Elspeth was no coward. This was her chance to prove herself. She would not let it pass her by.

She was twenty when she finally started at Durham University—the psychiatrists had selected Durham since it was a long way from the malign influences of home. The Van Leer name may have helped to get her a place but Rupert gave no other encouragement, though he never withheld financial support. She was allowed to spend only a month in Churston before going north; the doctors considered it "inadvisable" for her to stay any length of time in an environment so reminiscent of all her principal hang-ups. Thus she went from the clinic to the college, from one cloister to another, with hardly a stopover in the real world. Aunty Grizzle sped her on her way with ill-meant nagging and the observation: "As though your father hasn't had enough to bear." Rupert looked at her—when he had to—with an indifference that masked all feeling. Once, compelled to give an opinion, he said: "She'll never last the course. She hasn't the brains or the stamina."

"I'll show him," Elspeth vowed. "I'll show him what I can do. I'll achieve something. I'll be worthy of him. I'll make him love me . . ." This, she felt, was her sacrifice at Aulis, her far, far better thing: the task that would redeem her in her father's eyes. It had not occurred to her that she was not looking forward to it. She only knew that if she failed, everything that really mattered would be lost.

She failed.

It took two years—two years of lingering defeat before her tutor faced her with the truth. She could not cope. Artistic she might be, but the technical side of architecture baffled her. In a desperate attempt to force-feed herself with knowledge she would work too long and too hard, overtaxing her already fragile physique and, in consequence, succumbing to every passing germ. In a single winter she had two heavy colds and three doses of assorted flu, followed the next summer by a mild bout of glandular fever. She never heated her room properly, still ate too little, and forgot or ignored medical prescriptions, as though determined to accentuate the atmosphere of the cloister with suitably medieval hardships. One college physician, who had studied her case-history in some detail, startled his colleagues by remarking that she must be as strong as a horse to have survived all the damage she had wantonly inflicted on her own body. She had become obsessed with her private martyrdom, believing that only through self-punishment could she atone for her shortcomings as a daughter, for her sister's death, for whatever it was she had done wrong or failed to do right. Yet increasingly the impossible goal of Rupert's love receded from her, and she was lost in a darkness of her own making, exhausting her mind and abusing her health for reasons she could no longer clearly remember. If she had had any friends they might have helped; but she had no friends. In her view she had transformed herself from a fat freak into a thin freak, an attitude unlikely to give her new confidence. Her one attempt at taking part in the social life of the college did nothing to improve matters. There was a student on her course who reminded her slightly of Anthony, though he was far less beautiful, his colouring not so dark, his mouth fuller, his jaw less perfectly sculpted. His name was Keith Eager. Inevitably, Elspeth admired him. Study threw them together; she learnt he had a girlfriend of whom he saw little since she wasn't attached to the University. Possibly he implied that the situation bored him; possibly Elspeth read too much into his confidence. When he asked her out she was plunged into a state of panic, excitement, guilt: she could not leave her work, she shrank from the perils of physical attraction—but she liked him. In the end, she went.

They saw a film at the Arts Cinema which Elspeth pretended to appreciate, split the cost of an Indian meal which she barely touched. Afterwards, when he kissed her, she could taste the vindaloo. His full lips seemed to squelch around her mouth, covering her face with saliva. In his room, she concentrated on his resemblance to Anthony, tried hard to convince herself that she felt like making love. Keith appeared to take compliance for granted, sliding his hands through every gap in her clothes, sucking her nipple with all the vigour of a sink-plunger, rubbing her clitoris briskly through her jeans. She knew she ought to be aroused but she wasn't: the friction through the stiff denim was more painful than titillating, she imagined the flavour of curry invading her breast and turning her whole body as yellow as jaundice. When he removed her shirt and began to pull down her jeans she was merely thankful for the dark which hid her shrunken belly and protruding hip-bones. The scene had become a nightmare of tension and awkwardness; his cock rasped into her; his climax, too long delayed, filled her with an overwhelming relief. Yet she thought none of it would be important if he said he liked her, if he would offer her a single gesture of real affection. The next time they met, at a seminar, she lingered behind to talk to him. He seemed distracted but he walked with her down the stairs.

"Look," he said at length, "about the other night—it was fun, but . . . well, Lois and I have been together for three years. We're going to get married one day. It was fun, but that's all. Sorry."

He went away, leaving Elspeth to return to her room alone. It wasn't fun, she wanted to say. I only did it because I thought you liked me. It wasn't bloody fun. She didn't cry; she felt too bleak. This, then, was her punishment for neglecting her studies. She resolved to give up men and devote herself exclusively to her work.

All for nothing. At the end of her second year, they told her she would have to leave. She had failed.

Elspeth came down to London in the late afternoon and went straight to her father's flat in Knightsbridge. He had bought it some time before but he had never given her a key and she had to leave her bags with the caretaker. On the train, she had had some vague fantasy of a showdown or a miracle—an outpouring of lifelong bitterness or a magical transformation scene in which he would take her in his arms and tell her it didn't matter, she was his daughter and he loved her whatever she was, whatever she had done. She knew it was mere fantasy but when she was away from him she could still dream, even after long years of futility. Only now, when reality was upon her, would her dreams fail. She set off for his office like a zombie, trying to deaden feeling, imagination, heartache, shame; bracing herself for the devastation of her soul. This was the end: the end of hope, the end of all longing. Beyond, there was only despair. She entered the office building through the automatic doors, summoned the lift. When it came, she stepped in, alone, blank-faced and shaking, with the dreadful courage of a victim who mounts unaided the steps to the gallows.

He wasn't there. She found her voice sufficiently to ask where he was although she had no fixed intention of going to look for him. The receptionist gave her the address of a site on the South Bank. When she left the office it was five-thirty and the pubs were beginning to open. She picked one at random, perched uncomfortably on a bar stool, ordered a large Scotch. It was a while since she had had any alcohol; anorexia had put paid to that. She drank it neat, starting with sips and finishing on a gulp that burnt her throat. Then she ordered another. In the mirror beside the bar she caught a glimpse of the face she had learnt to recognize as her own: a gaunt face with too many shadows and a nose whose faint aquilinity had become a fixation with her ever since she lost weight. Long, rust-red hair, uncut and unkempt, straggled in its usual fashion down her back. I'm ugly, she thought. Whatever I do to myself, I'm ugly. Whatever I attempt, I fail. She swallowed her second whisky and waited to feel better; but she didn't.

By the time she left the bar was beginning to empty. Two men approached her as if about to initiate a conversation, but her expression was so stony that they moved away without speaking. She detached herself from the bar stool, picked up her things, and found to her satisfaction that she was quite steady on her feet. She knew she must be fairly drunk but she didn't *feel* drunk; on the contrary, her mind was very clear, clearer than it had been for a long time. She had made a decision, somewhere down her third glass, and now, having fixed on a definite course of action, she felt freed at last from struggle, from failure, even from pain. Outside, she wandered through a couple of streets in search of a taxi. When she found one, she gave the address of her father's building site.

It was growing dark when she arrived.

"Here?" asked the cab-driver, doubtfully.

"Yes," said Elspeth. "Here."

She paid him off and let herself into the site through a gate in the temporary fence which should probably have been kept locked. There were warning lights scattered here and there among half-covered trenches and improvised walkways; above, the building rose up some ten or twelve storeys, caged in scaffolding, solid walls glimpsed infrequently behind a fretwork of bars and shadows. She made her way cautiously in the treacherous dusk, walking around the building till she found an entrance. Inside, it was all bare walls, floors that echoed her footsteps, empty stairs zig-zagging upwards to nowhere. A building still only half shaped, dead rooms that had never yet lived, without atmosphere or purpose. One day, she imagined, boats full of sightseers would pass on the river, and guides would point and say: "That is the Technico building, designed by Sir Rupert Van Leer." And, if they were sufficiently knowledgeable they might go on: "It is a striking example of pure functionalism which . . ." I could never have done it, Elspeth admitted to herself, almost with resignation. Her visions had stayed on the paper: they had no power to grow into a reality of brick and concrete. She climbed the stairs, feeling her way in the dimness. At intervals light came in from outside, neither moonlight nor earthlight but a sickly orange light, faint as a stain on the walls: the nightglow of the city. On the topmost floor she found an opening and went out on to the scaffolding. Below—far below—the ground was almost invisible in the dark. The twin eyes of cars crawled down the street where she had come in her taxi; further away, the myriad city lights were scattered like seed pearls against a backdrop of night. None of it looked real. A poem she had read somewhere came into her mind; she thought it was called *The Suicide*. She repeated the last verse aloud, like an incantation:

> "I shall live out my life in a moment;
> I shall soar in the wind like a swan.
> Then the myriad stars of the city
> Will shiver; and I shall be gone."

She imagined falling, falling into oblivion, and the swift blink of a million lights that would signal the end. But she did not move. And then suddenly, with an onrush of terror that drove all such trivia from her head, she knew she was not alone.

Someone was breathing on her neck.

For a few seconds, such a fear gripped her that her knees seemed to liquefy and her feet were glued to the boards. Then came the voice—a voice as soft as the darkness, both alien and intimate, inexplicably familiar. Fear drained away too quickly, leaving her shuddering.

"It isn't like that, you know," said the voice. "Death wouldn't necessarily be instantaneous. You could lie there for hours with your spine crushed, in mortal agony. Not much fun."

"No," she whispered. Her romantic vision of suicide evaporated on contact with reality, like a raindrop in the sun.

"There are no shortcuts, even to eternity," he went on. "That's as it should be. Life is too precious to let it go without pain."

Idle wisdom. Both manner and voice stirred something in her memory, something she was half eager, half reluctant to bring into focus. She was conscious that although he—the voice—had not touched her, he was standing very close to her. Close enough to restrain her instantly, if she attempted to run. In the turmoil of her mind it did not occur to her that this might be for her own safety; she had practically forgotten the nearness of the drop, hardly a yard away, or her reckless fantasies. She was aware only of the presence behind her, a ghost whose breath was warm, and the voice which made her tremble with a sensation beyond fear. If she turned, she was suddenly sure that his face would be right in front of hers, eyeball to eyeball, as close as a kiss. The thought almost stopped her heart.

He waited.

She turned around. His face, as she had known it would be, was inches from her own. A face semi-visible in the dimness, pale—yes, definitely pale—with features that she could not make out clearly and yet seemed to recognize. A stone-grey stare, cold as November; a bloodless mouth closed as though upon secrets. She shivered, deep down inside, as she might have shivered at a caress, a touch as faint as a snowflake, as intimate as skin. Her conscious mind had forgotten but her body remembered—the body of a thirteen-year-old, both shrinking and awakening, threatened and aroused.

She said: "Michael O'Hara."

He did not contradict her.

"Do you—still work for my father?" He nodded. "You followed me here. You saw me at the office and you followed me . . . You must have." She sounded incredulous, not quite angry.

"No. I heard Sheila give you this address. I knew you would come here."

Telepathy, kismet, a lucky guess. But to Elspeth, worn out with trauma, bemused with whisky, it seemed like the hand of fate.

She asked: "What else do you know?"

"Well . . . I know you were chucked out of college, if that's what you mean."

"How?"

"Someone saw fit to inform your father. One of the lecturers, maybe; a colleague of his, I should imagine. I heard him discussing it on the phone in his office."

"And you thought"—she swallowed—"you thought I would come here, and kill myself."

"I thought you would come here," he amended. He had waited a long time in the empty building, doubting: but he did not say so.

"I wouldn't really have done it," Elspeth said. "I was just thinking about it. It gave me something to plan."

"I see." Perhaps he did. Abruptly, he took her arm. "Come on then. If you're not going to commit suicide, we may as well go. Come with me."

Elspeth hardly protested. It was quite dark now and he guided her down the stairs, still holding her arm, sure of his way. She went with him like a child bewitched by a goblin. His sudden appearance, his omniscience, his voice—the magic of the night, the fumes of whisky in her head—all combined to seduce her. She thought she detected a pattern, the intervention of Providence or of a genie in a bottle; whatever the truth, after the meaningless struggle of the past two years it was an inexpressible relief to let someone else take control, if only for a little while.

He put her in his car and drove her to a restaurant. She had dined out once with Anthony and Diana but she had never been to restaurant alone with a man. At the sight of the menu the familiar panic rushed over her; she said: "I don't eat much" but Michael paid no attention and ordered for her. When the food came she ate it, hypnotized by his unconsidered authority. The gourmet cuisine lay lightly on her stomach and the wine trickled easily into her bloodstream, and gradually she began to feel warmed and softened and insidiously relaxed. She found herself talking—talking as she had never talked before in her life—about her childhood, her sister, her father, her own failed hopes and empty dreams. With Diana, it had rarely been necessary to talk: the twins had understood one another without words. At the clinic, the psychiatrists had bored her with their routine formulae and textbook questions. No one had ever listened to her like Michael O'Hara, no one had ever prompted so gently, or shown such interest. She did not stop to ask herself why he should be interested: it was all a part of the pattern, a natural facet of his goblin charm. As she talked, she heard herself putting into words things she had scarcely known she felt, complicated tangles of love and hatred, jealously, resentment, wasted passion—all the secret desires of a starved heart and loveless body. Somewhere at the back of her mind a tiny voice whispered that this was a fatal mistake: she was betraying herself utterly to a stranger of whom she knew nothing; but she did not stop. The candlelight was too soft, the wine too strong, the pleasure of unburdening herself too sweet and unfamiliar. Elspeth talked; Michael listened; the wax ran down the candles and the clock ticked away to midnight.

The witching hour. Elspeth half expected her companion to turn into a toad and go hopping away across the floor, leaving her with the bill. But the transformation, if such it could be called, had happened, not suddenly on the stroke of twelve, but gradually, throughout the meal, with the slow bewitchment of her vision. He's not so very ugly, she thought, seeing the stony pallor mellowed by the candlelight, the cold eyes warmed (or so she imagined) by some inner feeling. His features were not particularly irregular; his nose was of normal proportions; his chin, while not the strong, manly chin of a Kirk Douglas or a Paul Newman, was neither weak nor receding: an adequate sort of chin. And his mouth might be narrow-lipped and rather bloodless, but at least it was not a full, sensuous mouth like

Keith Eager's, inflicting wet, sloppy kisses that drowned half her face in saliva. He smiled rarely, but sometimes when his eyes were serious his lips would move in a ghost-smile, faint as a shadow, hinting at some distant amusement of secret softening. Once, she had labelled his smile satanic; now, she was fascinated by the slightest twist of a lip. She felt no longer merely warm but hot; great waves of heat were radiating from a point somewhere below her stomach; her cheeks glowed with unaccustomed colour. She had an idea it would be prudent to go home but she had no key and it was far too late to ring.

"Come to my place," he said. "We'll share a toothbrush."

Dimly, she was aware that she was taking a step towards disaster—but it did not feel like disaster, not yet. It felt like sinking into soft cushions before you smother, or sliding into warm water before you drown: an escape, a release, a gentle glissade into a blissful limbo. This time, when he drove, she lost all sense of direction. He parked behind a small block of flats; in the lift, he put his arms around her. She could feel his crotch pressed against her, swollen and hard with anticipation, and she was filled with an onrush of desire that swamped all thought. She knew it was illogical: she had never experienced real pleasure with any man and Michael O'Hara was a stranger or near-stranger, a warlock who had waited in darkness to ensnare her. But she could not fight the dominion of her body. It was as if the pent-up passions of a lifetime had suddenly found an outlet, and she was swept away resistless.

He began to kiss her as soon as they were inside the flat. Even before they reached the bedroom he was pulling off her clothes, exploring her with his hands. In the past, she had always been embarrassed by such caresses, too ashamed of her ugly nudity ever to relax and enjoy herself—in her teens, too fat; later, too hideously thin, afraid to expose her anatomy to anyone. But this time she didn't care. She lay on her back and let him touch her with his hands, mouth, tongue, taking possession of her, inch by inch: her small breasts and sharp nipples, the hollow beneath her ribs, the soft post-prandial curve of her belly. And then he was opening her, nibbling her thighs, putting his tongue into the most intimate places, teasing, kissing, sucking at her like a bee trying to draw honey from a flower. She felt herself falling into ecstasy—floating—drowning—helpless and mindless with lust. The sweet stabbing pain in her groin intensified so that she could no longer bear it: her body was racked with spasms of glorious anguish, subsiding at last to leave her weak and shuddering and luxuriously supine.

He took her carefully the first time, nuzzling his way into her; the second time, he was less gentle, thrusting himself violently deep inside. Once, she gasped aloud and he stopped immediately, murmuring: "Did I hurt you? Did I?" and "I don't want to hurt you. It's just that you're so tight, that's all. I don't want to hurt you . . ."

"It doesn't matter," she said, meaning it. She thought she would have let him do almost anything to her, if it would give him pleasure. He could have whipped her, beaten her, tied her up: she would have been totally acquiescent. It was not love; yet she had never realized desire could be so complex, so inextricably tangled with the desires of another. Afterwards, she lay on the borders of sleep, still holding his cock, which remained obstinately erect; no longer stroking but clinging on to it like a child with a familiar toy. He lifted her hair from his face, settled her head more comfortably against his shoulder. There was a look in his cold eyes which she did not see, a little rueful, a little gentle, a little amused.

"All right?" he whispered.

But she was asleep.

Elspeth awoke the following morning with a shattering headache and a sensation of impending doom. Memory returned in fits and starts, hampered by her headache. Lifting her eyelids with an effort, she saw an expensive stack of bedside stereo, a sumptuous duvet billowing over her chest, and, to her left, a naked back. A man's back. Pale of skin, webbed with ridges of bone and swellings of muscle. Doom, she realized, was not impending: it had already struck. She thought of creeping away before the back woke up, but even as she moved Michael stirred and turned towards her. In the first light of day he was not an attractive sight, his adequate chin covered with unexpectedly dark stubble, his eyes narrowed to slits between puffed lids. Piggy eyes, she thought. Involuntarily, she imagined Anthony Stallibrass, sun-golden, gyspy-dark, beautiful—surely—even in the mornings. For a moment, she was afraid Michael might want to kiss her—it seemed reasonable, after the previous night—and panic engulfed her. But he only grunted, stretched, rolled over. When she was able, Elspeth got up.

She emerged from the bathroom after two aspirins and a cursory wash to find Michael in the kitchen, unhurriedly filling the kettle. He was dressed only in a pair of shabby jeans and his torso, she noticed, matched his back: pallid, tightly muscled, scantily haired. She wished he had put more clothes on. A few lank, fairish locks hung over his forehead; his eyes were still half closed with sleep. Perhaps that was why she did not catch their expression.

He said: "Coffee or tea?"

"Oh—nothing for me. I mean . . . nothing, thank you. I don't . . . Look, could you tell me—can I get a taxi round here somewhere? I really must go. Please."

He surveyed her with his arms folded, leaning against the sink. "I'll drive you," he said. "After coffee."

"No. No, thanks. I have to go now. I mean, I ought to . . . My father will be wondering where I am." An idiotic remark after the confidences of the night before, but even if she could not forget, she could pretend. It was the thought of that self-revelation—both mental and physical—which filled her with her present terror. She had to get away—before Michael touched her, trapped her, mocked her, blackmailed or reminded her. She repeated: "I must go now."

"All right." He grimaced, rather as if flexing his facial muscles to wake them up. He made no attempt to touch her, to blackmail her, even to remind her. Afterwards, she was to remember him as almost insolently relaxed. "Go down the road and turn left. Keep walking till you get to the lights. You might get a taxi there. It's a main road."

"Thank you," she said. "Oh, and . . . thank you for dinner last night. It was very nice."

She didn't wait to see him laughing before she bolted.

The ordeal of facing her father became somehow more manageable after her ordeal with Michael O'Hara: one horror belittling the other, or so she imagined. It did not occur to her that the events of that shameful, impossible night might have altered her perspective in some way. Her father did not shout at her (she almost wished he would): he merely looked at her with vexation, contempt, indifference, guilt—any or all of those, she could not tell and maybe nor could he. But not love. No love. As Michael had said, her news was no news; he had already heard. Even thin, he noted with an odd mixture of relief and disappointment, she did not really look like Diana. He said: "You'd better get a job, hadn't you? Do something with your life," but he made no suggestions and did not seem deeply interested. Afterwards, though it had all been less terrible than her fears, she found herself crying, as if his very calmness had robbed her of some distorted proof of affection.

A week later she rang the office and asked for Michael O'Hara. He had not tried to contact her and her panic had faded, leaving her with an uncomfortable feeling that, since he worked for Rupert, she ought at least to speak to him, dispose of the incident if she possibly could. Still, she did not give her name and was thankful the receptionist, a relative newcomer, would be unlikely to recognize her voice.

"Michael O'Hara?" Sheila sounded politely bored. "I'm sorry: he doesn't work here. You must have the wrong office."

"I—I beg your pardon?"

"There's no one here called Michael O'Hara. I'm sorry."

"But—there must be! He told me . . ."

"I expect you've got the wrong architect," Sheila said, distracted by the arrival of the second post. "This is Sir Rupert Van Leer's office."

"I know," Elspeth said tartly. "Thank you." But Sheila had hung up.

Elspeth was left staring at the phone in bewilderment. It occurred to her that she had driven to Michael's flat in a state of blind intoxication and left in a state of blind panic, leaping into the first taxi she saw. She had not even registered the name of the street. She might know it again if she could find it, but she was not really sure which part of London it was in. Michael had emerged from nowhere at the right moment in her life—and had evidently disappeared back into nowhere, without even leaving an address. She tried to dismiss the matter (after all, she didn't actually *want* to see him again, did she?) but it would not be dismissed. She was left feeling curious, unsettled, unfinished, as if she had been following a thread which was abruptly severed, leaving her

alone on a blasted heath when she had expected to find herself in a forest full of shadows and wolves.

She went to New York later the same year. Her Aunt Barbara
had turned up on one of her rare visits to London and, on an
impulse, invited Elspeth to spend some time with her in the
States. Elspeth had time enough and nowhere to spend it: in
due course, she went. Afterwards, she was to claim that that
one decision had changed her life—changed her *self*—forever.

New York was a fantasy city, an architect's dream-world
conceived in imagination and delirium, apparently untram-
melled by history or tradition or the restrictions of planning
committees. Old and new, stark and ornate, sublime and ridiculous—all stood side by side, art nouveau whorls and cur-
licues of stones facing soaring cliffs of metal and glass, St.
Patrick's like a huge, preposterous wedding cake decorated
with knobs and twists of icing and topped with spires of spun
sugar, mirrored in the endless windows of the Olympic Tower
next door. The streets opened like clefts in a mountain range,
streaming with sunlight, crawling with traffic, teeming with
people. Elspeth wandered around in a sort of trance, a Lilli-
putian in a world of fabulous gigantism, smelling the cooking
smells that seemed to proliferate on every street corner, drifting
into the Museum of Modern Art to spend an hour analysing the
squiggles in some abstract masterpiece, roaming through Saks
and Macy's and Bergdorf Goodman and looking in vain for
somewhere in Tiffany's to have breakfast. The automatic
friendliness dazzled her, the fevered crowds excited her, the
gargantuan buildings filled her heart. Distanced from her father, she could imagine herself closer to him, as if this vista of
contemporary daydreams constituted some species of revelation, giving her a new insight, a special understanding of whatever secret vision it was that drove him on. Had anyone asked
her, she could not have described that vision, or explained the
exact nature of her special understanding. But nobody asked.

And at home, there was Aunt Barbara. "Call me Barbara,"
she told Elspeth, on her first day. "*Aunt* makes me feel so old."
Elspeth remembered her infrequent appearances during childhood, bringing with her a whiff of perfume, a breath of glamour,
exotic presents, expensive furs. She remembered that night

when she was very little, and she and Diana had planned to run away. "We'll go to America—to Aunt Barbara." Now, she was a grown woman who had run away at last, and the welcome she had never dared to hope for was waiting for her here.

"It's lovely to have you," Barbara said, over and over again. "When the boys aren't at school they're always off skiing, or canoeing, or doing something uncomfortable—you know what boys are. And Richard works far too hard. It's *lovely* to have you." Long residence in America had given her a hint of an accent and a Florida sun-tan that never quite faded. The freckles of her teens had gone; the dimples remained. She had had two sons and several miscarriages (the last had coincided with Diana's death) and her marriage to Richard Heydon had survived in the way such marriages do: a lapse here, an affair there, a disillusionment, a falling in love again, a little laughter and a lot of patience. Doing something for Jo's children was one of those things she thought about in the middle of the night when she had nothing else to worry her. She felt sorry for Elspeth on sight, resolved to love her, grew to like her. No sentimentalist—or so she told herself—she tried not to fantasize that Elspeth would become the daughter she had always wanted and never had. But she enjoyed taking her out, buying clothes for her, half coaxing, half bullying her into hairdressers' and beauty salons—gradually beginning the transformation process from an ugly duckling into a tentative swan.

"More like a gosling into a goose," Elspeth said sceptically. But she did not refuse.

The portrait of Johanna Van Leer hung in the dining-room. As a Duny—one of his rare portraits—it had pride of place. Guests were prone to stop and gaze and air their artistic lore; some even offered to buy it. "It's my only sister," Barbara would say with unaccustomed coolness. "She's dead now. I could never sell." Elspeth, admiring, took a moment or two to realize who it must be. She had seen few pictures of her mother: it was generally accepted that Rupert found remembrance too painful, and at home there were only a couple of snapshots in old albums, face averted or out of focus under a blaze of hair. Elspeth sought for her sister's likeness, and was baffled to find features at once strange and elusively familiar. "I thought she would look more like Diana," she said.

"Oh no." Barbara seemed mildly surprised. "Of course, I

never saw much of Diana, but Grizelda sent me some photos. Apart from the colouring, I always thought she took after Rose. Mind you, that portrait isn't much like Jo: it has her eyes, her mouth, her cheekbones; but not her expression. She had a kind of serenity . . . It was as if she used her own face as a mask, and Duny tried to strip the mask away, but I was never sure that he was right about what was underneath." After a minute of serious consideration, she went on: "It's strange: you don't really look like Jo, but you look like her portrait. Your eyes are darker than hers, your bones not so perfect—but still, there's a resemblance."

An elusive familiarity. Later, contemplating her mirror, Elspeth almost believed she could see it. A poor imitation, she thought; a second attempt, botched by the sculptor. But it warmed her, just the same, to find her mother's ghost hiding behind her own reflection, like an unexpected proof of love after long years of loneliness. Her father couldn't have seen it, of course, but one day, back in England, she would know how to make him see.

That evening at dinner, Barbara told her: "I want you to have Jo's diamonds. Rupert gave them to me—I suppose he couldn't bear to keep them—but I've never worn them. I always intended to give them to you or Diana sometime. They're in the bank now, of course." And, since Elspeth looked a little blank: "Jo's diamonds. The diamonds in the picture. I want you to have them. I think it would have pleased her."

Elspeth said: "I've never had anything of my mother's."

"Nothing?" Barbara was rather shocked. "I thought—I'm sure—she had quite a lot of jewellery. What happened to it?"

"Diana had a pair of earrings," Elspeth offered. "I don't know where they are now." In the ground, she thought, suddenly certain. In a coffin with the dead, perhaps already fallen from ear-lobes that had rotted away. Buried with the leftovers of flesh and blood. No longer Diana, only a pair of earrings, and her father's love.

"I expect Grizelda decided it was unsuitable for you," Barbara was saying. "Silly bitch. I never liked her. Are you fond of her?"

Elspeth said: "No."

• • •

The next day they visited a beauty salon. In a variety of mirrors reflecting her from every conceivable angle, Elspeth sought for the ghost in the portrait. But the ghost faded under comprehensive lighting and eighties make-up, and the face that emerged was totally strange. A flush softened her hollow cheeks, shadows emphasized the slant of her eyes. Her lips were painted in, full and red, as startling on her thin face as a rose in a winter frost. Her hair was cut, shaped, curled, tumbled, sculpted about her head. Bemused eyes stared out at her from the depths of her reflection; to left and right, a profile with swan neck and Titian mane. Involuntarily her hand stole to her nose.

"What's the matter?" said Barbara. "You look lovely."

"My nose," Elspeth mumbled.

"What's wrong with your nose?"

"It's huge and ugly and I hate it."

"Change it," said the attendant beautician. This was America.

"*Change* it?" Elspeth stared. As if her nose was a jacket which didn't fit properly, or a dress which didn't suit her.

"Why not?" Barbara said. "If it would make you feel better. I know just the man . . ."

A few days later, Elspeth visited Just the Man. Her stay in New York was extended, her nose reduced. A passion for ice-cream sodas put on a pound or two, and Barbara's aerobics class began to restore her muscles. In England, Rupert read a long letter from his sister-in-law, stopped signing cheques, and arranged a credit card. On the other side of the Atlantic, Elspeth surveyed the magical sliver of plastic as if it was a ticket to maturity and sophistication. When the swelling on her nose had subsided, Barbara took her back to the beauty salon. The make-up artist went to work. Elspeth gazed at her assorted images without speaking. *Mirror, mirror on the wall, who is the fairest of them all?* On either side she saw a profile of nasal perfection. Her features grew under the painter's hand: Elspeth, yet not Elspeth; the same face—a different face. For the first time she dared to think: I look beautiful. I'm ugly, I know I'm ugly, but I *look* beautiful. I'm ugly, I know I'm ugly, but I *look* beautiful. I look beautiful . . .

After a while, Barbara said: "Well, what do you think? Are you happy?"

Elspeth tried to shrug and failed. "I look okay," she said. "Item two lips, indifferent red . . ."

"I don't think we have Indifferent Red," said the make-up artist. "Is it a new line?"

In 1981, Elspeth started an art and design course at the Cooper Union. Her father agreed to make her an allowance; in her second year, she moved into her own flat. This lifestyle was very different from her previous college days. This time, she tried to make friends, something that never came easily to her. She learnt to eat hamburgers, drink Jack Daniel's, go jogging in Central Park; she painted pictures of lines and spaces and produced odd, angular sculptures which evolved unexpectedly into functional objects. Fellow students called her Elsa; at first it sounded strange to her, but eventually she grew accustomed to it. She found it symbolic that in America even her name should be transformed. A new name; a new identity. Elsa Van Leer. She came to like being Elsa Van Leer. Elspeth had been ugly, solitary, unloved; Elsa had cover-girl looks and friends enough to feel at home in the world. Elspeth had failed at everything she attempted; Elsa was talented and potentially successful, a new focus of interest for society journalists and glossy magazines. Elspeth had been obsessed, unhappy, imprisoned in her own darkness; Elsa thought she was sometimes happy, hoped that at last she was free. And Elspeth—Elspeth had been the child her father did not want, could not love; whereas Elsa would return one day to be all in all to him.

Back in England, Rupert thought of her occasionally, when he could not avoid it, and trusted that New York would accomplish what the psychiatrists had bungled, and relieve him of his daughter for good.

5

Elsa was twenty-four when she embarked on her first serious affair—too inexperienced to be prudent, too generous to keep anything back, too eager to give away whatever was left of her heart. With Anthony Stallibrass, she had known unrequited love; with Michael O'Hara, unthinking lust. This time, she envisaged a meeting of both mind and body, a union which had to be total, must be forever. She threw herself into the relationship with the recklessness of adolescence and the passion of maturity. Even so, it did not have to be a disaster.

Grant Barrymore was forty-eight. His full name was James Grant Barrymore, but only lifelong friends called him Jim; he himself preferred Grant. The art director of an upwardly mobile advertising agency, he had come to the college to give twice-weekly evening lectures in a course which rapidly became the most popular of the year. The boys liked his colloquial style, his flippant dismissal of artistic convention, his large-scale visions of gloss and neon. The girls liked his broad shoulders (basketball), his electric blue eyes, the glimpse of chest hair when he wore an open-necked shirt. A short beard emphasized the squareness of his jaw and concealed the suspicion of a jowl—a carefully calculated beard, sufficient to make an intellectual statement while not long enough to label him a vintage hippy. His clothes were expensive but casual, the clothes of a man who liked to dress well but was indifferent to the impression he created—or such was the impression he wished to create. He prided himself on his sense of humour and his rapport with the students. Nowadays, he told them, Michelangelo Buonarroti would have covered the Sistine Chapel ceiling, not with images of God, but with scenes from *Dallas*. (Appreciative laughter.) "The Naked Maja" as Joan Collins on the centrefold of *Playboy*. The Coca Cola can had replaced the gilded chalice. Art moved with the times and the imagination of the artist must move still faster in order to stay ahead. His audience drank it all in. Only the tall redhead at the back never laughed at his witticisms, and he caught her smiling just once, during his third lecture, when the dynamic pacing which formed a part of his technique led him to stub his toe. He was intrigued. From a colleague, he found out who she was. He began to tease her in class, challenging her silence, inviting comment. "Miss Van Leer evidently doesn't agree." "Miss Van Leer, as usual, is not impressed." Elsa, at first unnerved, later flattered, did her best to answer back.

"I don't think da Vinci would have been designing soap cartons," she said once, with all the irony she could muster. "He'd have been more interested in the Concorde."

"Grant really likes you," another girl said afterwards, with a note of envy. Grant favoured first-name terms with his students; his use of "Miss Van Leer" was purely sarcastic. "Everyone's noticed. That's why he picks on you all the time: it's a form of sexual antagonism. Don't you think he's *gorgeous?*"

"He's old enough to be my father," Elsa said.

A fortnight later, he gave a cocktail party to which most of his regular students were invited. The party was at his flat in 1 Fifth Avenue; Elsa had only heard of the restaurant on the ground floor and was impressed to find twenty-seven storeys of redbrick architecture, oak columns in the lobby, and a glamour that was both solid and expensive. The apartment itself was furnished in manly browns with here a note of azure, there an undertone of sable. The bar was panelled in lignum vitae; the paintings, which were few and trendy, included a Howard Hodgkin and a Julian Schnabel; the guests, who were as carefully mixed as the drinks, encompassed a minor film director, a Wall Street whizkid, a psychiatrist, a publisher, a senator's wife. "Old money," whispered Elsa's self-appointed informant. Elsa spoke little, drank a lot, and was conscious from time to time of Grant's azure-blue stare (to match the keynote) picking her out in the crowd like a searchlight. She began to feel faintly excited, faintly sick. He *does* like me, she thought incredulously, still unaccustomed to the idea that an accredited catch like Grant could possibly be interested in her. But did she like him? Previously, she had been rather proud of her indifference. But she needed to be loved, to be "in love." She found herself looking for his good points: the exercise-rounded muscles, the sun-bed tan, still relatively wrinkle-free (there was a bottle of he-man moisturizer in the bathroom), the thick hair, streaky grey, an artistic *mélange* of pewter and silver. She didn't always agree with his views but she was pleasantly shocked and therefore stimulated by them, and wasn't it appropriate for a lecturer to shock and stimulate? And . . . "He's old enough to be my father," she repeated to herself. She had never had an older man. The thought attracted her.

Much later, lying among rumpled black sheets listening to Grant running the impulse shower, she knew this was different, believed it was special. He had proved a skilled lover, tenderly conscientious or conscientiously tender, evidently well grounded in Masters and Johnson. There was none of the mindless sensuality she had experienced with Michael O'Hara; this was intellectual sex, sensitive, caring and meaningful. She knew—because Grant had told her—that she was broadening the parameters of her physical awareness, while at the same time exploring the secrets of her inner self. Of course, Grant had a smaller cock than Michael, but such details were trivial and irrelevant in the context of a complete relationship and the conjunction of two minds. When he came out of the shower, capped teeth a-gleam in a swift, intimate smile, white towel round his lean hips, she concentrated on his mature good looks and the anticipated envy of female students. Even Anthony Stallibrass, after all, had been merely a beautiful boy, beloved in a fantasy by an undeveloped girl. Now she was an adult, a woman who needed a Real Man. Grant Barrymore, with the hairs on his chest and the crow's feet at play around his eyes, must surely qualify as a Real Man. This was serious. This was Love.

The next day, they dined off *nouvelle cuisine* at the Odeon. Grant pointed out Bianca Jagger and nodded to Andy Warhol. He dropped an extra name or two, carelessly, between crudités.

"But of course," he said—self-deprecating, a little mocking—"you're Sir Rupert Van Leer's daughter. You must know half the artistic establishment in London."

Elsa said nothing.

The affair progressed as Elsa presumed such affairs always did. They went to the theatre, to the cinema, to selected parties where Grant showed Elsa off to his friends, and for the first time she was made aware of the prestige attached to the Van Leer name. They dined out and in; Grant fancied himself as something of an epicure, both in the restaurant and in the kitchen. They talked about Life and Art and Sex; at least, Grant talked, Elsa listened. He was always trying to draw her out on the subject of her background or her father—but she told him little and let his imagination supply the rest, knowing he would get it wrong. He had fallen in love with Elsa, the tentative sophisticate with her cool manners and beautiful face; Elspeth—unhappy, unlovely, farouche—was part of a dead past: he must never catch even a glimpse of her, never suspect her existence. Grant Barrymore, gourmet, connoisseur of this and that, self-styled maverick in the world of traditional art, could have had nothing to say to the changeling child whom no one but her twin had ever been able to love, and whom no one had wanted at all. Elsa had a new personality, a new self; Elspeth she wanted only to forget. As for her father—Grant would never understand about her father. When he mentioned his own parents it was with a sort of compassionate superiority, a kindly contempt, gently belittling their way of life and their outdated attitudes, as if the peculiarities of his upbringing had happened to someone else and he was a psychiatrist reviewing the case with divine detachment. He seemed to be mildly fond of them, mildly bored by them: all mildness and disinterest. She could not possibly explain to him how she felt about her father.

The affair progressed, or at any rate, it continued. In the winter, they went skiing; in the spring, they jogged. They had rows: after the initial panic, Elsa felt rather proud to think that

she had a real relationship, with real rows. Barbara was introduced to Grant and pronounced him "charming"; Grant
thought Barbara "delightful." (Her husband, Richard Heydon,
thought him pretentious, but did not say so.) Grant tried teach-
ing Elsa to drive: they broke up for a week and got back together
again over asparagus tips in the conservatory at Raoul's; he
sent her a dozen long-stemmed roses and relinquished her to
a professional instructor. On the day she passed her test, he
was out of town. He had a beach house in the Hamptons which
she had never visited; once, only half jokingly, she had accused
him of keeping a secret wife there. He had laughed and with
genuine amusement, told her: "It's being redecorated" and
"We'll be able to use it in the summer. Anyhow, I can't stand
the beach on a bad day; it depresses me." Barbara's car had
been insured for Elsa's benefit and on an impulse she decided
to drive down and surprise him. It was the first initiative she
had taken in their relationship and she felt vaguely daring, but
passing her test had given her new confidence. Accustomed to
American notions of distance, the drive of a hundred miles or
so did not seem too far. She set off down the Long Island Ex-
pressway to Easthampton.

It was nearly evening when she arrived. She had found her
way with little difficulty, stopping to check her direction only
twice. Grant came running out of the house when she sounded
her horn. He was wearing a cashmere sweater with no shirt
underneath, as if he had dressed carelessly or in a hurry, and
a plastic apron which she did not recognize. "I passed my driving test," she said, "so I thought I'd surprise you." He looked
surprised. She went into the vestibule, still talking, and was
unnerved to find she had left him outside, standing on the front
step as though rooted to the spot. "Grant—" she called. And,
in a sudden access of self-doubt: "It's all right, isn't it?"

He didn't answer.

"You've been cooking," she said, trying for normality.
"What's for dinner?"

The kitchen was to her left, the door open. She walked in
without hesitation. Afterwards, she remembered vividly seeing
the young man across the room, half turned towards her, the
chef's hat squashed down over his blond curls, the pout frozen
on his lips. His apron was white cotton, with frills; under it his
torso was naked and honey-gold. Beside her was the chopping

board which Grant had just abandoned, with a little mound of diced meat and a bright knife, already bloodstained. She remembered it all in great detail.

She did not remember picking up the knife.

When it was all over, she was sent to Europe to recuperate. Her college course had ended in catastrophe, but Barbara still saw her as an artist and accordingly suggested a therapeutic programme of Great Art. She took her niece to see châteaux in the Loire, caves in the Dordogne, canals in Venice, ruins in Rome. Elsa did as she was told, remained generally docile, inwardly tense, outwardly quiet. "I might have killed him," she said, and it was impossible to tell if she was distressed, if she regretted it, or if she wished she had succeeded. After the accident (everyone involved called it an "accident") Grant had lost his nerve, found it again, staunched blood, called a doctor he knew. Elsa had been discovered wandering on the beach, washing her hands in the sea. Expensive lawyers kept matters out of the courts and out of the press; Grant did not want to lose his macho image and the unfortunate young man was offered little choice. Later, from the safety of his London office, Rupert sent in the psychiatrists. But Elsa was an old hand at psychiatrists: they had done her no good at the clinic and she was determined they should do her no good now.

"I hope you'll leave her with me," Barbara had written in a long letter to her brother-in-law. "Poor darling, she was violently in love with Grant—and Elsa isn't the type who falls violently in love easily. My own analyst tells me mere unfaithfulness might have been bearable, but the discovery of his homosexual activities would almost certainly prove devastating. I feel dreadfully guilty—Richard always told me he couldn't stand Grant, but I wouldn't listen. Anyway, you of all people must know how highly-strung Elsa is. She doesn't talk about it much, but I know she was absolutely shattered by her sister's death, and then she had bulimia, and failed at architectural college—and just when she was beginning to get her act together, *this* happened. It's no wonder she fell apart. I wish she would talk about it more, but I think it's important not to pressurize her. Right now she needs kindness, not questions."

And so kindness took her to Chenonceaux and Cheverny, to

Périgord, the Pitti Palace, the Colosseum. Finally, they arrived in Greece. "I ought to get back to the States," Barbara said, somewhere in the labyrinth of Daedalus. "It's Dicky's birthday in a fortnight." (Her son, not her husband.) "His eighteenth: I feel old just thinking about it. But . . . look, you don't have to come, if you don't want to. You could stay on for a couple more weeks, somewhere quiet. Lie on the beach, get a nice tan. You need to relax. We've been moving around such a lot, there hasn't been much time for relaxation. Would you like that?"

Elsa thought about it conscientiously, the way she always thought before answering these days. "Yes," she said at length, "I'd like that."

"You'll be all right on your own—*now*, won't you?"

Elsa considered it. "I'll be all right."

Before she left, Barbara found a suitable beach in the Cyclades, a cusp of sand hemmed in by crumbled cliffs, lapped by a creaseless sea. There were no luxury hotels, no airport. Instead, there was a shabby and overcrowded ferry which had evidently once been French, a fishing village with minor concessions to tourism huddled under a green mountainside, a villa with vines over the porch and centipedes in the bathroom. The landlady spoke few words of English so Elsa smiled more than was customary for her, to show that everything was fine. She caught the centipedes very carefuly in a tooth-mug and put them out of the window. She had breakfast on the porch under the vine leaves, black coffee (Nescafé, not Greek) and a slice of melon, and dinner in a diminutive restaurant, sitting alone at a corner table with a plate of fried squid, a Greek salad, a book. No one bothered her. And on the beach, she met the girl.

It was late in the season, there were few tourists left, and Elsa's cusp of sand was some way from the main beach and particularly inaccessible. On the first day, she was undisturbed. The girl came on the second day. Elsa had an idea she had noticed her on the ferry; island-hopping perhaps: her tan had the tinge of ochre that only comes from a whole summer out in the sun. Elsa's own tanning was a hesitant affair, with much caution and protective cream. The girl had a dilapidated bamboo mat to lie on and a very brief bikini, most of which she removed before sunbathing. Originally it had been shaded, yellow to orange, but on the bottom half much of the colour had been bleached out. Once, Elsa decided, it had been a nice bikini, probably expensive. Her hair was streaked blond, by art or nature, with a disintegrating perm and a salon cut that had long grown out of shape. But she seemed to belong, on the beach, in the village, in a way Elsa with her couture swimwear did not.

On the third day, she said hello.

"You've been here a long time," Elsa remarked after a while, "haven't you?"

"Here?"

"In the islands."

"Yes," said the girl. "A long time."

She did not sound happy or relaxed about it, like a casual beach bum or a free spirit roaming the Aegean on indefinite holiday. She sounded tired, tired to the bone, an unwilling gypsy condemned to wander, moving from one patch of sand to the next, from fishing village to identical fishing village, trapped in a maze of blue seaways and shabby ferries and green-and-golden fragments of land. It seemed to Elsa that she had come there to hide or to escape, and now her hiding-place had become her prison—a prison of interminable sunshine, cloying peace, deadly tranquillity. It was possible to have too much of anything, even Paradise. She was weary with the weariness of long desperation, her once glamorous clothes had grown threadbare, her money was almost gone. She was running away, Elsa thought, and now she is running in circles, and she cannot get out. Only a fantasy, of course: the invention of an idle moment. But: I suppose I'm running away too, after a fashion. And with that thought, faint as a shudder, like a droplet of cold water falling on her neck, came the feeling that they were akin.

On the fourth day they began to talk properly. The girl asked questions and Elsa answered. It did not seem to matter answering questions, here, with a stranger. She found herself thinking of a device in a C. S. Lewis story, a magical forest called the Wood Between the Worlds. This place, she decided, was like that, a place between worlds, outside time. Here, she and the other girl could meet and talk, maybe become friends, sharing their secrets, opening their hearts; and after they would go their separate ways, back into their separate lives, probably never to meet again. It was an illusion of the kind which had beguiled Elsa before, under different circumstances; but she did not notice.

"Are you on holiday?" the girl asked.

"I suppose so." Elsa was lying on her stomach, gazing at the sea; she did not look at her interlocutor. "My aunt tells me I'm convalescing after severe emotional trauma." She added: "People talk like that in New York."

"I've never been to New York," the girl remarked, with a hint of curiosity or wistfulness. Then—"I used to live in Paris."

"Where do you live now?"

"Here. There. Anywhere. Wherever I happen to be."

There were long pauses between question and answer, pauses during which the sea lapped, and the air shimmered, and tiny wavelets spread a thin foam like lace upon the sand. Presently, the girl asked: "What was your severe emotional trauma?"

Elsa hesitated, not—for once—set on reticence, merely picking her words. "I was in love," she said.

"That."

"Yes—at least, I think so. I thought so at the time. But . . . it's so easy to imagine things, isn't it?"

"Even when you imagine things," the girl said, "it still hurts."

"Mm. I daresay it hurt. It must have hurt. I don't really remember. You see, I found out he was living with someone else—with a *man*. I drove down to see him and he—the man— he was there in the kitchen. They'd been cooking together. Grant used to like that: sex first, then cooking. There was a knife on the chopping-board. So I stabbed him."

"Your lover?"

"No. His."

A further pause. The sea lapped. A dragonfly skimmed the beach like a small iridescent helicopter. Then: "Good for you," said the girl.

Elsa raised herself on one elbow, staring at her. No one else had said: "Good for you."

"Do you really think so?"

"Of course I do. I'd have done the same, if I'd had the courage. Did he die?"

"No," said Elsa. "I suppose I'm glad, really. I shouldn't have liked to go to prison." She went on: "The psychiatrists thought I'd gone off my head. Even my aunt thought so. 'Murder while the balance of her mind was disturbed'—that sort of thing. A fit of madness. Some of my ancestors were a bit mad."

"I don't think you were mad," the girl said positively. "I think you were quite right."

This time, the silence was definitely companionable. The dragonfly zoomed back for a second reconnaissance. Elsa remembered that in the story, the Wood Between the Worlds had been a place where past and future grew dim, where even your own name was forgotten. She felt comfortably distanced from herself, neither Elsa nor Elspeth, just a girl on a beach. Any girl. Any beach. She assumed her confidante felt the same.

"Why are you here?" she enquired, eventually.

"Why not?"

"Yesterday," said Elsa, "I wondered if you were running away. Like me."

"Maybe." The girl smiled thinly. "I'm in trouble. I always am. Running away from trouble . . . like you." And as she spoke, her voice altered, ever so slightly, though Elsa did not hear it. "As you say. Like you."

"What kind of trouble?—if you want to tell me."

"I don't mind." The girl might have shrugged if she hadn't been horizontal. "I was having an affair with a man who shot himself. A politician in the French government. You might have read about it." Elsa hadn't. "I knew they'd say it was my fault, so I ran away." And now, I have nowhere to go. She didn't say it but the statement hung in the air, as obvious as if it had been spoken.

"*Was* it your fault?" Elsa asked.

"Partly." Meeting frankness with frankness, Elsa thought, respecting her. "He told me he loved me. I wanted him to leave his wife. He said it would wreck his career. The usual scenario. Only . . . I never guessed he would kill himself. I didn't know his wife meant so much to him. Or I so little."

"When somebody kills himself," Elsa said, repaying reassurance with reassurance, "it's his choice. His fault. It's ridiculous to blame anyone else. It's ridiculous for you to blame yourself, too."

"I don't," the girl said, too quickly. And then: "At least, I try not to."

After a minute, she added: "Thanks."

Elsa said nothing. It didn't seem necessary to say any more.

They lay side by side in the friendly sunshine, turning themselves over now and then like fish under a grille. The girl applied protective lotion to the most inaccessible sections of Elsa's back. Elsa responded in kind with the last few drops from a bottle of cheap oil. "Tomorrow," she said, "you can share mine." She didn't have any more oil but she made a mental note to get some. There was a shop in the village. The girl produced a can of beer. It was lukewarm and flavoured with sand, and anyway, Elsa didn't like beer; but she drank it.

"It's a strange kind of coincidence," she remarked, "our meeting like this. Both of us here to escape from something. From an act of violence. And from men."

"Perhaps it isn't a coincidence," the girl said. "Perhaps it's fate."

Even as she spoke, Elsa knew a moment of *déjà vu*—a realization that, although the situation had changed, the *feeling* had happened before. A feeling of being part of a pattern, a fraction in the Great Equation, a dancer in the Dance of Life. Only this time, she sensed she was being manipulated, though whether by god or demon or her own subconscious cravings she did not know. In any case, the cat was out of the bag, the genie out of the bottle. She should never have mentioned coincidence: coincidence led inevitably to fate, fate to fatalism. And fatalism mesmerized the brain and sapped the will.

Still, here was no Michael O'Hara. Here was just a girl on a beach. Any girl. Any beach. The sea lapped like a cat which had got out of the bag and located a saucer of cream. Elsa was showered in warmth and light, bathed in air and silence. It was impossible to trouble about fate, on a beach in Greece.

"My name is Elsa," she offered, abruptly. "Elsa Van Leer."

"My name is Nicky Simpson," said the girl.

There was a pause—a pause unlike all preceding pauses. Lingering. Suddenly dreadful.

"I think I once knew your sister."

When the initial shock was over, Elsa found her reactions curiously ambivalent. The Nicky she had once imagined—the Becky Sharp with her wide eyes and deceptive air of meekness—had long vanished. Nonetheless, there remained an aftertaste of doubt; an occasional flicker of distrust, which she sought to overcome—like her sister, had she but known it—by proffering a little more friendship than the situation warranted, an extra milligram of generosity or confidence. Nicky, after all, was a link with the past, a witness to memory. She had been Diana's friend and in talking to her Elsa could revive, for a brief space, her sister's fading ghost. And so, over the next few days, she talked of Diana—favourite daughter, loyal twin— fearing to say too much, ashamed to say too little. They lay on the beach or sat at the corner table in the primitive restaurant, sharing a bottle of wine, or lemonade, or coconut-scented sun-oil, sometimes in silence, sometimes in leisurely conversation. Elsa resolved not to be drawn into any personal revelation, but in the event Nicky seemed neither oppressively curious nor passionately interested. She listened automatically, almost lazily, the way a lizard sunning itself on a rock, eyes half closed against the light, listens to the approach of a beetle in the grass. It is easy to talk to a lizard on a rock. Of course, often, when the beetle comes near enough, the lizard will snap it up for dinner; but Elsa knew little of jungle law. Gradually, even her doubts were forgotten or ignored. One day, it occurred to her that Nicky looked at her with Diana's eyes, rain-grey eyes changed to blue against the mustard-brown of her tan. She said as much to Nicky and Nicky laughed—a laugh that cut off abruptly as if she feared it was in bad taste. Elsa was to remember that laugh.

"I wonder if that's lucky or unlucky," Nicky said, "someone else's eyes. And . . . whose hands? whose destiny? whose heart?" Ah, whose?

Elsa looked up, startled; but the sea murmured of sleep and Nicky appeared to be talking to herself, and the tiny query in Elsa's mind faded into unimportance.

Time slid by. On the last evening Elsa gave Nicky her various addresses in London and New York, assuming they would remain unused. An end-of-holiday ritual, meaning nothing. "I would say I'll write," Nicky said, "but I won't."

"Do you know where you'll be?" Elsa enquired.

Nicky smiled mysteriously; she had a small mouth but many smiles, from the wide and dazzling to the inscrutable curve. "Oh—wherever the wind blows me," she said.

Elsa knew without asking that she had come to the end of her money, but when Nicky insisted on paying for dinner she felt it would be churlish to argue. It was a flamboyant gesture to a brief comradeship, and as such, sacred. In the morning Elsa went to Nicky's room in her villa while she still slept and tucked an envelope under her door. It contained five hundred dollars in fifty-dollar bills. Her own gesture, and, in her innocence, she worried that Nicky would see in it merely a rich girl's careless charity, and feel humiliated.

She left without saying goodbye.

Six months later, in New York, her money was returned to her. Five hundred dollars in fifty-dollar bills. It came by post from the UK, but there was no accompanying letter, no note, not so much as a compliments slip. Elsa banked it absent-mindedly, and forgot about it.

Elsa came back to England in the spring of 1984. She knew now that she had only been staying away, all that time, in order to plan her return. And somehow, although what Grant had done had hurt her, getting over it, finding herself undamaged, almost untouched, gave her strength and a kind of self-respect. "Good for you," Nicky had said. The words armoured her against all psychoanalysis and well-meaning pity. She gave an exhibition of paintings and functional sculpture: thanks to the Van Leer name, there was much interest and publicity; thanks to the publicity, over half the items were sold. Having that money—the first she had ever earned—was one of the best things that had happened to Elsa. All her life there had been money, not necessarily in her pocket but in the bank, in stocks and shares, in property and possessions and prestige, lots and lots of money, a safe, solid wall shutting her in, shutting the world out, imprisoning her, protecting her, isolating her. But this money was the product of her own efforts, her own creative thought: the currency of honour. With it, she felt she could face her father again, a woman he might be proud of, no longer a dependent child. She wrote and told him when to expect her. Two days before the date specified, she flew home.

Why she changed the date, she never knew. In her dreams her father was there to meet her. Perhaps, fearing even the faintest disillusionment, she decided to cheat her fantasy, and return early. She caught the night plane and saw the sun rise out of the Atlantic cloud cover, red in red sky. The air hostess brought her a breakfast which she couldn't eat. And then they were coming down to Heathrow, through a break in the clouds, into the chill brilliance of a spring morning. England. Her heart lifted, though whether in terror or anticipation or a little of both she was not sure. I am different, she told herself: everything will be different now. She had departed Elspeth, she returned Elsa. Elspeth had been a wretched scarecrow of a girl, with limbs like a stick insect, hair like bladder-wrack, clothes she could no longer remember. Elsa had a model figure, designer curls. Her complexion was by Shiseido, her sweater by Umberto Ginocchetti. A blouson jacket of imitation zebra, with a high collar and a plethora of metal studs, echoed faintly and ironically the motorcycle leathers of her teens. Impenetrable sun-glasses hid her eyes. She felt glamorous, tremulous, thankfully incognito.

The taxi drove her to Knightsbridge; the caretaker unloaded her luggage. "Miss Van Leer!" he said. "I didn't recognize you." And, on the way to the lift: "Your father left you the keys. You're a few days earlier than expected, aren't you? Perhaps you'll be able to make it after all."

"Make it?" said Elsa.

In the flat she shut the door, deposited her cases in the living-room. There was an envelope propped up against the telephone, addressed to her. She tore it open with suddenly shaking fingers. Inside was a single sheet of paper—office paper—crossed by a few lines of handwriting. A large, forceful hand using a wide-nibbed fountain pen and black ink: painfully familiar. Her father's hand.

Dear Elspeth—I shall be away for the next couple of weeks on my honeymoon. I was married on the 15th, at St. John's, Churston; I am sorry you were unable to be there. Yours, Rupert.

Shock held her rigid. Dreams fell apart; confidence, trust, hope vanished into the abyss. Somewhere, in the tiny corner of her mind that still functioned, she thought: He can't even sign himself Daddy. Just a scrawled note, an automatic regret: as impersonal as a memo. She had never had a Daddy. The rigidity broke into shudders; she leaned on the sideboard for support, still staring at the letter, reading it through, again and again, until words and phrasing became meaningless, a scribbled pattern on a page, a foreign language.

It was several minutes before she registered the significance of the date. The fifteenth. *Today.* Of course: her father had supposed she would arrive on the seventeenth, after the event—

Perhaps you'll be able to make it after all . . .

Urgency engulfed her like rage. She looked wildly around the flat, as though expecting a chariot drawn by dragons to materialize at her need. She thought of delayed trains, of unhelpful taxis, of the Ford Mustang she had driven in America . . . A car. Surely her father must have a car in the garage. She dashed for the door, hesitated, ran back to the phone. At Churston Grange, a new housekeeper answered. The wedding was at two. Glancing at the clock, Elsa saw she had little more than an hour and a half. She dropped the receiver and bolted without bothering to replace it in the cradle. The door slammed behind her.

Downstairs, the caretaker gave her the keys to Rupert's second car. A coffee-coloured Aston Martin: she hadn't seen it before. "It's insured for you, is it?" he asked belatedly.

"Bugger the insurance," Elsa said. She felt for the clutch, thrust the bar brusquely into gear, and drove off.

She arrived at the church only a minute or two after the hour. She had known the road since childhood and had driven the unfamiliar car with hereditary recklessness and little regard for the Highway Code. There was a long scratch on the coachwork but no one was dead.

"No, I don't have an invitation," she told the usher. "I'm Elsa Van Leer."

The name—and the defiant note in her voice—turned heads in the neighbouring pews. She walked up the aisle, her unsuitable studded zebra and black trousers attracting more curious stares and whispered comments. She did not notice. All she saw was the man waiting by the altar rail: the back of his head, hatless and unmistakable; the lion's mane, shot with grey and more carefully trimmed than usual; the giant shoulders, dwarfing those around him. Her father. As she drew near, the fury drained out of her, leaving only a sickening emptiness.

Briefly, she had been possessed, insane with desperation; but she had had no plan of action, no thought of what to say or do. Now, she realized that there was nothing *to* say, nothing to be done. She could not go to her father and remonstrate or plead, nor offer love, nor ask it, nor wish him happy, nor even say hello. At the sight of his back, terror filled her, useless longing, dying hope. She sank into a pew a couple of rows behind. People she did not know moved up to make room, murmuring objections she did not hear.

Her stiff poise disguised failing courage and weakened knees. In that moment she knew that Elsa Van Leer was only a mask, an artifice: under the Shiseido face, the designer clothes, she was still Elspeth. Still rejected, still alone, forever ugly. For a minute, she thought that was why the people round her were staring—they could see the ugliness showing through, the jutting nose, the sullen mouth; a changeling in their midst. She fixed her eyes on the altar, elaborately decked with flowers. The organist began to play the Wedding March from *Lohengrin*. Everyone craned to see the bride. Elsa had been so absorbed in her father, she had forgotten about the bride. She turned round.

She saw a white silk dress, deceptively plain: a virgin princess attired to meet her prince. A bouquet smothered her hands and a veil concealed her every feature. But Elsa was suddenly sure that the woman was young, nearer her own age then Rupert's. Through the semi-diaphanous chiffon, she caught a glimpse of red-gold hair—Diana's colour, she thought, with a shiver which might have been superstition. And as the procession passed, she saw or imagined the flicker of a gaze raised to hers.

The bride reached the altar; the organ reached a crescendo; the vicar preened his cassock for action. Slowly, the bride lifted her veil and turned towards the groom. Diana's hair framed a face of maiden pallor, mouth too small, cloud-grey eyes too far apart.

Nicky.

PART TWO

PART TWO

6

Nicky Simpson knew little about her mother, nothing about her father. The name on her birth certificate was Nichola Simpson, misspelt; her place of birth was given as Leeds; her paternity "not known." Muriel Simpson knew; but she would never say, closing her small mouth tightly on the secret as on so many things, until her lips grew pinched from the habit of constant pursing. Nicky had inherited the small mouth, but even as a little girl she made different use of it, flexing it into smiles for strangers or assorted grimaces for her mother. She was not a pretty child but she had a species of waif-like charm which beguiled most adults and would have been particularly effective on a charity poster: pale face, retroussé nose, straight wispy hair, round sad eyes. Originally undersized, she continued to give an impression of physical fragility and diminutive build even when she was grown-up and had passed five foot five.

She learnt early the importance of being a good liar. Her mother was not a good liar: little Nicky, with her quick ear and acute memory, often caught her out in self-contradiction or blatant inaccuracy. Collecting her daughter from school, Muriel would agree with another mother that yes, the West

Street bakery was the best, and didn't they have lovely chocolate cake; yet two weeks later she would aver that she preferred East Street, and personally she found chocolate cake far
too rich. Other women, preoccupied with their own affairs, did
not seem to notice; but Nicky noticed. In fact, they never had
cake at all, except on the rare occasions when visitors came.
Nicky, though critical of her mother's performance, absorbed
quickly the idea that cake for tea was an essential, and that it
was necessary to pretend. Muriel lied badly, without thinking,
keeping up appearances; Nicky lied fluently, extravagantly,
learning from her mistakes. "We had wedding cake last night,"
she told her classmates. "Chocolate wedding cake."

"Wedding cake isn't chocolate," said another girl, more
knowledgeable. "It's fruit cake, with hard white icing. I had
some at my cousin's. It's horrid."

"This was a *chocolate* wedding cake," Nicky insisted. "Chocolate cream in the middle and chocolate flakes on top."

Next time, however, she referred to wedding cake with scorn,
dwelling on the hardness of the icing and embellishing the story
with a cousin and a church and her own role as bridesmaid.
But secretly she was disillusioned: wedding cake ought to be
the nicest cake in the world, and that meant chocolate. When
I get married, she vowed, I'm going to have chocolate cake. I
don't care what anyone says. She tried asking her mother what
sort of wedding cake she had had, but Muriel merely answered:
"The usual kind," with that look on her face which she always
wore when she was telling a serious untruth, and Nicky did
not press her further. She doesn't know, Nicky concluded; she's
never had wedding cake either. The implications sank in gradually, insinuated themselves into her subconscious. She was
twelve years old when she first saw her birth certificate, after
picking the lock on her mother's dressing-table drawer. The
only part that surprised her was the mention of Leeds.

Muriel never talked about home or family. After the birth of
her unwanted daughter she had moved to a South London
suburb, leaving friends, relations, public disgrace or private
pity behind her. She called herself Mrs., wore a wedding ring,
worked at any job she could get in order to pay the rent and
avoid applying to the Welfare State. Perhaps it was a sort of
pride (she was just old enough to think of such financial assistance as "government charity"); perhaps she was reluctant to

divulge the necessary details of her personal life. She kept the flat clean but not as spotless as she would have wished: her successive jobs left her little energy for housework. Nicky was made to help with the dusting, but she grew expert at sweeping dirt under the rugs and ignoring the existence of nooks and crannies. Muriel dreamed of a cottage in the country with diamond-bright window panes, dahlias in the garden, a green view of hills; but of course it was not possible. There was no work in the country and she could never afford to buy a place of her own. Yet when the chance came, it did not make her happy. She told people it was a legacy from her godmother, and Nicky, assessing expression and manner with childish sagacity, decided this time that it was the truth. Long years of filtering out fact from fiction in her mother's stories had made her skilled at analysing every nuance of behaviour: she could spot honesty like a blackberry among briars. She did not want to leave London but she knew it would make no difference. Her mother talked about the merits of country air and removing Nicky from the "bad influence" of her present school. *I'm* the bad influence, thought Nicky, obstinately, and I'm going to be a bad influence anywhere else.

At Witherndean, the dream cottage proved to be three rooms above and two behind the tiny newsagent's and sweet shop. There was rising damp downstairs and falling damp upstairs. No matter how hard Muriel scrubbed and polished the plaster cracks remained, and the odour of mould, and the boiled-vegetable smells from her unenthusiastic efforts in the kitchen. Gradually, Muriel abandoned her vision of sparkling cleanliness, scrubbed only where necessary, and sat down in the evenings with a bundle of knitting to watch *Coronation Street*. She would have liked to knit bootees for the other people's babies but there was no one she knew well enough, so she knitted cardigans for herself and jumpers for Nicky. She wore the cardigans; Nicky lost the jumpers. The shop was popular because it was open for long hours, but she rarely smiled at her customers or said more than "hello" and made a cursory comment on the weather. Her appearance, always dowdy, grew dowdier. Lipstick only emphasized the compressed lines of her mouth and the wrong shade of face-powder lay like dust on her drawn cheeks. She was tired out, not just physically but mentally, tired of trying, tired of lying, tired of doing her best for the daughter she had been ashamed to bear and was ashamed to love. She could have had the baby adopted, but she did not believe in adoption. In keeping Nicky she would atone for the terrible thing she had done, or so she had intended; but both atonement and intention had grown blurred over the years, and increasingly she saw in her child not the innocent by-product of sin, but a nagging reminder of the sin itself, a symbol of guilt, maybe even a punishment. And so she punished Nicky, and Nicky punished her, until whatever love there might have been between them was shredded away.

As a very small child all Nicky's affection, all her hopes and dreams, were centred on her father. From a muddle of books and fairy-tales she created someone kind, handsome, invariably aristocratic, forced to desert her mother for a woman he did not love, living in a house as big as a palace surrounded by faithful retainers yet always longing for the child he had never seen. One day soon, the other woman would die in a car accident, or run away with a gigolo, and he would come to look for her. When she thought of his loneliness, in the big house full of chandeliers and red carpets, real tears filled her eyes. When she thought of the sunshine she would bring into his life, the gloomy curtains she would fling wide, the adoration she would inspire in everyone from butler to kitchenmaid, her heart beat faster with anticipation of happiness. Her mother faded from the picture: she and her father sat at a round table polished like a mirror, while she drank strawberry milk-shake from a silver goblet and beyond the tall window there was a green parkland and a perpetual spring. Her dream became the centre of her world, nurtured over months or years, reinforced by secret signs which only she could understand. When Muriel left a magazine open at a photo of a country mansion, that was because it reminded her of the place where she should have lived. When she bought a paperback with a hawk-face hero on the cover, that was what *he* looked like. Nicky was so certain, and everything seemed to add to her certainty. At school she was quick and eager to learn, wanting to become a daughter he could be proud of. Her teachers attributed her frequent naughtiness to high spirits, and hoped for great things from her. And then, when she was seven or eight, the day came when Nicky could no longer resist confiding her secret. The story did not sound so convincing out loud, but she embellished it with a wealth of detail and her selected confidantes were duly impressed. Other classmates were not. By the end of the week, Nicky was in tears; the form mistress was deeply concerned; Muriel was summoned. "It *is* true!" Nicky wept. "It is! It *is!*"

"She's always telling lies," Muriel said, between anger and weariness. "I can't think where I've gone wrong."

"It's *true!*" Nicky insisted. "Anyway, you tell lies. You tell lots of lies . . ."

At home, spanked and supperless, Nicky was sent to bed. Later, when Muriel looked in on her, she asked in a small voice: "Mummy—where is my daddy?" And, into the silence: "I do have a daddy, don't I? Where is he?"

"He's dead," Muriel said in a curiously flat voice.

Nicky did not ask again. She knew immediately, unquestionably, that it was a lie, but something in that flat tone frightened her. She was too young to recognize despair; she could only sense the greyness in her mother's soul, a greyness which reached out and touched her, turning her dreams to stone. There was no big house, no endless garden, no silver goblet of strawberry milk-shake. The truth—whatever it might be—was something dull and empty, the terrible revelation of a drab adult world. She no longer wanted to know. Truth always fell short of fantasy: truth was dreariness, loneliness, loss, a fading dream, a cakeless tea, a fatherless child. In the future, whatever stories she might invent about her father she would never again be able to believe in them herself. Her heart ached with deprivation.

In the classroom her teachers realized gradually that she had ceased to care. She spent lesson-times whispering, doodling, distracting her friends. If she learnt anything, it was by accident. She acquired a reputation as the form menace, and was proud of it; she had little else to be proud of. She became by turns cheeky and sulky, generally disobedient, often rude. By the time Muriel decided to move to Witherndean, a year or so later, the school was glad to see her go.

Meanwhile, Nicky sought her fantasies elsewhere. Her mother had always tried to keep her from playing in the streets, and the long evenings at home, without company and before they could afford a television, had made a voracious reader of her. She graduated early from fairy-tales to adventure stories, borrowing from friends books which she usually forgot to return and working her way through the children's section of the local library. In Witherndean, she found a junk shop which sold second-hand paperbacks half-way to disintegration and hard-backs well-thumbed and long coverless. The owner, a kindly man, soon learned Nicky's tastes and took care to save any Malcolm Saville or Enid Blyton for her. She liked school stories best, the kind where there was a beautiful bitch with golden hair and china-blue eyes who got her comeuppance in the end, and a plain, quiet girl who would suddenly blossom and be-come the most popular in the class. She often wondered if the posh school nearby was anything like the schools in books. In common with the other children from the village primary she affected to despise the "snobs," shouting insults at the younger ones when the chance offered and even snatching a panama hat to toss into the gutter, but secretly she admired and envied them. The bigger girls sometimes came into her mother's shop, and she would watch them with huge eyes and tight mouth, half resentful, wholly fascinated. They all seemed to have beau-tiful skin, shining hair in plaits or ponytail, high, clear voices with perfect diction. Nicky had lost most of her cockney accent on leaving London, but although she could imitate them in mockery she knew she would never be able to speak quite like them. They brought with them the subconscious echo of a dream that had failed, and Nicky would watch them leave with a hungry, angry feeling inside her, both envy and rejection.

As she grew older, *What Katy Did* and *The Fourth Form at St. Clare's* gave way to *Forever Amber,* Anya Seton's *Katherine,* a succession of *Angéliques.* Nicky began to see herself as a dif-ferent kind of heroine, a heroine who would fight misfortune, rise above humble origins, win through to riches and happiness by her own wits and astonishing beauty. She was not quite satisfied with the astonishing beauty, but blusher could supply the bloom she lacked and her light-brown hair could be bleached golden or flaxen, if only Muriel would allow it. Her eyes, it was true, were neither violet nor emerald, but nor were anyone else's. They were grey, she decided, like deep pools reflecting clouds, like sparkling rain, like anything that was grey and sufficiently romantic. Grey was not a glamorous col-our, but Nicky did her best. She visualized herself arriving in Paris—in her dreams, it was always Paris—a beautiful un-known of eighteen or twenty, with her eyes like grey pools and her long silver hair. She would have many lovers but only one true love—a film star, a prince, a hero tailored to her ideal. Paris, she imagined, was the city of romance, something between Victor Hugo's alleyways and shadows and Hollywood's Gay Paree. Her school reports reflected an unusual enthusiasm for French, and her mother scolded her for trying out a blond rinse on her hair. It went into uneven streaks the colour of dirty sulphur, which Muriel said ought to be a lesson to her; but Nicky closed her small mouth, thought of Marilyn Monroe, and said nothing.

She was thirteen when she sneaked out on her first date, fourteen when she first slept with a boy. She was not in love but everyone slept with their boyfriends nowadays, it was prudish and old-fashioned not to, and anyway, she wanted to do it before the other girls in her class. In the event, it was not very exciting. She had sex because her contemporaries expected it, because her mother prohibited it, because it made her feel unconventional and daring; but it did not warm her heart or stir her blood. Her coldness troubled her a little, but she hoped it would disppear when she fell in love, and in the meantime she learnt quickly to put on an act, panting and gasping in all the right places. The pain of awkward positions, cramped muscles, and sore vagina all lent a genuine flavour to her fervid moans. It was only when she was in her own room, lying on her bed, imagining, that she could make herself feel the way they felt in books. She would picture a man, usually in period costume, ruffled shirt unlaced across his chest, satin breeches straining over a bulging groin, forcing her down beneath him and pushing his hand into her bodice. Presently, her small breasts would burst from their confines, her nipples would nestle into his palm, tight and hard with desire. There would be a ripping of silk petticoats, and then she would feel the urgent thrust of his cock inside her, and waves of effortless pleasure flowed down her loins. She would touch herself, through her knickers, more gently, more sensitively than any boy, feeling for the tip of her clitoris, rubbing against it very lightly, until her knickers were wet and a slow, shuddering orgasm jerked her body and then released her to curl up into a ball like an animal in hibernation. She would lie with her legs closed, dreaming of spreading them open, her body empty, dreaming of being filled. Afterwards, if she drifted into sleep,

the fantasy sometimes invaded her slumber. But once or twice
the face of her unknown lover changed, growing older, kinder,
his eyes no longer passionate but tender, his hair grey-streaked,
the phantom lover she hoped to find becoming the phantom
father she had lost. From a stranger to a stranger. And Nicky
would wake with a warmth between her thighs and a sensation
of elusive well-being which vanished all too quickly.

The first time she saw Diana Van Leer she was cantering
through the school grounds on her pony one afternoon in
spring. Nicky had climbed the wall for a glimpse of privileged
territory, and now she sat perched on the top, a leg on each
side, feeling mildly daring since the wall was school property
and technically she was trespassing. In the distance she could
see a stretch of playing-field, white goalposts, an ivy-covered
outbuilding. Nearer at hand there was only short grass, well-
spaced trees and sprawling patches of yellow and purple cro-
cus. Among the bare branches there was a green glimmer of
opening buds; the light of the falling sun picked its way between
the tree-trunks and flecked bark and turf with gold. It was long
after tea-time and apart from the pony and rider there was no
one else in sight. The pony was dappled every shade of silver,
mane and tail flying in the wind of its speed. The rider wore
jodhpurs and a hard hat; under the peak her face was very rosy,
her lips slightly parted as though to drink the air. A swatch of
hair, red as strawberries, bounced against her back. She looked
as free as a wild bird and as remote as a princess. Nicky, watching her, felt the old familiar ache to be like that, to be rich and
careless and happy, riding through a private park on a pony
of her own. Then the rider veered off to the left and vanished;
the leaning hills snatched the last veins of sunlight from between the trees. Nicky slid down from the wall and went on
her way.

It was about a year later that she and Diana actually met.
Nicky had always made friends easily, not perhaps lifelong
friends but the more superficial variety, admirers rather than
intimates, who were briefly dazzled by her smile, her secrets,
her defiance of petty authority. She used the same charms on
Diana, having no others, determined to make the most of the
one friend she really wanted. She enjoyed talking about her
among the lesser lights of her social circle: "My friend, Diana
Van Leer"; she found a piece about Sir Rupert in a book on

modern architecture at school. With Diana herself she was careful not to appear too keen or push too hard, handling the relationship more cautiously than any of her casual affairs. Boys might come and go, but a girlfriend was for keeps. She dreamed of being invited to Diana's home, of meeting the famous father who obviously adored her, the fussy aunt, the twin sister she mentioned so defensively. "You're fooling yourself," Muriel snapped, sensing her daughter's thoughts. "I daresay she's a nice enough girl but she's not your kind. Leave her be."

"*She* comes to see *me*," Nicky retorted. "She likes me. Some people do."

"For the time being, maybe. It gives her a chance to escape from school. Have you met her parents? Has she suggested you stay with her in the holidays? Of course not. She hasn't and she won't. Different classes don't mix. Be content with your own sort. Time you stopped mooning over what you can't have and grew up."

"She'll ask me," Nicky said confidently.

But she didn't.

Nicky never knew exactly what it was she had done wrong. There was a day when Diana took her to the stables to admire her pony, and Nicky actually sat on his back while Diana led them round the yard. She was feeling a little nervous but she would have died rather than let her companion see it. She sat straight in the saddle, shoulders squared valiantly, leaning to pat his neck and ruffle his mane as if to the manner born. Diana liked horses, therefore Nicky would show that she liked horses too. And then suddenly it was easy. She found she was enjoying herself, sitting up above the world looking down even on Diana, with the sun in her eyes and the wind in her hair. She could imagine leaping the gate and galloping off through the trees— as free as a wild bird—somehow transformed by the magic of the ride into Diana's equal, her class, her kind, a real friend and not merely an opportunist. "I am like her," Nicky thought, exhilarated. "I don't care what anyone says. We are the same. We *can* be friends." But when she eventually dismounted there was a constraint in Diana's face which she did not understand, and after that what remained of their friendship gradually faded away.

Nicky read about her death in the newspapers two years later. It was a front-page story in the locals, a tearjerker in the tabloids, a minor-item in the nations. The image of a poor little rich girl falling to her death after a wild orgy of boozing and drug-taking seemed to have little to do with the Diana Nicky remembered. There was a photograph with most of the articles, a studio portrait of a budding debutante in evening dress with pearl-drop earrings and swept-up hair. The picture was what Nicky would have anticipated; the tragedy wasn't. She wondered what sort of a person Diana had really been, behind the ponytail and the perfect diction, and how she could have died in such an accident when, to all appearances, she had always been so much protected and beloved. A faint chill touched Nicky's heart, the echo of a half-forgotten disappointment, or the sudden proximity of death—death which had been, in the past, so remote as to be almost unreal. In the week that followed, she regularly checked the papers in her mother's shop for further details. With coverage of the funeral, there were other photographs—Sir Rupert, a blurred white face pitted with craggy shadows, shoulders hunched against the onslaught of publicity; the boyfriend, lowered eyes and dramatic cheekbones under a mop of dark hair. He's gorgeous, Nicky thought, taken aback. Somehow, she would not have expected Diana to attract quite that calibre of young man—the sort of dusky, romantic type she might have dreamed of for herself. She studied both men for a long time.

There were no pictures of Diana's twin sister.

Among her friends, Nicky referred to the tragedy with regret, making much of her brief association with the deceased. After all, she and Diana *had* been quite close, if only in passing. Acquaintances were suitably impressed by the reflected lustre of fame and calamity. She herself never stopped to wonder if any of the regret was genuine, perhaps afraid to probe beneath the surface of her feelings in case there was nothing there.

Nicky's inclination had been to leave school at sixteen and get on with life, but after various career discussions, she had come to terms with the fact that, in the modern world, she could not graduate automatically as a courtesan or an adventuress, and she had been forced to compromise with secretarial qualifications. She did both O- and A-levels and went on to a course of Business Studies at the nearest technical college, with

typing and shorthand on the side. Her typing was bad and her
shorthand worse, but she got a job in Tunbridge Wells with a
finance company who did not seem to mind. She worked fairly
hard when she wanted to; mostly, she didn't want to. In any
case, her boss was more interested in the tautness of her skirt
across her small bottom, and the hint of erect nipples under
T-shirt or sweater. He was in his mid-thirties, comfortably married, with two cars, two point six children, premature baldness
and a paunch. His name was Mr. Parfitt. He had a tendency to
lose his place while giving Nicky dictation, particularly if she
wriggled in her chair and showed her thighs through the split
in her skirt. Sometimes, in a spirit of mischief, she would ex-
periment with the effects of a scoop neckline, unfastened but-
tons, a transparent blouse. The office manager, Deirdre Lang,
looked disapproving and occasionally made a spiteful comment; but Nicky would only laugh and ignore her, secure in
her youth and conscious of her charms. Deirdre, in her late
thirties, divorced, smart if not glamourous, seemed to Nicky
both middle-aged and dull. With unerring female instinct
Nicky knew that Ms. Lang "fancied" her boss—perhaps they
had had an affair—but she found the passions of a thirty-eight-
year-old woman and bald man with a paunch merely ludicrous,
a matter for sport rather than serious consideration. On one of
the scoop-neckline days Mr. Parfitt was leaning over her shoulder in the throes of dictation, ostensibly studying the hiero-
glyphics on her pad. His right hand had come to rest as if by
accident on her bare skin, instead of on the back of her chair.
Nicky was just wondering if he would attempt to explore further and was preparing herself to repulse him in virginal confusion when the door opened and Ms. Lang came in. Mr. Parfitt
looked guilty; Nicky didn't. Deirdre's face assumed an unpleasantly blank expression. Later, Nicky expected more spite and
was slightly taken aback to receive instead a gush of friendliness. Over tea, she was offered half a Kit Kat and invited to
admire Deirdre's rings, two diamonds from her broken marriage and a garnet from her grandmother. Nicky was suspicious
but she duly admired.

   That was on Wednesday. On Friday, at around four o'clock,
Deirdre complained loudly that the rings were missing. She
had taken them off in the Ladies to wash her hands and must
have forgotten to put them on again, and now they had dis-

appeared. The cleaning-woman, feeling herself accused, presented a picture of outraged virtue worthy of Sarah Bernhardt. Nicky, bewildered by events, said nothing.

"She went into the loo just after me," Deirdre said. "I remember now. Yes, and she was admiring my rings only the other day. *She* took them."

Mr. Parfitt, an unwilling participant in the commotion, was assigned to search Nicky's handbag. Out came wallet, purse, hand-mirror, lipstick, comb, tissues—and the missing rings.

"I'm sure this can all be settled quietly," Mr. Parfitt said, with a droop in his voice.

But the cleaning-woman, determined to vindicate herself, had already called the police.

Nicky was arrested.

The room was small, bare and palely lit. It was probably an interview room, but to Nicky it felt like a cell. She had been there for a very long time. They had taken her fingerprints and removed her shoes; she had an idea they always removed prisoner's shoes in case they hanged themselves with their laces, but her shoes had no laces so that couldn't be right. Her bare feet made her feel diminished and disproportionately vulnerable, as if her height had lost vital inches, her body essential armour. Perhaps that was the intention. She was trembling, partly from cold, partly from shock. The two policemen interrogating her were in plain clothes, a detective-inspector and a detective-constable. The inspector was fat, the constable thin. Laurel and Hardy, she had thought at the beginning, when she was still scornful and relatively unafraid. She repeated it to herself now—Laurel and Hardy—trying to recapture both fearlessness and scorn.

Only these two weren't funny.

"I didn't do it," she had screamed on her arrest, with all the fury of a habitual liar who—for once—is telling the truth.

"I didn't do it!" she reiterated for the twentieth time, no longer sure what she might or might not have done, clinging on desperately to her wavering certainties. Her face was puffy with crying, mascara smeared under her eyes. She rubbed them with her knuckles, making matters worse, her appearance long forgotten—a pathetic child protesting more and more feebly against some terrible but well-founded accusation.

The constable wrote it all down.

"If you didn't do it," said the inspector, speaking slowly as though addressing a moron, "how—did—the—rings—get—into—your—bag?"

"Someone must have put them there."

"Of course. Someone put them there. It's a frame-up. We've heard it all before. You've been watching too much TV."

"*I* didn't put them there, so someone else must have."

"Who?"

"I expect Deirdre did it herself."

"I see. She stole her own rings and put them in your handbag. Fascinating. Hates you, does she? Office passions? Where did you get this stuff—some TV soap?"

"She's jealous of me."

"Why should she be jealous of a little tart like you?"

Nicky's hand clenched into fists; a broken nail drew blood from her palm. "Because I'm young and pretty and she isn't. Because Mr. Parfitt fancies me. Because she fancies him." She added: "I think they must have had an affair."

"I understood Mr. Parfitt was a happily married man. Kids, too. Generally respected and all that. But *you* say he had an affair with Ms. Lang. Caught them at it, did you?"

"No, I . . ."

"Of course you didn't! There wasn't any affair except in your imagination. Think a lot of yourself, don't you? 'I'm young and pretty and she isn't. Mr. Parfitt fancies me.' You don't look up to much now, all red eyes and snotty nose. Shall I bring you a mirror?" He thrust his face towards her, beetroot-tinged and threatening, like some grotesque gargoyle. "You make me sick! You're not content with pinching other people's things; you want to smear them in your own dirt as well. You carry on like you're the heroine in a novel—everyone has to be either in love with you or conspiring against you. You're living in a dream world! The truth is you're just a common little sneak-thief who can't bear being found out. You'll bleat out anything that comes into your silly head to put the blame on someone else. You stupid bitch: do you really think you can fool *me*?"

It did not occur to him that it might be Nicky who was telling the truth. Detective-Inspector Bullard was not much concerned with truth: his object was to get a conviction. He had a suspect and he had evidence. The result was a foregone conclusion. A conviction, even on such a trivial matter, was another crime solved, another useful statistic in the local detection rate, another point on the way to his advancement. Of course, it would be best if he could get a confession; that was the quickest and tidiest solution. It looked good in the files. Crime—discovery—confession: every policeman's ideal case. He had obtained several confessions under similar circumstances and he was justly proud of his interrogation technique, learnt at police college and perfected over the years. "The suspect must be confused and humiliated in order to weaken his resistance," he had been taught. "Do not allow yourself to be diverted by excuses and protestations of innocence. Deprive him of his sense of identity. Belittle him. Fear gets results." The detective-inspector employed various tactics: pushing his face close to the suspect and shouting, sinking his voice to a menacing whisper, looming over his victim—he was not particularly tall but made up for it by the solid expanse of his stomach, built up on a lifelong diet of junk food—or turning his back and making contemptuous remarks, as if the suspect were of less importance than the dust on the floor. He rarely used violence: it was too risky, and besides, he liked to boast that more could be achieved by psychological methods. He was relieved that Nicky had not thought to insist on a lawyer. Inexperienced, he concluded. Lawyers were liable to cramp his style.

When he grew bored by Nicky's tears and obstinacy, he remembered to offer the obligatory phone call. "My mother," Nicky whispered. "Please." The thought of Muriel was safety, familiarity: it filled Nicky with a rush of rare child-like longing. *I want my mummy!* Her mother did not often embrace her but this time, surely, she would manage a quick, tight little hug. Nicky's whole being ached for a hug like that.

Someone else made the call and in due course Muriel arrived. Nicky read through her statement without seeing it, signed on the dotted line, heard that "for the moment" she could go. Muriel did not hug her. She looked at her daughter with clamped lips and new lines about her mouth. "How could you?" she hissed, when she could speak. "How *could* you?" And, to the inspector: "She's always been dishonest. The lies she told, when she was little . . . I tried, I really tried, but it never did any good. That's how she is."

They left the police station in silence.

• • •

In the small hours of the morning Nicky rose and dressed. The events of the previous day had culminated in an appalling row with her mother which left her feeling exhausted and rather sick. Afterwards she lay in the dark, unable to sleep, while slow numbness spread through her, blanketing pain. She thought vaguely that the pain was neither new nor strange; it was more like an old, old wound, crudely ripped open and bleeding agony, which would presently close again, not to heal but to fester. And sure enough, close it did; feeling was dulled; a scab of anger and resentment formed over the top. Gradually, her mind began to function again. She made plans. When she finally got up, she had come to a decision.

She found the passport she had acquired for a Spanish holiday the year before, threw it into a bag with a few of her things. Downstairs, she removed a key from its hiding-place under a jar of liquorice and unlocked the till. She stuffed the notes in her wallet and as much of the change as she could into her pockets and purse. Then she hitched the strap of the bag on to her shoulder, unbolted the door, and let herself out into the night.

Half-way down the road she paused, turned, looked back. She promised herself that she was never going to come home.

7

Nicky met Stephane Maglioli on the beach at Saint-Malo. She had caught the ferry to Calais and had spent the summer idling along the coast, staying in cheap rooms or even sleeping out, eating at other people's expense, determined to have a good time. One day it would be necessary to do something about getting a job, possibly in a bar or café, or finding herself the sort of rich man she had always dreamed about to take care of her. Meanwhile she practised her French, streaked and permed her hair, tanned every available inch of her body. Any nightmares she might have had about the police or her mother trying to search for her were dispelled by the sight of her reflection in the mirror, her normally pale face peanut-brown and glowing under a mass of tousled waves, her grey eyes ice-blue against her tan, her peroxide streaks already running white in the sun. On the beach the French boys stared and whistled; in the cafés they flocked to buy her drinks. And among them was Stephane Maglioli.

Stephane was not rich and seemed unlikely to be interested in taking care of anyone but himself. Nicky, when she first met him, assessed him from experience as volatile, probably spoilt, much too conscious of his good looks, with a heart as light as a soap bubble. Determined not to fall in love with him, she was ensnared by her own resistance, bewitched by charms which she knew it would be wiser to ignore. She was too young for caution, too feckless to be wise. Gradually her vision blurred: his defects shrank to minor failings, his qualities were pepped up to suit her recipe. She looked into his large brown eyes and saw strength, intelligence, ambition—all the virtues of her kind of hero. She need never be the mistress of some wealthy older man, sleeping her way to success; she and Steph could achieve her dreams together. His dreams she took for granted, reinforced by careless fragments of conversation over cheap wine and late-night coffee. She wanted to be rich; so did he. Magical coincidence. She was hungry for glamour and excitement; he had an *envie* to be a racing-driver. (One of his Italian cousins worked in racing.) She had run away from a mother who did not understand her; he was trapped by parents who kept trying to understand him. They were obviously soul-mates. When she told him she wanted to go to Paris, he said, "You must stay with me." Nicky was eager to accept. Two months later, they got married.

Arriving in a city which was bigger, uglier and dirtier than anything romantic fiction had led her to expect, Nicky found herself in the midst of a numerous family of Italian immigrants, all staring at her in horror and shouting over her head in a variety of languages. She said little, too unnerved by so much vociferous disapproval either to protest or turn on the charm. "I told them we were getting married," Stephane explained later. "That really did it. My mother doesn't like you—she says you're a tart. She says that about all my girlfriends. My father thinks you're all right."

"Why did you tell them *that?*" Nicky asked faintly.

"Oh, I don't know. I was sick of all the fuss. They treat me like a child." He was lying on his back, unconscious of triteness, gazing at the ceiling. Suddenly, he turned towards her. "If we got married my uncle Luca would let us have the flat above his restaurant. I daresay you could get a job there. What do you think?"

It was not the kind of proposal Nicky had ever imagined. Still, it was a proposal. And Stephane, she reminded herself, was not given to articulating his feelings: love, like everything else, was all choked up inside him, hidden under the veneer of carelessness and the quick-change moods. With him, she must learn to perceive the depths beneath the shallows.

"Okay," she said.

They were married in late October. It was a Catholic wedding, so Nicky became a Catholic. She wore a cheap white dress with too much lace and an unsuitable quantity of eyeshadow and lipstick. Stephane's mother continued to disapprove, but fortunately in Italian. Nicky did not care. The reception was held in the restaurant above which the young couple were to live, and instead of a wedding cake there was a gâteau Saint-Honoré, a huge pyramid of profiteroles, cobwebbed with spun sugar, studded with sugared almonds, oozing crème pâtissière. Almost a chocolate cake, Nicky thought. Almost.

Afterwards, she was never able to remember much about her first experience of married life. Disillusionment set in before the last of the crème pâtissière had congealed, but it was not the disillusionment that frightened her so much as the drabness. Ever since she was a small child, when she had seen the revelation of a bleak reality in her mother's face, she had feared to find that reality waiting for her, behind the excitement and glitter of her dreams: a reality of dullness, loneliness, despair. Worse than a broken heart she dreaded a heart in decay; worse than poverty, monotony; worse than death, an endless withering into old age. Sometimes, she imagined she was imprisoned in a grey world, shut away from colour and light, and the greyness was seeping through her like a shadow, reducing her inexorably to little more than a dingy wraith. And now here she was in Paris, the city of romance, and Paris, too, was grey. She lived in a cramped flat above an inferior restaurant. Stephane had a job in a garage; she worked as a waitress for his uncle. In the evenings, Stephane went out with his friends while she scribbled orders, wiped tabletops, spilt soup. She learned to swear fluently in French and passably in Italian. Luca Maglioli pinched her bottom too often and too hard. She complained about it to Stephane but he just laughed and said: "Let him have his fun." Nicky did not find it fun, any of it. Somewhere, she knew, there was another Paris, a Paris of glittering nightclubs, exquisite clothes, playboys and gigolos, caviar and champagne, where the ghost of Gershwin's music hovered around every corner and romance hung like perfume in the lamplight under the trees. The Tour Eiffel, the Quartier Latin,

the Tuileries, Yves Saint-Laurent, Régine's, the Folies Ber-
gères—the names which had enchanted her were all jumbled
inside her head, yet she knew no more of them than if she had
stayed in Tunbridge Wells. Stephane never took her sightseeing
and she rarely had the opportunity to explore on her own. One
Sunday she sneaked off to visit the Louvre: she had only a
casual interest in art, but at least, when she was there, she
could feel this was truly Paris. The "Mona Lisa" disappointed
her, it was so small (Nicky thought famous pictures should be
on a grand scale), but she was impressed by Géricault's "The
Raft of the Medusa," which produced in her the same agreeable
curdling of the blood as a good horror film. Back home, Stephane was waiting (for once) and demanded to know where
she had been. "Paintings!" he said when she told him, managing to sound both amazed and bored. Nicky did not go again.

Stephane himself was even less exciting than Paris. She
thought she was in love with him, she wanted to be in love
with him—maybe she *had* been in love with him, for a fleeting
moment, half a night, half a dream—but the illusion was gone
with summer and the dregs tasted as uninspiring as dregs always do. They argued frequently: not gorgeous sexy rows cul-
minating in bed but silly bickerings, sulks, mutual spite and
indifference. Nicky tried to resist it, but she knew the indifference was there. For all Stephane's Italianate good looks she
had begun to notice that his neck was too thick and too short,
his lips girlishly full, and his round brown eyes under their
drooping lashes reminded her more of Bambi than Sylvester
Stallone. Away from the beach, he was too indolent to bother
with regular showers. His chestnut curls were often shiny with
grease and his clothes, which she was expected to wash, smelt
of sweat and oil from the garage. As for sex, she had hoped
desperately that one night the magic would happen. It didn't.
Naked, his body was burnt to the colour of cinnamon, except
for the brief pallid area which had been covered by his swimming trunks. Yet his beauty seemed to stop with his tan: within
that pale triangle his genitals lay like shrunken fruit unripened
by the sun. Nicky had read in the more forthcoming magazines
that quality was more important than quantity, and she tried
very hard to be aroused by his limited erection. But after
matrimony Stephane's foreplay grew increasingly perfunctory,
his ecstasies virtually automatic. Nicky lay on her back and

even thought of England, when she had nothing else to think
of. She decided that it was all a part of the dreary fate which
pursued her: the banality at the heart of adventure, the truth
about real life. Real life was tedium in Paris and a beautiful
man with an inadequate erection—an inexorable succession of
let-downs. With Stephane, adventure stopped at his navel. She
was puzzled, too, by his habit of vaunting his sexual prowess,
both to her and to his friends, boasting of his meagre assets as
if he had the equipment of an erotic Titan. Since he could
scarcely hope to deceive her, she concluded he was unaware of
his own inadequacy—or, if he knew, he was trying to brazen
it out, drawing her into a conspiracy to protect his ego. When
he bragged to her, she was noncommittal or merely silent;
when he bragged to his friends, she was embarrassed. Nicky
might make up fantasies herself, but she liked to feel she could
believe in them.

One of their nastiest quarrels was about sex. Stephane enjoyed fellatio, not just as a preliminary to intercourse but sometimes as a substitute, although he never responded in kind.
Nicky found it both boring and vaguely distasteful. That night,
she said she was tired and didn't want to. Stephane called her
a selfish cow, an English prude, and finally—illogically—an
espèce de pute.

"Your cock is so small," Nicky said, forgetting herself, "when
I suck it I'm always afraid I might swallow it by mistake."

Inevitably, he stormed out. He did not come home all night.
Nicky lay on her own wondering if he had gone to another
woman—there was an ex-girlfriend she had met once, a heavy
brunette with a moustache—and realized she didn't care.
Lately, there were too many things about which she didn't care.
An old nursery rhyme of Muriel's came back to her:

> Don't-Care was made to care,
> Don't-Care was hung;
> Don't-Care was put in the pot
> And boiled till he was done.

Still, she didn't care.

They never really made up that quarrel. Others followed, not
only about sex but about Nicky's job and Stephane's job, his

family, the flat, any and every aspect of their life together. Stephane might resent his relations but he would not allow his wife to criticize them; he might complain of his mother but he quoted liberally from her growing catalogue of Nicky's short-comings. He had flung himself into marriage as a way of escape or a gesture of rebellion, but the gesture—like all his gestures—proved ineffectual, and he was lured back to the fold by his own apathy and the very maternal coddling against which he had rebelled. His ambition to be a racing-driver was yet another escapist fantasy. His cousin Gino, Nicky discovered, was only the most junior of mechanics, and Stephane would obviously have been quite content to emulate him, wearing blue overalls and Formula One grease and standing at the edge of the track to watch other men win. Once or twice she taunted him, in an attempt to spur him on to something, but spurring simply made him obstinate and sent him running to his mother or his friends. Uncle Luca did not help: he had taken to grabbing Nicky from behind and rubbing his crotch vigorously between her buttocks. "My nephew is no good, *hein?*" he would say (perhaps he had overheard some of the rows). "They are all the same, these young boys. No experience. You need a *real* fuck." In retaliation, Nicky wore very high heels and stamped on his feet as hard as she could. It did not appear to put him off. It worried her that he had a key to the flat, but she did not think he would come in when he knew Stephane might be there.

And then the day came when Stephane wasn't there.

Nicky found the letter on the table when she finished work one afternoon.

> Dear Nicky—Going to Italy to join Gino. Thierry is going too—we've both had enough of Paris. I'll fix up a divorce when I get there. Uncle Luca will look after you. Steph.

Nicky had been half expecting, half hoping this would happen; nonetheless, she had to sit down for a minute or two, feeling curiously blank. Her first marriage (she trusted it was only the first) seemed to have come and gone so quickly that she had hardly had time to assimilate it. The episode had streaked across her life like one of the Ferraris for which Stephane's soul hankered, knocking her sideways and leaving her temporarily stunned. It surprised her a little that Stephane had summoned up the initiative to go; possibly the initiative had been supplied by Thierry, his mate at the garage. And now what? "Uncle Luca will look after you." The sting in the tail. Idle malice or sheer stupidity? Suddenly, Nicky wondered if Stephane had left a note for Luca as well. She thought viciously that it would have been just like him.

The footsteps on the stairs came while she was still sitting there, trying to decide what to do. There was a knock on the door—a cursory knock, the knock of someone who intends to come in anyway. She did not answer. A key rattled in the lock and the door was pushed open. Luca's head poked through the gap. "Nicky? You are all right?" When she still made no answer he came and sat down beside her, much too close. He smelt of sweat and garlic and halitosis, and his very eyeballs seemed to be swimming in olive oil. In the past, Nicky had merely found him disgusting. Now, she felt frightened. "Stephane has gone, no? Don't worry. He was no use, my nephew. Lazy—full of himself—no use to anyone. It is a good riddance: you will see. You are unhappy now but it will pass. You stay here; I take care of you. I take *real* care of you."

To her astonishment Nicky realized she was supposed to be upset. She had not had the forethought to produce any tears but she managed a small, pathetic voice and huge mournful eyes. "Thank you: you're so kind. I'm afraid I—I haven't taken it in just yet. I need to be alone for a bit: do you mind?"

Luca nodded understandably and patted her head. He thought visibly about patting other portions of her anatomy, but for the moment he refrained. That could come later: the decencies must be observed. Nicky knew a sudden urge to laugh hysterically. It was all a ludicrous comedy: surely he must see that her maidenly distress was as phoney as his own avuncular concern. Yet they both continued to ham their unconvincing roles, Nicky, her tan long faded, achieving a tragic pallor, and Luca offering insincere consolation. "You finish early tonight if you want," he told her, generously. "I go now but I come back after work. We have a nice quiet talk."

"*Trop gentil,*" Nicky murmured.

As soon as he had gone she wedged a chair under the door handle and began to pack her bag. She reflected that she was getting all too experienced at unobtrusive exits. This time she had no plans, nowhere to go. When she looked in her wallet she found Stephane had taken all her money. Fate getting its own back. The front stairs connected with the restaurant but a window in the bedroom opened on to a fire-escape. Nicky climbed out, clattered down the steps, and fled.

It was February. Paris at the fag-end of winter was a city of grimed stone façades, snarling traffic jams, wide streets choked with exhaust fumes, narrow streets overhung with shadows. A bare, cold, leafless city, black and white like an old film. Nicky went from café to cocktail bar, from brasserie to bistro. She met bored faces, blank gazes, an endless variety of shrugs which all meant the same thing. No. We won't need any extra help. It's a bad time of the year. *Bonne chance*. The pallid day dwindled into a premature dusk. Lights sprang up in the windows of shops and around palaces and monuments, splashing the leaden twilight with garish colour. The city decked herself out in lights like an ageing courtesan hiding her corroded beauty under the sparkle of too much jewellery. Behind the glitter, the faces changed. Gone were the boredom and blankness; instead, the darkness brought leering glances, knowing smiles, slyness, mockery, lechery, all manner of petty evil. The relief of escaping Luca had long worn off. Nicky began to be more afraid than she had ever been in her life—even more than when she was under arrest. She had nothing to eat, nowhere to sleep, hardly any money. She told herself, with desperate optimism, that something would come up, something *must* come up; but it didn't. She remembered Linda Radlet, a favourite heroine of hers, who had sat down on a suitcase in the Gare du Nord and had been picked up by the Duc de Sauveterre. But no *ducs* came for Nicky. There were only the nightmare faces winking from darkened doorways, a jeering laugh, a clutching hand, her own footsteps, running, walking, running through a maze of street-lamps and shadows. Eventually, she went into a bar, ordered a bowl of soup. At the next table someone had left half an omelette. Nicky would have liked to ask the waiter if she might finish it, but embarrassment prevented her. She wondered if anyone had ever died of starvation because they were too embarrassed to ask for food. Two boys bought her a brandy but when she inquired if they knew somewhere she could spend the night they lost interest.

"Where do people stay," she said in a would-be casual tone, "when they have no money?"

The familiar shrug. Nicky was growing to dread it. There

were places, they said. Hostels. They didn't know exactly where. Some people slept out.

"In the Métro," offered one.

"Under the bridges," said the other.

Nicky shivered. To sleep on a beach in the summer was one thing. But this was winter, in a city of stones. She turned away so they should not see her fear.

A man in a tan leather jacket bought her a second brandy, then a third. He wanted to take her home but said his wife would object. It was gone midnight when the waiter threw her out. "We don't want your sort here," he said. "Go ply your trade somewhere else."

It is not respectable to be destitute.

"I need a place to sleep," Nicky said. "Please help me."

Inevitably, the waiter shrugged. "This isn't a hotel."

A long time later, Nicky found herself on the river bank. The fumes of brandy were clearing; she was very cold and her feet hurt. Under the bridges, the boy had said. There was a bridge ahead of her; the light of the street-lamp showed darker bundles in the shadow beneath the arch. People. People huddled in sleeping bags or coarse blankets. Tramps, junkies, down-and-outs. The dregs of the city. As Nicky drew closer she saw there were four or five of them. She stopped a little way away, staring. She could not speak. Dimly she was aware that this was the absolute nadir of existence. This was what it meant to have nothing, to *be* nothing. To have is to be. She had lost everything, and in so doing she had lost herself. Here under the bridge was a reality more terrible than any tedium. She stared, and was silent, and did not move.

Just inside the arch there was an old man propped up against the wall between two dogs. They must have been Alsatians but they looked like wolves: one brindled, one black. They sat so still that it was a few seconds before she realized they were real and their unblinking eyes reflected the light like yellow opals. The old man said something in a cracked voice with a Bordelais accent which Nicky did not understand. One of the dogs shifted at a gesture and he patted the space in between. She hesitated only for a moment. She was too tired and wretched to walk away. He proffered part of a musty blanket and a swig from a bottle of some unidentifiable spirit. It was so fiery it took the skin from her throat, but afterwards a sort

of glow began to permeate her insides and her teeth no longer
chattered with cold.

"English?" he asked her when she mumbled her thanks.

Nicky nodded.

"You should go home," he said. "Go home to your parents.
This is no place for a young girl like you."

"I'm an orphan," Nicky said, avoiding explanation.

He shook his head, sighed. "You should go home," he repeated.

She made no response. Exhaustion and alcohol were taking
effect. On one side, the old man's slight bony body felt like a
pile of dry sticks folded up in his clothes; on the other, the
warm flank of the Alsatian was pressed against her. She
thought: I shall fall asleep, and when I wake this will all have
vanished like a hideous dream. In due course, she slept.

She woke up. It wasn't a dream. Over the edge of the blanket,
a bitter air cut her face. Her eyes were clogged with yesterday's
mascara and parts of her body had gone numb, possibly from
cramp, possibly from cold. When she tried to move, the Alsatian
beside her produced a low-key rumble which might have been
a growl.

It disturbed the old man. In daylight, Nicky saw he was *very*
old, his skin so mottled and webbed with lines that it looked
like a map with all the minor roads pencilled in. She was sure
he smelt but her senses had ceased to register such details. He
gave the dog an order and she got to her feet. "Tonight," he
asked, "you come back?"

Nicky had begun to shiver again. "No," she said. "I'll find a
job."

He wished her luck.

There was no luck. She got a cup of chocolate and a wash in
a small café and set out, trying to feel confident. But it was a
duplicate of the previous day. The same streets, the same faces,
the same negative shrugs. This time, she enquired not just in
restaurants and cafés but in shops, offices, anywhere that might
have a vacancy. "I can type," she said. "I do shorthand." But
she was used to an English typewriter, English dictation. They
thanked her and were sorry. In the evening, she went back to
the bridge. The worst thing, she reflected, was how quickly you

adapt. Already, such was her desolation, it felt almost like going home.

The old man did not seem surprised to see her. He moved over so she could curl up against the wall, and offered her a drink. Nicky had decided the spirit must be absinthe, but he told her it was something called marc. He asked if she had eaten and she said yes, but when he produced a croissant from a paper bag she accepted it and did her best not to wolf it down too quickly. It settled in a doughy lump on her empty stomach, as if her digestion, already unaccustomed to solid nourishment, did not quite know what to do with it. She asked him how he managed to feed the dogs; he told her there was a private charity which provided them with regular meals. They provide meals for dogs, Nicky thought, but not for me. Doubtless there was some French equivalent of social security, but social security meant officialdom, and officialdom, where she would promptly be arrested and thrown in gaol. Nicky wanted nothing to do with officials.

The evening was long and cold. She was tired; but she did not sleep. Later, in the world beyond the bridge, she saw white flakes falling slowly through the darkness. Snow. A couple of gendarmes came past: they turned over a youth who was rolled up in a sleeping-bag and started to question him, but when one of them approached the old man the dogs stirred and made soft subterranean grumbling noises, and the gendarme retired hastily. Nicky's relief was so great it almost made her warm.

The old man noticed, but he did not comment. He had stopped suggesting she should go home. *"Les flics,"* he said, "they know me. They leave us alone."

He told her he had once been a soldier: he had fought at Verdun in the First World War and in the Second he had joined the Resistance. When he pulled back the lapel of his coat she saw a string of medals pinned to a moth-eaten sweater. "I fought for my country," he said. "I should have died. They called us heroes—heroes of France. Now, it's not important." His voice had sunk to a wheezing whisper; it was impossible to tell if he felt resentful, or angry, or merely philosophical. Nicky wondered if any of it was true.

She slept fitfully, and woke to another day even more hopeless than the last.

• • •

It was a grey morning, with turbid clouds sagging low over the city and the thin snowfall already melting or turning to slush in the gutters. Nicky went to the café she had used before, ordered hot chocolate and had a scanty wash. The spotted mirror over the sink showed her face both pinched and haggard, with new lines around the mouth and pits of shadow under the eyes. She put on a lot of lipstick in an attempt to combat her pallor, but it only made matters worse. The light was too poor for her to risk a touch of blusher; she would be sure to get it uneven. She drank her chocolate, hoping her scalded tongue would bring colour to her cheeks. Tomorrow, she supposed, she would look even paler and dirtier. She could not visualize tomorrow.

When she had paid for her chocolate, she discovered she had only a few centimes left. This was the end. No tomorrow. Nothing existed beyond the abyss of today. She asked about work in one or two places, knowing the answer in advance. People stared at her as if they could see she had been sleeping under a bridge. Probably they could.

Outside a charcuterie, she paused to gaze wistfully at the range of delicacies in the window. Smooth pâté mantled in yellow fat. Coarse pâté under a glaze of jelly. Slices of galantine flecked with truffles. Cold roast chicken. Sausages of all shapes and sizes. The sight of so much food filled her with shivers of hunger stronger than any lust. She pushed open the door and went in. She wanted to say: "I'm starving. Please give me something to eat"—but of course she could not. Instead, she stammered her usual enquiry about work. The man behind the counter was in his forties, not fat, but packed in a firm padding of flesh, like one of his own sausages. She saw the shrug begin around his middle, and tears of disappointment and futility sprang into her eyes.

But the shrug was never finished. In a room at the back of the shop, the telephone rang. The man called: "Jean-Claude!" but no one came and the ringing persisted. The charcutier threw Nicky a preoccupied glance, muttered: "Excuse me," and bustled out. For an instant, Nicky wavered; then she slipped behind the counter and reached for the nearest sausage. She did not hear the click next door when the man rang off. Even as she retrieved her trophy, his hand fell heavily on her shoulder.

In the back room, seeing the sausage to which she had come so close plucked away again, helpless, ravenous, overwhelmed with despair, Nicky dropped her head in her arms and sobbed her heart out.

The charcutier looked at first nonplussed, later horrified. Between sobs, Nicky gave him a suitably expurgated version of her story. The absent Jean-Claude arrived and was despatched to mind the shop while M. Cochelin alternated between shocked exclamations and consoling pats on her shoulder. Nicky did not really like being patted—it reminded her unpleasantly of Uncle Luca—but she was too immersed in misery to object. He produced a supply of paper napkins and when she had cried herself out she mopped up the tears and the last flecks of her mascara, blew her nose furiously, and felt a little better. M. Cochelin sent Jean-Claude out to the nearest café for bread, butter, and strong black coffee, and himself produced a hunk of pâté de foie and assorted slices of cold meat. Nicky thought it was the most heavenly meal she had ever had—indeed, her subsequent craving for pâté de foie dated from that occasion, though it would never taste quite the same again. The charcutier watched her eat, giving little nods of approval. "You will be all right now," he told her. "I give you a job. He is a nice boy, Jean-Claude, but very stupid. I can always use a bright girl like you. It's not much pay, you understand—I have my overheads—but it's a job. Better than the streets, *hein?* When you are ready, we find you somewhere to live. There is a place near here—they have rooms for single girls. The landlady is a good friend. In a minute, I take you there."

Nicky said: "You're very kind."

He looked kind. But she wasn't sure.

Half an hour later, Nicky found herself in a species of shabby bedsit, whose closed windows and stifling heat made her really warm for the first time in days. A small basin and single gas ring enabled the room to be categorized *"tout compris;"* down the corridor there was a communal shower and primitive lavatory. The furnishings were dominated by two decrepit wardrobes: one would not open, the other would not close. Beyond the window there was a vista of similar windows, set in a dun-coloured wall along which weather and city smokes had traced the usual tidemarks of creeping dirt. But the double bed had clean sheets and the lumpy mattress was softer by far than hard stones. Nicky paid little attention while M. Cochelin and the landlady came to some arrangement; they seemed to be on familiar terms. And then she was left alone. Alone in a warm room with a real bed. At that juncture, it was all she wanted, the sum total of her dreams. She undressed, rolled into bed, and plunged instantly into a fathomless well of sleep.

It was one of the happiest moments of her life.

Nearly two weeks passed before M. Cochelin climbed into bed with her. By then, Nicky was prepared for it; she had had time to think things over. Sleeping under the bridge with the old man and his Alsatians was infinitely worse than accommodating the charcutier occasionally. She had learned her lesson only too well: nothing is for nothing. He had been kind and now he expected her to be grateful. After all, he was a kindly man, neither as old nor as repulsive as Uncle Luca, probably very good-looking before he put on weight. He still had plenty of hair, eyes as bright and dark as a squirrel, and an echo of the impish smile with which he had once charmed every female in the *quartier*. He explained, with a lugubrious sigh, that he had married money—the daughter of the charcuterie's previous owner—and he had evidently been consoling himself with extramarital romping ever since. His wife was a *femme formidable*, the mere mention of whom provoked a positive earthquake of shrugs; his four children were all *adorable* and he frequently brought photographs of them for Nicky's benefit. In the shop, his manner to her was generally brisk and business-like; in bed, he obviously fancied himself as a great lover, spending far too long on foreplay she would rather have done without. She just wanted it over, quickly. After the first few times she no longer found their union distasteful, merely dull. She moaned, gasped, shuddered in simulated orgasm, sensing he would be disappointed if she did not put on a show, yet secretly despising him for believing in it. Stephane had cared little whether she pretended or not, provided his public façade remained intact; M. Cochelin preferred to be deceived. How many women before her, she wondered, had moaned and gasped and faked in this way, to make him think he was so wonderful?

How many women throughout the world did the same, night after dreary night, with men who never stirred them, never reached them, never knew? It was a reflection which depressed her all the more since no man outside her fantasies had ever given her anything but boredom and pain. She was sometimes afraid no one ever would.

She had not intended staying very long at the charcuterie but time passed and habit or the terrors of the bridge held her prisoner. Bernard (in private, she was allowed to call him Bernard) paid her rent and with food from the shop she was able to save a large part of her wages; but she worked hard and was too tired after hours to look for another job. Leaving with no job to go to had become unthinkable. Strangely, she was less dissatisfied than she'd been in Uncle Luca's restaurant, partly because her expectations had diminished, partly because she was always planning to quit—next week, the week after, next month. But autumn came round again, and she was still there. And one night, she went back to the bridge.

She did not know what drove her: conscience, curiosity, or some deeper compulsion which she could not explain. Criminals revisit the scene of the crime; would-be suicides return to the cliffs where they tried to jump; Nicky went back to the bridge. She told herself repeatedly that she would not go; but the idea continued to haunt her and in the end it was easier to succumb. Nicky invariably succumbed to demons of any kind. She filled a carrier-bag at the shop after M. Cochelin had left and set out, disdaining the bus so that she would have time to change her mind. When she reached the path along the river bank her footsteps faltered, slowed, and finally stopped. It was evening, as it had been before. She was sober. She could see with dreadful clarity the intervals of darkness between the street-lamps and the black water heaving in the river below. It seemed strange to her that she had never noticed how terrible the place was, with its treacherous shadows and the cold depths of the Seine, ominously near. Yet she had not noticed: hunger and misery had filled her to the exclusion of all else. She had lain down in the shelter of the bridge like any other vagabond, indifferent to the phantoms of the imagination, her hopes and fears reduced to her most basic needs. And that, somehow, was more terrible than all the rest. Peering ahead, she thought she could discern huddled figures under the arch. She pictured the old man, still sitting there, no longer a man but a skeleton, with stony grin and empty eyes, stretching out fleshless hands to hold her. And on either side of him the two dogs, patient and unmoving as Cerberus at the gates of Hell. She feared to go on; yet she could not go back. She went on.

The old man was not there. The arch had only three tenants, one already snoring in an alcoholic slumber. The others watched her warily, natives of a shadow-world scrutinizing an intruder. She deposited the carrier-bag on the stones, looking at them without words. When she turned to leave, someone called after her. She did not listen, did not stay. She was hurrying along the river-path, her feet breaking into a run—running towards the steps and the haven of the street. At the top, she paused and leant against the wall, getting her breath back. Gradually, her pulse decelerated, her shaking limbs relaxed. She needed a drink. But not here. Nowhere near here. She got into a passing bus without noticing the destination and got off in the vicinity of the Pompidou Centre.

In a side street she found herself a bar—an ill-lit, dingy bar patronized almost exclusively by men. Their eyes swivelled after her as she crossed the room. At a seat in the corner she drank her Pernod, feeling the evil liquid trickling slowly through every vein in her body. Maybe her face betrayed her tension; a young man at the next table who had been studying her for a few minutes leaned over and offered: "Cigarette?"

Nicky was not a habitual smoker. In her teens, she had started because she thought it was grown-up; now she did it to occupy her hands. It was more sophisticated than knitting. But she did not really enjoy the taste of smoke and French cigarettes, she had decided in Saint-Malo, had all the elusive aroma of vintage animal dung. However, there were still times when she told herself she felt like a cigarette. She hesitated.

"Marlboro," the young man said, moving his fingers so she could see the packet.

Nicky found herself smiling at his quickness, in spite of her nerves. "Yes, please."

He extracted a cigarette for her and slid into the chair opposite in order to give her a light. The move was accomplished so smoothly, with such unthinking assurance, that Nicky felt a twinge of shock—she thought it was shock—somewhere in the region of her stomach. None of the seaside charmers of two summers ago had ever approached her with such careless certainty. He did not insinuate himself, he did not push, he contributed neither sweet talk nor excuses. He simply sat down, drew his chair towards her, flicked his lighter. The flame sprang up on cue, straight and tall. Nicky lit her cigarette. It evidently hadn't occurred to the young man that he might meet with a repulse and Nicky didn't attempt to repulse him. In any case, she was not entirely sure she wished to.

"You want another drink?" he said, observing the inroads she had made on her Pernod. He ordered without waiting for an answer, catching the barman's attention with a wave and addressing him by name.

"Do you come here a lot?" Nicky enquired.

"Here—there—everywhere. Paris is my backyard. Everyone knows Alex." He considered her, head on one side. "But you— you are English, I think."

Nicky nodded. She expected him to pursue the matter, but he didn't.

Their drinks arrived: his looked like whisky with too much ice. "You see," he remarked. "I am French: I drink Scotch. You are English: you drink Pernod. This is what they call cultural exchanges."

Nicky laughed. "Alex doesn't sound very French," she said.

"It's Al-lex-andre," he explained. "Like Dumas. Alexandre Fauvelle. I prefer Alex. And your name?"

"Nicky."

"Nikki. It's pretty. I knew a Nikki once, in Marseilles. She had very nice legs—Nikki what else?"

"Nicky Maglioli. I was married to an Italian—a French Italian."

"*Was.*" Alex smiled suddenly, a wicked vivid smile. "That's good. I like 'was.' Anyway, the Italians are all *cons*. What happened to him?"

"He ran off to Italy—to become a racing-driver."

"Oh, *merde!*"

Nicky found she was laughing again. Alex was someone whom it was easy to laugh with. Not good-looking—crooked features, irregular bones, black-asphalt eyes which turned down at the corners—but attractive in a way that was oddly unnerving. He seemed at once very old and very young: old in cynicism, world-weary, dissipated, yet underneath, some instinct told her, morally and emotionally immature. A corrupt choirboy, a dissolute urchin, light-hearted in mischief as an infant but with a face creased and puckered like that of an ancient monkey. Between smiles, his expression held a trace of wistfulness, of deceptive candour—an echo, had Nicky but seen it, of her own waif-like charm. Perhaps that was why, though attracted, she was not bewitched; though intrigued, she maintained a certain detachment. She might believe she had learnt from Stephane—indolent, easy-going Stephane with no depths beneath the shallows—but in Alex her subconscious had recognized something of herself, a kindred spirit, and as such untrustworthy, irresponsible, unsafe. In the dim light Alex's skin was sallow from the fading of a Riviera tan and his black eyes crackled as if with electricity. His smile was as blinding as Nicky's, less beautiful maybe, but far more disastrous. He was small and slight in build but he gave an impression of wiry strength: the strength of an alley-cat who can climb any wall and is used to the quick getaway. And despite his jeans and black leather jacket he looked expensive: there was a gold earring in one ear, gold rings on several of his nimble fingers, graven initials (not his own) on the cigarette lighter; and the wallet he had tossed on the table had deprived some endangered reptile of its skin.

When Nicky was halfway through her second drink he ordered more, once again without asking her. From time to time he was accosted by various people, all of whom seemed extravagantly pleased to see him. Nicky, regarding him in a sudden flash of clarity, realized with a kind of fascinated horror that there were no good qualities in his face at all, no vestige of courage or integrity or kindness, only the hallmark of assorted vices. He's picked me up, she thought, and I've let him do it. The idea both alarmed and allured her. Much later, when she was fairly drunk and had just remembered she hadn't eaten, he said: "Let's go."

"I'm hungry," Nicky said. "I feel like pâté de foie."

"There's some in my fridge."

They went.

The following week, Nicky had a terminal row with Bernard. Perhaps her subconscious was doing overtime, driving her forward where in the past she would have shrunk back. Her mind had made itself up, independent of her control, and when catechized over her depredations on the stock of charcuterie she lost her temper. The subsequent quarrel, conducted in the shop during business hours, was aggravated rather than restrained by irregular interruptions from Jean-Claude and a string of customers. Jean-Claude, with a sort of clumsy tact, did his best not to notice; but the customers were less discreet. Finally, Nicky said that if she didn't get a substantial pay-rise she would call on Mme. Cochelin and tell her everything. Whether she would actually have done so was a moot point; M. Cochelin evidently took the threat seriously. That afternoon when Nicky had left early, Madame herself turned up at her lodgings, a mountain of a woman with the musculature of an all-in wrestler, determined to oust her from both work and home. In his lunch-hour Bernard had obviously taken the opportunity to confess, braving the tidal wave of his wife's displeasure, and now cowered like a rabbit in his burrow while she sallied forth to do his dirty work for him. Afterwards, Nicky speculated that such was his regular practice, when an affair had run its course. The landlady looked bored, as if she had seen it all before; the other residents chattered excitedly. Nicky, seeing little alternative, packed her things—including her savings, which had escaped Madame's gimlet eye—and left with what dignity she could muster. Dignity was not one of her strong points, but under the circumstances she felt that it was called for. Someday, she decided, she would learn to make a graceful exit, instead of always running away, with or without an avenging Fury in pursuit. Someday.

She went to Alex.

He hadn't asked to see her again; indeed, she doubted if he would recall more than her christian name. And she had money enough to pay for a room while she looked for another job—if another job was what she wanted. But she made her decision with only the briefest hesitation. She went to Alex.

She found the street easily enough: the rue Quincampoix— she had noticed the sign when she left Alex's flat in the small hours. It was a gloomy place even in daylight, little more than an alleyway between antique stone tenements which seemed to lean towards each other above her head, squeezing the sky to a narrow path of blue. The stone was crumbling, many of

the upper windows were broken, the buildings looked long un-
occupied. But on ground level, in addition to the bars, there
were art galleries, a discreet restaurant, stretches of recent
paintwork and sheer glass between mouldering pilasters. In
such a street Nicky could imagine the misshapen figure of Quas-
imodo fleeing over the cobbles, the bandit Calembredaine lurk-
ing in some shadowed postern, Mme. La Voisin, with her crystal
ball and her poisons, waiting in an inner sanctum for clients
who came veiled and clinking softly with diamonds. Here, D'Ar-
tagnan might have been ambushed, Arsène Lupin assumed his
thousandth disguise, Maigret lit his pipe. By night, Nicky had
strayed into the street without seeing it, even as children in
stories cross the border into fairyland. She had left in a hurry,
dimly aware of furtive lights and dark recesses where gnarled
stone faces peeped and vanished—half awake in a kingdom of
dreams. Returning by day, she knew at once that this was
what she had been seeking, the Paris of story and fantasy
which she had never been able to find. She put her bags on
the ground and looked around her, breathing in the atmosphere. Fate, whose intentions she had so often doubted, must
have schemed to bring her here. Her last reservation disappeared; she picked up her things again and set off in search of
Alex's flat.

She was on the point of retracing her steps, believing she
must have missed it, when she came to a heavy door on her
left, inlaid with weatherworn carvings set in a circle. She only
glanced at it but retained a vague impression of a grinning
kobold-face peering out from a maze of interwoven shapes. The
door stood slightly ajar: beyond, through a twilit passageway,
she could see a gallery hung with slabs of what looked like
plaster-sculpture and a miniature courtyard half full of rubble.
This was it. Her heart beat faster in spite of all her would-be
confidence. She pushed the door further open, went down the
passage, clutching her bags, and mounted the crooked stair
which skirted the courtyard up to the first floor. A couple of
windows showed signs of occupation; behind drawn curtains
there was a glow of artificial light. At the top of the stair there
was a door, a plain new door, painted black. It sported an iron
knocker in the shape of a hand and an electric bell. Nicky chose
the bell.

When the wait had begun to seem interminable, the door

opened. Alex. He stared at her, his expression neither friendly nor unwelcoming, merely blank.

"Nicky Maglioli," she said. "I expect you've forgotten. We met last week. Can I come in?"

Possibly he was reassured by such limited expectations. He drew aside reluctantly and motioned her to enter.

Inside, the apartment had been carefully restored and decorated. White walls, scarlet curtains, black velvet sofa, black lacquer desk. Several pieces of avant-garde ceramics overflowing with cigarette ash. A litter of newspapers and magazines, a dirty coffee cup, a bottle of Scotch and a tumbler, half empty. A carpet patterned with pseudo-cabalistic designs; cushions ditto. Two or three lampshades of blood-coloured glass. Last time, Nicky had noticed little more of the flat than she had of the street outside; now, she scanned the room with interest. Her attention was caught and held by the painting hanging above the sofa. About six feet by four, a sombre abstract with will-o'-the-wisp threads of green and scarlet caught between amorphous masses of jet. Off-centre, there was the suggestion of a face, lineaments only half formed, emerging from the surrounding shapes like the kobold on the street door. A wicked little face, puckered like a monkey, tugged awry by the swirl of the pattern. Perhaps it was in Nicky's imagination that it resembled Alex.

She put her bags on the floor and sat down on the sofa. Alex eyed the bags with disapprobation. He did not sit down. He did not offer her a drink. He propped himself pointedly against the wall by the door. "What do you want?"

It didn't sound promising. Nicky stammered over her rehearsed speech and discarded it in favour of bald frankness. She had a feeling that Alex—this new, hostile Alex—would see through anything else.

"I was living as this man's mistress," she stated simply. "He wasn't very exciting, but he paid for my room and I had a job in his shop. I didn't like it much, but before—when my husband left me—I had to sleep on the streets. So you see . . . Anyway, the room was a hole and the job was boring. I asked for more money but he wouldn't give it to me. He told his wife and she threw me out. And so—I came here." She faltered. Alex appeared increasingly unsympathetic but Nicky, groping for the words to express her needs, was not looking at him. "I don't mind being someone's mistress," she burst out, "but I want it

to—to be *worth* it! I want clothes and money to spend and a
proper apartment to live in! I don't want a horrid little bedsit
and a dreary job and a fat *salope* of a wife chasing me down
the street. I want to be the mistress of a different kind of man,
someone rich and—and *interesting*. I want him to give me furs
and diamonds and take me to nightclubs and buy me the best
champagne! I want to have *fun!*" She ran out of words and met
Alex's suddenly inscrutable gaze almost fiercely, her fists
clenched in passion. "I thought"—she took a deep breath,
plunged—"you know everyone. You said so. I thought—
maybe—you could help me."

Alex was still standing by the door, one shoulder hitched to
the wall. But his expression had changed. "Maybe," he said.
The swift, calamitous smile irradiated his face. "You are not
such a sweet little girl after all, are you?" And in his eyes there
was a sort of recognition, the acknowledgement, in his turn,
that they might just possibly be two of a kind.

He unhooked himself from the wall, went to the kitchen for
another tumbler, and poured her a generous measure of whisky.
Nicky drank valiantly. She didn't like whisky.

"You need it," he insisted. He selected another prop, this
time the black lacquer desk, and produced the inevitable packet
of cigarettes. Frowning abstractedly, he threw one to Nicky, lit
one himself. "You want me to find you a man," he summarized.
"Someone rich and *interesting*. Which is to say, rich—and pow-
erful. Money—so you can have fun. Power—*eh bien*, power is
fun too. Power is status. Power is glamour. And power is vulnerable. It is important, that he should be vulnerable. Someone
who can be used. Someone who can, if necessary, be blackmailed. A man of position. A man who needs a mistress." The
smile again, glittering with hidden wiles. "I daresay I could
find you such a man."

Nicky looked up hopefully.

"It depends"—Alex sucked deeply on his cigarette—"what's
in it for me."

Nicky said: "Anything you want."

"Anything," Alex said, "is much too vague a term. But for
the moment it'll do. Meanwhile, I suppose you want to stay
here?"

Nicky had been in France long enough to pick up the national
gesture. She shrugged.

"You might as well," Alex decided. "It will be more conve-

nient. You have a lot to learn. You can sleep on the sofa; I don't
like too much company. Remember: this is *my* flat, you're only
an uninvited guest. Never tidy up, never dust the shelves, never
wash my shirts. I'll teach you to make coffee: the English hav-
en't a clue. Otherwise I don't want you cooking in my kitchen."

"I'm a rotten cook," Nicky said.

"Fine." Alex glittered at her. "I think we understand each
other. Yes? *À la bonne fortune!*" He drank.

Nicky followed suit, grimacing at the taste of the whisky.
"Bonne fortune," she echoed.

In the succeeding weeks Nicky learnt a little more about Alex.
Sometimes, after sex or over a joint, he would tell her certain
things about himself—details of his past as carefully tailored,
she suspected, as anything she chose to confide from her own
history. Not necessarily untrue, merely abridged, or glamour-
ized, or distorted. His father was a rich industrialist on his
second marriage who had provided his only son with every
luxury except attention and had cast him off at the first sign
of trouble. Now, they did not speak. *"Il me fait chier,"* Alex said
dismissively. His mother lived on alimony in a villa in the Midi.
She obviously adored him and gave him whatever he asked
for—usually in cash. His stepmother also supplied him with
funds on occasion, though it was not clear why. He did not
appear to work, but many of his low-voiced colloquies, in bars
and clubs, were reputedly concerned with *"mes affaires."* Frequently, people came to the flat, midnight visitors who used
the knocker, not the bell, and on whose arrival Nicky was supposed to make herself scarce. The black lacquer desk was unlocked; small quantities of this and that changed hands; there
was always plenty of money. Nicky, remembering Kipling on
another kind of contraband, reflected that "them that asks no
questions isn't told a lie" and accordingly watched the wall.

If Alex was evasive about such dealings, he was equally evasive about many other features of his existence. Nicky guessed
that he had a love of intrigue for its own sake, preferring to
wrap himself in the cloak of the conspirator even if he was
merely going out to tea, and returning an enigmatic answer to
most direct questions as a matter of course. Thus all his confidences were invested with guile, his meetings were invariably

clandestine, and an atmosphere of contrived mystery pervaded his social life. If he took Nicky out with him he would never introduce her to his friends: they stared curiously at her, and she stared curiously at them, and everything was left to conjecture. He had a lot of friends. In the seediest café-bar, in the smokiest cabaret, in the smartest nightclub, there was always someone sidling up to him with a furtive greeting, or hailing him with a shout from across the room. Pale young men with haggard eyes, dark young men with expensive hair-cuts, older men with face-lifts, disillusioned men whose faces had sagged beyond recall—even a smattering whom Nicky recognized from the television or from cinema hoardings. And girls—some pretty, some tarty, some chic—all of whom Alex kissed or ignored with equal nonchalance. Nicky was glad she was not in love with him, and so did not have to worry about the girls. Occasionally, Alex let slip morsels of information regarding these friends: that man was a journalist, this man a film producer, that girl was sleeping with a certain actor, this girl with a certain politician. He implied he had business connections with a couple of rock groups, with a film studio, with a particular newspaper; Nicky wondered if he sold titbits of scandal to roving gossip columnists. But if she distrusted Alex she was also impressed by him. She saw him as a spider at the centre of a glittering web, a shape-shifter moving with the skill of a chameleon between high fashion and low life. And behind all his masks she detected a core of cold common sense, an intelligence without affection or scruple. She noted that, for all his illicit deals, he took cocaine only rarely and never touched heroin. He drank, but not to excess—except for coffee, which he liked as strong and sweet as black treacle. He ate little. He had a motorbike on which he would roar down the boulevards, but he was chary of arousing the enmity of the police. Nicky gathered he had once done a spell in gaol, though he would not say what for. "You have been in trouble too," he remarked, "haven't you?"

"Maybe," Nicky said, imitating his own equivocation.

He laughed. "You learn too fast," he said. "You begin to resemble me. I have a sister, did you know? She is ugly and virtuous and stupid. Three deadly sins. She married an *espèce d'enculé* who won't have me in the house because he says I'll get money out of her. I should, of course, but why does he care?

He can afford it. And it gives her pleasure, poor stupid ugly woman. You would have made a better sister than that. We could have had a good time. *N'importe.* Come to bed, little sister—pretty sister. Let's make incest."

Theirs was a partnership, not a relationship. Nicky—the uninvited guest—never dusted, never tidied up, never cooked in the kitchen. They had a row once when she inadvertently put a camembert in the fridge ("The ex-mistress of a charcutier should know better!"), but otherwise they co-existed comfortably enough. Alex's comments were always barbed, often mildly cruel, but Nicky remained more or less unaffected. His little cruelties, she saw, were distributed with impartiality, a part of his image rather than a specific attempt to hurt anyone. His whole manner was shaped and honed as a weapon against the world, but whether defensive or offensive she was never quite sure. Once he understood that she would not try to encroach on his life he began to relax with her—sometimes. She might sleep on the sofa but when awake she was frequently in his bed. "You're a lousy lover," he told her, the evening she arrived. "I thought so last week. You fake it like a third-rate whore. Did you ever see a film called *Klute?* Jane Fonda in bed with some man, looking at her watch. With you, I can see the watch. Think of yourself as a million-franc screw and fake it like that. Don't just pretend you're having an orgasm—*imagine* you're having an orgasm. Fake it like *Garbo.*" And, later, "To fake is good: it means you are not involved. Orgasm makes women sentimental."

"And with you?" Nicky murmured.

Alex grinned. "With me, it's different. I make the rules: I can break them. Think of it as masturbation. I am your familiar spirit, your *âme damnée.* Don't love me. Give yourself to me. Do it with me and you will know how to pretend with other men. And then whoever you may lie with I shall be there, in the bed beside you, between you, not two lovers but three, flesh and phantom intertwined in the darkness, and it will be my shadow that possesses you, enjoys you, dissolves into the daylight, while the other man will never be more than an onlooker. Always, little Nikki: do you understand? Give yourself to me now and I shall have you always. *Always . . ."*

And Nicky gave herself, without love, fascinated by his certainty and his distorted lust. His hands moulded her, his mouth devoured her, his tongue entered her, and she came and came and came, riven by slow tremors of pleasure and terror. This was the dark side of passion, the abandon of a witch who sells her soul to the devil through an act of sexual degradation. Once she had dreamed of finding pleasure through romance, but romance had failed her and only in the embrace of a warped desire did she discover, at last, the ecstasy she had sought for so long.

8

Nicky collided with Théophile Montador outside the Galeries Lafayette a week before Christmas. It was a carefully planned collision: she had been awaiting him for half an hour. She dropped a bottle of aftershave, which broke; he began to apologize; she showed signs of bursting into tears. She knew already, from her experience with Bernard, how effective that could be. Montador was suitably affected. He bought her a cup of coffee to calm her down, and she launched into a tangled explanation of how the aftershave was for her boyfriend, who didn't love her any more, and she wanted to leave him only she didn't know where to go, and it was so terrible to be unhappy when it was nearly Christmas. She was—of course—an orphan, she had met her boyfriend on holiday and had given up her job to come to Paris with him, she had no one to turn to, and so on. Montador took her back to the Galeries, bought her a replacement bottle of aftershave and some perfume for herself, and gave her his card. He was going away for Christmas but would be back shortly afterwards: she was to call him if there was anything, anything at all, that he could do. Nicky achieved a brave smile and dewy eyes, wished him—in a trembling voice—a *very* happy Christmas, and staged a graceful exit.

"It will work," Alex assured her on Christmas Day. "You'll see. He needs a woman very badly, that one. He has a beautiful wife who has lost interest in sex; they have separate bedrooms and exchange polite kisses at the breakfast-table. His tastes are too rarefied for common prostitutes and in any case, he has a spotless reputation to maintain. *Pauvre homme:* it must be very tiresome to have a spotless reputation."

"If he's so upright," Nicky said, "surely he won't want a mistress."

"He doesn't know what he wants," Alex said coolly. "We have to teach him. First, we offer him the opportunity to be chivalrous. You are in trouble; you need help. For a man like that, helping people is part of his code. Afterwards—you are grateful, you cling to him, you look at him with worshipful eyes. Before he knows where he is, you are in his bed. It will be easy."

"Grateful . . ." Nicky echoed, lingering over the word. Fleetingly, she wondered if there would ever be a man to whom she did not have to be grateful. Stephane, she thought, had expected her to be be grateful to him for marrying her, Uncle Luca for offering to take care of her, Bernard for giving her a job and a place to sleep. And now Théophile Montador, he of the spotless reputation and chivalrous instincts, was going to require her gratitude. Open your legs, Nikki, open your legs and be grateful. Close your eyes; close your mind; sigh; gasp; fake it like Greta Garbo. *Et voilà.* Gratitude.

Even Alex . . . no, with Alex "grateful" was not the word. Already she felt herself bound to him with bonds stronger than sex, deeper than feeling. He might snap those ties as carelessly as he would brush away a spider's thread, but she feared suddenly that if she tried to struggle the bonds would still hold her, enmeshed in his fantasies like a butterfly in a web. *Give yourself to me now and I shall have you always . . . always . . .* When you are young, "always" is a term lightly used and swiftly forgotten, a commitment for an hour, a month; a game. But even an empty vow can endure. Abruptly, Nicky reached for the wine, shaking off her nebulous fears with a movement that was almost a shudder. Alex, sprawled on the black velvet sofa absorbed in his own schemes, did not notice.

He was reticent about his sources but Nicky gathered his principal informant on Montador was his son Eugène. Alex called him a *copain*, implying a friendship which she did not quite credit; she was almost sure Eugène was one of the furtive clientele who visited the flat after dark, knocking softly and slinking away afterwards into the shadows of the rue Quincampoix. But Alex's information, however obtained, appeared to be accurate. Montador—he said—was ideal for their purposes: the gently upward trend of his political career, his reputation as a family man, his unquestioned integrity, his inherited income. His wife Isabelle was a lady of impeccable pedigree and cold, elegant beauty, interested in charitable projects and Saint Laurent suits. Montador was in his late fifties, Madame a few years younger: the right age, Alex declared, for the woman to lose enthusiasm and the man to develop an itch. Physically, Nicky thought he resembled an antique knight, tall, thin and silver-haired, with remote blue eyes, and aristocratic profile, a skin of old ivory. An unexpectedly gentle smile etched lines of wry humour in his sunken cheeks; his voice was deceptively quiet; a flawless courtesy concealed any violence of feeling. When Nicky came to him in the New Year, flaunting a bruise on her temple supposedly administered by her boyfriend, the quiet voice acquired an edge, the blue eyes an icy glitter. The bruise was genuine: Alex had provided it, removing his rings so as not to break the skin, and Nicky had laughed even when it hurt. Montador went with her to collect her few possessions from a couple of rooms borrowed solely for that purpose and installed her in a hotel at his own expense. He wanted to call the police but Nicky shrank from the publicity and, after brief reflection, so did he. "You've been so kind," she told him, sniffing valiantly through a smattering of tears. "So *kind* . . . In my whole life, nobody ever—nobody ever—" Here she gave up on speech, shaking her head and retreating hastily behind the handkerchief which he proffered across the tea-table. It was almost too easy to lose herself in her imagined predicament, to be moved by lies that had their roots in comfortless truth. Scraping together a semblance of personal pride, she went on: "I don't know what I'll do now. I suppose I ought to try and find myself a job . . . ?"

Montador responded without thinking to the hint of a question. "You don't have to worry about that," he assured her. And: "I'll take care of you."

Familiar words—lapping her, for the first time, in an unfamiliar warmth. He wouldn't hurry her, he wouldn't force her, he wouldn't quibble at the cost. He was a man of his word: he would take care of her. She believed him.

She could not cling to him: the table was between them, loaded with fine bone china, a half-eaten *tartelette aux fraises*, a pot of scented geisha tea. But she looked at him with worshipful eyes, only slightly reddened from crying and made to appear even larger by the smudges underneath. "I've never met anyone like you," she said simply.

It was true.

Looking back on the two years that followed, Nicky knew she should have been content. She had an apartment in the avenue d'Eylau with period furnishings and modern central heating, a wardrobe full of clothes, a dressing-table stacked with perfumes and cosmetics. Montador made her an allowance which was generous enough even when Alex had taken a cut, and on special occasions he gave her jewellery, all of which Alex had valued for her. He was a punctilious lover, always arranging visits in advance and arriving more or less on time, so that in between she was free to do as she pleased without fear of discovery or inquisition. Indeed, there were times when security made her reckless, and Alex's departure almost coincided with the return of Théo. He had given her a fourposter bed when she related a childhood fancy, and Alex made love to her on the embroidered sheets, striking Rodin poses in the Louis Quinze mirror. And on certain evenings they still went to Paris nightspots, where she spent her money on overpriced champagne and danced with other men. Montador took her out only rarely, since his political position made discretion essential, but to begin with she did not mind. During sex, he was gentle and considerate, arousing her to unexpected pleasure— not the frenzied climaxes she attained with Alex but a more temperate rapture, warm and sweet and satisfactory. It was as if Alex had tuned her senses as a musician would with a faulty instrument, and now any man who was sufficiently painstaking could pluck the right notes. Montador cosseted her, spoiled her, occasionally confided in her, and Nicky, in response, played the little girl who adored him—played the role so perfectly that she never noticed when it became a reality. With Alex, she was always a bright girl on the make, nimble in deceit, a cour-

tesan in bed; but increasingly she felt that it was this Nicky—
Alex's *petite Nikki*—who was acting a part, a part for which
she experienced a growing distaste. She wanted to become the
person Théo thought she was, a kitten wrapped in luxury and
fed on cream, more loved than loving, untouched by fears of
the future or shadows of the past. There were even moments
when she wondered if she could forego the night-life and the
bedroom antics with Alex, and find security and permanence
with Théo. But the problems seemed insuperable. She did not
think seriously about breaking with Alex; for the present, that
was impossible. But she thought about Isabelle. She bought a
good many magazines and Isabelle's picture appeared from
time to time on the society pages, the picture of a poised woman
in clothes of an impeccable simplicity, with high cheekbones
and swept-back hair the colour of pale mink. She was usually
portrayed at some charity function, cutting a ribbon, cam-
paigning diligently for this and that: one-parent families, drug
addicts, the elderly, the homeless, whatever was in vogue. Even
Nicky appreciated the irony of such activities, when her son
was rotting his nasal cartilage with cocaine and her husband
sought relief in the arms of a girl from the streets. She took to
cutting out the pictures and keeping them, hidden in a drawer
under her knickers where Alex would be unlikely to find them.
Left too much alone, she brooded. Théo loved her—she was
sure of it—so why shouldn't he leave his wife and marry her
instead? She visualized herself on the society pages, wearing
immaculate suits and presiding at appropriate functions. The
idea made her laugh, but it attracted her just the same. His
marriage was empty—he had not said so, but the fact was
implicit in their whole relationship—and nowadays both Cath-
olics and politicians often got divorced.

But Montador did not want a divorce.

"I love my wife," he explained, a little sadly. "I am a man,
I am weak, I have betrayed her; still, I love her very much. You
are a sweet child, Nicky, but you have to grow up. Things are
not always as simple as they should be. You must understand
that it is possible to love one woman and to need another—"

"You love *me*," Nicky whispered, a sudden chill in her face.

"Yes—in a way. You are very dear to me. But one day we
will say goodbye and you will find a younger man to make you
happy. That is as it should be. Isabelle—Isabelle is a part of
my life."

"I don't want a younger man!" Nicky protested. "I want you! I *love* you!"

"Nicky . . . don't lie to me. Not this time. *Ma pauvre:* did you think I didn't know? Oh, nobody spied on you; I met him one evening, coming out of the lift. The concierge told me he was here often. It hurt, but only a little. I felt it was natural enough that you should want someone more attractive—someone your own age. And you have always seemed pleased to see me: that meant a great deal. I appreciate your company—your consideration—but let us not pretend it is anything more."

She stared at him, too shocked for tears. "You don't understand . . ."

"I understand very well. You have told me a number of pretty stories; I have not checked them, nor questioned you, but I am not a fool. It didn't take me long to see . . . Anyway, no more stories, please. I had not really intended to discuss these things—it has been extremely pleasant, being with you, and I didn't want to spoil it. However, maybe it's for the best. You are very sweet, Nicky, with all your fibs and weaknesses—God help us, we are both weak—but I think it's time to talk of parting. I suppose I have known it for some while, *au cœur*. Only I am fond of you, and so I put it off. But it can't be put off much longer."

Nicky felt a cold hand squeezing her heart. She repeated in a low voice: "I love you," and in that moment, she believed it.

He smiled—a rueful, melancholy smile tracing the familiar lines across his face. Nicky longed to kiss away that faint melancholia, but she knew it was too late.

"That's very charming of you," he said. "But then, you have always been—very charming. Don't overdo it now."

She did not tell Alex. Not yet. When Montador had left she sat huddled in the middle of the huge fourposter, with the satin quilt sliding to the floor and a white nylon pussycat sprawled across the pillows, and she shivered like a lost child in a cold place. Her security was gone; beyond the comforts of her flat she saw old horrors lying in wait: a sordid bedsit, a tedious job, and at the back of all her fears the shadow of the bridge. She had saved no money, made no plans. Théo had said he would take care of her, and she had trusted him. She sat for a long while without moving. Eventually, she got up and went over to the dressing-table. In the left-hand drawer there were several small velvet cases embossed with the names of various jewellers. She took them out and shook their contents on to the painted tray in front of her: opal and pearl ear-drops, a ruby pendant, a snake bracelet with emerald eyes, two or three brooches. No rings: he had never given her a ring. But at least it was some kind of insurance.

When Alex came the next day, she did not want to make love. He looked at her sideways under his black lashes, and went away.

Three weeks later, Montador told her about his promotion. He had been appointed *chef de cabinet* at the *Ministère des Finances;* she inferred he must have known something about it for the past month. "I am sorry, Nicky," he said, as gently as he could. "I cannot afford to keep you here. You will have to make other arrangements. It isn't just the responsibilities of my new position: there are family problems. My son, Eugène . . . I should have seen it long ago, but I was so self-absorbed, so blind to the needs of others . . . No, it is not your fault; but I have done very wrong. He requires treatment; it will be expensive. I'll give you some money, I'll do all I can to help you, but you have to leave. Soon."

Nicky said slowly: "I see," and that was all.

That same night, she called Alex.

"It's been coming for some time, hasn't it?" he remarked when he arrived. "I saw it in your face. You looked as if you were getting sentimental."

"I am not sentimental now," Nicky said, plucking absently at the fur on the white nylon cat.

"Good . . . Well, don't worry. You still have me. We are partners: remember? I chose M. Montador with care. And this promotion—the *Ministère des Finances:* I heard it on the grapevine—it could not be better." Glancing at him, she saw his face was alight with a perverse satisfaction. "We have him in a trap. The lobster in the lobster-pot. It is almost too perfect."

"They are sending Eugène away for a cure," she interposed, without comment.

Alex waved it aside. "Let them waste their money if they want. It happens all the time: the cure, the new resolutions—

and after one month, two months, he will come back again, more desperate than ever. If not, there are always others. Anyhow, it's not important. For now, we are concerned with Montador, not his son. Listen: you will tell him you are happy here, you do not wish to move. Don't threaten: merely convey to him—through your tears—that if he throws you into the street your natural distress may well compel you to visit his wife. If you cry a little, if you *show* distress, it makes the whole thing less calculated. And should he still claim he cannot afford you, tell him there is the public purse—the purse which will be handed to him at the *Ministère des Finances*."

"He won't do it." Nicky blanched before the enormity of such a demand.

"He has no choice." Alex's sparkle waxed to a flame. "You have only to tell the world that he was using government money to pay for you all along and he will be finished. Even if he cleared his name, the scandal would ruin his career—and probably his marriage as well." He added, consideringly: "I think—I am almost sure—he loves his wife. That was one reason why I picked him."

Nicky said bleakly: "Was it?"

After Alex had gone, she rehearsed the forthcoming scene with Théo in front of the Louis Quinze mirror. But when the time came she couldn't weep, couldn't pretend.

"This is blackmail," he said quietly, when she had finished.

"Maybe." She regarded him steadily, her small face set and bitter. "You said you would take care of me. That's all I want." I would have loved you, and you rejected me. Just like the others. But she didn't say that. The realization of what she was doing left her rigid with horror, an automaton with its nervous system stuck on absolute zero. She was incapable of any dramatics, real or faked.

He said in the same quiet voice: "You seem to be quite good at taking care of yourself."

She did not reply.

He paced the room, turned—his tone altered to one of appeal and growing certainty. "Nicky, you cannot do this. I don't believe you could even think of it—not on your own. This young man of yours, did he suggest it? Did he persuade you—pressure you? Whatever hold he has over you, don't be afraid to tell me. I won't abandon you."

Nicky's fingers tightened; she responded: "You said that before."

"Oh, Nicky . . . Nicky . . ."

They stood at opposite ends of the room: he leaned on the mantelpiece, his head in one hand. She looked at him with eyes that scarcely saw, her whole body stiff with fear.

"If you can't afford me," she reiterated, "the government can. Governments spend billions. They won't miss a few thousand francs a week."

He made a gesture of repudiation. "I cannot possibly do such a thing. It would be to abuse my trust—to rob the taxpayer of schools, houses, medical care, all to finance my own pleasure. You must see . . ."

"Rob the taxpayer of weapons," Nicky said, recollecting one of Alex's more light-hearted arguments. "He shouldn't mind that."

"Don't joke about this: it is too serious. I won't—I *can't*—do what you ask. God knows I am far from perfect, but . . ."

"If you don't," Nicky said, "I'll say you've been swindling the government already. I told you. I'll ruin you."

"*Une connerie.* I can disprove any such allegation easily enough."

"It will be too late." She stood like a stone; only her voice continued to function. A flat, alien voice that did not sound like hers at all. "Mud sticks: you know that. Your reputation will be destroyed, your marriage over. I have contacts. If you won't help me, I swear to you the story will be in the *Canard Enchaîné* next Friday. I swear it."

They faced each other for an endless minute. She could not speak any more. In his expression she saw, as if from a great distance, disgust, weariness, blame and self-blame. It didn't touch her. Presently, he went out: she heard the door close softly behind him. Even now, he would not slam it, would not abate either his courtesy or his restraint. She slid to her knees where she stood, half fainting with reaction. It would have been a relief to cry, but the tears seemed to have frozen inside her.

When Alex came round, he said: "Well done."

"I didn't do it well," Nicky said. "I was too frightened."

Alex grinned. "You need practice."

• • •

The following evening he took her out to dinner. Medium-rare steak and Beaujolais Villages. Over the brandy, Nicky said: "What happens if he won't give in?" And: "I couldn't really go to the newspapers. I *couldn't.*"

"You won't have to," Alex said with confidence. "Drink up. This is no time to lose your nerve. I brought you out to encourage you, and you just sit there looking sick."

"I feel sick," Nicky said.

She bade Alex goodnight in the street and went up to the flat on her own. She had forgotten to double lock; the front door opened at a twist of her key. That meant nothing: she often forgot to double lock it. Then she saw the light in the sitting-room. She knew she hadn't left a light on. She called out: "Théo!," willing him to be there, knowing that in her present state of alcoholic depression she would cast herself on his chest and sob out her penitence, telling him she couldn't do it, she had never meant to go through with it, she loved him and she would try to live more cheaply if only he wouldn't send her away . . .

No one answered. The door stood slightly open; the light— a reading-lamp, maybe—threaded its way furtively through the gap. The effect was somehow sinister. Suddenly hesitant, Nicky touched the handle—then she pushed the door open and stepped into the room.

He was sitting in the armchair facing her, the lamp at his elbow tilted down so that the light spilled across his knees and onto the carpet, leaving the upper part of his body in shadow. He had evidently fallen asleep: she thought he looked old and helpless in the indignity of slumber, with his jaw sagging and his head lolling sideways. He even appeared to be dribbling. She said again: "Théo!" and leaned forward to adjust the lamp. The light splashed full on his face.

He wasn't asleep. His eyes glared in ferocious blankness and the dribble that ran from his mouth was red and clotted. Behind, where his head touched the cushion, there was a wide stain, already darkening. As she started back, she saw where the gun had fallen from his hand in the shadow of the chair.

She didn't scream. She had never seen death, let alone violent death, and until that moment it had been little more than a cheap sensation or a fleeting shadow. Even in front of those terrible eyes and crusted lips she half expected her vision to shift and the horror to melt away, leaving Théo merely dozing in her chair. But the eyes were still glazed, and the mouth drooled with all the trappings of reality. When she was able, she moved her gaze; then her limbs. She tottered into the kitchen like someone recovering from cramp. Over the sink, fighting nausea, she changed gear. From horror to panic. She had to get out. Now.

An hour or so later, she was stumbling up the stairs to Alex's apartment. She leaned on the bell and shouted and presently Alex opened the door. He hadn't been sleeping—he was a chronic insomniac—but the music-centre was on, a joint smoked in an ashtray, and he obviously didn't want to be disturbed. Nicky flung herself past him into the flat like a bat out of hell.

"Nikki—"

She dropped her hastily packed case, sank on the sofa. She was trembling and incoherent; Alex took one look at her, administered a large whisky, and became abrasive. "What's the matter? What are you doing here—and with this?" He kicked the suitcase. "Pull yourself together. You're not running out on this one."

"He's dead!" Nicky sobbed. Alex froze. "Why do you always give me bloody whisky? You know I loathe it. Of course I'm running out—what else can I do? He's dead—oh God, he's dead—"

Dear God make it not true. Please God . . .

Alex said: "How do you mean—*dead?*"

"Dead. Not breathing. Kaput. Dead. For Christ's sake, get me a gin."

"Nikki, be sensible. Slow down. How did he die—a heart attack?"

She shook her head. "—shot himself."

"What?"

"He shot himself. In the flat—my flat. I got back and he was there in the salon, just sitting there—I didn't see until I moved the light. There was blood coming out of his mouth, and his eyes . . ."

Alex stood over her, very still. She could see all the lines in his face—lines normally lost in a flickering mobility of expression—suddenly petrified, his ski-tan blanched to a yellow pallor. He looked old and drawn and ugly. When he spoke, his voice sounded oddly deliberate.

"*Quel vieux connard. Quel connard de merde.*"

He took Nicky's whisky and drank most of it himself. Then he went into the kitchen and poured her a gin, neat. Later, when she was calmer, he said: "You can't stay here."

"N-no, I suppose not."

"Look, in due course the concierge will call the police. The police will want to talk to you. If you were tougher, you could brazen it out; as it is—you'd better get away for a while. The police might let it drop soon enough but the press are more tenacious. I don't want you leading any of them to me."

"I wouldn't—"

"I can't risk it. The suicide of a respected politician—the *canards* will be on to it like locusts. Did he leave a note?"

"Not with me."

"Hmm. That's something, anyway. I wonder why *your* flat. Revenge? Atonement? *N'importe.*" Dismissing conjecture, he took another gulp of whisky. "The concierge. He looked practically blind, but I daresay he noticed me. He can probably manage a description. *Merde.* I'll have to clear out for the summer myself."

"Can I come with you?"

"Why?"

"Well, I . . ."

"No way. You're on your own now, little one. I don't carry dead wood. Maybe some day we'll get together again, but not for a long time. You can sleep here tonight; I suppose that will be okay. In the morning, you go."

Nicky whispered: "Where shall I go?"

"Wherever you like. I don't care. You've got money; you'll be all right."

"I'll have to sell my jewellery." She fumbled in her shoulder bag for the embossed velvet cases. "Will you—could you—?"

Alex hesitated. "I shouldn't bother," he said, after a pause. "It's all fake."

"*Fake?* But Théo—"

"Not Théo: me. Did you really think I'd be happy with a cut of your pocket money? I didn't help you out just for the fun of it, little idiot. I had the stuff copied and sold the originals. Oh . . . all except the ruby—it's a big stone: I thought Montador might notice. I'll give you cash for it now, if you like."

Nicky said, in English: "You bastard."

Alex shrugged, tossed her a smile. "I taught you a lot, Nikki. Next time you will know to be more careful."

"Bastard—*bastard*—"

In the morning, she gave him the pendant. He paid her considerably less than its worth, kissed her goodbye. "Here's the address of a friend of mine in Marseilles. He'll get you on a boat somewhere, if you want. Italy, maybe."

Nicky said, savagely: "How kind of you."

Alex flashed her his shattering smile. *"C'est la guerre."*

Nicky took the address, descended the stair for the last time into the rue Quincampoix. The Paris of story and fantasy. So much for daydreams. Once again, she was running away.

Italy was too expensive. The Greek islands were cheap, and populated—in Nicky's imagination—with shipping millionaires wandering the Med in luxury yachts, on the lookout for beautiful girls. In fact, she found herself surrounded by drunken English tourists and oversexed natives. She had read all the details of Montador's suicide in the newspapers, but it seemed like an incident from another world. Here on a beach in Greece she felt like a girl with no history, no future. At first, it was a relief; later, she began to be afraid. She went from island to island, feeling increasingly lost. Each time, she hoped for something new, someone different, a Cinderella-story or just a lucky break. Each time, it was the same. Her money was running low. At night she was gripped with a panic that was depressingly familiar. Where had she gone wrong? She had promised herself there would be no more undignified exits—yet her last exit had not even the semblance of dignity, a desperate flight pursued by the spectre of Montador's death and the memory of their final confrontation. She told herself that was the worst the gods could do: there could be nothing else lying in store. Stretched out on her bamboo beach mat she had all the long, slow days to reflect, to agonize, to watch her fears gathering like clouds on the blue horizon. Her life unravelled before her like that of a drowning man: it seemed to her that she had been little more than the plaything of a cruel providence, a constant victim of her own impotence, her naivety, her misguided treachery and misplaced trust. She had poured herself into every mould that was offered in an attempt to find some fairy-tale ending—Stephane's bride, Bernard's mistress, Théo's little girl, Alex's *intriguante*—and in so doing she had lost her true shape and her real identity had trickled away like water into the sand. Next time, she vowed, she would use her own wits, not somebody else's. Next time, she would make her own mistakes, in her own image. If there was a next time.

And then on a shabby ferry-boat, chugging between islands, between beaches, from one No Through Road to another—she saw Elsa Van Leer.

Nicky recognized her almost at once. She had seen her picture in a French magazine, part of an article on the children of celebrities trying to "go it alone." Because of Diana, she had read the article with some attention. Elsa, she remembered, had been going it alone in New York, evidently in style. There had been mention of an abortive attempt at architecture and a photograph of a clutch of metal tubes apparently intended to serve some useful purpose, though Nicky could not recall what. Beside this expression of her individuality Elsa had posed as effortlessly as if she had been doing it for years, which, Nicky thought, she probably had. Without actually saying so, Diana had always conveyed the idea that her twin was plain, but the girl in the photo was as beautiful as care and money could make her. A face like a model with a strong jaw-line, cheeks slightly hollow, narrow eyes aslant under sweeping brows. A matt white complexion and wine-dark hair straying in corrugated curls on to the shoulders of an exotic sweater. This was no Diana, with her healthy, ordinary prettiness—or if so, it was a Diana fined down to the bone, shadowed and highlighted for dramatic effect. But the camera can lie, Nicky had reflected, dismissing the matter. On the boat, she knew the camera had not lied.

Elsa stood on her own at the rail. The ferry was fairly crowded but somehow there was a space around her, a space inhabited by the breath of Chanel perfume and the curiosity and admiration of nearby passengers. Where others were in jeans or shorts she wore a cream trouser suit obviously designed for Saint-Tropez, flawless Italian shoes, and an air of unconscious aloofness, as if she were a junior member of royalty trying to pass incognito among the populace, fondly imagining a pair of dark glasses would conceal her regal bearing. Nicky wondered if she was really as oblivious to the vulgar herd as she appeared. How wonderful to be like that, she thought wistfully, almost hungrily. To know you're so bloody special you don't have to give a damn. *The cow*, added her inner demon, and she smiled to herself. She contemplated speaking to Elsa, maybe striking up an acquaintance ("I knew your sister:" that sort of thing); but the aura of distance and disinterest intimidated her. It was not until they had disembarked and she heard Elsa giving a direction to the taxi-driver that she saw her chance. She had no plans and few hopes, but she was growing desperate. And any chance was better than none. She picked up her suitcase and went to look for a bus that was going the same way.

On the beach their acquaintance developed naturally. Nicky, with no Alex to direct her schemes, saw Elsa initially as a temporary meal-ticket, someone whose generosity would spare her dwindling funds. She sunned herself, took her time, asked few questions. Given the opportunity, she insinuated the idea of a certain fellowship—they both had man trouble, which was always a common denominator. However, she was wary of Elsa in a way she had not been of her twin: Diana's nature had been sunny and relatively straightforward; Elsa, under the beautiful mask, seemed to have depths which Nicky feared to plumb. Yet for the same reason Nicky came to admire her, not simply for her glamour and her rich indifference to the opinion of the world, but for the strength and recklessness with which she fought back against disaster, regardless of the consequences. Nicky saw in her both passion and courage, the stuff of heroines, and secretly yearned to emulate her. When she told Elsa: "Good for you," she meant it. She remembered all the times she might have lashed out, had she only thought of it—had she only been sufficiently careless and fearless and hot-headed. Granted, she had no wealthy family to rally round her, no team of lawyers and psychiatrists to make her excuses; she merely had valour with discretion, and a talent for running away. It had got her nowhere. Elsa, whatever the cost, had tried to rough-hew her own destiny. And beneath her sophisticated exterior Nicky sensed a more primitive creature, untamed and unpredictable—the legacy, perhaps, of ancestors who had roamed a wider continent, white savages among black, making their own laws and killing to live, and to rule, and for the pleasure of the kill. Nicky's unknown forebears, she thought dispiritedly, had probably done little more than pick pockets, with an occasional knife-in-the-back in a dark alleyway. And suddenly her longing to be like Elsa, to be strong and dangerous, filled her with a new determination. She shifted on her beach mat like an animal flexing its muscles. It was the late afternoon: Elsa was talking, idly, about Diana, and her father. Nicky listened.

The idea crawled gradually out of her subconscious, haunting her by night, taking shape by day. Through Elsa's memories of Diana the figure of Rupert loomed like a distant giant, larger than life yet a little out of focus, haloed in his own legend. Rich and famous—and lonely. It was obvious that he had adored the daughter he lost while he and Elsa were at odds from some unexplained cause—Nicky did not know what and for the moment did not care. Back in her room, she studied her reflection in the mirror and wondered how she would look with red hair. It would make a change, she told herself, evading commitment, afraid to take her idea too seriously. And: "You have Diana's eyes," Elsa had remarked, giving her a sudden shiver, as if a devil was walking over her grave. Still, it was something to dream about, something to plan. And it was a long time since she had been in England. If she could find the money to get there—if she could avoid the authorities—there were too many ifs. And anyway, her scheme was surely too wild, too impossible ever to succeed.

On Elsa's last evening, Nicky said rather rashly that she would pay for dinner. She had only a hundred francs left and it was no time for a gesture, but ouzo had made her expansive. She hoped Elsa would refuse, as she had invariably refused such offers in the past, but Nicky's luck was out. And then the next morning she found the envelope. Five hundred dollars. Relief flooded through her—followed by anticipation. Five hundred dollars wasn't much, but it would do. She could go to England overland—coach was cheap—find a room and a temporary job in London, and explore the terrain. Her scheme might be impossible, but there was no harm in a preliminary investigation. She could always draw back.

Nicky presented herself at Rupert's office one morning in September. "I've come about the job," she told them. There wasn't a job, but it seemed like a plausible excuse for a closer look. And she didn't expect to see Rupert. She was not at all sure she felt ready for such an encounter.

He emerged from another room just as his secretary was giving Nicky a tactful brush-off. Evidently he was going to lunch: he gave his secretary some orders, refused to take a phone call, and did not so much as glance in Nicky's direction. Like Elsa, she thought, uninterested in lesser mortals. He was even bigger than she had imagined and his presence filled the room. She retreated towards a window, feeling small and insignificant. It seemed suddenly presumptuous of her even to be there. And then he turned, and saw her.

The helpful sunlight poured through the window, making a golden nimbus around her rufous hair. The remnants of a sun-tan, pepped up with blusher, had given her a complexion of peach-bloom hues; reddish eyebrows (the salon had been thorough) arched above smoke-grey eyes round with shock. Perhaps it was her recoil, which she could not dissemble, that completed the illusion. Rupert saw, not Diana, but a girl of identical colouring, slighter, not so tall, more lissom about the neck and waist. But he persisted in seeing Johanna's ghost in her daughter, so—in those first few seconds—he glimpsed his daughter's ghost in this unknown girl. And she was looking at him with the startled expression of someone who sees a familiar apparition in a strange place—almost as Diana might have looked had she come back to life and found him. Or so he liked to believe.

He asked: "Who are you?"

"It's Miss—Miss Simpson," said his secretary. "She came about a job. One of the agencies seems to have made a mistake . . ."

"I asked *her.*"

He towered over Nicky. The combined impact of his physique and his personality was shattering: the primitive creature which in Elsa was glossed over with civilization here appeared in the raw—a rugged Titan of a man, ferociously intelligent, visibly ruthless, with a glance as sharp as an auger under a scowling brow and a jaw that might have been chipped out of rock. His reaction terrified Nicky; already, she felt as if her futile plots were laid bare before that coruscating gaze. But it was too late: her fantasy had overtaken her and now she was being swept away.

"My name is Nicky Simpson." She licked dry lips. "I thought—I was told—there was a job here. Typist. There must have been a mix-up."

"Do you know me?"

"Not—not really." She wanted to escape but his eyes held her, interrogated her, mesmerized her. "I've heard about you. Naturally. And—I knew your daughter."

"Diana." A statement, not a question. It could only be Diana. "How . . . extraordinary. You're very like her."

"It's the hair," Nicky said, perjuring her soul.

"And you came here—for a job?"

"That—that was coincidence," Nicky stammered. "Only . . . I was sort of keen, because of knowing Diana."

He took her arm, without asking, and barked a dismissal at his secretary. "Come to lunch." He did not wait for an answer. Nicky went with him, a brief exhilaration tingeing her fear, unsure if she was being clever, or foolhardy, or merely carried along with the tide.

She had not registered, among the office minions, a man leaning in the doorway; a man in shirt-sleeves and loosened tie, with dull blond hair hanging in his eyes. He stared after them and remarked thoughtfully: "How very interesting. It must—yes, it must—be the hair."

"That hair," said the secretary, with the unerring perception of the female sex, "is dyed."

"Is it?" said Michael Kovacs.

In the restaurant, Nicky was recovering a little of her confidence. There was a gin-and-tonic inside her, wine in an ice-bucket, an art nouveau starter of green mayonnaise and pink shrimps decorating her plate. Rupert's height was less daunting when he was seated, and a gentleness had invaded his manner which she found both exciting and frightening. So might a tiger play tenderly with his prey. Here was no elderly aristocrat like Montador: in Rupert's face, she thought she saw a strength and power which disdained the withering of age, as well as the remorseless quality of true genius. Nicky's reading had led her to believe that great talent always manifests itself on a grand scale, with ardours too fervent for the normal mind to compass and vices of an Olympian magnificence. Rupert's eyes burned in their caverns and the set of his mouth was inflexible beyond the measure of ordinary inflexibility. He drank the wine as indifferently as if it were water, ate as though impatient with the necessity for food. Nicky felt scorched by the proximity of so much fire and fame.

"You knew my daughter," he pressed her. "Where? At school?"

"On no." Nicky flinched, blushed, stared into her wineglass. "We—we were quite poor: my mother could never have af-

forded the fees at Brayfield. We lived nearby. Diana and I became friends . . ." She couldn't mention the shop: Rupert, she
was sure, was sublimely unaware of anything as commonplace
as a newsagent's. Poverty should be romantic, a matter of
stitching by candlelight in a Dickensian garret. Her background
had been merely shabby and depressing.

But Rupert was uninterested in poverty, romantic or otherwise. "How well did you know her?"

"Quite well. She used to come round after lessons; I think
she felt she could talk to me. She told me a lot about her
family—about you." She added: "I never had a father. I always
envied her."

"What happened to your father?"

"He died," Nicky said. "Before I was born. I don't really know
much about him: my mother wouldn't tell me anything. I suppose it was too painful for her."

"Yes," said Rupert, a flash of understanding illuminating
sombre thoughts. "It might be . . . too painful. Where's your
mother now?"

"She's dead too," Nicky said hastily.

"So you're alone," Rupert murmured.

He didn't show any compunction, or offer to take care of her.
Nicky, reacting to some element in his brooding gaze, abandoned her little-girl act and lifted her chin. "I'm all right," she
said.

If he was touched or impressed, he did not show it.

"It's incredible—" he reverted without warning to the subject which mainly absorbed him "—about your hair. Exactly
the colour of hers. Your eyes, too."

"Sometimes," Nicky said, "people mixed us up."

He nodded, very slowly, as if affirming something of great
significance. Nicky toyed with her lamb noisettes during a
heavy pause. Rupert did not appear to find it heavy.

"So," he said at last, "you need a job. What were you doing
before this?"

"Secretarial, mostly," Nicky replied. "I was living in Paris
until recently, learning French. At the moment I've got a bar
job in the evenings—it leaves me free to go for interviews during the day."

"I'll see what I can do." His intentions appeared to be purely
avuncular but there was an undercurrent of some unknown
emotion which continued to disturb her. She felt he was too

incalculable, too dangerous, too gigantic both in spirit and in frame for her little schemes. Yet her own snare had caught her: she could not run away. Not this time.

"Where do you live?"

"Balham. It's not very nice, but . . ."

"Phone number?" He had extracted paper and pen from an inner pocket.

"There isn't one. I—I could call you."

"Do that," he said. "Tomorrow. Without fail."

She didn't call. She went to the pub where she worked, stood by the phone, twisting a glass in her fingers. It was early for gin, and the drink did not make her feel brave, only ill. When she picked up the receiver her throat tightened and her pulse began to thump uncomfortably. It was no good: she could not do it. After Montador, she had been able to flee from disaster; with Rupert, there would be no escape. She had gone fishing for mackerel and hooked a leviathan, and one lash of his tail would destroy her. "I can't," she told herself. "I dare not." And she replaced the receiver, and went and hid in her room, as if down any street she might encounter Rupert, come to hunt her out and destroy her.

A fortnight later, he came. She was behind the bar washing up; it was gone closing time. And there he was, looking down at her. Her hands froze in the tepid water; she returned his stare with enormous eyes. He said: "I've found you." His voice held no anger, only a rough gentleness and an absolute satisfaction. There was nothing avuncular about him any more. "Why didn't you call?"

"I was afraid . . . I thought . . ." She felt drained of lies, denuded of all masquerade. She could not think of either explanation or excuse.

"It doesn't matter." To what he attributed her fears, she never knew. "At least I've found you. It took long enough: none of the agencies seemed to have you on file and there are a good many pubs around Balham. If it hadn't been for your hair— but everyone notices hair like that."

"I'm sorry," she said on a rush of sincerity. "I should never have come to your office. I don't want another job. I don't really need any help . . ."

"You came to find me," he said, "didn't you?"

And in his face she saw her dream made flesh—she saw certainty, understanding, fate. Shock held her speechless. She was suddenly aware of his body—huge shoulders, hard muscles, overwhelming virility, terrifying charisma. The inevitable mixture of excitement and nerves tied itself into a knot somewhere in her groin.

He said: "You've finished here. Come with me."

Like a sleepwalker, she obeyed.

She spent one night in his flat in S.W.1 and thereafter moved to a place of her own nearby. He did not try to make love to her and his kisses, for all his strength, were merely tentative exploration, as though he was always holding back. In his arms she felt an arousal close to panic: she longed to be in bed with him and yet at the same time she was continually afraid—afraid of desertion, of disappointment, of being broken to pieces on the torrent of his lust. Perhaps it was the fear which aroused her: in sex, it was a novelty, a different kind of thrill. But she waited in vain for consummation. By day, she shopped with his credit card; in the evenings, they usually dined out. Rupert talked at length about art and architecture and Nicky listened dutifully, knowing herself privileged to be the recipient of such intellectual outpourings. In one of her haphazard gestures to a species of personal honour, she amassed the five hundred dollars Elsa had lent her and sent them to America. She told Rupert, truthfully enough, that it was for an old debt. The sly humour of paying the daughter with money obtained from the father occasioned her only a fleeting smile. The thought of what would happen when Elsa came back was a further cause for apprehension.

At Christmas, Rupert gave her a ring with an emerald as big as her thumbnail and as dark as the waters of the Styx. "How beautiful!" she gasped, suitably stunned, certain the proposition must come any minute now.

But he did not ask her to be his mistress. He asked her to marry him.

PART THREE

9

The wedding reception was held at Churston Grange, in a room on the first floor which had originally been designed as a ballroom. On arrival, Elsa found herself joining the queue to shake hands with the bride and groom. Nicky, she thought, was one of those people whose hairstyle can transform them beyond all recognition: the strong colour emphasized her pallor and the piled-up curls, interspersed with tiny white flowers, made it look as if the weight of her head would be too much for her slender neck and slight body. A far cry from the sun-browned girl with her tattered blond mop whom Elsa had known in Greece. Their hands clasped automatically: Elsa's firm and strong, Nicky's soft and shrinking as that of a child. On an impulse, Elsa's grip tightened; she leaned forward to press a cold kiss on that cold cheek, leaving the imprint of her lipstick behind like a smear of blood. The kiss of Judas: but the treachery belonged to Nicky. For an instant, their eyes met—then Nicky's gaze slipped away from her and Elsa moved on. To her father.

Afterwards she realized that his initial blankness of expression was because, quite simply, he did not recognize her. She tried to recapture anger and defiance but instead there was a hollowness about her heart. The blankness faded and a familiar look of withdrawal took its place. He did not comment on her new-found glamour, possibly he did not see it. Under his eye the last of her confidence dissolved: she felt ugly and awkward, her clothes all wrong, her face the painted mask of a clown. Their communication was empty of feeling, a string of mechanical formalities.

Elsa said: "Congratulations."

"Thank you." And: "I didn't expect you to make it."

You didn't ask me, Elsa thought with silent rage. You didn't want me. You never wanted me . . .

She said: "I flew home early. Is it all right if I stay at the flat?"

He hesitated. "While we're away. After that—call Langley and Mayhew. I've made arrangements. They'll help you out."

Too kind. Too generous. Too everything. Elsa burned inside. "Have a lovely honeymoon."

He merely nodded. "Elspeth, you're holding people up . . ."

Her white face went even whiter; but she moved away. Dimly, she was aware of the reception eddying round her, people chattering in front of her, behind her, through her. She felt like Coleridge's Ancient Mariner, stalking the feast in a desert of his own memories. *A thousand thousand slimy things Lived on; and so did I*. A waiter offered her a glass of champagne; she drank it, and took another. Now and then she saw someone she knew: "Elspeth! Good God, I hardly recognized you . . ." No one does, she thought, no longer encouraged. She lit a cigarette and put it out again, declined a smoked salmon sandwich. And then, through an opening in the crowd, she saw Aunty Grizzle.

She was sitting at one of the small tables round the edge of the room, crumbling a fragment of pastry on her plate. She was not looking at the pastry, or the plate, or the wedding guests: her eyes were vacant. Beside her sat a young woman whose clothes were tidy rather than smart, and who dabbed at her charge's mouth from time to time with a napkin. The young woman appeared kind and competent. Elsa stared in horror. Of course, Aunty Grizzle had always been elderly, her hair grey, her face lined, her mouth creased with age and peevishness, but throughout Elsa's childhood and adolescence she had hardly changed and it had been impossible to imagine she ever would. Her wispy hair had always been unsuccessfully

curled in the same late Forties hairstyle; her lipstick had remained the identical shade of nondescript pink; for social occasions, floral hat had succeeded floral hat rather like the Queen
Mother. She still had a hat but it had slipped sideways, her
lipstick had gone, her mouth slackened in a face no longer
capable of expression. I've been away three and a half years,
Elsa thought. That's all. Three and a half years. She had not
believed she could regret the niggling, nitpicking great-aunt
who had so often made her wretched; yet she regretted. Not so
much Aunty Grizzle herself as what she symbolized: the passage of time, the shadow of change. For Elsa, this was her long-
awaited homecoming, and instead of home she had found a
nest of monsters: all the people whom she had thought so familiar and immutable had turned into serpents and they slid
away from her. She knew a sudden longing for her sister—a
feeling so strong that for a moment it seemed there was a voice
in her ear, a hand on her arm; she had only to turn and Diana
would be there. Tears came to her eyes. She walked across to
Aunty Grizzle and sat down beside her.

"Aunty—it's me: Elspeth. Do you recognize me, Aunty?"

A species of thought dawned behind the vapid features: they
assembled themselves with an effort into a parody of expression. "Elspeth . . . She was a pudding. Always eating. Greedy,
you know. Greed is wicked. She was a wicked girl. Rude to
me—rude to everyone—a bad influence on Diana. Yes, she was
wicked . . ."

The attendant said: "I'm afraid she wanders a bit. She doesn't
really know what she is saying."

Elsa nodded. The faded eyes suddenly fixed themselves on
her face with an attempt at focus; a thin hand lifted to touch
her hair, leaving a flake of pastry in her curls. Elsa detached
it carefully.

"Diana?" Aunty Grizzle whispered. "Diana . . . ?"

"Yes," Elsa said. "I'm Diana."

"So pretty," Aunty Grizzle murmured. "Such a pretty girl.
Such a beautiful woman. Pretty Diana . . . Listen." She waved
a choppy finger aimlessly, leaning forward as if to mumble
secrets. "Don't go with her. She's wicked, your sister. Greedy
and wicked. She's jealous of you. *Don't go with her.*"

Elsa's red-rose mouth tensed; she fought an age-old pain. But
when she spoke, her voice was soft and noncommital.

"I'll be careful," she said. "I promise."

She rose to her feet. The attendant took a fresh napkin and began cleaning Aunty Grizzle's hands. Elsa went in search of another glass of champagne.

The voice caught her off guard. As always. She had retreated to a window and was staring out, thinking that the view at least was the same—green and brown fields, clusters of trees where a smattering of early leaves were aflutter in the wind, hills sloping smoothly towards the sky. And the inimitable English weather up to its usual antics, with the sun glancing briefly between hasty flurries of cloud. The sun was in her eyes when she heard the voice. Right behind her. As always.

"Hello, Elspeth."

She turned sharply, spilling a little of her drink.

"You."

"Are you surprised? I still work for your father, you know." He looked her over thoughtfully. "I saw you in church."

Elsa waved that aside. "You *don't* work for my father," she insisted, her frustrations released in a sudden rush of anger. "I phoned—I asked for you." She checked, started again, conscious of disastrous self-revelation. "It wasn't that I wanted to see you—I just thought we should talk. The receptionist said there was nobody at the office called Michael O'Hara." And, indignantly, ridiculously, she added: "Who *are* you?"

Michael did not answer immediately; she feared he was amused. It was, she realized, the ultimate morning-after question, crude in its humiliation. And with that thought certain memories returned in hideous detail; embarrassment gripped her; a faint colour rose in her pale face. Michael saw it, and for a full minute he looked her straight in the eyes. To her fury, she felt the flame in her cheeks grow hotter; a pain as abrupt and unexpected as an arrow stabbed at her groin.

"Michael—" she began, breaking off abruptly when she realized she had forgotten what they were talking about.

"I'm adopted," he said, reverting to her question with an effort. "O'Hara was my adopted name. When I left the A.A. and stopped being dependent I went back to my own. Michael Kovacs. I didn't think to tell you." And, after a pause: "So you wanted to see me."

"It was ages ago," Elsa said. "Before I went to New York. It doesn't matter now."

"America seems to have suited you," Michael remarked. "I thought you might turn out beautiful, one day. Evidently I was right."

There was a further pause. Elsa fished desperately for something to say. Something polite, and neutral, and free from any uncomfortable nuances. She could think of nothing.

"When did you get back?" Michael enquired.

"Today."

"Just in time?"

Elsa nodded. "Just in time." She was concentrating once more on the view, if only to evade his gaze. A cloud-shadow swooped down from the hills; the sun vanished. It had reappeared again before he spoke.

"Shall we go now," he said lightly, "and miss the speeches?"

"Go where?" she should not have asked.

"My flat."

This time, Elsa faced him. "I'm not going to your flat," she said. "I'm not going anywhere with you. I don't like you. I only went to bed with you that night because—because I was drunk, and unhappy, and you took advantage of that. It's never going to happen again: do you understand? Never again."

She gave him no chance to reply. She turned away and fled blindly into the bosom of the party, almost colliding with a waiter carrying a tray of glasses. Automatically, she helped herself to more champagne. It was beginning to take effect, but Elsa was past caring.

The speeches were perfunctory: a colleague of Rupert's stood in for the bride's father, the best man—an old client—knew too little of the couple to elaborate, and Rupert himself had never been given to articulating his feelings. The toasts were duly drunk; Nicky disappeared upstairs and subsequently reappeared in a Princess Diana going-away outfit; the bride and groom drove off in a Rolls for a honeymoon in Scotland. The left-over guests gathered themselves into cosy little cliques to polish off the champagne and canapés and speculate about the marriage. Elsa caught sight of Michael occasionally but carefully avoided him. Aunty Grizzle had apparently been removed by her attendant. Presently, Elsa wandered downstairs with a young man in tow and fetched up at random in front of the Picasso in the hall.

"Very fine," said the young man, who had artistic leanings.

"Of course, in his later years he did nothing *new*. And you can see here his obsessive eroticism . . ."

The picture showed a haphazard tangle of limbs and breasts and eyes, all twisted together in a complex image of Cubist sex. It seemed to Elsa that sex was everywhere she turned: unthinkable sex with Michael, unimaginable sex between her father and Nicky. On the staircase, every bannister was a phallic symbol. Even the young man, despite his artistic leanings, had a distinctly heterosexual glint in his eye. She wanted to escape to London but she knew she was far too drunk to drive.

Michael found her in a sitting-room, with her head on a cushion. "I won't," she told him, in the car. His car. "I don't like you. I don't find you attractive. I don't want to go to bed with you. Just take me to my father's flat. Did you hear me?"

"I heard," Michael said.

After a couple of miles, she fell asleep.

When she awoke the car had stopped. She was in a subterranean darkness; somewhere, a door clanged. A garage. Michael came round the car, opened the door and hauled her to her feet. Her head cleared slightly; she said: "This isn't Knightsbridge—is it?"

"No."

His face was dangerously close to hers. One arm held her against him, imprisoning or supporting her; his other hand was in her hair. His lips were slightly parted; she knew he was breathing hard. They seemed to be drawn together without will or movement, as if by some gravitational pull. Their kiss felt like a kind of drowning.

"I'll take you home," he said at length, "if that's what you really want."

Elsa thought of the great-aunt who called her "Diana," the father who had not recognized her, the friend who had deceived her. She said: "I have no home."

In the lift, when he let her speak, she told him to call her Elsa.

"If you like." His voice was very soft, a ragged whisper, a grating purr. "Elsa. Elsa."

"This isn't the same place," she said, with a flash of lucidity. "Last time, there wasn't a garage."

"I've moved."

This flat was larger, more expensive. Michael flicked the

lights on and off as they crossed the living-room: Elsa caught a glimpse of wood finishes, bookshelves, Japanese technology. The bedroom was very similar but with fewer books. She tumbled onto the duvet, kicking off her shoes. Michael tugged at his clothes with shaking fingers and threw himself on top of her, only half undressed, clumsy with desperation. His jacket, hastily discarded, slid to the floor, spilling keys and loose change over a French lace bra and a Kurt Geiger shoe. Neither of them noticed: Michael was kissing her with a passion close to anger, tongue-wrestling inside her mouth, his hands on her breasts, on her back, kneading her with a roughness that should have hurt but instead only excited her. His body seemed to be all strength and urgency, hot flesh and hard muscle. Already his cock was thrusting for entry, foreplay irrelevant and forgotten, slithering in the wetness between her legs. His arms were locked around her in an embrace that almost cracked her ribs; his perspiration sucked at her stomach. She writhed under him, half in struggle, half in submission, biting and clawing at him in a raw expression of lust. And then he was inside her, forcing himself into her, invading her, possessing her, filling her. The cry of his orgasm shivered through every fibre of her being: his tremors became hers, welding them together for an endless, unendurable moment and then sinking gradually until they collapsed at last in a wallow of exhaustion and sweat.

As sensation ebbed out of her, Elsa found she was partially sobered and wholly awake. Some hazy undercurrent of feeling warned her she had just collaborated in a terrible act of self-betrayal, but her body felt too limp, her mind too stunned for her to think clearly about anything. She sought for a phrase with which to dismiss the situation and found none. Eventually she said with strained sarcasm: "Did the earth move for you too, darling?"

The ghost-smile which she remembered suddenly so clearly brushed across Michael's face. "Hell moved," he said. To complete her discomfiture he kissed her, slowly and thoroughly.

"I'd like a drink," Elsa said afterwards.

Michael got up, absent-mindedly pulling on his trousers. "There's wine or beer in the fridge," he said. "Also vodka, Scotch—"

"Wine."

He fetched the wine for her and beer for himself and sat on

the edge of the bed drinking from the can. After so much passion and turbulence she was unnerved to find him apparently cool and undisturbed.

"Do you always make love like that?" she asked abruptly.

"Like what?"

"So—so"—to her annoyance, Elsa felt herself flushing—"so *uncontrolled.*"

"No. With some women, you have to hold back. They need delayed action—a certain gentleness. It's a question of temperament. The first time with you, I was more—cautious. Now, I know I can do what I feel."

"How do you know?" she whispered.

"Instinct."

A pause. "Do you have many other women?"

"Depends. Do you care?"

"No, of course not."

The light catching his face from below etched a further smile: satanic, she thought. She had always known he was satanic. She could see the pull of the sinews in his neck, the ridge of his Adam's apple, the indented shadows around collar-bone and pectoral muscles. He's ugly, she told herself, obstinately. Beauty was a gypsy-dark student in flared jeans, an intellectual man-of-the-world with a sun-bed tan and electric blue eyes . . . But Anthony had belonged to Diana, and even when she was wildly in love with him Grant had not been able to arouse her as Michael did. He's ugly, she reiterated, clutching at her repulsion as if it was the most precious element in her feeling for him. Repulsion that trickled through her loins, scrambling her nervous system and seeping through every pore in her skin . . .

Michael put down the beer can and removed the wineglass from her unresisting fingers. Then he took her hand and placed it between his thighs. His cock stirred at her touch; it was already hard. She began to kiss the planes of his breast, the stiff nipples, the sparse hairs growing down towards his stomach. Presently, he took his trousers off and climbed back into bed. This time he was more leisurely, even tender; she came at the caress of his tongue and he entered her almost immediately, climaxing in the aftermath of her pleasure so that all the sweet anguish came flooding back to her like a wave returning from the sea.

"I don't like you," she said later, a little drowsily. "I don't need you. I never meant to go to bed with you."

"Too late."

"I know."

It was a long while before they finally drifted into sleep.

Waking up the next morning was even worse than the last time. Elsa dragged herself from a bottomless pit of slumber and unstuck glued eyelids on a scene of painful reality. The bedroom, though different from the one in the other flat, bore familiar signs of Michael's taste: multiple stereo, discreet luxury, no keynotes, no undertones, no frill. Even beside the bed there were books on architecture: a biography of Le Corbusier, a textbook on the New Brutality, two or three on Post-Modernism. Michael himself lay with his face half buried in the pillow, one arm thrown across her chest. A bleary eye blinked at her out of a tangle of tallow-coloured hair. Her headache was so appalling she was afraid to move in case her skull fell apart.

"Are you going to depart in your usual fit of panic," Michael enquired sardonically, "or will you have coffee first?"

"Coffee," Elsa murmured. "Two aspirin. Glass of water. Please."

Michael gave a short laugh which exploded inside her head like a burst of gunfire. "Champagne and jet lag," he deduced. "I wonder why you feel you have to get drunk in order to go to bed with me? Next time you should try it sober."

"No—next—time."

"Sorry. I forgot."

After coffee, she was able to get up. The bathroom mirror revealed unsurprisingly that her face was a mess, vestigial trails of make-up under her eyes and her thick hair matted into elf-locks. She looked like a witch after a heavy night's Devil-worship. How was it, she asked herself, that Michael always did this to her? Grant had been able to make love to her without so much as smudging her mascara. In her present frame of mind, she decided it was a virtue.

"I think it would be best if we don't meet again," she told Michael on her way out, with a dignity that sounded more like petulance.

"Why? Are you afraid of me?"

No. I am afraid of myself.

But she didn't have the courage to say it.

Elsa spent the next few days moving into a new flat in Fulham. Langley and Mayhew had acquired it for her, ready furnished, on a one-year lease. "Your father thought you might go back to America," explained Mr. Mayhew, with a deprecating cough. "The lease is, of course, renewable."

"Thank you," Elsa said. "I don't think—I don't intend going anywhere just yet."

She rented herself a studio in the King's Road to work in, then telephoned her way through a long list of professional and social contacts provided by friends in New York. On Sunday, she caught a train down to Churston to retrieve Rupert's car. And in slack moments, she tried very hard not to think about Michael. She was not sure exactly why he disturbed her so deeply—whether it was his cold-blooded self-command or his elemental self-abandon, the violent response he evoked in her, his obscure connection with her father, his unknown motives and incalculable emotions. Whatever the truth, he was not the kind of man she had dreamed of: no contemporary princeling with glittering good looks and invincible charm, wearing his integrity on his sleeve and his heart in his smile. Michael had invaded her life like a disease and had got under her skin like a parasite, and she wanted only to be free of him.

Ten days after the wedding, she called her father's office.

"Michael Kovacs," she requested.

"Who is it?" the receptionist enquired automatically.

Elsa hesitated. "It's personal," she offered at last. "A friend." She could not possibly give her name.

The phone clicked; her pulse thumped. Then came Michael's voice.

"Hello."

"Hello . . . It's Elsa."

"Yes, I know."

How did he know? How dared he sound so sure? Her nerves vanished. "We have to talk."

"Certainly. How about tomorrow—dinner?"

"No—no, of course not. I mean, tomorrow will be fine, but not dinner. Just a drink."

They arranged to meet in a wine bar and Elsa rang off, feeling she had not appeared as cool as she would have wished.

The following evening, over dinner, she tried to remember not to drink too much. Michael had dignified the occasion with a tie, knotted half-way down his chest with his shirt collar undone. At the wedding, Elsa recalled, he had been dressed with strict formality; previously, she had only seen him in jeans. She thought of Grant, whose clothes had been a symphony in designer casuals, every empty buttonhole and rolled-up sleeve the result of sartorial deliberation. Michael appeared to dress for comfort rather than style—yet the clumsy tie looked like silk and she could tell from the abundance of creases that his shirt was pure cotton. Perhaps he was out to create an effect quite as deliberately as Grant. Anyway, she felt reassured by his detachment.

"I just wanted to tell you," she said, "that—well, that it's over, but . . ."

"You hoped we could remain friends," he hazarded.

"No! We can't remain friends when we've never *been* friends—we hardly know each other."

"Do you want us to be friends?"

"*No.* I want—I want us to be able to meet without embarrassment. That's all. I want us to behave like sensible people and not—"

"End up in bed together. Fair enough." He cracked a prawn. "Tell me about America."

Three and a half years disappeared in a blur. "I had fun," Elsa said.

"So I heard."

She glanced up, suddenly wary. Michael was sucking on a claw. "Your unhappy love affair," he explained presently. "What was his name?—Barrymore. James Grant Barrymore."

"Who told you about that?"

"Your father." And, into the ensuing silence: "I've been with him more than ten years, remember. Student, assistant, junior partner. He's used to me. There are times when even he needs someone to talk to. Who knows? . . . maybe he trusts me."

For a few minutes, Elsa said nothing. All the usual emotions were there—the goblins that reared their heads whenever her father was mentioned—jealousy, resentment, the sense of betrayal. She thought: he'll talk to anyone except me. And the ugly image of Rupert discussing his problem daughter with her occasional lover darkened her mind, an image fraught with insidious possibilities. "Maybe he trusts me . . ." *I* don't trust him, Elsa told herself, as though making a resolution. Nor should my father. And she asked, harshly: "What do you want from me?"

Michael nearly grinned. "I thought you knew."

She made a brusque gesture of dismissal. "Not *that*—I mean, what do you really want? Not now but next week, next year. What do you dream of? What do you plan? Whenever I look at you, I seem to see—shadows. Shadows within shadows. Veils over your thoughts. I know nothing about you—nothing." An earlier remark suddenly registered; she added: "Did you say junior partner? My father's junior partner?"

"Why not?"

It was like an aftertaste of old failure, an inscrutable manoeuvre on the part of fate the chess-player. She said, "He doesn't know anything about you either—does he?"

"Perhaps not." Michael picked up the tail of a prawn, dipped it in mayonnaise and ate it, slowly, shell and all. "Sometimes," he said between mouthfuls, "you're very like him. Self-absorbed. Single-minded. Obsessive. He's obsessed with architecture: imprinting his cloven hoof on the cityscape of the world. You—what are you obsessed with?"

"Don't change the subject." Elsa dropped a croûton in her soup, pushed it around for a while, and then abandoned it. In the past, it had not occurred to her to see Michael as anything other than the demon who plagued her life, plunging her into turbulence; she had never imagined him as a separate individual, with a life and traumas of his own. Reticence was so much a part of his personality that she had simply accepted it, without curiosity. Now, she tried to picture him, a child or a schoolboy, lonely, uncertain, afraid, afflicted with spots and vanity, growing pains and teenage love. But the secrecy of his nature blocked off all insight.

She said: "You told me you were adopted. Did you know your real parents?"

He shrugged—a species of capitulation. "I knew my mother. Briefly. She died when I was four. That was in a refugee camp near Lübeck—1950 or '51. I think she was fair and not very pretty. Like me." The echo of a smile. "She left Poland to escape the Russians and got stuck in Germany after the war. There were thousands like her. Or so I'm told. I don't remember very much about those days: just moments, here and there. She always said my father was a British officer—at any rate, that was the story in the camp. I spoke better English than German."

"I had no idea," Elsa said blankly, incapable of visualizing such a childhood. She stared at him as if he were a Martian, unsure whether pity was required of her, or sympathy, or anything she knew how to give. For perhaps the first time in her life she was conscious of being privileged, of being rich and spoilt and selfish. She fumbled for words of commiseration; but even in her head they sounded artificial, almost indecent.

Eventually, she said: "Your mother—how did she die?"

"How does any refugee die? Shortage of food, shortage of clothes, shortage of medicine. Epidemics of this and that. A hard winter; a dose of flu. Conditions, as they say, were primitive. The weak died; the strong lived. I lived." Unexpectedly, he went on: "She used to cough a lot—all those cheap cigarettes scrounged from the Americans. I remember her coughing. I smoked too, when I was five or six. I didn't like it much but cigarettes were gold dust—and far more grown-up than chocolate. Besides, if an adult caught you with one they would always take it away, tell you it was bad for you, and then smoke it themselves. There's nothing like forbidden fruit."

Elsa said: "You don't smoke now."

"Not much."

"How did you come to be adopted?"

"It must have been—'53. International Year of the Refugee: something like that. They planned to empty the camps. Children orphaned by war and sickness were being sent all over the place to good homes and a proper education. Dread words. I wasn't having any of it. I was living on the streets of Lübeck most of the time, running errands for the black marketeers. When I grew up, I was going to be another Harry Lime. I was too smart to get caught by the do-gooders." Once again, the tail of a smile. "My foster-father—Matthew O'Hara—was with the Red Cross. He'd been in a good many campaigns, patching up the mess after the grenades and the glory. He used to offer me a drag of his cigarette and tell me tall stories. Irish blarney. I never thought of him as a do-gooder. I suppose that was how he hooked me; I'd have run away from anyone else. He had a young wife back in England: they'd been told she couldn't have kids. So they had me instead."

His attitude seemed distant, dispassionate, almost as if he

were talking about someone else. Elsa asked: "Did you love them?"

"I expect so." Not much of an answer. "It was just too late for me to change. They say your character is formed in the first five years, and I was seven. I'd already lived. I knew it all. Hardened, so to speak. Oh—after that I had every advantage. Public school, the A.A.—whatever I needed. My father's family were Catholic landed gentry, my mother's English upper middle class. There was plenty of money, plenty of opportunity, plenty of parental encouragement. I daresay I was very lucky."

"You sound cynical."

"Do I? I felt grateful. And—yes, I loved them."

"Past tense. Are they dead?"

"No. But I don't see them much now."

"Why not?"

"I don't know. It isn't necessary. When I'd been with them about three years, my mother found she was pregnant after all. Result: my brother William. Just like his father, all charm and dash and blarney. It wasn't that they stopped loving me, but . . . I suppose he was easier to love. He gave more in return. As William grew up, I felt they didn't need me so much. So— I didn't need them."

"Was that why you changed your name?"

"Not entirely. I told my foster-parents it was for the sake of my real mother, but—looking back—I don't think that was true. My mother's dead: it wouldn't make any odds to her if I called myself Charlie Chaplin or Leo Tolstoy. The real reason— oh, I wanted to be alone and separate, to sever any ties with a family unit and what I saw as an artificial background. I wanted to be myself, with no labels attached that didn't belong to me. In a sense, it freed me to be fond of my foster-parents without feeling owned by them."

And, after a pause: "Why did you change *your* name?"

She looked blank.

"Elspeth to Elsa—why?"

"I liked it." She sucked her lip. "I think—I wanted to be someone else. Not Elspeth. Not myself."

Michael said gently: "Elsa is yourself too."

"Is she?"

There was a silence while Elsa studied the dimples of light in her wineglass and wondered about her own identity, and

Michael's, and the relationship she wished to terminate. "What about architecture?" she enquired at length, reverting to her interrogation. "What made you go for that?"

"I liked it," he mimicked her. "You ask too many questions." The main course had gone cold and the waiter was hovering with offers of dessert. "How about a brandy and a change of subject? You still haven't told me anything about America."

This time, she told him—about college, and Barbara, and functional sculpture, if not about Grant. Later, in the car, she said: "You know, we did everything in the wrong order. We should have talked more first, and gone to bed after."

"Not necessarily. We did what felt right to us. Besides, you talked enough that night you thought you were going to kill yourself."

Elsa's face clouded, possibly at an unwanted reminder. "I'd forgotten."

Following directions, Michael drove to her flat, parking in a side street.

"Would you like more coffee?" she suggested, a little shyly.

"Maybe. Can I park here all night?"

"If you want," Elsa said.

In bed, with Elsa sleeping beside him, Michael found all the memories which she had disturbed floating to the surface of his mind like mud churned up in a pool. His early childhood did not haunt him; mostly, he never thought of it. He knew the details because his foster-parents had told him, always answering his questions, never seeking to build a wall of false security between himself and his past. Perhaps it was *because* it did not haunt him that he felt troubled: those memories that drifted upwards were annoyingly fragmentary, elusive, like a name on the tip of his tongue which he could not quite recall. The faces of his mother, his playmates, the soldiers and the wild boys whom he had admired—all such things had faded, leaving only a flash here and there to illumine the shadows. Running down a street pursued by some manifestation of authority—the taste of his first orange—the smell of a forbidden cigarette. Hide-and-seek on the bomb-sites of Lübeck, destroyed by the RAF in 1942. And among the rubble, a wall still standing, empty windows, blackened carvings—the leftover

husk of another world. He had never known anything but rubble. Yet out of that rubble had sprung his desire to build, his
dream of a city made whole, a city of the future with bones of
steel and flanks of glass and horns that touched the sky. It had
been a boy's dream, unrecognized for what it was—until he
was twelve years old and a schoolmaster at Winchester had
asked him what he wanted to be. "An architect," he had answered, without pause for thought. And suddenly he had known
it was true. Here in a new life of gentle pressures and academic
achievement the distant images of the past acquired meaning
and purpose. He would be an architect, and create something
useful and beautiful out of the rubble.

Now when he tried to look back, the rubble was all he remembered. Fractured beams, tumbled masonry, crawling
weeds, the dust of ashes long scattered to the winds. He had
started with dreams and the debris of war and created—what?
A vista passed before his eyes: a bastion of concrete, a gridiron
of glass, angular contortions of metal and plastic jabbing at
the clouds. "What about architecture?" Elsa had asked. A question he had evaded. He had made factories sprout from quiet
fields, had superimposed a ruthless symmetry on the jumble
of ancient cities—but for a long time now he had felt his dream
turn sour. He reviewed his endeavours and it seemed to him
he had produced only a man-made ugliness little better than
the man-made destruction which had inspired him. He knew
disillusion in every stroke of the pen. Somewhere, something
had gone wrong. Somewhere . . .

Rupert Van Leer had been his idol. Michael had few idols:
cynicism had been bred into him from boyhood, when he saw
that the streets of war-torn Europe had no heroes, only survi-
vors. There were men he had liked or admired, a few he had
respected, but he considered himself as smart as or smarter
than any of them and well able, once he was old enough, to
hold his own in an adult world. But from his first glimpse of
Stallibrass House (a picture in a book of contemporary art),
from all he could read and learn and analyse, he sensed that
Rupert was a man worth looking up to, genius among talent,
stature among littleness, not merely part of an artistic rebellion
but its leader, its principal inspiration. Michael determined
that one day he would work for him, work *with* him—and when
the chance came, he made the most of it. He performed menial

tasks without complaint, bided his time, patient, implacable, absorbing Rupert's skills and ideology and using custom and his own talent to insinuate himself into Rupert's confidence. Yet gradually, in constant proximity to the man he had idolized, he began to see that the stark inhumanity of his work mirrored something in his spirit, an element of coldness or blindness that reduced him, in Michael's eyes, until he was less than a colossus, even less than a man. And, as he had come to perceive ugliness in the artist, so he came to perceive ugliness in his art. Every structure seemed like a physical rejection of the environment, a clenched fist in the face of past civilization. Instead of simplicity, he saw crudity, instead of functionalism, barrenness, instead of austerity, ruthlessness. He still admired Rupert's demonic energy, his one-track passion; but he no longer wished to emulate him. Dissent had grown slowly in his soul, and, as with all slow-growing things, its roots had gone deep. Long ago he had planned to marry Rupert's daughter—the plain one, not the pretty one: plain girls were easier to manage—and thus secure his position as Rupert's logical successor. He had met the daughter and assessed her, coolly enough, as suitable material: ardent, unhappy, not her father's favourite, but what did it matter when she was a Van Leer? But that was long ago. Years had passed, the plain daughter had turned into a beauty, his idol had fallen, and the very shape of his ambitions had changed. Some days, he felt he would like to tear down every stone Rupert had ever built, and obliterate his iron hand from the landscape for good. He turned over in the bed, studying Elsa's sleeping face—wondering why he was there, if he had no further use for her. But he was not sure any more what he wanted, or whom he wished to use. Once, he had thought her the key to Rupert's inheritance. Now, he sensed she was the by-product of his flawed nature, victim or legatee, the weak link in his armour.

He contented himself with the reflection that it was always interesting to probe a weakness.

Sir Rupert and Lady Van Leer spent the first night of their marriage in a country-house hotel near the Scottish border. The bedroom boasted a huge bed and a panoramic view. In the restaurant, they were served with fresh-caught trout, home-grown vegetables, well-hung venison. Nicky, picking at her food, thought: I've married this man and I've never been to bed with him. Tonight will be the first time. The very first time. The idea deprived her of all appetite and sent a deep shiver of excitement through her body. Rupert was so tall, so dominant, so overwhelmingly masculine that she felt as if all the others had been mere substitutes for men, whose tentative penetrations had left her essentially untouched. She glowed like a virgin at the thought of a total violation.

Upstairs she wrapped herself in a satin negligée, principally so that Rupert could take it off. She even blushed when he loosed the sash and surveyed her nakedness, cupping her small breasts in his big hands, pressing his lips very gently against her mouth, her eyes, her hair, lifting her into his arms as if she weighed no more than a child. In bed, she groped urgently for his substantial penis, making use of all the skills she had learned so carefully, eager to please and be pleased. It had not occurred to her that he might find her too skilful, or too experienced—or too eager.

There was a moment when he drew back, his mouth hardening. His eyes narrowed. Then he was on her, without gentleness, without restraint. His embrace crushed her, his kisses left weals on her skin. She could no longer respond or resist; she was battered by lust and rage, helpless, terrified. "Whore," he said, striking her across the cheek so violently that stars exploded in her vision. *"Whore."* She tried to protest but he did not listen; his eyes burned into her and through her as though he saw, not Nicky his wife, but some image in his mind, a phantom of his own creation, whom he both loved and hated, ached to possess and wished to destroy. She thought a madness had seized him; arousal vanished in fear; she could not fight, could not even struggle as he rammed his cock into her, tearing dry flesh, plunging like iron into her vitals. His orgasm rocked like an earthquake: the quiet that followed was the quiet of desolation, the ruin of her hopes, the end of her dreams. He breathed great rasping breaths, shuddered seismic shudders. "Diana," he whispered, scarcely aware he had spoken. "Diana . . ."

The next morning they went downstairs for breakfast. Rupert was polite, distant; if he felt any remorse, he did not show it. There was no mention of the previous night, no apology. Nicky, taking her cue from him, said nothing, forcing herself to nibble toast and sip coffee like any bride after her first night. Her brain would not function, her emotions had turned to stone: social necessity programmed her like a robot. Opposite her, Rupert ate sausages, bacon, tomatoes, mushrooms, eggs. He appeared invigorated, like a man on a regime of fresh air and healthy exercise. Nicky felt cold to her heart's core.

Through Elsa's eyes, she had seen Rupert's preference for Diana as something based on her supposed resemblance to her mother—on her sunny nature, her radiance, her effortless lovability. A normal father-daughter affection which could easily be transmuted into an equally normal passion for a new, young wife. Nicky had not realized in her game of swapped identities that she might be calling up demons. Even now, she shrank from the implications of what had happened. She tried to tell herself that she had mis-heard or imagined that whispered name; that next time, maybe, everything would be all right. But she did not really believe it.

Back in London, Nicky gave a dinner party. She was determined to behave as she supposed the wife of a successful man should, still carrying at the back of her mind a picture of Isabelle Montador, wearing Saint Laurent suits and opening bazaars. She employed a caterer to do the food, attendant minions to wait at table and wash up afterwards. All she had to do was choose the menu and buy a new dress. Rupert, after his initial surprise, appeared to concede that the idea was reasonable and supplied the names of suitable clients for her to invite. "You can ask Michael, too," he concluded as an afterthought.

"Michael?" Nicky was at sea.

"From the office."

Left with an imbalance of the sexes, Nicky had the excuse she needed. She called Elsa.

Knowing nothing of Elsa's deepest feelings, she could not know the depth of her own treachery. The recollection of that cold kiss at the wedding chilled her a little, but she still hoped the first flush of anger would pass, still fantasized that she and Elsa might somehow remain friends. What, after all, had she done? Dyed her hair and married Elsa's father—something any woman might have done during the preceding twenty-six years.

And she had married him, not simply because he was rich and famous, but because he had personality, genius, charisma. In her own vocabulary, Nicky had fallen in love. Surely Elsa could not blame her for that. Struggling to ignore the pitfalls already opening in her marriage, Nicky would not or could not see the chasm that gaped between herself and the other girl. In Greece past and future had not mattered: there had been an illusion of comradeship. In England, past and future were all: Nicky had transgressed rules she could not read, and she would never be forgiven. Resolved on a course for disaster, she even dismissed as trivial the tension between father and daughter, spinning herself a daydream in which she was a miniature chatelaine, Rupert's wife, Elsa's friend. She picked up the telephone, and held out her feeble olive branch.

Playing back the message on her answering machine, Elsa felt as if that olive branch was being rammed down her throat. She could only assume Nicky wanted the opportunity to triumph over her, to flaunt her stolen victory and revel in Elsa's humiliation and hurt. Or maybe her father had instigated the idea, from motives she dared not imagine. Either way, she reacted to the invitation like a wealthy cardinal bidden to a Borgia supper.

Nonetheless, she went.

She had not expected to see Michael. He was there when she arrived, looking, she decided, neither handsome nor striking but presentable, wearing his dinner-jacket without awkwardness, as though wearing a dinner-jacket was a chore to which he was accustomed. The female director of Technico to whom he was talking—a glamourous fifty-year-old with colour-fast hair and a Jean Muir evening dress—seemed unwilling to relinquish his company. Evidently that too was a chore to which he was accustomed. He gave Elsa only the faintest acknowledgement, but she felt warmed. For the first time, she found herself thinking: He's attractive. He's ugly, but attractive. Other women were clearly attracted to him. The man who can attract other women always becomes that much more desirable—illogical, and Elsa knew it; still, it reassured her to find him there.

She needed reassurance. Nicky came forward to greet her, conscientiously polite, playing the perfect hostess. She was dressed in white, possibly to emphasize her bridal status; her

huge eyes were shadow-coloured and held a faint sparkle like
light frost; her face was very pale. Only her hair flamed in
violent contrast. Elsa wondered all over again about the transformation from brown-legged beach girl to this snow-spirit
with her fire-red curls, a transformation that was more than
just hair-dye and different clothes—that was, perhaps, something in her very substance, an essential fluidity of character.
It seemed to Elsa that she had an unhuman quality, as if she
were an ambiguous spirit who could re-shape herself in the
form of every man's secret dream. Elsa had assumed Rupert
had seen in her traces of Diana, traces of her mother; yet Diana
had been a creature of earth, and Johanna Van Leer, from her
portrait, had had the solidity of a marble statue. Nicky, however, was as light as air, as formless as water. Maybe she had
changed the dream, subtly, using all her physical charms; or
maybe Rupert himself had allowed his memory to fade with
the passage of time and the demands of work, until it was
sufficiently blurred to be adaptable. But Nicky's face betrayed
neither subtlety nor triumph; her expression was bland and
innocent; her conscience might have been as spotless as her
dress.

Elsa wore black.

She was curt with Nicky, and gave her father a greeting that
sounded like a challenge. He nodded indifferently, switched his
attention elsewhere—paused, turned back, stared. Others, too,
were staring. Against the plain black, without pleat or pattern,
Elsa wore diamonds. Real diamonds. Far too many diamonds.
Clusters of them weighing down her ear-lobes, glittering
strands encircling neck and wrists, two rings on her right hand,
one on her left, with a single stone as big as a hazelnut. They
flashed from the hollows of her bronze hair like furtive stars,
dripped from her arms like beads of ice. To many of the guests
they were a vulgarity, a needless ostentation, an object of envy,
a colossal insurance risk. But Rupert recognized them, though
he had not seen them for so long. Van Leer diamonds—Johanna's diamonds.

He said in a low voice: "Where did you get those?"

Elsa lifted her chin. "Aunt Barbara gave them to me. She
said, as they were my mother's, she thought I ought to have
them."

"They must be worth a fortune," remarked the female company director, briefly diverted from Michael. "How did you get here—Securicor?"

"Taxi."

"You'd better go home immediately." Rupert's undertone was taut with restrained fury. "Take them off, lock them up for tonight, put them in the bank tomorrow. Is there no end to your folly?"

"I was invited to dinner"—Elsa's voice, unlike his, was meant to be heard—"and I'm staying to dinner."

It was not a comfortable meal. Nicky, baffled by undercurrents she did not understand, stumbled over her small-talk, and Elsa's ill-fated diamonds glittered away in the candlelight as if in deliberate provocation. Half the table separated her from Rupert, but that did not prevent him glowering fixedly at her during every lull in the conversation. There were many lulls. Exquisite course succeeded exquisite course, but no one noticed. Michael, next to Elsa, asked no questions but offered with unstudied nonchalance to "see her home" later. Elsa agreed absently.

"I look like my mother," she thought. "Aunt Barbara said so. At least, I look like her picture. Which means I must be more like her than Diana—certainly more than Nicky. But he won't see it, won't admit it. He hates me wearing her jewels—he hates me looking like her."

Over dessert Nicky considered speaking to Elsa, saying something friendly; but she knew it would be no use. Even Rupert's anger when he heard Elsa had been invited had not prepared her for this. She assumed she was the sole cause, the spark which had fired Elsa's resentment; the diamonds meant little more to her than the stigmata of wealth. Her own resentment rose in return: Elsa had everything, she had nothing, yet her new stepdaughter grudged her even a small share in unearned luxury. What did Elsa know of hunger and desolation, tedium and panic? Life had rolled her in clover and hung her with jewels, but she could not bring herself to accommodate a stranger at her board. The coffee-pot found them side by side in the drawing-room—Odette and Odile, the white swan and the black. Only here, it was the white swan who was the interloper, the black swan who was the true princess.

But Nicky knew nothing of Odile. She still believed she was Cinderella.

Afterwards, when nearly everyone had gone, Rupert confronted his daughter.

"Your behaviour tonight has been inexcusable. Wearing those diamonds . . ."

"They were my mother's," Elsa said. "I have the right."

"You—have—no—rights. From tomorrow, I shall discontinue your allowance. There is a trust fund set up for you by your grandmother: you can live off that. In the meantime, you are not to come here any more: do you understand? *I never wish to set eyes on you again.* Never. Now get out." And, seeing Michael in the background: "Take her away."

Michael complied without comment. In his car, Elsa sat speechless and shivering. Presently, he put his arms around her. "It's all right," he murmured inadequately. "I'm here."

"Take me home," Elsa whispered. "No—I have no home. Take me . . . somewhere."

He took her to his flat.

10

During the months that followed, Elsa began to make a new life for herself in London. Not a life such as she had had in New York—a social whirl of people and parties interspersed with outbreaks of intellectual kitsch—but a life. In America, she had begun to establish her artistic reputation (not difficult, said the scathing, for the daughter of Sir Rupert Van Leer) and now, back in England, art galleries showed signs of interest, and invitations from the glitterati came flapping through her letter-box. Finances were still no problem: the flat was already paid for and her grandmother's legacy had accumulated comfortably over the years. "The income has been yours since you were twenty-five," explained Mr. Mayhew. "But your father was empowered—he did not wish—that is, I believe he preferred to pay your allowance himself." Conscience money, Elsa thought with a new depth of bitterness. I could half kill myself with anorexia, fail at college, stab someone in a lover's tiff—none of these mattered. But when I wore my mother's diamonds, I committed the ultimate sin. Now, his conscience is clear: he can cast me off without guilt. Possibly she was right. Rupert had always found signing cheques a way of upholding his responsibilities, while keeping her at a distance. She tried not to think of him, not to brood over his nearness, but in her King's Road studio the pain she strove to ignore went into her work, distorting it from its original bleak purity. She found herself producing objects that served no useful function, coils of plastic and twists of metal knotted together into meaningless shapes of anger. She made a centrepiece of broken china, with all the jagged edges fanning outwards like the leaves on an artichoke; it was spotted with blood where she had cut herself during the work. And she bought a red-gold wig, snipped off individual curls, and attached them round a hollow, featureless mask of smooth plaster which she called "Women with Dyed Hair."

"You know," Michael said, dropping in one afternoon without warning, "lately, your work has become more interesting. Crude; but interesting. You used just to copy your father."

Elsa went white. "What do you mean—copy my father? I gave up architecture. I was no good."

"Your father is a functionalist. You went in for functional sculpture. A small-scale version of the same thing. No emotion, no ornament, everything to a purpose. You deliberately stifled your natural romanticism. Now, some feeling seems to be getting through."

Elsa said: "I hate you."

Michael smiled. "Put it into your work."

She did—constructing a huge plastic phallus which she packed in newspaper and had delivered to his door. He sent back a message: "Is it a good likeness?" Elsa laughed, and for a minute or two she forgot her pain.

Her relationship with Michael continued, but in a style very different from her affair with Grant. At times it seemed hardly a relationship, more a curiously prickly friendship which would lapse without warning into bouts of furious sexuality. There was no jogging, no skiing, no seeing and being seen in trendy restaurants. If they dined out, they did so unobtrusively, in dark corners. Mostly, they just shared a bottle of wine, talked, made love. The love-making was, for Elsa, both a release and a problem: the need troubled her, the violence shocked her, the surrender frightened her. Over and over she told herself: "This is it. The last time"—but it never was, and she knew it even as she made the resolve. Her body had learnt total gratification, and now it could not go without. Frequently, Michael left it to her to get in touch, knowing she would call in the end, resentful perhaps, but conscious that she had chosen: she had not been either coaxed or forced. Her freedom was important to her and Michael made no attempt to restrict it. He did not ask if she were faithful or profess faithfulness himself; he did not expect to meet her friends or introduce her to his. They made no plans, long-term or short. Rupert was rarely mentioned between them, but she never forgot that Michael was his junior partner. Maybe that was the real reason why she clung to him, against her judgement, even against her will: he was her last tenuous contact with her father and throughout that period of enforced separation Michael, for all his reticence, seemed to carry with him some remnant of reflected glory. She did not ask about Rupert; she could not. But now and then Michael would relate something he had said or done, studying her all the while with chilly detachment, and she would look bland and say nothing, and indulge in a bittersweet secret suffering. For the rest, she could not decide how she really felt about Michael, or how he felt about her. He was just there. Whenever she wanted him. Whenever. He was there, and that was good. She gave up on further speculation.

Once he asked her about Nicky. "You knew her, didn't you?" he said.

"Yes."

"She told him she'd been a friend of Diana's, but I thought she must have known you, too. She'd worked out all his weak spots. Her inside information had to be up to date."

"If you saw what was happening," Elsa said, "why didn't you warn me?"

"Why should I?" Michael retorted with an irritating aloofness. "Anyway, what could you have done?"

Something. Nothing. Elsa was silent.

"Don't waste time hating her," Michael recommended. "She won't hurt him: he'll hurt her. Sooner or later, he'll crush her like an egg-shell. She's not wicked: just weak and greedy and short on morals. Hatred is too valuable to throw away on someone like her. Hate is like love: if you spread it around too much you cheapen it. You should save your hate for important things."

"Such as?" Fleetingly, curiosity made her forget her own concerns.

"Injustice. Inhumanity. Cruelty. The abuse of power or position for selfish ends. The stupidity that lets men get away
with it. The ego which says: I am unique, I am special, I stand
head and shoulders above my kind. My life is worth more than
other lives. That sort of thing."

"Whom do you hate?" Elsa whispered, and for a terrible
instant she thought she knew.

"No one," Michael said lightly. "I was a brat from nowhere,
and the world has been good to me. I have little cause to hate."
He added, more seriously: "Nor have you."

Haven't I? Elsa thought. What about treachery—lies—the
abuse of trust? Is that not cause enough?

Later, back in her studio, she took out the empty mask with
the red hair. Crude, Michael had called it. Emotional. Maybe
he was right. An expression of hate, not art: more vulgar than
primitive. She looked at it for a long moment. Then she began
to tear off the red curls she had stuck on so laboriously. Denuded of its hair, only an eyeless crust of plaster remained, a
hull, a rind, without identity. She picked it up and hurled it
across the room.

Nicky was not crushed like an egg-shell. Experience had
made her pliant: she bent, and did not break. After that first
time, Rupert's love-making had become abnormally gentle, as
if he were always having to hold in check the violence and
savagery that was a true expression of his sexuality. His gentleness came to frighten Nicky almost more than his brutality: it
had the ominous quality of a cloud that hangs over the horizon
before a storm—a last ray of sun slashes through, and the light,
usually so warm and friendly, turns the cloud to indigo and
tinges the world with an evil ochre glare. Rupert's rare gestures
of tenderness began to seem somehow poisoned, his very touch
a threat. Once or twice, he lost control—for example, after
Nicky's fatal dinner party—and she was left with bruises dark
as pansies on her breasts and thighs which did not heal for
days. But she was resilient. At times she dreamed of breaking
through to some hidden wellspring of genuine love; at others,
she concentrated on the advantages of her position, wealth,
status, the Stygian emerald on her left hand, the credit card
in her right. Initially, Rupert's attitude baffled her; but as the

months passed she scarcely thought about it. She had expected, after their hasty marriage, that he would try to understand her as an individual, at least in so far as she dared to be understood. Having fallen in love with her hair and her face he would surely want to unfurl the petals of her personality, so that their bizarre relationship would become a gradual voyage of discovery, as in some of the novels she had read where strangers marry and learn to know one another afterwards. But Rupert seemed content to know nothing. He encouraged her to give a few more dinner parties (with the guest-list now carefully edited); ignored her at breakfast and talked to her at supper—or vice versa—in neither case requiring any particular response; looked at her from time to time as if she was someone else and stroked her red-gold hair, not as a man fondles a puppy or a beloved object, but more as he might caress an antique vase of considerable beauty and hopeful authenticity. She was careful never to let the roots show. She did not think he suspected it was dyed but occasionally she wondered if he suspected *her*— if without effort or insight, he had anticipated something from their aloof, fragmentary union which he did not find. When she realized she was bored, it was as if she had known it, subconsciously, for a long while. Behind the glitter of a dream achieved the tedium she feared in her secret heart had seeped in, and now a grey existence stretched ahead of her for a lifetime of inescapable matrimony.

Boredom and fear make dreary bedfellows. Nicky's other dinner parties, for all the designer labels and the food she did not have to cook, were surpassingly dull. The talk was all of art and architecture, the newest play, the latest book; but Rupert never took her to see the plays and she had not read the books. She felt like a part of the Spode dinner service or the silver cutlery, decorative, functional, inert. At the parties to which they were invited (those Rupert bothered to attend), it was the same. Her mirror told her she looked good, but the male guests were usually elderly, besuited, ascetically thin or expensively portly, drearily civilized and conventionally polite. Once, she drank too much, just to see would would happen. She pulled her dress down off one shoulder and flirted wildly with a fiftyish company chairman—a Van Leer client—who appeared both titillated and shocked by her. She filled her shoe with champagne and attempted a toast, but the champagne ran out of the peep-toe over his waistcoat and Nicky shrieked with laughter. Rupert promptly bundled her into a taxi and took her home. In the bedroom she waited for him to strike her, call her a whore, tear her clothes off—half afraid and half defiant, feeling that at least in this mood she could reach him, in some perverted way, break through his unrelenting façade, touch his soul. But he only surveyed her with a disgust that was both angry and cold. "Get to bed," he said. "And in the future, stay sober."

That night, she slept alone and unmolested.

In Churston matters were no better. There was nothing for Nicky to do by day except fidget with a novel and order dinner, and at night the old house was full of creeping draughts that searched the back of her neck with chilly fingers and little snufflings in the wainscoting and little creakings on the stairs. Her imagination strayed inevitably to fictional heroines she had encountered—in everything from the Brontë sisters to Victoria Holt—whose husbands had closeted them in Gothic manors for sinister ends. The idea did not either comfort or divert her. Mantled in the shadows of the house Rupert's size became monstrous, his dark moods still darker. Yet when she was alone Nicky hated the place even more. Mrs. Skerritt—Nicky called Aunty Grizzle Mrs. Skerritt—hardly counted as company: she was locked in a room upstairs to prevent her wandering off and could be heard from to time beating on the door panels and crying out. The attendant insisted she was harmless, merely a little vague and muddled, but Nicky was not so sure. She was brought down to tea on one occasion and horrified Nicky by plucking a strand of her hair and saying: "Dyed." Fortunately, Rupert was not there. After that, Nicky asked the nurse if Mrs. Skerritt could have all her meals in her room.

One afternoon, she went to look at Stallibrass House. Her interest in Rupert's work was limited—she was more concerned with his aura of genius than with genius itself—but she had heard the place spoken of as his first significant work and anyway, what else had she to do? "Call it a house," muttered the daily. "Wouldn't fancy it meself, living behind all them glass walls. Like a tomato in a greenhouse."

"Who *does* live there?" Nicky asked.

"Nobody—now. Used to be Miser Joe—him what had it built—but he died, two years ago last spring. The widder still owns it, only she don't go there much. Lives with one of her daughters, up north somewhere. The son, he should of got the place, but he quarrelled with the old man. Pot 'n politics— much like any other boy of that age, but Miser Joe wasn't having any. I heard the son became a Commie at one time— that wouldn't do for his dad. Anyway, they quarrelled, and that was that. Miser Joe died not long after. His own fault, if you ask me. Sour old basket." After a minute or two, she went on: "The son—Andrew, Anthony, something like that—he used to be a boyfriend of one of the girls. Diana—the pretty one. Hair like yours." Perhaps it was Nicky's imagination that a sceptical gleam flickered briefly in her eye. Nicky was ultrasensitive about her hair. "Heard a rumour they got engaged."

"What happened?" Nicky said, intrigued.

"She died. Climbing up to his window after some party—I daresay she'd had a bit. Playing Romeo and Juliet, only the wrong way round. That's what comes of all this Women's Lib. He wasn't even there, or so they said. It was in all the papers."

"Yes," said Nicky. "I remember now." She had never forgotten. "So they got engaged, and then—she died. Just like that."

"That's what I heard."

She was thinking of this conversation when she reached the gates of Stallibrass House. They were locked. There was little to be seen between bars set too close together but the driveway disappearing behind a belt of shrubs and a remote gleam of plate glass. The daily, she recollected, had said something about the best view being obtained from the hill above. Nicky, like Elsa the child so many years before, retraced her steps along the road and climbed a steep path that brought her eventually to a point where she could look down on the house. Time had not weathered or worn it; Nature still kept her distance. It stood alone, apart from the surrounding countryside, a piece of sculpture all angles and windows, a fragment of some space city which had broken off and fallen like a meteor amongst the gentle southern hills, where it endured, intact and unchanged. The swimming-pool was drained; even at that range Nicky could see where the creeping green fingers of weeds and mosses had begun to claw at the edge of the terrace. But the house itself appeared as stark and barren as the day it was built. She found herself thinking that it might be more than a product of

Rupert's imagination—that it might be, in some way, an image of his soul, the very core of his self translated into glass and stone, all angles where there should be planes, and planes where there should be angles. She had reached for that self in vain through his impenetrable charisma, fumbling like a child with a puzzle that is too complicated, coming up against hard surfaces and sharp edges that hurt and baffled her. Looking at the house, she almost thought she understood him—not his feelings perhaps, but his substance, the stuff of his nature. It did not help her. Her mind flickered back to the daily with her fund of gossip. He built this house, Nicky thought, and it killed his daughter. Was that somehow symbolic? Had Rupert wanted his daughter dead—the daughter he adored—because she was going to marry and leave him? Or had the boyfriend killed her, from some obscure motive of passion—the boyfriend who claimed he had not been there? Faintly she recalled the darkly beautiful face pictured in the press. And Elsa? What of Elsa? Surely one of the reports had said she was with her sister at the time. Had Elsa killed her twin? The daily had said that as a child she was fat and plain. The plain sister and the pretty one—an age-old story. And now the pretty one was dead and the fat larva had turned into a beautiful moth—a jungle moth with exotic eye-markings that glared at you suddenly as its wings unfolded. Nicky had never really like moths.

"It's all fantasy," she told herself, wishing she could believe it. Beneath the tedium of her everyday life she sensed the undercurrents of drama—but not the kind of drama she had always longed for, with glamour and romance and a happy ending. This was something dark and ugly, the threads of a plot she could not untangle, a clue here, a hint there, a veil she did not want to lift, a shadow she would not try to penetrate. For a moment, she wished that Rupert loved her, that Elsa liked her, that she herself was the person she always pretended to be. But it was no use: the script had already been written. Elsa hated her. She hated Elsa. She had realized after that fateful dinner party that her own schemes had forced them into enmity. And between her and Rupert was a wall of concrete and plate glass which reflected her own lies back at her, blinding her to whatever lay beyond.

"It's all fantasy," she repeated, suddenly and irrationally angry. "It's just the house."

But that evening, facing Rupert across the dinner table, she found herself seeing the echo of his design in the very modelling of his skull. There were no curves in his face, no softness; even his mouth was a rigid line, his eyes as impenetrable as stone. It was as if he was a physical manifestation of his work; concrete and steel had grown into him and become a part of him. Which came first, she wondered with rare profundity, the artist or his art? Had Rupert created Stallibrass House or had the house created him? And this is the man I married, she thought. For a fleeting moment, truth confronted her in all its ruthless clarity. Her appetite vanished; she pushed her plate to one side.

Rupert, as always, did not notice.

"I saw Stallibrass House today," Nicky said. Suddenly, she wanted his attention.

"What did you think of it?"

"I thought . . ." She was aware that she was supposed to make some educated comment, but she had no educated comment to make, and what she really thought she dared not say. "It's the first thing you did, isn't it? I wondered . . . what it meant to you."

"I've built better since. The Technico building was more ambitious; the church of St. Mary Magdalen was far more innovative. Stallibrass House was simply a preliminary essay, a four-finger exercise in brick and mortar. The first draft of ideas I improved on later. When I'm drawing, I usually scrap the first draft."

"Still," Nicky hazarded, "it's real, isn't it? A building, not a drawing. It must be a little bit special to you."

A peculiar smile touched Rupert's mouth, a smile that thinned and straightened his lips instead of curving them. "In a way," he said.

The following winter Rupert caught flu. Like most people who are rarely ill he was a bad patient, going to work when he should have stayed at home and being brought back to the Knightsbridge flat in a taxi by Michael Kovacs, feverish and on the point of collapse. Nicky was flustered and unnerved— it seemed so incredible to see Rupert thus enfeebled, buckling from his enormous height like a pillar turned to sand. Fortunately, Michael was strong enough to get him to bed, calm enough to summon a doctor. "I'll wait with you," he said, re-placing the phone, assessing Nicky's incompetence (she thought) with a dispassionate eye.

"I can manage," she insisted. She was not quite comfortable with Michael.

"I'll wait."

The doctor came, wielded thermometer and stethoscope, sounded Rupert's heart and lungs. "I'm afraid he's very sick," he told them afterwards. "The flu's pretty bad this year. Always the same: a wet winter, not cold enough to kill the germs, and some new strain hatches out and rampages around getting under everyone's immune system. Give him plenty of fluids, keep him warm, not much else you can do. Basically, flu just has to burn itself out. He's got a strong constitution: he'll be all right. Only one problem: seems he has an irregular heart-beat. Don't know if anyone's picked it up before. He should be taking something for it. I don't know if"—he glanced doubtfully at Nicky—"an illness in the past, perhaps . . . ?"

"I've never seen him ill before," Michael said, "but I believe he had rheumatic fever after the war. He was invalided out of the army."

"That would be what did it. I'll have him into the surgery when he's over the flu—give him a thorough check-up. In the meantime, young lady"—he turned back to Nicky, scribbling a prescription—"you'd better start giving him these."

"He thinks you're Rupert's daughter," Michael said later, with malice aforethought.

Nicky decided it was best not to answer.

Michael went out to get the medicine while she sat at Ru-pert's bedside like a dutiful wife. Watching him, she realized for the first time that he was old, visibly old, his normal healthy colour—from being on site in all weathers—faded to an uneven pallor, broken veins stretched like red webbing across his gaunt cheekbones, his sweat-sodden hair now predominantly grey. In sleep his jaw sagged, as the jaw of Théo Montador had once sagged; the skin of his neck bunched into empty wrinkles; the mouth was no longer rigid but merely an open hole through which his breath came in wheezing gasps. The short February day dimmed towards evening and in the ashen twilight a shadow slid over him; for a while, left alone with the sick man and her own doubts, it seemed to her that his face had a look of death. She had never before thought about Rupert's death.

On the doctor's next visit she asked him: "Is it dangerous, an irregular heartbeat?"

"Not necessarily. He's in pretty good shape overall; you don't want to worry. Overworks himself, of course; all these dynamic types do that. Doesn't do them as much harm as you'd think. Nothing like work for keeping a man interested in life. Half the time, it's the retired ones who just curl up and die. He'll probably live to a hundred and still be upsetting the old fogies. You'll see."

"Yes, but"—Nicky looked brave—"you said: *not necessarily*. That means, there's a chance, a possibility—please tell me the truth. What *could* happen?"

The doctor said frankly: "A stroke. But it's 'could,' not 'will'— and strokes, heart attacks, they can happen to anyone. Hazards of the game. When you reach the end of your life you die, one way or another. We've yet to come up with a cure for that." He reiterated: "Don't worry. Doesn't help, worrying. Ten to one, he'll go on fine."

"I shan't worry," Nicky said.

That winter was long and dreary, a winter of slush and rain, of thick brown mud in the country and thin grey mud in the city, of dripping trees, gritty streets, splintering winds. At Churston Grange, the dampness and the chill crept into every corner. Nicky wrapped herself in expensive furs, but they did not warm her. In London, she closed all the windows and stifled, escaping from reality by reading a succession of bodice-rippers and romantic melodramas, eating too many chocolates, watching her favourite films over and over again on the new video. She dreamed of running away again, or having an affair, but she knew wherever she ran Rupert would find her, whoever she slept with Rupert would know. Her dyed hair marked her like the brand of Cain and her experience with Montador had taught her to be wary of male omniscience. When Rupert came home he talked, she prompted; in bed, he continued to make use of her body. He's old, she told herself in the sleepless hours, listening to his rasping breath, not quite a snore, more the heavy breathing of some huge animal whose slumber intimidates the forest. He's old. One day he'll die. Maybe soon—and inevitably her imagination would leap ahead, gilding the future (He must leave me *something*. He might leave me everything.), seeing herself rich and free, still young, still beautiful, at last able to be herself. Whoever herself might be. *He's old.* Insidious hope. He might die. He could have a stroke. People had strokes. (He might live for years.) At the end of your life, you die. No cure. She did not wish him dead, but she dreamed him dead, and the dream kept her warm, until spring followed on the dragging footsteps of winter and blossomed overnight into a wet green summer. Summer '85. A year of international disasters, of sinking ships and crashing planes, of private and public tragedies, of flood and storm and heartbreak. The year of which someone quipped grimly: "Stay alive in eighty-five." And one stuffy June day in London Nicky picked up the phone to a familiar voice.

"Meet me at the wine bar round the corner. Angelo's. In five minutes."

Alex Fauvelle.

She ought to be angry with him, she knew; but her anger had long gone. He had been her lover but not her love: there had been no sentiment between them, no false promises, no act of kindness, no debt of gratitude. He was her partner and he had cheated her: it was in his nature to cheat. At bottom, she had always sensed that. He had said: "Next time you will know to be more careful." Well, this was next time. She would be more careful. She put on lipstick and perfume, picked up her bag, and walked round to Angelo's. She did not hurry.

She saw him as soon as she went in. He was sitting at a table at the far end of the bar, drinking red wine. He looked seedy: his skin had the dead-leaf tan of three seasons ago and the wizened-monkey lines seemed to be etched deeper into his face. His clothes, normally so sharp, had grown shabby; the black hair hung further down his back and into his eyes than she remembered. On the table, a packet of cigarettes, a box of matches. The lighter had gone. He looked unmistakably French and as out of place—even in cosmopolitan London—as a visiting parakeet. A slightly faded parakeet, whose bright plumage had dulled with a weary flight or drab captivity. Beside him, she felt suddenly fashionable, self-possessed, cool. She found herself thinking: *J'ai réussi.* In his terms, she had indeed succeeded. She had married money and position, hooked her kit-

ten-claws firmly into the good life. The shadows in her existence
began to recede: she saw herself reflected in Alex's eyes and
felt a warm, sweet glow of satisfaction. She was even pleased
to see him. His motives for getting in touch were doubtless self-
seeking, possibly sinister, but for the moment she could dis-
regard all that. Her memories of Paris altered with her moods:
today, she saw it as one continuous party, nightclubs, champagne, romance and intrigue in the rue Quincampoix. Time
dimmed her fears, reduced the horrors to obstacles which she
had (mostly) been able to surmount. And she had been free.
Nostalgia rushed over her. She sat down opposite him, said:
"Hello."

His smile mirrored hers. The familiar vivid smile, a little
worn about the edges. It was odd how comfortable she felt with
him. Alex with whom she never had to pretend.

"I hear you've done all right."

"Yes." Away from Rupert, she allowed herself a little com-
placency. She fingered the ring on her left hand.

"Very pretty," Alex said appreciatively. "Would you like me
to get it valued for you?"

He laughed, so she laughed. It was easy to laugh with him.
His betrayal shrank to a mere peccadillo, frivolous, unimportant. Lightly committed, lightly forgiven. A joke.

She asked: "How have you been?"

He shrugged. "Not so bad, not so good." She knew he
wouldn't say any more now. A cryptic remark maybe, later, a
name dropped here, a place there. The usual element of mystery. Fleetingly, she wondered if he had been in gaol.

She drank some of the wine—it was warm and vinegary—
and they talked about Parisian friends and acquaintances, old
days.

"Isabelle makes a lovely widow," Alex told her. "Everyone
says she is very brave. If you have no feelings, it is easy not to
give way to them. She looks lovely in black."

"She would," Nicky said. And: "What about Eugène? Do you
still see him?"

But Alex brushed Eugène aside, changed the subject. "I like
the hair," he said, pulling a red-gold curl. "A nice touch. It suits
you, too."

"Thank you."

"Clever Nikki." The smile flickered, like a tired candle-flame.
"His first wife's hair was that colour, wasn't it?"

"Uh-huh."

"It was a good thought. I taught you a lot, didn't I?"

Nicky said: "Everything." She didn't know if it was true, but it didn't matter. She felt homesick for Paris, for freedom, for the good times. Whatever good times they had had.

Alex stroked her cheek. His fingertip was like a snake, curling over the contours of her face. He murmured: "He is an attractive man, too—*Sir* Rupert?"

"Charismatic." Her tone was indescribable.

"Good in bed?"

Nicky copied his shrug.

"Does that mean you won't tell me, or—?"

"It means I won't tell you." She waited for more questions, but he didn't ask. His eyes looked straight into hers and she saw that they were quite black, with no visible alternation of colour between iris and pupil. They did not look real eyes at all. Tiny reflections swam in the blackness, like glints of light caught in a button.

She had half expected him to try a little friendly blackmail— we were partners, you struck gold, share and share alike: after all, I know too much about you—but he did not. He didn't even try to borrow money. In the end, seeing his shabbiness, she offered. It made her feel good, peeling ten-pound notes from her wallet, as if ten-pound notes meant less to her than a sheaf of scrap paper. "Take it," she said. "I daresay you can use it. It's nothing to me."

He made a face, took the money—as if circumstances beyond his control forced him into unwilling acceptance. Nicky recollected suddenly that all the women in his life gave him money. Maybe he was just being devious.

She said: "I'll call you some time. If you give me your number . . . ?"

He had told her he was staying with a friend. Apparently, the shadowy throng of Alex's friends extended even to London.

"No number." A farewell grin, thrown over his shoulder, on his way out. "I'll call you."

Inevitably, he had left her the bill.

Over dinner that evening, it occurred to Rupert that Nicky looked animated. He distrusted her animation, as he had come to distrust anything unpredictable in her behaviour. He had realized, on his wedding night, that the woman he had married was a mirage; but he hoped—if he kept his distance, if he asked no questions, if he closed his eyes—that the vision might linger for a while. He suspected that behind the image which had temporarily bewitched him was a human being far different from the phantom he had conjured, but that very suspicion made him draw back from any intimation of the truth. He was like a man in a blindfold who squints cautiously from under the rim of the bandage, doggedly blinkered, warily deceived. When he was with her, he concentrated on her face. After all, it was a pretty face, rather piquant, with its milky skin and wide eyes, grey as a winter's evening. And the hair—well, he had always admired Titian hair. Sometimes, he remembered that Diana's face had been far from piquant, and in her grey eyes—surely?—there had been a fleck of hazel. But these thoughts—like all unwanted thoughts—he pushed away from him. It was not difficult. Work, as always, dominated his life; marriage and family came a long way second. Perhaps that was why he made so many misjudgements—because he never gave more than a fraction of his attention even to those he loved best, never saw them clearly, never learnt their feelings or understood his own. His emotions were a maelstrom of pagan instincts, animal passions and subconscious traumas which rarely saw the light of day or were subjected to either intelligent analysis or civilized control. His art, being devoid of emotion, focussing on the pure logic of form and function, gave him no outlet for the darkness of his spirit. Once, when he was a young man, caught up in the nightmare of war, every moment free from fear, every skirmish with death had filled his heart. But since then he had bound himself in bonds of his own making, and the delusion of his marriage was merely another chain which he would not strive to break. He might register Nicky's unusual liveliness; he would not speculate on the cause.

After his illness, he worked even harder, as though—like Nicky—he had some premonition of his own mortality. But he was a Van Leer: he knew the Great Reaper would await his convenience, at least for a time. And he had a new project on his board, a vast and exciting project for a media company moving to a site in Docklands. Already, he visualized a huge construction whose windows would outglitter the stars and whose horns would top the Post Office Tower. With this, he would leave his mark on the skyline of London forever. He had no leisure—even if he had had the inclination—to worry about his marriage. Or his daughter.

He thought of Elsa from time to time, when he could not help it. In the still small hours her spectre would intrude, creeping out of the dark places in his mind to torment him. He had long forgotten (if he ever really knew) why it was he disliked her or what she had done wrong. It didn't matter. Her face on the borders of his thought had become inexplicably associated with that tumult of inchoate feeling—an ugly face grown unnaturally beautiful, whose painted immobility revealed nothing, gave nothing. The face of Nemesis. One night he dreamed he was climbing an endless stair, and suddenly he saw there was blood dripping down the steps towards him, and between the open treads he saw that same face. Elsa's face. Her mother's face. And on several occasions he dreamed of Diana, riding away from him on her pony, only when he called out she turned and it was her sister. In such dreams he felt for Elsa what he had once felt for Diana: he reached out to take her, to strangle her in his arms, absorb her in his body . . . and he awoke, always, in a fever of baulked desire, which gradually drained away into horror and self-disgust.

Alex called Nicky again nearly a week later. This time, they arranged to have lunch—an extravagant lunch in a Soho restaurant with walls of sugared almond and ceiling of crystal and exquisite food in minute portions. A morsel of pâté de foie, a wafer of steak Diane. A thimbleful of chocolate mousse under a globule of cream. The champagne frothed its way up the long glasses and into Nicky's head. After all, she told herself, even if someone does see me, why shouldn't I have lunch with an old friend? There's no crime in having lunch. "Your Honour," she declaimed, "the accused is charged with having lunch. How does she plead?"

"Guilty," said Alex.

"Guilty," Nicky echoed, taking a further gulp of Bollinger.

"So," Alex said, "you are afraid of him."

In the ensuing pause Nicky heard the champagne bubbles hiss against the side of her glass. Inside her head, the bubbles had burst. "Sometimes," she admitted at last. "He—he isn't like Théo. Théo knew about us but he was just—disappointed. Rupert . . ." She came to a halt.

"Does he love you?"

"No. I don't know. He likes to look at me. He loved . . . the person I remind him of."

"His first wife."

Nicky nodded. She wished it was true.

"The trouble with marriage," Alex continued after a moment, "is that it makes *your* position vulnerable. If you were his mistress, we could have managed something. As it is . . . He's quite old, isn't he? Is he likely to die? He might have a bad heart— or perhaps it's the liver. In France, everyone has trouble with their liver." Through his raised glass Nicky saw his smile studded with bubbles. "What do you think? Can we arrange for him to die?"

"You haven't asked me," she said coldly, "if *I* love *him*."

"Of course you don't. Oh—maybe you fooled yourself, to begin with. But not now." His voice softened—sank to a note of perilous intimacy. "When you lie with him, Nikki, do you think of me? Am I there beside you—between you? Not two lovers but three . . . Do you remember, Nikki? Do you remember me in the dark?"

She had long forgotten those words of idle seduction, but she did not say so. She picked up her spoon, scraping the last of her mousse from the dish. After all, she didn't have to say anything. How could she tell him that when her body lay between Rupert's hands all she could think of was whether his control would break—whether some day he would squeeze her muscles into clay and crush the very breath from her lungs? There was no question of pleasure, real or feigned. No space in her mind for sensual fantasy. *Do you remember me in the dark?* Do you remember me in terror, in tension, in doubt? Do you think of me on the rack?

Like hell.

She said, compromising: "Maybe."

He looked at her without smiling, a strange expression on his face. A curiosity that was almost sensitive, an unaccustomed trace of compunction. "What has he done to you, Nikki? If you have forgotten me, why don't you laugh? Laugh at me, *petite putain. Tu as réussi.* Why don't you laugh?"

"I don't want to laugh," Nicky whispered. A tear welled in her eye and slithered unexpectedly down her cheek.

Alex said: "I think we should go now."

"Go," Nicky repeated dully. "Go where?"

"Bed."

Back at the flat, in the bed she shared with Rupert, Nicky clung to him with the hunger of despair, filled her mouth with his kisses, opened at his touch. He squirmed into the wet softness of her and they writhed together like eels copulating in the tide, twisted in the crumpled sheets, slimed in each other's sweat. The curtained window created a stifling dimness that was filled with gasps and groans and murmurs in both French and English—an indrawn breath, an exhaled sigh, the creak and shudder of heaving bedsprings. Afterwards, Alex smoked a cigarette, Nicky lay in empty abandon.

"How long have we got?" Alex asked, tossing his cigarette end into the wastepaper bin.

"Oh . . . ages."

They did not hear the banging of the front door. Rupert had been on site, missed his Dictaphone, come home to collect it. They knew nothing till he was in the bedroom. Nicky saw his face looming suddenly over Alex's shoulder and began to scream, but it was too late. He picked up a chair—she saw him swing it into the air, saw it smashing down on top of them— heard Alex yelping like a dog as Rupert belaboured him with the broken chair-legs. He rolled off the bed, tugging the sheet with him in a futile attempt at protection, but Rupert went on beating him while he lay twitching and whimpering on the carpet. Then Rupert turned to Nicky. Her screams were cut short; she whispered: "No—please, please—" but he did not listen. She tried to curl herself into a foetal position, arms crossed over her head. He raised the chair. The first blow jarred her forearm to the socket: her spine seemed to snap. The second lashed her thigh with torn wood—blood flowered along the scratches. She waited for the third blow but it never came. In the act of lifting the chair again Rupert's whole body went rigid—his face contorted with something more than fury—he pitched forward as if in slow motion and slumped heavily across the foot of the bed. Nicky sat up, biting her wrist in fear. Alex was pulling himself off the floor, tears of pain on his cheek. He said: "What's happened? What's happened?"

"I think he's dead."

"*Bordel de merde!* Why does everyone around you always die? Try his pulse. Perhaps it's a fit. He's crazy—really crazy. A psychopath. I think all my ribs are broken. He could have killed us both! Where are my clothes?"

"I don't know how to find a pulse. Alex—"

"Don't cry. There isn't time. You can cry later: it'll look good. I've got to get out of here."

"Shall I call an ambulance?"

"*No!* Not till I've gone. You'll have to tidy up—dress—cover those grazes. And get rid of that fucking chair. *Then* call. For God's sake don't let them see you like that . . ."

Much later, in the hospital, Nicky sat looking pale and shocked. She sat for a long time, just waiting. Her arm hurt and the cuts on her thigh were sticking to her skirt. A nurse brought her a cup of tea and made soothing noises. He's had a stroke, they told her. It's serious. He's paralysed down his right side. When the doctor admitted he might never recover, her relief was so great she had to duck her head between her knees. The sister thought it was distress and ordered more tea, very strong and sweet. "You're so kind," Nicky mumbled. And: "Has he said anything?"

"I'm afraid his speech is impaired. It may improve, but—don't hope for too much."

Nick took a deep breath. "I see. Thank you. I mean, thank you for telling me."

"You can see him now," the doctor said.

It was Michael who broke the news to Elsa.

For a full minute she stared ahead of her, stiff and silent. Then: *"She did it.* She did it . . ."

"He had an irregular heartbeat," Michael said gently. "As I understand it, that increased the likelihood of a stroke, particularly under stress. He always worked too hard." Like Nicky, after Rupert's bout of flu he had checked the medical details.

"It was *her*," Elsa insisted. "She must have done something. He was always so strong. He'll get well. He'll get well and then . . . then he'll leave her. I can look after him . . ."

"Balls," Michael said comprehensively, deciding gentleness was a waste of time. "He's in hospital: they'll look after him. It's their job. You concentrate on looking after yourself."

"And you," Elsa said, switching to accusation with disconcerting alacrity, "who are you looking after? What's in it for *you?*"

"I'll look after his work," Michael said drily. "What else?"

"You wanted this." Her eyes searched his face as though looking for cracks in a wall. "You're glad he's in hospital—sick—out of the way. I suppose—you wanted control. What was it you said to me once—about hating people? Have you always hated him? Have you always hated *me?*"

"Stop it. Stop it *now*. I won't be made a scapegoat for your father. He never gave a damn about you—"

"You're lying. All this time, you've been lying. Lying to him, lying to me. Creeping, scheming, using me against him. Waiting your chance. You bastard. Creeping, scheming *bastard*—"

She pounded him with her fists—he seized her arms to restrain her, shaking her like a rag doll. It made no difference.

"Get out!" she panted. "You loathsome shit! I never want to see you again. Get out! Get out! *Get out!*"

He went without another word.

In the hospital she sat by the bed, gazing down at the wreck of her father. His right hand—his drawing hand—lay still on the coverlet. It would lie still now forever. His countenance seemed to have collapsed sideways as though his features were no longer fixed but sliding down his face. His thick hair looked both lank and brittle; his skin both pale and red. Transparent plastic tubes connected him with transparent plastic bags. Liquid nourishment dripped into him; urine dripped out of him. She could not tell if he slept or woke. Sometimes he stared at her out of half-closed eyes, without rejection, without reaction. He was her father and in her fantasies he had loved her, but now there would be no more fantasies, no more hope—neither love nor forgiveness, neither fulfillment nor redemption. It was all over.

And his soul from out that shadow that lies floating on the floor
Shall be lifted—nevermore . . .

It was a private room: the nurses let her sit. Until they came to give him a wash. In the corridor outside she found Nicky. For a few minutes they did not speak: Elsa because she felt too much, Nicky because she felt nothing at all. Only a vague prickling of fear.

"It was you," Elsa said. "You did this. You."

Nicky shook her head, but her eyes were guilty.

"I'll take him from you," Elsa vowed. "I swear it. If he lives

I'll look after him, if he dies I'll call him back. Somehow I'll take him from you. You think you've won but you haven't. I won't let you destroy him."

The door opened; a staff nurse poked her head out. "Miss Van Leer—Lady Van Leer—"

Elsa turned to go. "I mean it," she said. Her face was white, her voice blank with pent-up emotion. Nicky could almost see her struggle for self-control.

When she had gone, Nicky went into the room, sank down in the chair. She propped her forehead in her hands and stared at the floor, at the window, at the flowers in the vases, the fruit in the fruit-bowl. Anywhere but Rupert. Anywhere.

11

"She can't do it," Elsa said. "She can't do that to me."

Mr. Mayhew looked unhappy. "I'm afraid she can. The—er—rift between you and your father was—well, not common knowledge, but *known*, you see." Elsa was silent. "She claims your presence distresses him. It's very plausible."

"*Plausible*. Precisely. She's always been plausible. She wants me out of the way." Elsa fiddled with a pen lying on the desk, pulling the cap off and ramming it on again. "She never loved him. She's just using him."

It was Mr. Mayhew's turn to be silent.

"What about these lawyers of hers?"

"Schnurrer, Greenbaum and McTavish. Yes. Well. Not really a reputable firm—off the record, of course. But they know the law. She's his wife: she's within her rights. We could always contest the injunction, but it would be very messy. A lot of vulgar speculation. The press . . ." He paled at the thought.

Elsa said: "I don't care about the press."

"They dig things up, you know . . ." With superhuman tact, he failed to specify exactly what. "The lawyers, too. All sorts of skeletons tumbling out of the closet. It really could be most unpleasant."

"I don't care."

"Why don't you leave it for a while—give everyone time to adjust? Perhaps Lady Van Leer can be induced to change her mind. In the long term it won't look good, keeping you away like this. Might even look as if she has something to hide. Best to avoid a public confrontation, if you can. Later, we'll see if we can persuade her—appeal to her better nature—that sort of thing. Discreetly. You know."

Elsa said: "She hasn't got a better nature."

Mr. Mayhew did not comment. Possibly he agreed. "He'll be well looked after," he offered, attempting reassurance, "down at Churston—just the place for him. Regular nurse, local doctor on call, his own chap down from Harley Street now and then to give him a check-up. Nothing to worry about there."

"Will the nurse live in?"

"I—believe not. Lady Van Leer doesn't seem to like live-in staff. The nurse—I think it's a man—he'll stay if necessary, naturally. Of course, people don't want to live in these days. I suppose they feel it ties them down. Things aren't—"

"—what they used to be," Elsa supplied brusquely.

Mr. Mayhew looked disposed to forgive her rudeness. After all, she was very upset. And he had known her as a child.

Presently, Elsa asked: "What's happened at the office?"

"For the moment," Mr. Mayhew said, "the junior partner has taken over. Michael . . . Michael Kovacs."

"I know Michael Kovacs," Elsa said.

At Churston Grange, Rupert sat in a wheelchair with his head on a cushion. His right arm was arranged on the armrest almost as if he had put it there himself; the fingers of his hand hung down like a bunch of sausages. He had tried writing with the left hand, but Nicky took the piece of paper away. "He gets frustrated when he can't do things," she explained, "and that distresses him. I think it's best if he doesn't try." The nurse, a doe-eyed Pakistani youth fascinated by Nicky's wistful charm and heroic devotion, assented eagerly. Rupert, with horrible effort, made a series of shapeless noises that would not quite coalesce into words. "I understand what he says," Nicky added, "most of the time." The nurse believed her. After a few weeks, she had ceased to fear that Rupert might recover the power of speech. But she had an instinctive dread that Elsa, if allowed to visit, might understand him—that for all their conflicts there might exist between them a familial telepathy, a comprehension not of the ear but of the blood. She knew it was dangerous—it was inviting suspicion—but she wanted Elsa kept away. She had been afraid of her stepdaughter, that day in the hospital: not just of what she might find out but of Elsa herself, Rupert's child with Rupert's uncontrolled passions. She felt overburdened with too many little fears, too many shadows of the unknown. Only in Elsa's absence could she begin to relax. "I'll make him comfortable," she promised herself. "I'll do my best." After all, he had never loved his beautiful daughter. Alex suggested the lawyers for Nicky; the lawyers told her what to do. And now she was secure. For a little while.

Churston Grange had become a house of the sick. Upstairs, Mrs. Skerritt beat on the walls of her asylum, or stared vacantly ahead of her with what was left of her mind. Downstairs, Rupert sat hunched up in the prison of his body, his wheelchair creaking as the nurse pushed him from room to room. Well-paid servants took care of their needs: Rupert's nurse, Mrs. Skerritt's attendant, the housekeeper, the gardener, the daily help. And in the midst of it all there was Nicky, an unlikely queen in a kingdom of invalids. For the first time in her life, she was in charge. The staff answered to her; she answered to no one. She gave orders and held consultations, sat beside Rupert, a picture of caring concern, smoothing his brow and holding his lifeless hand (she did not touch the other one lest he should pull it away). She bought striped pyjamas for the nurse to dress him in, obtained videos for him to watch, books for him to read. Sometimes, she would glimpse her reflection in a mirror, and be caught unawares by her own strangeness. The red blaze of her hair (she had never quite grown used to it), the white stillness of her face, a new poise in her slight body, a new assurance in her manner. Now she was indeed a chatelaine—no Isabelle Montador, perhaps, but a self-possessed ruler in her private domain, endowed with magical health amidst sickness, eternal youth beside age, vivid modern glamour amidst Gothic decay. The Pakistani nurse adored her, the other staff deferred to her, Rupert and Mrs. Skerritt were in her power. Gradually, her confidence grew: she even began to enjoy herself. When she wanted, she could escape to London;

in between, it was a novel experience to be a ministering angel. She came to like the image of herself sitting at Rupert's bedside being devoted, and her patience with Mrs. Skerritt also increased. The housekeeper said she was "a dear little thing. Can't be much fun for her, living with a couple of invalids. She looks so delicate, too, yet she's hardly ever cross or tired." Nicky, overhearing, made a resolution never to be cross or tired, always to look delicate. She bought plenty of black to emphasize her seriousness and her pallor, tried to avoid—at least in the country—low necklines and tight skirts. She had her detractors (the daily help was always sceptical) but most people commended her; a woman's magazine even interviewed her on her Florence Nightingale role. And at night—at night when she was left alone with the crippled man and the demented woman—the kingdom was all hers.

Rupert's nurse, Geoffrey Patel, usually left last, at around nine. Nicky would give Mrs. Skerritt her sleeping pill, lock her door, take Rupert his tablets—simple duties which made her feel she was involved in the actual nursing. Then she would go to her room (since Rupert's stroke she had moved into the bedroom which had once been Diana's), strip off her demure clothes, put on a sleazy sweatshirt and jeans or a wisp of Janet Reger lace. Downstairs, she would pour herself a drink and eat the supper the housekeeper had prepared for her. There were moments when the solitude and the night-murmurs of the house still frightened her, but the chatter of the television chased her fears away. Alex would come about eleven. The sound of his motorbike snarling down the country lanes was loud and unmistakable—but only to Nicky. Many of the village boys had motorbikes. Indoors, Alex helped himself lavishly to Rupert's whisky, propped his feet on Rupert's table, wrapped his arm round Rupert's wife.

"I could get you a job here," Nicky suggested. "Chauffeur maybe. I don't have a chauffeur."

"*Quelle merde.*" Alex smiled sleepily. "I don't want a job. Anyway, it's too risky. I prefer to remain invisible."

"But you must get so tired driving down from London."

"I don't always come from London." As ever, he didn't explain, and she knew not to ask.

Later, they would make love—on the sofa, watching a pornographic video, in Diana's bed, in Elsa's bed. "I want to fuck you," he whispered once, "in every room in the house." He took her into Rupert's room, stared down at the prone figure. "Is he awake? Can he see us?"

"I think so."

There was a white gleam under Rupert's eyelids; his mouth opened; the breath rattled in his throat.

Alex put his hand inside Nicky's sweatshirt, feeling her breast. Watching Rupert.

"Alex—no . . . Stop. Please stop."

She struggled, half resisting, her erect nipple showed clearly through the clinging cotton. Presently, he pushed up her sweatshirt, began to kiss the exposed breast. "I want him to see . . . I want him to see what I am doing to you." He ignored her mumbled protests, her uncertain attempts to thrust him away—undid her zip, pulled down her jeans and briefs, opened her to his tongue. All the time, he hardly moved his gaze from Rupert. Her hands writhed in his hair—but whether to repulse or caress him she did not know. She felt his tongue probing, savouring her: a gentle sucking drained all the resistance from her body. Orgasm came gradually, as though her very revulsion had slowed her responses, drawn out her pleasure. She twitched and jerked and tugged his hair till he cried out. Afterwards, she would not look at the bed.

"There," Alex said. "You enjoyed that, I enjoyed that—I expect he enjoyed it too. If he can't do it he can at least watch. Now I'm going to take you, here, on his bed—where he can see . . ."

"No!" She pulled up her jeans, tore herself free of him.

"Nikki—"

But she had already fled from the room.

He found her downstairs, pouring vodka. "Nikki, come on. We were having fun. It's too late now to be a prude. Let's go back . . ."

"No"—she swallowed the alcohol neat—"no—*no*—"

"Calm down. You liked it, didn't you? I just wanted . . ."

"*No!*"

She had never said no to him in that way before. He looked her over thoughtfully, shrugged, allowed himself to relax. "Very well . . . If you won't, you won't. Sometimes, I wonder why I come down here."

"So do I," Nicky snapped.

He tried another tack. "This sudden affection for the old man . . . The shock might have killed him: have you thought of that? Finding us in bed gave him a stroke; sharing his bed with us might have finished it. Then"—he made a poetic gesture—"all this would be yours."

Nicky said flatly: "I don't want him to die."

Some time later, as if his words had started a new train of thought, Alex asked about Rupert's tablets.

"Digoxin, digitoxin. Heart stuff." Nicky was vague. "They don't make you high or anything."

"All the same"—Alex frowned—"I've heard of that. I must check . . ."

In the mornings he was supposed to leave before the staff arrived, but all too often he went out of the back door as they came in through the front. On one occasion he overslept the advent of both nurses and the housekeeper, only waking when the daily started the Hoover on the landing. He climbed down the Virginia creeper below Nicky's window, laughing at her panic, retrieved his motorbike from its hiding-place behind a shed, and roared off down the drive, leaving Nicky smouldering at his reckless indiscretion. He was with her two or three nights a week, but although she disliked her periods of isolation she decided, after the incident in Rupert's room, that she was relieved he had declined her offer of a job. Had he accepted she would have had no way out. As it was, she still fooled herself that she could tell him to go, if she really wanted to. It troubled her a little that he had so swiftly renewed his hold on her, insinuated himself into her life, taken possession of her domain. Her feelings towards him were a strange mixture of trust and suspicion, comradeship and hostility. She was both repelled and tempted by him, doubtful of what he might do yet reassured that he was there. For all his past failures, he was on her side. Two of a kind. And after all, she reminded herself, this time, he could only advise, not compel. This time, *she* was in charge. Or so she believed.

In September 1986 Elsa gave her first solo exhibition in London. She had taken part in three joint exhibitions since her return from the States, but this was to be something on a more ambitious scale. The critics were interested but unappreciative; the mildest wrote: "Ms. Van Leer has yet to discover her-self," while others spoke of her "lack of direction" and the most waspish described her "trying out different artistic styles like a woman in a dress shop." Elsa paid little attention. The art world came to admire or be spiteful; name-droppers and trend-setters bought all her best (and some of her worst) pieces; friends told her she was "breaking new ground." It was a kind of success. About two weeks after the opening she wandered in, ostensibly to keep an eye on things, actually to look at her work, and brood, and wonder if she was any good. It was mid-afternoon and the gallery was almost empty. There was only one other person present, standing with his back to her study-ing the principal exhibit. A young man.

The exhibit consisted of moulded plastic tubes vaguely re-sembling a female nude with metal bolts piercing her anatomy in judicious places. It was called "The Second Coming." The young man was about six foot tall, slim, with a mop of black hair worn too long and carelessly trimmed, an ex–army jacket left over from the seventies, faded denims. Even from the back he seemed to hold himself with a certain grace, like a gymnast or a dancer. He appeared totally absorbed in her artwork. After a while he moved, walking round to look at it from another angle. She saw his profile: straight nose, clean-cut jaw, out-thrust cheekbone. Recognition came gradually, like a film winding down into slow motion. He stood immobile, as though caught in a freeze-frame.

Elsa came forward, stopping a couple of yards away. Her heels clicked on the floor. He looked up.

She said: "Hello."

It was several seconds before he realized who she must be. "Elspeth . . . ?"

"Anthony."

At first, she thought he was still beautiful; then she decided he was less beautiful but far more attractive. There were lines around his mouth, not smile lines but the drawn lines that come from pride and determination and a constant stiffening of the upper lip. His gentle eyes had hardened, his gypsy wild-ness given way to the aloofness of the hermit and a faint ar-rogance that suggested voluntary poverty. His clothes did not matter because he did not care; it was impossible to imagine Anthony in conjunction with designer casuals, loosely knotted silk ties—ties of any kind. He would not have noticed if the shirt on his back was made of cotton or sacking. In his teens, he had had an image—the image of his generation—but he had evidently omitted to update it and it had worn out, over the years, until all that remained was the man. Or so it seemed to Elsa. Whatever the truth, her heart shivered at the sight of him.

As for Anthony, he knew her solely from a blurred photograph in an arts magazine. Only her mouth was familiar—a mouth he remembered set in sullenness in the middle of a pale, solid face. Now, the sullenness was transformed into a kind of frozen pout, painted copper against a face etched in pastel tints like shadows on snow. He saw bone structure, glamour, a nymph-like slenderness, wine-red hair. He said: "You look lovely."

You too, Elsa thought. She pulled herself together. "Did you know this was *my* exhibition?"

"I read about it somewhere." A pause. "You call yourself Elsa now—?"

"I never liked Elspeth. A maiden-aunt sort of a name . . ."

Anthony said: "I liked it."

He might as well have said: I liked *you*. Fat, plain Elspeth, the unwanted child. She recalled with exquisite pain how kind he had always been.

She said: "Perhaps . . ."

He said: "Perhaps . . ."

They both hesitated, both laughed. His laughter softened him, taking the new-found hardness from his face. He said: "We must get together. Soon."

Elsa could only assent.

Over the next few weeks they saw each other with increasing frequency. He bought her spaghetti in cheap restaurants—although he was very broke he did not like her to pay—or they talked half the night in some seedy bar. They discussed environmental pollution, nuclear disarmament, racism, sexism, Marxism—subjects Elsa had never touched on except to echo fashionable views. Anthony was well-informed, opinionated, passionate. He claimed that the use of wealth as an incentive to labour only encouraged greed and self-interest, that people should work for each other, for the good of the community. In a perfect society there would be neither rich nor poor: everyone would have enough. But that was Utopia—something to believe in, something to strive for, not something to impose on the reluctant and the ignorant by force. He had outgrown the rigidity of Communism: he saw that violent revolution leads only to violence, destruction can only destroy. The important thing was for every individual who cared to do his best, no matter how small and ineffectual that best might seem to be. In the end, if enough individuals tried, failed, succeeded—then they might make a difference. As he spoke, she saw in his face the shades of past disillusionment, the awareness of futility—she saw stubbornness, persistence, courage. His ideals had survived the transition from theory into practice, the wear-and-tear of reality. This was the inner fire which had burned away much of his gentleness, yet that very flame could also transform him, making him far more than merely beautiful. If he had charm, it was irrelevant. She was bewitched by his sincerity, drawn into an alien world where her priorities tumbled and her tragedies shrank to passing misfortunes. As once before, with Michael, she felt inhibited by her own privilege. But Michael's was a standard success-story, from the gutter to the top of the heap. Anthony had rejected privilege, deliberately opted for penury. She knew in her heart she could not do it herself. But she could listen, admire—fall in love.

His father had disinherited him during his dalliance with Communism; afterwards, despite pleas from his mother and sisters, Anthony had made no attempt to mend the breach.

"I suppose," Elsa said slowly, "you could say my father disinherited me. I had an allowance and he stopped it. And I doubt if I feature in his will."

"What made him do it?"

I wore my mother's diamonds. How ludicrous it sounded. They were in the bank now, locked away; she would never wear them again.

She said: "He didn't like me. You know that."

"Yes, I know." Distracted from his principles, Anthony looked thoughtful and sorry. "It always upset Diana, being the favourite. He was a fool: you're much brighter than she was. More beautiful, too."

"Do you still miss her?"

"Not often." He was almost regretful. "I haven't had the time. I think of her now and then: her laughter, her vitality—how easy she was to be with. All wasted. It makes me sad, remembering. But it was over ten years ago. None of it is very clear any more."

Elsa said: "I miss her."

Later that night, when they were in bed, she fancied Diana was watching over them, even imagined she would be pleased. Twins share everything. Anthony's love-making was instinctively considerate, tender rather than fierce, a long way from the savagery of her relationship with Michael. Evidently he reserved his fervour for his politics; in sex, he used an intense concentration, a slow development of pleasure, sensitivity, control. When it was over he slid into sleep like a child, his arms around her, his head on her breast. This was her dream come true. She dozed fitfully, her mind taking wing, afraid to relinquish a single moment of her happiness.

One day, he took her to visit the drugs rehabilitation centre where he worked. Two junkies on the cure were repainting their own common-room; under the tattered dust-sheets Elsa glimpsed second-hand furnishings with stuffing leaking from split cushions and bald patches on the arms. The unfinished wall was mustard-coloured and spotted with damp, and there was a musty smell which even the sharp tang of the paint could not vanquish. A half-caste girl with light eyes in a dark face made them coffee: Anthony introduced her as his co-worker, Cathleen Mirza. The atmosphere was friendly, even welcoming; but to Elsa it all seemed unbelievably sordid. The worst cases, Anthony told her, were upstairs, under medical supervision. They had fourteen beds, too few full-time staff, nowhere near enough money. Elsa remembered the clinic where she had been sent in her teens—white rooms, green garden, endless psychiatric sessions—and asked hesitantly what funds they had.

"It all comes from private donors. Charities. We get a government grant, but it's only a token amount—so they can claim they're supporting us. It hardly pays the electricity bill. Most clinics charge, but our junkies don't exactly come from the wealthy section of society. If they had to pay, they couldn't afford it." He added: "Taking the cure is still a rich man's luxury."

I was even a privileged bulimic, Elsa thought. She said: "I'll write you a cheque."

The scorn faded from Anthony's expression; he said gently: "I didn't bring you here to get money out of you."

"It doesn't matter. I'll write a cheque anyway."

"No. You told me your father discontinued your allowance. And I can't believe your sculpture is all that commercial."

"I've got money from my grandmother. Please, Anthony—I must do *something*."

"All right. But not now. Later."

Over tea, while she wrote the cheque, he asked unexpectedly: "Do you still see your father?"

"No. We argued—that was when he stopped my allowance. And since the stroke, I'm not allowed . . ."

"Stroke? You never said he'd had a stroke."

She hadn't wanted to tell him about Rupert. Most of all, she hadn't wanted to tell him about Nicky. But he was looking anxious, concerned, involved. She would have to explain some time.

Nicky was sitting in the drawing-room when the housekeeper ushered him in. "Mr. Stallibrass to see you." She started to her feet, thrusting her Jackie Collins under a cushion. In historical novels, she thought irritably, the butler always gave you the opportunity to say you were not at home, or at least to prepare yourself. Stallibrass—the Mean Millionaire. Died two years ago. What on earth—?

It was a moment or two before she realized who he must be. Diana's fiancé, Andrew or Anthony, the original of that newspaper photograph which she had never quite forgotten. The Romeo who had been absent when his Juliet tried to climb the creeperless wall. Those dramatic cheekbones were unmistakable. Fleetingly, she wished for a mirror—for a minute's grace to examine her complexion, brush out her hair. She pulled her fingers through the curls at her neck, managed a tentative smile. "I'm sorry, I—I wasn't expecting you, was I? I was just— was just—"

"Did I disturb you?" His manner would have set her at ease if she had been less distracted by his looks. "Were you asleep?"

Nicky remembered that she was never cross or tired. "Oh no . . . Just thinking. Please—do sit down. You're the son of Joe Stallibrass, aren't you? I'm afraid I don't—?"

It was Anthony's turn to falter. But a lifetime of unflinching idealism had given him plenty of self-assurance. "This is a bit difficult," he began, obviously picking his words. There was a pause: he smiled at Nicky, she smiled at him. He said irrelevantly: "You're not at all what I expected."

Elsa's description had been very brief. Young, pretty, on the make. She had mentioned dyed hair; she had not said that it was red. Without really thinking about it he had visualized a bimbo with a short skirt and too much mascara. But the girl in front of him—she seemed scarcely more than a girl—was quietly dressed, soft-voiced, large-eyed, her face apparently in a state of nature, her hair colour matching her eyebrows. Perhaps Elsa had said it was dyed out of an obscure jealousy, because she could not bear anyone to compare with her beloved twin.

Nicky asked a little shyly: "What *did* you expect?"

"I don't really know . . ." She saw he was looking at her with interest—perhaps the normal interest that one person might feel for another, perhaps something more.

She said: "Would you like some tea?"

"No thanks. I must explain why I came. I don't know Rupert very well, but I was once engaged to Diana. I gather you were a friend of hers, before I met her?"

"Yes." It was the truth, but she felt suddenly guilty, as if it were a lie.

"Her sister is also a very close friend of mine. She told me you don't get on—I suppose it's traditional for girls to hate their stepmothers. And Elsa was always very emotional: she over-reacts to things. Anyway, as I was down here, I thought it was worth coming to see you. I couldn't believe anyone could be so deliberately unkind as to refuse her access to her father."

Nicky stiffened; but Anthony did not notice.

"She wants to see him," he said. "I think she has the right, don't you? Whatever disagreements they may have had. She loves him very much—probably too much. And . . . he may not live long."

There was a short silence. Nicky felt rather than saw his gaze fixed on her face.

She said: "I didn't mean to be unkind."

"Then prove it. Let her see him."

"The doctor said . . . he mustn't be upset." She couldn't recall if the doctor had said anything of the sort, but she had used the excuse often enough to believe in it.

"His brain isn't affected, is it?" Evidently Anthony was determined. "He's had plenty of time to think things over. He may have changed his mind. Fathers do . . ."

Nicky saw the lines about his mouth flex themselves, as though from a tensing of the muscles, a brief recollection of useless pride. She said abruptly: "Did yours?"

He looked disconcerted. "You listen to gossip."

"What else have I got to do?" And again: "Did your father change his mind?"

"So my mother says. She sent for me, but I wouldn't go. He died very suddenly. We had no chance to forgive each other." The tension about his mouth might have been firmness or pain. Or both. "One of my sisters said that I wouldn't have behaved to a tramp or a stray dog the way I behaved to him."

Nicky thought of her own mother, whom she had not seen in so many years. She whispered: "That was an awful thing to say."

"She was right. The sins of the fathers shall be visited on the children—but we should at least try to forgive them. Give Elsa her chance. Give Rupert his."

Nicky nodded dumbly. Faced with a direct plea, with gentle persuasion, with Anthony's eyes, she could not say no. Her heart quailed inside her.

"I'll have to tell the lawyers . . ."

"Never mind the lawyers. I'll tell Elsa; we'll call you to fix a date. Lady Van Leer . . ."

"Nicky."

"Nicky—thank you." He took her hand, she hoped he might kiss her cheek; but he did not.

"Are you sure you won't have tea? Or—or a drink?"

"No. I've got to get back to Stallibrass House. My mother's finally putting it on the market—she wanted to make it over to me, but I couldn't let her do it. The old man cut me out and that's that. Anyway, she's come down to sort through a few things. I don't see her often, so I said I'd help. I'm glad I did; otherwise I wouldn't have come here."

"I'm glad too," Nicky said. She essayed a note of irony. "You don't still think I'm the wicked stepmother—do you?"

Anthony smiled. "Not any more."

She saw him to the door. "By the way," she enquired as he was leaving, "are you Andrew or Anthony? Local gossip couldn't remember."

"Anthony."

Anthony . . . I like that, Nicky decided, lingering by the door. Better than Andrew. She had once been out with an Andrew who had been particularly boring.

Anthony got into his car—a battered Mini with ingrowing rust and a chronic sore throat—waved, and drove off. Nicky stared after him until the dust had settled on the drive.

She thought: "He said Elsa was a close friend. I wonder how close . . ."

Back in London, Elsa heard the good news in silence. She could not tell him how bitterly she resented taking any favours from Nicky—how deeply she hated her. It did not matter what Michael thought but it mattered about Anthony. She said: "You just *asked* her—and she agreed?"

"I think you misjudged her," Anthony said. "She might well have married him for love. It isn't unheard of: a young girl and a much older man. It's a form of hero-worship."

Elsa refrained from comment. She had told him as little as possible of the background to the situation: Nicky was "an acquaintance of Diana's—I met her once abroad"; nothing more. Anything she said would give her away.

"According to my mother," Anthony added, "they speak well of her in the village. They say she takes good care of him. I know it's hard for you—it's always hard in these cases—but Nicky isn't the fairy-tale villainess you seem to imagine. She's—"

"*Nicky?*"

"She told me," Anthony said, a little surprised, "that was her name."

"And you used it," Elsa murmured.

Nicky. Nicky the shape-shifter, slipping through your hands like water, turning on you like a serpent with forked tongue and poisoned tooth. Nicky the defenceless, the deceiver, the sun-burned blonde, the porcelain redhead. Perhaps Anthony, like Rupert, saw in her some warped reflection of Diana. And now, history would repeat itself, the wheel would turn full circle: Elsa struggled in the grip of a deadly fatality. Conflicting jealousies raged inside her—Diana was her sister, whom she loved, yet it was Nicky the stranger who had borrowed her

identity and used it to destroy her twin. The dead cannot betray; yet she felt betrayed. Past and future were catching up
with her; she fought against her apprehensions, clinging to
present happiness, but her brief security was gone. If it had
ever been there.

She went to Churston during the week before Christmas.
Anthony did not come so she drove down alone. The housekeeper let her in; Nicky stood waiting at the foot of the stairs.
A shaft of light bisected her face, leaving her eyes in shadow;
Elsa fancied they sparkled strangely. She wore a dark dress
which came well below her knees, making her appear very
fragile, very young, a wistful orphan from some Dickensian
novel. She did not look glamourous or even especially pretty.
Elsa was once more bewildered by her ability to mould herself
to any role she wished to play.

It was Nicky who said hello. She made a movement as if to
extend her hand, then apparently thought better of it.

Elsa stood silent and inflexible, hating the position she was
in, the obligation she did not feel—hating Nicky most of all.

When the pause had lengthened beyond bearing, Elsa said:
"I'd like to see my father now."

"Yes. Of course." Nicky seemed to be jerked out of a trance.
"He's upstairs. I'll take you."

She set her foot on the bottom step but Elsa forestalled her.
"Thank you. I know the way." Her voice was so bleak that the
sarcasm was lost. Nicky shrank from her as she brushed past
and hurried up the stairs.

The nurse admitted her to Rupert's room and left her alone
with him. His dressing-gown was bundled up on the chair so
she sat down on the edge of the bed, cautiously, almost afraid
of a repulse. But he could not repluse her any more. He looked
less deathly than he had in the hospital, but in his home environment, trapped between the bed and the wheelchair, he
appeared to her more broken. She imagined him living on in
his wretched body with who knew what torments of rage, frustration, remorse, imprisoned by his sly young wife, pampered
like a sick animal by his nurse, maybe even mocked or mal-
treated when there was no one around to see. The eyes that
stared out of his twisted face were bloodshot and fierce. She
looked down at his hands: the right lay palm upward, fingers
curled; the left was clenched. She reached out as if to touch

it—the left hand that was his only means of communication, the one instrument with which he might convey his feelings or his needs. But even now, she did not dare. There had been too many shattered hopes, too many vain fantasies. She said: "I want to help you" but in her voice was the pain of endless disappointments. His lips moved: a harsh sound came out, meaning nothing. She did not speak any more; there was no point. Her mouth tightened and her eyes filled. She sat on the bed, feeling useless, wondering how to stay, how to go, how to live with this moment through all the moments she had left.

And then his hand moved. It crept across the quilt towards her, closed over her own. All the strength in his body seemed to be concentrated in his fingers: he squeezed until she thought her bones would break. She did not care. The tears spilled from her eyes and poured down her cheeks unheeding. She bent her head and sobbed: "Daddy . . . Daddy . . .": she who had never called him Daddy in her whole life. He clung to her hand as if it was all he had left in the world.

The nurse disturbed them about half an hour later.

"I'm going to get him up now. I usually push him round the garden. He likes that."

Does he? Elsa thought. How do you know?

She said: "Isn't there anything—*anything*—you can do for him? Physiotherapy, or electric shocks, or—"

"He has physiotherapy. We do everything we can."

"What are these?" She picked up a bottle of tablets from the table.

"Digoxin. For his heart."

"Are they—all right? I mean—do you give them to him?"

"The dosage is carefully regulated. Lady Van Leer likes to administer them herself."

Elsa said: "I see," and her tone was suddenly cold.

She went slowly back downstairs. There was no sign of Nicky, but in the front hall the daily help was dusting assiduously. Elsa paused in front of the mirror to wipe the smudges from under her eyes. She said: "Is Lady Van Leer anywhere about?" She didn't want to say goodbye or thank-you but she felt she should make the attempt.

"In the garden." The daily had stopped dusting and was staring avidly at her. "You don't want to see the old woman, then?"

"Not—not this time."

"Been crying, have you?" Elsa did not answer. "Don't see much of that in this house. Only crocodile tears."

Elsa said sharply: "I thought Lady Van Leer was supposed to be so devoted?"

"She acts sweet enough when it suits her—I almost swallered it meself. But we don't know what she gets up to when she's away, do we? And then there's her young man."

"Young man?" For no specific reason, Elsa had a feeling of impending horror, as if shadow from the future was thrown across her path.

The woman nodded vigorously, pleased to find such an audience. "I've seen him leaving in the mornings two or three times. I reckon he comes down from London."

"What does he look like?"

"Dark. Might be foreign. Brown skin and black hair. Bit like our Paki."

"*Is* he?"

"Don't think so. Just dark. Very dark. You know."

"I know," Elsa said. She felt slightly sick. After all, she told herself, London was full of dark young men. And Anthony would never deceive her: he wasn't the type. Anthony . . .

"You all right, dear?" The daily help was peering inquisitively at her. "You look a bit pale."

"I'm always pale," Elsa said.

She left without seeing Nicky.

Reaching London, she went straight to the office of Langley and Mayhew. Mr. Mayhew was busy; Jonathan Sterling, the most recent addition to the firm, supplied her with coffee and bore the brunt of her vehemence. "We *must* help him. He wants to get away from her—I know he does. There must be something we can do."

Jonathan said tactfully that Mr. Mayhew would be free in a minute. He was rather dazzled by Elsa, but in her present mood he found her a little overpowering. She said: "Did you know *she* is in charge of his tablets? Digoxin—I've read about that somewhere. In a detective story. It's made from foxgloves. A small dose is a stimulant, but a big dose is lethal. And *she* gives them to him . . ."

"I'm sure Lady Van Leer would never—"

The advent of Mr. Mayhew was greeted by Jonathan with relief, by Elsa with passion.

"Do you realize," she stormed, "my father may be *murdered?*"

But Mr. Mayhew did not think so. In real life, he assured her, people were very rarely murdered. Certainly not among his clientele.

Elsa went home in a blaze of anger and desperation, which wore itself out in pacing the floor of her flat, sudden gusts of crying, a smashed coffee-cup. She had said she would phone Anthony, but although she picked up the receiver she did not make the call. Instead, she spent a long time cradling her right hand, bruised from the savagery of Rupert's grasp.

Christmas Day. In Churston, Nicky sat down to dinner with Rupert, Mrs. Skerritt, and their respective nurses. At the instigation of Geoffrey Patel, who was a Muslim, there were crackers and paper hats. Somehow, they only served to emphasize the atmosphere of hopelessness. The nurse cut Rupert's turkey into neat small cubes and he fed himself awkwardly with the wrong hand. Mrs. Skerritt dribbled. Nicky ate little and left the table early, careless of her image. Alex was in France for a couple of weeks; there was nothing to do but watch television or read a book: the same things she had been doing for a year and a half. By now she was bored with her responsibilities, her devotion, even her stolen nights with Alex—she wanted to be free again, to have something new to plan. Something like Anthony Stallibrass . . . He liked me, she thought, remembering his frank interest, the warmth of his smile. He did like me. She slid into a daydream in which Rupert died and she was liberated at once from her marriage and her past, from Elsa's enmity, Alex's domination. She pictured the countryside blanched with snow like a Christmas card, and Anthony coming up the drive in an anorak with a fur-lined hood—she was sure he would wear an anorak—with his eyes narrowed against the silver glare. She tried to recall the length of his lashes, and whether his irises were dark like dessert chocolate or lighter like cappuccino. She herself would be dressed in black—not modest, respectable black but a black that was both subtle and exotic, suitable for a mysterious widow. A flowing veil, a velvet cloak, a cloud of fur . . .

If Rupert died.

Alex had told her about the tablets, long before. "It is very dangerous, digoxin. A small overdose could kill him. Of course, nobody would know. Another stroke—a fatal stroke—would be quite natural. No doctor would be very surprised."

"I won't!" she had said. "Don't mention it again—don't even *think* of it."

But she thought of it. In a daydream, in a fantasy, in a tale of dark romance. She thought of it.

Elsa paid her second visit on January 1st. Once again, she was on her own. She had avoided Anthony over Christmas, making excuses, filling her mind with her father. She came down in the afternoon when her New Year's hangover had worn off. It was almost dark when she arrived.

This time she sat for ten minutes with Aunty Grizzle, responding politely to her ramblings and being addressed as Diana. Then she went to see her father. He was in bed again, slumped across a mound of pillows, his grey face looking even greyer in the evil dusk. She imagined he was pleased to see her. She took his hand of her own accord; wept a little, without words. The twilight sombred into night and a thin wind whined under the eaves. All the draughts came out of the corners to frolic with the curtains and rattle the ill-fitting door. It was the sort of evening, Elsa thought, when hope fails, and depression lingers, and all endings are sad.

Later, when she went downstairs, she saw there was a fire in the sitting-room, a flickering glimmer of light. There was someone by the fire, ensconced in the big armchair. Not Nicky.

"Michael."

His presence affected her like a malediction.

She said: "What are you doing here?"

"I come down now and then—to keep an eye on things. Anyway, I was his protégé. I'm supposed to be fond of him."

"You're very late."

"So are you."

"I had a hangover . . ."

"Snap."

His gaze roamed over her, seeing too much. Sparks of fire glinted in his eyes.

She asked: "Where's Nicky?"

"Avoiding you. Or me. I would offer you a lift back, but I saw your car in the drive."

"Thanks," Elsa said, "for the thought."

She drove off into the dark, wondering if he would follow her; but he did not.

One by one they went away, leaving the house to the draughts and the shadows. Elsa, Michael, the two nurses. Nicky sat by the fire with a drink, her feet curled under her. She had switched off the electric light and the flames made tiger-patterns on the wall and limned her face in gold. Presently, the roar of a motorbike mingled with the wind; gravel spat and crunched; a slight figure slipped into the house like a returning phantom. They lay in the firelight, playing games with the shadows, hearing nothing but their own pleasure. The flames hissed against the coals like little bright snakes; outside, the trees moved and muttered.

In his room upstairs, Rupert died alone in the darkness.

PART FOUR

PART FOUR

12

They had loved him, hated him, used and been used by him. And now he was dead. Yet in death he seemed somehow more present, more positive than the cripple with the fierce eyes whom they had all seen on that last evening, or the dynamic giant who had dominated their lives. His magnetism seemed to hold them to the graveside: the spectre of his charisma, a latent menace, a lethal fascination, drew them almost to the lip. Flakes of snow spiralled into the grave and were swallowed up. He was down there, down in the dark, nailed into the coffin, a prisoner straining against the leaden bonds of his inanimate body and the confines of his brass-handled cell, fighting to escape the eternity trap into which he had been plunged so abruptly. It was as if he wanted revenge—for his life, for his death, for his long sickness, lost hopes, broken faith, wasted love. His anger emanated from the grave like a visible force. A gust of wind sent the snow whirling like a dervish round them; voices woke briefly in every angle of the crooked church. From the trihedral bell-tower came a faint clang, the echo of an echo, as if the huge bell had been brushed by some invisible hand.

It is a sign, Nicky thought, and shivered, deep down in her furs.

It is a sign, Elsa said, too softly to be heard.

The tension between them had shifted, becoming one undercurrent among many, a part of the pattern but no longer the focus. Rupert's memory, Rupert's death, Rupert's presence filled their minds. Nicky was pale, but Elsa was white, white as the snow itself, her unpainted mouth mauve with cold, her flared nostrils slightly pink. Her eyes were like slits of rage, dry and hard. She did not look at Nicky any more, nor at the grave: her gaze went beyond, into the thickening snowfall, where horizon and distance were lost and sky and rooftops blurred into one. The wind prowled the churchyard, mewling. The last of the journalists had fled. The other mourners waited, locked in their cars—all except the art dealer in the lynx coat, who, having shown his support for the modernist cause, had given up and gone home. The vicar, with some justice, looked long-suffering. And Elsa stood there, in a silence that was not prayer, teeth clenched so they would not chatter, gloveless hands buried in the folds of her coat. Waiting. Watching her, Michael knew why. She would be the last to leave, though she waited till her very blood had turned to ice. Only a gesture—a stubborn, futile gesture. But in that moment he knew it meant so much to her she would have died for it.

He thought: Let her have her gesture.

"Come on." He laid a hand on Nicky's arm.

For an instant she hesitated, as if drawn to compete with Elsa even for this meaningless victory. But Michael's hand was firm, and the wind bitter, and she wanted to get on with her life. They walked out of the churchyard to their respective cars: the chauffeur held the door for Nicky to enter her hired Daimler, Michael slid into his Merc, reached for the safety belt.

Ten minutes later, stiff-legged with cold, Elsa followed.

At the Knightsbridge flat, mourners were offered sherry, tea and sandwiches. The minor duchess drank three glasses of Bristol Cream and embarrassed everyone by patting Nicky's cheek in farewell and commiserating on the loss of her father. When the guests had gone, Mr. Mayhew read the will. Rupert had cousins in South Africa and Barbara Heydon in the States but few close relatives in England: only his widow and his daughter were present—and Michael. They sat around the dining-room table, sherry copitas in front of them, the two women pointedly ignoring each other. Nicky started to smoke and then stubbed the cigarette out with an abrupt, nervous movement. In the background Mr. Greenbaum rubbed his hands. Mr. Mayhew had flu, but it was only at Elsa's insistence that he had allowed Jonathan Sterling to deputize for him at the funeral, and he began to read with a rigid determination sustained by frequent mouthfuls of tea and a handkerchief laced with eucalyptus. There were several pauses while he coughed, and blew his nose, and fiddled with his spectacles. Nicky was assailed by a sudden fancy that he would die before the will was read and in consequence the whole document would be mysteriously invalidated.

The will had been made at the time of Rupert's second marriage. Michael was nominated to take over the architectural practice; Rupert's share passed to Elsa as a sleeping partner. Mr. Mayhew, almost tearfully, had begged him to leave her something, and perhaps as an ironic souvenir of her abortive degree Rupert had chosen this—the symbol of his success to remind her for all time of her own failure. But the decision might equally have been made by chance, the product of little deliberation and little interest. Where architecture was concerned, Rupert believed in the principle of "Après moi, le déluge."

Everything else was left to Nicky.

Even though she had been expecting it, Elsa sat cold and silent. Her father's voice out of the past could not hurt her, not while her fingers still ached with the memory of his last handclasp, and his suffering eyes still seemed to burn into hers. It was Nicky who was responsible for this final indignity, Nicky who had schemed and lied and cheated, Nicky who had taken from him health and strength, manhood and fatherhood, love and liberty and life itself, and who now robbed him of all that was left. To Elsa, it was not she who was deprived but Rupert: she saw her stepmother as a scavenger on a battlefield, picking over the body of a fallen king for his crown and signet. And there she sat, barely a yard away, gold-digger and corpse-robber, a little tell-tale colour coming and going in her normally colourless cheek. Even the lipstick that shaped her small mouth was a part of the pickings.

Gradually, Elsa became aware of the silence: she realized the others were awaiting her reaction. She got to her feet. This time, unlike her words earlier in the graveyard, she spoke to be heard.

"You thief," she said, very slowly and distinctly. "You cheap, shoddy, lying, sneaking little thief."

Nicky gazed at her, fists clenching with rage or nerves. She remembered a girl who had come to a dinner-party dripping with diamonds, a girl who had everything yet who begrudged her anything. She remembered a rejected olive branch, and five hundred dollars that now seemed not generosity but condescension, an act of lofty charity from an aristocrat to a peasant.

She said: "Take me to court!"

"I will," Elsa retorted, colder than ever. "But not for this."

She drove herself home, shaking from the chill or the horrors of the day. Anthony had left a message on her answering machine, but she didn't want to see him, not yet. She went to bed early and dreamed vividly. She was back in the churchyard of St. Mary-the-Whore, and it was spring. The snow melted before her eyes. The funeral flowers took root and flourished, clawing their way across the graves, entwining the standing stones. A bell rang in a bell-tower that seemed to be distorted into a maze of interlocking perspectives like an Escher print. On Rupert's grave, the green coverlet of turf heaved and broke, crumbling into earth. Spears of torn wood thrust up from below. And suddenly there was Rupert, springing up like the flowers, shaking the crumbs of soil from his hair. Hair no longer grey but tawny—limbs agile and strong—cheeks tanned. Only his eyes held the same fierce light they had held when he was a cripple trapped in his sickbed—eyes fixed on Elsa, as they had been then, in a hungry, angry stare. He leapt towards her across the graves, arms outstretched. In her dream, she was frightened. His embrace gripped her like a boa-constrictor; she was crushed against his chest; she could not breathe. She struggled, but it was no use. She thought: he's suffocating me . . .

She woke up. Her face was half buried in the pillow, and in her restlessness she had wound the duvet around her body so tightly that she could hardly move. When she had disentangled herself, she found she was too alert and unsettled for sleep. She needed someone to talk to, someone who would not mind being disturbed in the middle of the night. Of course, she could always call Anthony. Anthony would listen and sympathize, come round if she asked. But then, he would do the same for a drunk who wanted company, or a would-be suicide, or anyone lonely and desperate enough who knew his phone number. Besides, there were too many things she could not say to Anthony. Who was there whom she could turn to, whom she could talk to . . . ?

She picked up the phone and pressed out Michael's number. Although it was a long time since she had used it, she still had it by heart.

"Hello."

She noted with a strange satisfaction that he sounded sleepy and cross. "Michael?"

"Who else?"

"It's me. Elsa."

"I *do* know your voice. What do you want?"

"I had a bad dream."

"I'm not surprised. I was having one myself, till you disturbed me."

Elsa said: "Sorry." She did not sound sorry.

"Why didn't you call what's-his-name?"

"Anthony." She didn't want to explain. "I don't know. Because I called you."

"Well, I'm awake now. Tell me about this dream."

"I expect it'll sound very stupid," Elsa said, suddenly reluctant.

"Tell me."

"I was back in the cemetery, and the grave opened, and my father jumped out and hugged me. And I was afraid. That's all."

"Symbolic," Michael remarked cryptically.

"And when I woke up I was sort of fighting the bedclothes, and my face was squashed in the pillow so I couldn't breathe."

"That probably explains it," Michael said, which was what she wanted him to say. But his tone was unmistakably dry and she wasn't reassured.

"Sorry I bothered you," she said hastily. "Goodnight."

"Elsa—"

"Yes?"

"Stop panicking. You wanted to talk, didn't you? So talk to me."

"I hate telephones."

"How about lunch? We ought to discuss your connection with

the practice, anyway. Meet me at the office—tomorrow at one. All right?"

"All right," Elsa said, adding belatedly: "Thanks."

They went to the same restaurant, had they but known it, to which Rupert had taken Nicky on their first meeting. Michael ordered cassoulet to keep the cold out, and burgundy. Elsa cut the fat off a lamb noisette. Michael noticed that much of her usual antagonism was gone, forgotten, maybe, in the chaos of other obsessions. He wondered if it would be amusing to try and revive it.

They scarcely mentioned the practice.

"It will give you a good income," Michael said. "If you need it."

"Mm? Oh—yes. I don't know. My grandmother left me plenty of money."

Money, Michael reflected, a little wryly. The secret of unworldliness. She could throw away the lot on a point of honour, because she didn't really know what it meant to be without. He knew. It was a long time ago, but he knew.

He went on, testing her: "What about the rest of your father's fortune? You seemed to feel strongly enough about that—yesterday."

"I don't want it for *myself*." She looked startled that he needed to ask. "I just don't want *her* to have it."

"So I inferred. You called her a thief—and other things."

There was a pause. "You heard that."

"Yes, I heard."

This time, the pause stretched from seconds into minutes. A waiter replenished the wine in their glasses. Elsa took a morsel of lamb, chewed, swallowed. Michael waited. "Maybe I was wrong," she said at last, voice and expression curiously blank. "Maybe she didn't actually kill him. But she *caused* his death. She brought on his stroke, one way or another. She nursed him and coddled him and mocked him and tortured him—"

"How do you know?" Michael was carefully noncommittal. "Have you any evidence?"

"Have I *evidence*?" Elsa's eyes flared with anger.

"That she tortured him."

"I don't need evidence! Do you think it wasn't a torture to him, to be imprisoned in that useless body, unable to control his own physical functions? Do you think it wasn't torture, to be deprived of all communication, cut off from those who loved him, walled in on every side by her sweet smile and saintly demeanour? Rupert mustn't be disturbed, Rupert mustn't be upset, Rupert must remain effectively bound and gagged and helpless—at her mercy. *Mercy.* She wouldn't know what it meant. She has a boyfriend—did you know?"

"No," Michael said. "Who—?"

Elsa shook her head: she seemed to feel she had said too much. "Anyway," she continued, "she *might* have killed him. She had everything to gain—her freedom, his money. And it would have been very easy. Only a quick autopsy would have detected poison; digoxin doesn't stay in the system. I asked a doctor friend of mine."

"Were there any pills gone from the bottle after he was found?" Michael enquired.

"I thought of that. His nurse said the bottle was practically full, but Nicky could have topped it up with aspirin or something. And later, *she* was the one who threw it away."

"Inconclusive," Michael said, sounding slightly bored.

"All right I can't prove it. I can't prove anything. Still . . ."

"Have you tried?"

Elsa gazed at him, uncomprehending. "What do you mean?"

"Well," Michael said slowly, as though selecting not only his words but his thoughts with caution, "it does just occur to me that if you really suspect—whatever you suspect—you could try getting a professional to look into it. It might be a waste of time, but it's better than speculation."

"A professional?"

"A private detective."

Elsa's lip lifted in a faint grimace of distaste. She said: "I thought private detectives were only for sordid things—divorce and so on. Not for—"

"Not for murder and mayhem among the privileged classes?" His shadow-smile mocked her. "Isn't gold-digging sordid? Isn't adultery sordid? I should imagine there are some fairly sordid details in Nicky's past, too. She's hardly a beginner. I'm only surprised no one ever suggested checking up on her before. Your lawyer, for instance."

"Mr. Mayhew? Oh—oh no. No, he wouldn't. He's very old-fashioned and stuffy. He'd be horrified at any hint of scandal. And once Father and Nicky were married, I supposed he saw it as a *fait accompli*. Anyhow, he'd visualize private detectives as—sort of seedy and dishonest. He wouldn't have anything to do with people like that."

"Like you," Michael murmured.

Elsa ignored the gibe. They had reached the coffee stage and she stirred the liquid in her cup pensively, although it contained neither milk nor sugar. Eventually she said: "If I wanted to hire a private detective, how would I go about it?"

"Yellow Pages," Michael suggested.

"I might get the wrong kind," Elsa said. "I might get—someone seedy and dishonest. How could I tell?"

"I daresay I could arrange it for you," Michael offered. He had always intended making the offer, in the end. "Someone honest and—er—seedless. Don't worry. I'll fix it."

"I rely on you," Elsa said, adding without visible humour: "I don't trust you, but I rely on you."

"What about Anthony?" Michael knew it was unwise, possibly unkind, but he could not resist asking.

"I—love him."

"I see." As ever, Elsa thought, he saw too much. "You love him, but you don't trust him either—or rely on him."

That finished the conversation. "I have to get back to the office," Michael remarked, waving a hand for the bill. He had a meeting with the surveyor doing the report on Stallibrass House, but he did not mention it. He had had more than enough of the Stallibrass connection.

"About the detective," Elsa said, hesitant and chilly, "you'll call me?"

"I'll call you."

Afterwards, in the taxi home, Elsa thought about Anthony. She had arranged to see him that evening, partly because such a meeting was long overdue, partly as a sort of insurance against any reawakening of sexual attraction for Michael. The image of Anthony's beauty would surely keep all such feelings at a distance. In the event, she had been too preoccupied with other matters to experience any conscious lust. Only now, when he had gone, did she find herself wondering why she had wanted to see Michael, and what their discussion had really been for. "I rely on you," she had said. I need you. Anthony was an ideal to which she could aspire, a fairy-tale prince, a thorn in her heart, a love sharpened with pain, strengthened with doubt.

She longed for him, dreamed of him—but she did not need him. The realization filled her with a sudden certainty: because she did not need him, he would never truly belong to her, never make her happy. Anthony was a yearning that could not be fulfilled, another in a long list of fruitless loves.

She tried to push the thought away, but it persisted.

Anthony Stallibrass had dealt with the problem of his exceptional good looks long ago, largely by ignoring it. There had been a moment of revelation, somewhere in his teens, but his sensitive soul had recoiled from it in horror: he did not want empty adoration, satisfied vanity, a swollen ego. He wanted to be loved with discrimination, for the fine temper of his spirit rather than the fine chiselling of his profile. And since no woman ever told him the truth he was able to fool himself, at least on the surface. As he grew older, the delusions of a confused adolescent became a part of his creed: where a medieval monk might have gone in for sackcloth and flagellation, Anthony cultivated little martyrdoms, wanton indulgences in self-denial. He shaved with a cut-throat razor, rarely had his hair trimmed, bought his clothing in jumble sales, patched and re-patched his jeans. All of which did his appearance no disservice at all, only adding a certain macho carelessness to the perfection of feature and bone. "He's so *sweet*," women whispered. "He *doesn't know* . . ." He had to work at not knowing, every day, every hour. Lovers came and went in his life in a routine that he fondly believed to be normal: he began each affair with liking, attraction and tenderness, and ended with regret, tenderness and the anguish of inflicting pain. In bed, he was always gentle and considerate; he would have been gentle and considerate with a whore. He remembered Diana, sometimes, with a vague sense of guilt, not for her death but for the inadequacy of his own grief. Because of her, he avoided the drift into involvement, reluctant to offer any woman only a tiny piece of his heart. But underneath, there was an unacknowledged awareness: the conviction that when he wanted it, love would be there—the certainty that he would never be rejected—the mystery of how such a rejection might feel.

Elsa had not called him over Christmas, had refused to weep on his shoulder when her father died. Other girlfriends had reached for that shoulder on the death of hamsters or fifteenth cousins, for a broken ornament, an overcooked roast. Elsa, faced with a real tragedy, had turned away. It was a novel sensation for Anthony. He even began to wonder if this might be love: this faint bewilderment, this frustration, this desire to hold and kiss and comfort, baulked—for once—of its object. His elation when she finally telephoned and made a date startled him. He had always felt Elsa was special—but then, he tried very hard to feel that every girl was special, in her own way; he abhorred the concept of casual relationships, of replacing one woman with another as if he were a businessman changing his car. Fortunately, Elsa's uniqueness had required little effort on his part: she was Diana's sister, he had known her a long time, he saw her past shadowed with tragedy, her beauty as an enchanting transformation. (He was not afraid to admire beauty in others.) And in the recesses of her spirit he sensed hidden sorrows, all the more alluring for being unspecified. Anthony was invariably attracted by hidden sorrows.

She arrived at the house which he shared with three others (including Cathleen Mirza) at around five o'clock. His room was in the basement; his bed, a mattress on the floor. A small electric fire gave out insufficient heat, its red-gold bars glowing with misleading fervour in the dim light. Elsa sat beside it, keeping her jacket on. The white-washed walls were hung with posters, scattered cushions did the work of chairs, a strip of thick curtain over the window shut out the snow-pale evening and the most vicious of the draughts. There was a bookcase sagging under the weight of too many books and a conspicuous gap beside it which had once contained a music-centre, Anthony's only luxury. He had sold it to help a single parent just off amphetamines to furnish her new flat, and now all he had was a useless pile of records and tapes, with the Messiaen his mother had given him for Christmas, and which he had never been able to play, on top. Whenever he spoke to her he had to remember not to mention the matter, since he knew she would insist on replacing the music-centre immediately. It was very difficult, he thought bitterly, for the rich to achieve true poverty and self-sacrifice. His conscience had only to look the other way for a second and the gap would be filled, the chords and discords of Messiaen would reverberate through the basement room, blotting out, for a little while, the dilemmas of a bleak reality. He wondered if Elsa would notice the absence of the music-centre, but although her gaze flickered over the pile of records she did not appear to register the anomaly.

Elsa was thinking, as always, how brave he was to live here, how *committed*, how admirable. And how uncomfortable. She could not have endured it, not in the grip of winter, with only the ineffectual fire and the passionate slogans of lost causes to warm her. The songs lied, she reflected. Love doesn't keep you warm.

Anthony plugged in the kettle to make coffee, opened a bottle of wine.

"I missed you," he said. He sounded as if he meant it.

Her heart turned a quick somersault. "Did you?" She kept her voice nonchalant. Her suspicions of him seemed almost ridiculous. Almost.

"Why didn't you answer my calls?"

"Oh, I don't know. After—after it happened, I just wanted to be alone. I'm used to being alone."

He said awkwardly: "It must have been dreadful for you." He wanted to sympathize with her, to ease her pain, but somehow he couldn't. She looked so cold and untouchable.

"Dreadful," she repeated. She wanted him to hold her, to kiss away all her doubts and fears and sorrows. But she could not ask, dared not trust him. Her feelings seemed to ebb and flow in a tumult of conflicting currents, like the waves of different seas fighting one another for the same ragged shore. She was tossed upwards, sucked under, pulled hither and thither by impulse and emotion. She could not let her expression change because she was afraid of what it might betray.

Anthony gave her the coffee, which was hot enough to scald her tongue. She clung to the mug for warmth. Suddenly, she felt it was the only warm thing in the room.

"Before your father died," he said, "there was something wrong, something you couldn't tell me. Can't you tell me now?" And, when she didn't answer: "Was it—seeing him? Was that what upset you?"

"Let's not talk about it," she said.

"You ought to talk about it." His manner was both gentle and insistent. "Get it out of your system. If you bottle things up inside they fester, like poison in a wound. Yes, I know it's a cliché, but it still applies. You really will feel better if you can . . . unburden yourself."

He's said it before, she thought. A hundred times, with a hundred unhappy people. I'm one of a queue.

He would say it to Nicky, if she were here . . .

She said: "I won't discuss it. I want my burdens. They're *mine.*"

"Elsa." Unexpectedly, he looked hurt. She had not realized she could hurt him. "Please, Elsa . . ."

She put down her coffee-mug. "I'm hungry."

"We could go for a Chinese. Or some spaghetti."

"Let's go to my flat," Elsa said. "My kitchen; you cook. I've got eggs and things." Anthony was a good cook.

"All right." He was surprised—normally, she followed his suggestions—but he didn't mind. "I'll bring the wine."

At Elsa's flat Anthony cooked an omelette, Elsa drank the wine. Afterwards, they left the washing-up in the sink and sat down in front of the fire: an immaculate fire of artificial logs licked by real flames. No wash, no smoke, no fuss. Central heating enfolded them. Outside, half-thawed snow froze into grey ridges on the pavements. Anthony was too warm and much too comfortable, but this once it did not trouble him: he had other things to think of.

"I was worried about you," he told her simply.

"I'm sorry. I didn't mean you to worry. Nobody ever worried about me much. Only Barbara . . ."

"Well, I worried. I always will. I don't just want you to tell me your problems for *your* benefit—I want to know you, to know all about you. I want to *understand.* I'm not some fly-by-night lover who's only interested in your body: I care for you. I think—I care very much. Elsa, do you—could you—like me?"

His dark eyes pleaded, compelled, bewitched her. She saw longing there, ardour, a shadow of doubt. The doubt was the most bewitching of all.

"Could you live here?" she asked, after a long pause.

"Here?" He looked round at the imitation fire, the expensive furnishings, the curtains hanging in immobile folds over the draughtless windows. He didn't say any more because it wasn't necessary. The expectation that had hovered briefly between them faded from the atmosphere, leaving only the central heating.

They finished the wine.

"It's my immortal soul," he said at length, half flippant, half desperate. If this was love, this thing he was about to lose, this twisting pain inside, he could not just walk away. He owed her more than tenderness or guilt. If this was love. "You can't live my life and I can't live yours. There's no way to compromise. You're asking me to abandon everything I believe in. It's too much. Please understand."

She nodded. She didn't need him, but she wanted him— wanted him with an aching hunger that seemed, in that moment, to fill up the world.

"I'm so sorry," he said. And abruptly, violently: "I'm so *fucking* sorry."

Suddenly, she did understand. In that one savage word she heard a self-hatred and hopelessness to echo her own—a lifetime's struggle to escape that which could not be escaped, to reach a goal which could never be reached. To become *someone else* . . .

She said: "It doesn't matter," mainly for something to say. The second's intuition vanished, leaving an after-taste like a reminder of her own failures.

"I'll always be your friend," he assured her.

He means it, she thought. He, alone among men. Poor Anthony.

When he went, he kissed her with restraint, promised to call. Elsa closed the door and went back into the living-room. She sat down on the carpet beside the fire, clutching a cushion to her stomach, rocking slightly to and fro. Presently, she began to cry, though whether for herself or Anthony, in wretchedness or relief, she did not know.

Michael produced the detective the following week. Elsa was annoyed when he insisted on staying while she talked to the man, but she concealed it as best she could. Michael, she knew, would only be amused by causing her annoyance. She hoped he wouldn't ask about Anthony.

He did.

"How's Tony?"

"*Tony?* Oh—Anthony."

"Everything okay?"

"Yes. Yes, he's fine. I'm fine. Everything's fine. It's none of your business."

The presence of the detective put paid to further exchanges. He was a short, chubby man of fifty or so with a suit a little too small for him and a wafer-thin moustache maintaining a precarious existence on his upper lip. When he stared at her directly, he blinked a lot. He was like a shy door-to-door salesman, a furtive street-hawker, a retiring debt-collector. He looked not quite honest, not quite dishonest, neither seedy nor smart. His name was Herbert Mowle.

Elsa detailed the circumstances as concisely as possible and tried to explain what she wanted.

"Everything?" said Mr. Mowle, as one seeking after exactitude. "You want to know everything?"

"A full investigation," Michael supplied, sounding faintly bored. "Past and present."

"Everything comes expensive," said the detective.

"The practice will pay," Michael put in.

"Why?" Elsa was startled.

"Because I say so."

"This is *my* investigation—" She checked herself, turned back to Mr. Mowle. "You'll report to me," she ordered, in a would-be imperious tone that was more like temper. "I'll give you the addresses of the Knightsbridge flat and Churston Grange. I should think she'll stay in London but you'll have to go down to the country to find out about—about my father's death. My great-aunt still lives there. Mrs. Skerritt. She's senile—she has to have an attendant. And there'll be the rest of the staff."

"More gossip in the country," offered Mr. Mowle sapiently.

"Yes," Elsa said. "They say in the village she—my stepmother—has a boyfriend." Her face was expressionless. "I want her watched all the time. *All* the time."

"Expensive," murmured Mr. Mowle, by way of a leitmotif. "About her past—you got any ideas? What's the official story?"

"I don't know." Elsa hesitated. "I mean, I don't know what she told my father. She told *me* she'd been in Paris. There was something about a man who shot himself: a French politician, I think she said. But she might have made it up. She tells lies."

"Why the hell didn't you look into it before?" Michael asked, evidently exasperated.

Elsa was thrown on the defensive. "I just didn't. I didn't think about it. When she married my father—nothing else mattered. Whatever she'd done in the past, it wasn't important. Besides, I thought—I assumed she was lying. She's the kind who always lies."

"I daresay," Michael said. He glanced at the detective. "It might be true. Even liars tell the truth sometimes—it fills in the gaps between the untruths. Check it out."

Herbert Mowle looked tired, as though in anticipation. "If it's true," he said, "I'll find out."

Elsa and Michael parted, as usual, in mutual unfriendliness. Michael found himself both irritated and concerned, a disturbing mixture: Elsa rarely managed to irritate him and he despised his concern for her as weakness. He was using her obsessions to fill her mind, blinding her with her own narrow vision—yet during the meeting he had known a sudden urge to shake her till her designer jewellery rattled, to swear at her, to jerk her eyes open on a new reality. It seemed to him dangerous for someone to see so little and feel so much, out of all proportion, like the python's hug in the coil of an earthworm, or a mountain crushed into a handful of stone. He wondered, not for the first time, what had possessed her to become involved with Anthony Stallibrass. Michael had never met him, but he knew about him by way of the multiple tendrils of the grapevine, and although he told himself that Elsa's passion was merely another adolescent hangover which would pass in due course, that, too, troubled him in ways he did not like. It was easy to smile at the picture of Elsa living in idealistic penury; it was less entertaining to think of her gazing hungrily into Anthony's face, perhaps as she had once gazed at her father—an unrequited love which might yet be requited, and then who knew what monstrous form it might take? Such love would wither if returned, Michael reassured himself cynically: it was a fire that fed only on pain. Elsa would tire of Anthony. Preoccupied with her vendetta against Nicky, one obsession would gradually exclude the other. Rupert dead would be endowed with her jealousy, demanding all her love. Michael did not like it but it served his purpose.

Back at the office he found a file on his desk marked "Stallibrass." He knew its contents only too well. Seeing it he felt haunted, and confused, and full of doubt.

• • •

In Knightsbridge, Nicky sat on the Regency sofa as she had
sat every afternoon since the funeral. On the table at her side
lay the remote control for the television, two paperbacks, and
a box of chocolates. But the television was switched off, the
paperbacks thumbed and discarded, the chocolates scarcely
touched. She played with the lid of the box, which was of
quilted silk decorated with a silken rose, more perfect than any
real flower. That day, she had been shopping, and a new cocktail dress was thrown across the end of the sofa, its chiffon skirt
billowing like blood-coloured foam from a bodice heavy with
sequins. She had seen herself in it, transformed, her skin very
white and her red-gold hair shrieking at the colour as if in
defiance—utterly different from the woman in the demure costume of devoted wifehood or the black glamour of mourning.
But where was the party? where the fiddlers to play for her?
where the dance to spin her away? She imagined returning to
Paris, a beautiful widow protected by her wealth and her famous surname, going from nightclub to nightclub in her flaming dress, the sparkle of her sequins mingling with the sparkle
of champagne. Her eyes were made of diamond and her lips of
coral, she was Nana, Angélique, Madame de Pompadour: Paris
was at her feet. But her daydreams had grown thin and tired
with repetition, and there was only the unworn dress tumbled
over the sofa, and the greying afternoon. Outside, what was
left of the snow thawed or froze according to its mood. Briefly
she almost wished she was back under the bridge, penniless
and free, with the doorway to Adventure standing half open
before her. The wish was little more than a twinge of fancy, as
unreal as romance, but it startled her. She looked round the
room as though seeing it afresh, reminding herself how far she
had come, how much she had achieved. As long as she did not
think about it everything would be all right.

She tried very hard not to think, playing with the television
controls, opening and closing a book, grasping at the fraying
threads of her daydreams. But the thoughts kept creeping back,
infiltrating her mind. She visualized her life as a succession of
parties, into which she had sneaked like a gatecrasher, using
every trick in the game, and from which she had fled on the
stroke of midnight, her glittering clothes turned into rags for

all the world to see. But this time, she resolved dramatically, this time she was not running away. This time she was going to walk out with her head held high and her dignity intact— to walk out in her blood-red dress even though there was no pumpkin waiting, no new parties to invade. Whatever the past, whatever the future, whatever the cost . . .

The shrill of the telephone was so sudden in that silent room that her heart jumped.

She lifted the receiver on the third ring. "Hello?"

"Hello, Nikki," said a familiar voice.

He arrived at the flat twenty minutes later. He had bought her a spray of lilies, the kind that look most at home on the lid of a coffin. "Flowers," he said, "for the sorrowing widow."

They had not met since the night Rupert died. Alex had left in the early morning, before the housekeeper had brought her the news; he had not heard till the evening papers appeared. Subsequent obituaries had been lengthy, old artistic dissensions had been taken out and re-aired, old scandals resuscitated; but no one had suggested there was any mystery about the actual death. Still, Alex had stayed away. Being careful.

She offered him tea; he took whisky. "I'll pour it myself," he said, mocking her.

"What do you mean?"

"Nothing, pretty Nikki. Nothing at all. Rupert was an old man, he was sick, he died. It was all perfectly natural. And you—you are young and beautiful and rich . . . and free. I could almost marry you myself. Al-most." He toyed with the whisky but did not hurry to drink it.

"I wouldn't marry you," Nicky snapped, "even if you asked."

"I haven't asked." He raised his glass to her, smiled, drank. Their eyes met in a gaze laden with meanings that neither really wished to understand.

"A natural death," Alex reiterated. "Let us leave it at that. No police, no trouble. So convenient. So much tidier than poor Montador."

"Théo shot himself," Nicky said, caught off guard. "You know he did!"

"Of course he did."

"*Of course* he did."

"Don't worry." The provocation was gone from his manner: he sounded calm and deliberately nonchalant. "I am your friend: I won't fail you. We've always been partners, haven't we? I shall be as secret . . . as the grave."

The words left behind them a little silence which lingered uncomfortably.

"You knew about the pills," Nicky said at last, in a voice hardly more than a whisper. "You found out what they were, what they could do. You, not me. You were there and you knew what to do. You were there when he died."

The suggestion, once spoken out loud, seemed to grow huger and more terrible. In a sudden flash of clarity Nicky saw Alex's face drained of its evil laughter, yellow and crumpled like an ill-fitting mask.

"We were both there," he said slowly, significantly. "We both knew. *Both of us.*"

She neither protested nor agreed. The winter's day was fading swiftly now and she had not put on the lights: the only colour that endured in the dim room was the cocktail dress, still lying where she had left it. The two of them stared at each other unmoving, grey shadows in a grey dusk.

He said: "Was the bottle empty the next morning?"

Nicky knew without asking to what he referred. "When the nurse found it," she said, "it was nearly full. Just as it should have been."

"What did you do with it?"

"I threw it away."

Alex moved. It was only a little gesture, a quick motion of the hand, but it jarred in that stillness like something breaking. He picked up his whisky, finished it, resumed in a lighter tone: "That's that then. Whatever happened, it's over. Rupert is dead and buried and he will not rise up like Lazarus to accuse us. Let us talk of other things. What will you do now?"

"Sell, I suppose." She got up and switched a light on; the atmosphere changed completely, like Technicolor flooding into a black-and-white film. "Sell up and leave." She nearly added "gracefully," but she did not think Alex would appreciate it.

"No hurry," Alex said. "You'll have to get rid of the old woman first."

"Get rid of her?"

"Put her in a home. You can't sell a house with a sitting tenant." His mockery returned, teasing her, testing her. "There's nothing to be afraid of, Nikki. She is just a mad old woman. No one will listen to her."

"Why should they?" Nicky said, involuntarily touching her hair. "She talks nonsense."

"What about other relatives?" Alex enquired. "This daughter who was so fond of her father—will she make trouble?"

Nicky shrugged—not the exaggerated French shrug that she had learnt in Paris but an abrupt, uncertain movement. She remembered Elsa staring at her across the open grave and a whisper quieter than the fall of a snowflake. *Murderess . . .* There were moments when she imagined that wherever she went, whatever she did, that whisper would follow her, a voice on the edge of hearing, a threat on the borderline of fear. Resentment, anger, fever came in its wake. But she showed none of it to Alex. He knew too much already.

"She wants the money," Nicky volunteered. "She doesn't need it—she's stinking—but she wants it anyway. She may take me to court."

I will, but not for this.

Nicky's fists clenched, perhaps in determination. "She won't get it."

"*Le bon* Greenbaum will take care of that," Alex said easily. "You can trust him."

"How much?"

Unexpectedly, the soulless, heart-shaking smile lit his face. "As you would trust me."

He got up, helped himself to more Scotch, wandered into the kitchen for ice. Returning to his chair, he flicked the red dress with an idle finger. "What's this? Escape? Triumph? Mourning?"

It was too soon to triumph and too late to escape.

"Mourning," Nicky said.

The detective's information came in trickles, by telephone and by post, as tantalizing to Elsa as tidbits before a feast. She learnt the available facts of Nicky's childhood, the present circumstances of her mother, her brief encounter with the police. She learnt of Montador's political career, the official and unofficial accounts of his death. Herbert Mowle sent her copies of newspaper cuttings and even photographs of Isabelle and she pored over them, drawing the wrong conclusions, like someone with a few fragments of a jigsaw puzzle most of which has long been scattered. She learnt that Rupert's male nurse suffered from a youthful adoration of Nicky and believed his patient's demise had been a merciful release. She learnt that Aunty Grizzle had got out of her room on the night it happened and drifted round the house, seeing little or nothing. She learnt that village gossip was divided between adherents of the tragic widow and a few loyalists who claimed that the poor daughter had always had a raw deal.

After about a month Herbert Mowle said he had something special for her and proposed a meeting at her flat. Perhaps because the practice was paying his fee, he also notified Michael. Elsa decided not to mind. She had seen Anthony two or three times in recent weeks: after their abortive love scene he seemed more beautiful and more painfully unattainable than ever. There was no need for her to be disturbed because of Michael.

She was not the sort of person who usually noticed such things but it occurred to her that he was looking very tired, his grey-fair skin somehow greyer and lines dragging at his eyes. His sleeves were rolled up for work and she could see the hard swell of muscle in his forearm and the veins bulging outwards as though he was permanently in the grip of tension. Yet his hands lay limp, the fingers uncurled—not the long, tapering fingers generally attributed to the artist but blunt, calloused and ink-stained, evidently familiar with both the drawing-board and the building-site. She wondered idly what Anthony's hands were like and realized she didn't know. She caught herself thinking that it was he, no doubt, who had the long, tapering fingers of the artist: such was the luck with which he had been burdened.

Michael said hello; she said hello; Herbert Mowle blinked and got on with his report. The chances of proving murder, he said, were virtually non-existent. Obviously he was determined to start with the bad news. "It could have been done," he explained. "That's the problem. It would have been almost too easy. She might have upped the dose of digoxin slightly over a period of three or four weeks or lost her head and given him a whopping great overdose. Mashed in his food, shaken up in his drink—he might even have simply swallowed what he was told like a little lamb. Sick people do sometimes." He sniffed dubiously; Elsa imagined his flimsy moustache waving and twitching on a scent like antennae. "Nothing left in the body now," he went on. "No point in digging him up. His heart was a bit dodgy and it did for him. Just what the doctor ordered."

"I would have requested an autopsy," Elsa said, "only I was told it would be useless."

"Too easy," the detective repeated. "It's a crime, making murder as easy as that. Temptation. Seems to me she might be a sucker for temptation, Lady Van Leer."

"Did you find out about the boyfriend?" Elsa asked. Her throat tightened as she said it, even though she knew her fears must be false.

Mr. Mowle nodded, his eyelids fluttering like a butterfly's wings. "Followed him from her flat. He's a Frenchie—a chum of hers from Paris days, at a guess. Name of Alexandre Fauvelle. I had him checked up at the other end. Nasty bit of goods. Got a record—possession of cannabis. Suspected of being a pusher. Killed someone with his motorbike when he was too young for a licence. Daddy's rich but doesn't want to know: threw him out when he was eighteen. Plenty of funds but not too clear where they come from. My contact says he lives in one of those picturesque slums, all art galleries and restaurants. Got his own flat. Don't know Paris too well myself but apparently that means money."

"Is he very dark?" Elsa asked in a voice which made Michael look sharply at her.

"Black hair. Black eyes. Sallow. Not too tall. Ugly little runt if you ask me, but women go for them." He spoke with a touch of actual bitterness, but Elsa ignored this potential sidelight on his personal life.

"Could he have done it?" she demanded. "Was he there—in Churston—at the right time?"

"Maybe. The gardener lives down the lane: remembers hearing a motorbike very early in the morning. Fauvelle has a bike over here. He's staying in a grubby little bedsit in London. Downmarket. Might be broke. Might be dangerous. They could be in it together—or separately. He could be blackmailing her. Should've thought blackmail was more his style than murder, but you never know with the French." Regretfully, he reverted to his original point. "You'll never prove a thing. Put a hundred detectives on it for ten years: it won't make any difference. She's guilty of adultery but that doesn't mean she's guilty of anything else—it just gives her an excuse for looking guilty. As for him, he's careful. Slippery customer. Slide through a net like an eel." He added, rather unnecessarily: "Can't stand Frenchies."

"Is that the lot?" Michael asked brusquely.

"Not quite. Been saving the best part. Got something else from Paris." He paused, twirled in vain at his insubstantial moustache, went on. "Seems she got married while she was there. Not Fauvelle: another one. Lots of men in her life, Lady Van Leer. This one's an Eytie. Bummed off to Milan and left her flat. Got his address somewhere." He groped through a couple of pockets and produced a folded piece of paper. "Here we are. Stephane Maglioli." He pronounced it Maggy-lowly. "That's him. Thing is, far as I can tell she never got a divorce."

"What?" Elsa's cry was very faint.

"No record of one in France or Italy. Nothing here. We'll have to talk to him, of course, but I thought I should report to you first. If it's true—well, your father wasn't married, so no widow to inherit. You're home and dry. You can't hook her for murder but you can sink her with bigamy."

Michael laughed—a tired sort of laugh that wore out in the middle. Elsa managed only a smile. There was a sudden flush under her make-up but she was very quiet.

"Like catching Al Capone for tax evasion," Mr. Mowle offered.

"Well done, Elliott," Michael said, getting to his feet. "If that's all, I'm going back to the office. Miss Van Leer can take it from here. Send in your account."

Elsa saw him to the door. He paused on the mat, surveying her with a sort of grim reluctance, his mouth tightening on words that did not wish to be said. He spoke softly, but his voice grated. "Call in the lawyers. Mayhew will sort out the mess for you. Get back to your own life. Get back to bloody Anthony if that's what you want. Don't keep pushing a murder you can never prove. You've got the means to defeat her now: she won't get the loot she killed him for—*if* she killed him, which isn't certain. Let the lawyers finish it. Leave Nicky alone."

"I'll deal with her," Elsa said, "in my own way."

Michael hesitated. Her hand was on the brass knob, closing the door against him. Afterwards, he wondered if things would have been different if he had stayed. But there was work on his desk demanding his attention, a session with clients in half an hour. He went.

Back in the living-room, Elsa studied the piece of paper with Stephane's address.

"A lot depends on the wording of Sir Rupert's will," Mr. Mowle was saying. " 'My wife, Nicola' is pretty specific. Just 'Nicola' would give her a bit of leverage in court. But she hasn't any money of her own: if she fights the case and loses she can't pay the costs. Anyway, you can go to gaol for bigamy. She's in plenty of hot water however you look at it."

Elsa didn't appear to be listening. "Have you contacted this man?" she asked.

"Not yet. Told you, thought I should report first. We can get a deposition from him this week."

"No." Elsa's tone startled him. "We'll bring him over here."

"Over here?"

"Tell him—tell him I'll make it worth his while. Isn't that the right phrase? If he isn't rich he'll be greedy. He isn't rich, is he?"

"Well—"

"If he was rich she'd have hung on to him. He's poor and he's greedy. He *must* be. Get him over here. And . . . bill me for the ticket, not the practice." Her hand closed on the crumpled paper as if it were the key to Bluebeard's chamber. "I'll talk to him."

Elsa rang the office before visiting the new Cable Star building, taking care not to speak to Michael. She was "just interested," she said. After all, the practice supplied her with an income and was in some part her responsibility. No, she didn't want a guided tour. Only a quiet look round. It didn't matter if Michael heard about it later, she reasoned, as long as he didn't insist on coming with her now.

This was the Dockland project which had been on Rupert's desk before his stroke—a project Michael had subsequently taken over. For him, it was a vital testing ground. He had impressed the client but he also had to impress the world, to show that Rupert's firm could survive without Rupert, to prove that he himself was more than just the copycat legatee of the Van Leer ideology. Seeing it for the first time, Elsa was disconcerted. She had chosen this venue for her plan in memory of that night on the South Bank when she had contemplated suicide, and subconsciously she had been expecting a sister to the Technico building, a place of uncompromising outlines, zigzagging stairs, uniform windows. Instead, she saw a long curving façade with a concave roof that dipped in the centre and sloped upwards to the towers at either end—towers designed not to dominate the skyline but to share it. Where the scaffolding had been removed walls interceded with windows and a wide archway sheltered the main entrance. Elsa stared at it for several minutes before she realized the truth. There was nothing of her father here. This was all Michael, only Michael. Her father's designs must have been screwed up and thrown away years ago, even as the paralysis first seized on his body. The anger which filled her was so deep and so violent it left her feeling physically shaken. *"Et tu, Brute?"* she murmured, with a bitterness that robbed the phrase of any flippancy, thinking that she had never trusted Michael, never believed in his loyalty. In that instant she saw the whole building as an act of destruction: the destruction of Rupert Van Leer. And Michael had made her part of it. He had ravished not only her body but her spirit, inching his way into her feelings, stealing her from her father. Even now she found it all too easy to turn to him. This was the final betrayal—a betrayal in which she too had been ensnared, without her knowledge, against her will. If she could have vomited up her own heart she would have done so.

It was some while before she remembered her real reason for being there.

Nicky arrived at the rendezvous around two o'clock on Saturday. The gate in the security fence was unlocked: inside, the earth was raw; a plank vibrated underfoot; huge piles of blocks, mysterious lengths of metal tubing, a motionless cement-mixer were scattered around like the relics of long-dead dinosaurs. The building rose up ahead of her, the vast inverted arc of the roof silhouetted against a white-washed sky. Passing the section still criss-crossed with scaffolding she came to the entrance, halting on the steps for a moment to look up at the glassless windows through which she could see the skeleton of endless rooms and grey faces of unpainted plaster. There was no sign of life. The shadow of the archway was cold; beyond, there were doorways without doors, stairs without stair-rails, passages interlocking with passages, all identical, all filled with the same chill air and pallid daylight, like something in a maze. The grumble of traffic was reduced to a murmur in the background: Nicky imagined her footsteps echoing down the stairwell and pattering ahead of her on every untrodden floor. "If there was someone here," she thought, "surely I would hear them. I would hear them *breathe*." But there was only the tapping of her new heels, and the squeak of her leather shoulderbag, and the thump of her heart.

She climbed to the top floor, seven storeys up. Turn right, the caller had said, and keep walking. She hadn't recognized the voice; it had been too muffled. A handkerchief over the receiver, perhaps; she had read about such things. There had been no hints or threats; just instructions. "Come." Nicky came. Curiosity, fascination, fear drew her. And now there was nothing, only the strangeness of this hollow place, a shell fretted with holes through which cold and light and sound travelled unhindered. She entered a large room with three tall windows rising from floor to ceiling; outside, she glimpsed a filigree of scaffolding cutting off the pale afternoon. This room was darker than the rest, barred and patched with shadow. She stopped for a minute, as if some noise, too slight for certainty, had fallen on her ears. But she was alone, quite alone. She was almost sure of it.

The figure of a man appeared in the third window virtually without warning. She knew he had been waiting for her, he had come to find her just as she had come to find him, but still, it was a shock. He loomed black and featureless against the light. She moved towards him, to see better, and experienced a further surprise. Whatever she had expected, it was not this. A man of thirtyish, running to fat, his jeans fitting too tightly across his plump thighs, a bomber jacket billowing over his paunch. A heavy jowl blurred his jaw-line, his mouth was full and sulky, his thick curls cut and blow-dried as if he had just come from the hairdresser. Somehow, she knew that his collar was dirty. His attitude suggested a false bravado, masking apprehension. Her fear vanished. She was a yard away from him before recognition came.

She whispered incredulously: "Steph?"

Of course. The bravado was familiar, the sensuous mouth, the dirty collar. Those were the long-lashed brown eyes, now sagging in little pouches, which she had once found so melting. And looking at the bouffant hair-style, she thought: he's made an effort. She was conscious of horror at what a few years could do to a man, relief that she had not been there to see it.

He said: "Come outside."

"Why?" She stepped obediently through the window, resting a gloved hand on the frame. She felt small and elegant beside his fleshy coarseness. "What are you doing here? What's this all about?"

He glanced round nervously although there was obviously no one else there. Then he turned back to Nicky, studying her with a mixture of resentment and admiration.

He said: "You've done all right."

She hugged her fur collar close against her cheek in unconscious imitation of a picture of Garbo she had seen somewhere. She could imagine what he saw, what he was thinking. He had deserted her in ignominy and now he would have given anything to get her back. And anything he had to give would not be enough.

He reached out to touch her but his hand fell back, as though her very glamour defeated him. "You've changed your hair," he said, searching desperately for faults. "I liked it better blonde."

"Oh?" Nicky did not care.

"You look . . . so different."

"So do you."

The phrase slipped out before she could check it, cruel as truth. He flinched as if she had struck him. She saw the latent rancour bubbling to the surface in his expression; his mouth worked between petulance and spite.

"*I* didn't marry money. I didn't screw my way into *la dolce vita*. I've done an honest job for an honest wage. It may not be much but at least I'm not a paid whore!"

"You haven't done so badly," Nicky retorted. "Plenty of beer and spaghetti. With that stomach I shouldn't think you've seen your prick in years—not that there was ever much to see."

His face twitched with conflicting passions: the effect was both horrible and ludicrous. Restraint won; his eyes shifted from side to side as though he suspected some unseen auditor might creep up and witness his shame. He said: "I didn't come here to argue with you. All that is in the past. If you didn't excite me that was your problem. Maybe you did better by your next husband." If there was a slight emphasis on "husband" Nicky missed it. "I came here to talk business."

"What business?"

He repeated, deliberately: "You've done all right."

"I've been lucky."

"*Si*." He made the word into a hiss. "You have been lucky and I haven't. Perhaps—perhaps it is time for you to share some of your luck."

This was what she had anticipated. Blackmail. But after Alex, Stephane was child's play. "Why should I?" she said in a voice as cool as the air. "Rupert is dead. You can't tell him anything. You're too late." And, the ultimate insult: "Sorry, Steph."

"I know he's dead." Stephane made an impatient movement. "I'm not stupid. I hear things. He's dead and you inherited all his money."

"Yes."

"As his widow."

"Yes."

His smile grew slowly, a mirthless grin full of evil relish. "Only you're not his widow."

"What do you mean?"

"You're not his widow." The grin widened. This was his moment, his triumph. Stephane had known few triumphs. He savoured it like the first taste of caviar. "I never divorced you. When you married him, you committed a crime. You are a criminal. Maybe you committed another crime, when he died so conveniently. All for nothing. I have only to reappear, and it will be—all—for nothing."

For a whole minute she stood without speaking. In the spinning panic that filled her brain she was aware of only one thing: she must not lose control. The ground beneath her had become a quicksand; but somehow she must stay calm, stay sane, think clearly. She could not think at all.

"I don't . . . understand. You said you would get a divorce. You said it in your letter."

She had never heard from him. With a divorce, there would have been forms to fill in, papers to sign. She had assumed it was over and had forgotten him completely.

"I *said*." He shrugged. He was relaxed now, leaning against the metal rail. "I didn't bother."

She thought. What shall I do? *What shall I do?*

Possibilities flashed through her mind—Mr. Greenbaum—Alex. Alex might stand by her. If it was worth his while.

She said: "How much?"

"Depends." He was settling into the role of blackmailer with ease. "You want to be a rich widow. I just want to be rich. Perhaps something can be arranged. I understand the late Sir Rupert left a lot of money."

"How much?"

He ignored her. He seemed to be producing a speech long thought out, carefully rehearsed. He enunciated each statement as if he were listening to himself. Although he would have been more at ease in French they were talking mainly in English; it did not occur to Nicky to wonder why. "You have done a great deal to get what you want. It was very well timed, your husband's death—your husband who was not your husband. They say he was an invalid, and you gave him his medicine. You gave him his medicine every night. Too much medicine can be poison. They say—"

"Who says?" Her long nails, painted silver, dug into her fur. The threat had changed shape: reverted to something more familiar and more dreadful. Like a nightmare where the scenes alter without meaning or sequence, plunging her from one horror to the next. "Who says?"

"Nobody." Stephane seemed to be jolted; his answer came too fast. "Anybody. I told you, I'm not stupid. I read newspapers. I hear rumours. I can guess. Anyone can guess."

He was standing quite close to her and suddenly she smelled his sweat. She wondered why he was sweating when it was so cold. But he had always sweated easily.

"I know you," he went on. "You wanted money—I remember, when we met, that was all you talked about. Dreams and schemes. Not just a little money but lots of it. You wanted to be *filthy* rich." His own frustrated greed sounded in every word. "If you couldn't make it you would steal it or screw for it—or kill for it. Isn't that true, Nicky? He was a sick old man and you killed him, bit by bit. You caused his stroke and you nursed him to death. Isn't that true?"

Incredibly, she saw fear in his eyes—as though he had terrified himself with the rashness of his accusations. She seized on it like a drowning man clutching a broken lifebelt.

"What if it is?" Despair had made her reckless. "No one can prove it. No one can prove anything." And again: "How much do you want?"

He swallowed. "If something is worth killing for," he said, "then it's worth a lot—isn't it?"

She waited.

From inside his jacket he produced a long envelope. "Our marriage certificate. Make me an offer."

In the chaos of that moment, the proposition appeared suddenly, miraculously straightforward. She forgot there would be other records of the wedding, other witnesses. It seemed to her that she had merely to destroy a piece of paper and she would be free. She held out her hand. "Let me see."

What followed was never very clear in her mind. He snatched the envelope away; she grabbed for it. And then somehow she lost her balance, or her foot slipped on the icy planks, and she fell, grasping his jacket for support, dragging him with her. They were falling together, fighting each other or trying to get up. His weight was on top of her but she had hold of the certificate and she kicked and shoved in an attempt to thrust him away. He swore softly and his breath was hot and stale on her face. She pushed harder and his weight shifted—he rolled sideways, under the rail—she heard his startled cry, saw his outflung arm. Then he was gone. Gone.

It happened so quickly that it was several seconds before she could take it in. The scream, abruptly cut off. The crash. Silence. She struggled to sit up and found she was shaking. The envelope was in her hand; her fur coat was matted; there was an ugly weal on the pristine leather of her boot. She felt sick. A long time passed while she waited for her pulse to slow down. When she could move, she crawled to the edge of the planks and peered over. Fortunately, there was little to see. The body had evidently dislodged a stack of blocks, bringing them down in its wake. Hence the crash. Only the legs and a portion of jacket protruded. Nicky called out: "Steph!" although she knew he would not answer. She had spoken quite quietly but it sounded very loud to her, and she shrank from her own voice. But there was only the echo whispering through the empty building. Nothing moved. No one came.

She scrambled unsteadily to her feet, cramming the certificate into her bag. She must get home, destroy the evidence—

tidy up. She told herself that there was no way the police could connect her with Stephane, not now. Someone else would find the body and it would be duly identified and written off. That would be the end of it. But the dreadful trembling would not leave her; she stumbled down the stairs, clinging to the wall, and hurried across the open site looking neither to right nor left. Only when she was some two hundred yards down the road did she slacken her pace and begin to look for a taxi.

In the room beyond the one where Nicky had met Stephane, Elsa listened until the sounds of her departure had died away. The tape recorder stood on the window-sill in the corner of the frame; she hadn't used the machine before and she wasn't sure how well it would work. After a while she remembered to switch it off. She felt as if the bare concrete and bitter air had struck their chill into her very bones. Her plans had been amateurish, optimistic rather than cunning: whatever she had hoped for, it was not this. Not this. Eventually, because she knew she must, she climbed out on to the scaffolding and leaned over the rail to look down.

She, too, left without alerting the police.

That evening, Nicky packed a bag and left London. She did not want to be anywhere in the vicinity when they found Stephane: she did not want to see even a small paragraph in the *Standard* or hear a postscript on the regional news. She wanted to put it out of her mind, out of her life. She went to Churston because she had nowhere else to go.

Sunday was grey and damp, a muddy country day. In the house there were draughts and boredom and Mrs. Skerrit, brought downstairs by her nurse so the latter could watch television. Nicky waited for the phone to ring, hoping to hear from Alex; but it didn't. In desperation, she went for a walk. Nicky was no enthusiast for country walks but at Churston Grange there was little else to do. Besides, she thought, if I go out Alex will call. Sod's Law. Then when I get back at least there'll be a message or a number. She needed someone to confide in, someone she could trust. In lieu, she would take Alex.

The last of the snow had melted and low clouds chugged

ominously across the sky, promising rain. The downs were dirty green and the bare trees dirty brown. Everything dripped. Nicky thought of Greek islands scattered like leaves on a sea as blue as a jewel, of arid golden hills and purple evenings and the smell of dust. Her usual ability to transform her memories took over: she dismissed frustration, *angst,* shortage of cash, and recalled only the radiance of an endless summer. And the world was full of islands and evenings and summers which she had yet to see. For the thousandth time, she reassured herself: It'll be all right. There's nothing to connect me with Stephane. Nothing. But the islands slipped away and a flurry of rain awoke her to reality. For no particular reason she had been walking towards Stallibrass House, but she was less than half-way there when she decided to turn back. It was raining stead-ily now and the Aquascutum coat which she had once consid-ered suitable for Caesar's wife afforded only limited protection. Icy drops of water ran down inside the collar and the wind plastered strands of her hair across her cheek, gluing them to her lipstick. When she heard a car hoot behind her, she merely moved closer to the verge. The car pulled past her and stopped: an ancient Mini which looked vaguely familiar. The window on the passenger side was wound down and a face from her most optimistic daydreams leaned across to look out. "Get in," said Anthony Stallibrass. "I'll give you a lift."

She got in. As they drove away it occurred to her that once again he had caught her unprepared. On this occasion, she reflected crossly, she was as dripping and bedraggled as a half-drowned kitten. Anthony himself had damply curling hair and raindrops glistening on his donkey jacket, but he glowed against the dingy afternoon like a warm fire on a cold day. She tried to think of a conversational gambit that would instantly fascinate him, and failed.

He enquired, politely: "Down for the weekend?" and, when she nodded: "Are you going to stay on at Churston?"

"N-no. No, I'll sell. I should have done something about it already, only . . . it still seems a bit soon. Anyway, there's Mrs. Skerritt."

"Mrs. Skerritt? Oh—Aunty Grizzle. That's what the twins used to call her. Grizzle by name and grizzle by nature. I suppose she meant well but I don't think she was much good with children. How old is she now?"

"I don't know. Old." Nicky snuggled deeper into the dry interior of her coat. The car was underheated and a ripple of cold air was creeping in somewhere round her ankles. "Why are you down here? Has your mother sold the house yet?"

"It's on offer." Perhaps it was her imagination that the phrase sounded curt. "She's got her own surveyor on to it. I came down to talk to him."

He turned into the driveway of Churston Grange and pulled up before the front door. "Here you are. Chauffeur service. All you need is a butler with an umbrella."

Nicky remembered how she had wished for a butler on his previous visit, and involuntarily she smiled. "It's a bit late," she said. "I'm soaked."

They both hesitated, faltering on the edge of further exchanges. Nicky was conscious of a chance waiting to be taken, the hint of a promise.

"Come in," she suggested. "Have some tea."

"Okay."

Alex hadn't called but it seemed less important now she had something else to think about. The housekeeper came only infrequently since Rupert's death so Nicky made tea herself and they drank it in the kitchen. They were sitting at a table of unvarnished wood which Anthony claimed he remembered from his days with Diana; an Aga stood against the wall beside them; opposite were the fan oven and microwave which had subordinated it. The room was warm and it should have been friendly but instead it looked abandoned, as if nothing was ever cooked there any more except ready-meals and things out of packets. There were no flowers on the window-sill, no fruit in the fruit-bowl. In an old-fashioned dresser the best china was gathering dust.

Anthony said: "You must be lonely here."

"Sometimes. I'm used to being lonely." A little to her surprise, she realized it was true.

Elsa had said something similar, Anthony recalled. *I'm used to being alone.* Perhaps the two of them had more in common than they knew.

"Were you in love with him?" he asked. "I know it's a bloody rude question, but . . . I wondered. You seem upset, but not really sad. You can tell me to mind my own business if you like."

She shook her head. "I thought I was," she explained. "At least, to begin with. He was charismatic and—sort of godlike." She searched for the right words to tell her story, not exactly lies but a form of presentation that would make the facts more attractive. "The trouble was, he was obsessed with his work. I suppose all great artists are." The truism scarcely grated on Anthony's ear. "He gave so much of his energy and his—his *passion* to architecture that he didn't have any left for loving *people*. He expected me to be there and look pretty and that was all. He didn't give or take. He didn't even *know* me."

"He missed a lot," Anthony said gently. He was thinking how young and defenceless Nicky appeared, with her hair drying in crinkles and the make-up washed from her face by the rain. Very different from the bimbo Elsa had led him to imagine.

Automatically, he took her hand.

"I wanted s-so much to be a part of his life," Nicky stammered, wrung by the pathos of her own invention, "but he wouldn't let me—he just wasn't interested." Tears chased one another down her cheeks; she gulped bravely. Anthony, faced with a situation to which he was accustomed, moved round the table to offer his shoulder.

The back door slammed, but it did not occur to them to spring apart. Elsa found them there—Anthony leaning against the kitchen table, Nicky sobbing quietly into his sweater. She knew that sweater: she had clung to it herself. One of his sisters had given it to him, years ago; it had shrunk in the wash so that the sleeves were too short and there were holes in the armpits clumsily darned, probably by Cathleen Mirza. Elsa could remember the very smell and texture of the wool.

She found herself thinking of another kitchen, another couple caught off guard. Grant Barrymore in a cashmere sweater with no shirt underneath . . .

She said in an unnaturally flat voice: "I'm sorry . . . I didn't know. I saw the car outside, but . . . I didn't know. I'm interrupting. Sorry . . ."

"Of course you're not interrupting." Anthony looked surprised but not guilty. "I'm glad you've come, Elsa. I hoped you would. It's time you and Nicky tried to make up your differences."

His misconceptions horrified her. Groping for an escape, she said the first thing that came into her head.

"I came to see my great-aunt."

Nicky looked round at her, and her wide eyes were suddenly dry.

That night, Aunty Grizzle's bedroom door was left unlocked, and she wandered downstairs into the garden. She was found by the main road the following morning. The car that knocked her down did not even stop.

The inquest brought in an open verdict.

The affair was of purely local interest: the county press composed headlines like "Double Tragedy" and "Dead Man's Aunt in Fatal Ramble," but the nationals could find little to excite them in the commonplace fate of an unknown woman, no matter how illustrious the nephew who had predeceased her. Only rustics crammed the village hall in the hope of further sensations: they sat sucking sweets instead of straws, muttering and pointing. Aunty Grizzle's former nurse wore black from Next; Nicky wore black from Brown's of South Molton Street. The coroner criticized the nurse for her carelessness and exonerated Nicky, commending her "rare sense of responsibility" for someone not actually related to her. Nicky might have blushed if she had not been too distracted by other problems. Elsa had been called for the official identification; she admitted to visiting her great-aunt on the evening of the accident and she, too, received praise for her thoughtfulness. It was peculiarly ironic, declared the coroner, that this woman, surrounded by so much care and attention, should nonetheless have managed to come to such an unhappy end.

Afterwards Nicky got up to leave in a hurry, hugging her

sable collar round her ears in a gesture which no longer mimicked Garbo but merely sought to hide her face. She moved towards the exit, hoping to pass out in the crowd, shielded from the small but eager clutch of journalists and photographers. But the crowd drew away from her to stare and Elsa was waiting by the door. In the short period since Rupert's funeral the nature of their antagonism had changed: it had become something naked and ugly, a raw enmity which no onlooker could mistake. This time, when they confronted one another, there were no whispers, no undercurrents, no rigid self-restraint. Glittering eyes met glittering eyes; each face was pale and bitter. In Elsa, hatred burned with a still, cold flame; in Nicky, it flickered and flared, nourished on old rancour, new fear, the lust to survive.

She said: "Excuse me." The words were a courtesy but the tone was not, and the paradox lent a touch of grotesque comedy to the situation. Elsa did not laugh.

"You're not going to get away with it," she said—a standard line, and she knew it sounded ham.

"Let me pass."

"Did you unlock the door for her? Did you help her into the road when a suitable car came along? Two deaths so close together: it's a little too much for coincidence, isn't it?" The grating sarcasm was painful to hear. "Did she know something, somewhere in the pathetic muddle of her brain—or was she just a burden you wanted to dump, an impediment to your golden progress?"

"She was *old*. You said it. She was old and senile and muddled. She hardly knew who I was."

"She got out of her room the night my father died. What did she see? Did she see you give him his pills—too many bloody pills? *Did she?*" She seized Nicky by her padded shoulders, crushing the coat in her hands. Perhaps because it was fur it felt like a live thing, not Nicky's clothing but a part of her, an outer skin which could be torn and hurt. Nicky thrust her violently away, just as someone moved out of the crowd to separate them.

"You killed him!" The accusation was out in the open. The spectators looked both embarrassed and eager; two policemen began to converge on the group. Elsa's voice held all the fury of a fighter in a cause which has long been lost. "He was sick and helpless and you killed him, bit by bit. You caused his stroke and you nursed him to death. You killed him—you killed him—"

Against reason, against sanity, Nicky recognized the words. Stephane's words. Rage and terror rose in her in equal measure.

"*Get out of my way!*"

She pushed Elsa aside with a strength that was more than natural to her. By the time the police came over she had gone. One of them said to Elsa: "What's the trouble, miss?" but she didn't answer. Behind her, the person who had moved forward to prevent a possible skirmish drew nearer and laid a hand on her arm. A well-known hand, strong and blunt-fingered and ugly with calluses.

"Come on, Elsa."

She glanced around. "What are you doing here?"

"Taking you back to London."

The glitter seemed to have gone out of her even as her anger failed: she looked suddenly listless. She said: "I've got my own car," but there was no real resistance in her voice.

"I haven't," Michael said. "I came down by train. Give me your keys. In this mood, you'll drive too fast and smash yourself to pieces."

"I always drive too fast."

"I know. You might also smash somebody else to pieces, which wouldn't be quite fair. Give me the keys."

Surprisingly, she obeyed. Outside, he swept her briskly past the waiting press and pushed her into the car. Nicky had already left in a taxi for Churston Grange. Elsa knew she was staying there since she had called in at the house before the inquest. It's my home, Elsa thought, and she's there. The cuckoo in the nest, the interloper, the supplanter. In *my home.*

She said nothing at all most of the way to London.

They drove to Michael's flat. Elsa did not demur. She did not want to make love: she felt too empty, so empty that she could not imagine ever wanting to make love again. But love-making between her and Michael had ended long ago, leaving a bond less transient, less exciting, close as blood. She was too tired to argue, tired not in body but in will. Michael was there and the flat was there and she had to go somewhere. They descended into the garage, out of light into the dark. Behind them, cumbersome metal doors settled into place with a dull clang. She had heard that clang a hundred times before but for the first time it struck her as ominous, doors of steel thudding into grooves of stone, shutting her in a dungeon. A nebulous doubt brushed the edges of her mind, waking her to a new alertness. But it was the same garage she had seen so often. The same lift to the same apartment, four storeys up. The same Elsa. The same Michael.

She found herself studying him in a way she had not done since the night they met in the Technico building, so many years before. She had seen him always with the eyes of memory, as a projection of her own emotions, never with true detachment. He *is* the same, she thought, always the same, since I was thirteen. The idea troubled her: it seemed he had been there all her life, growing into the infrastructure as a tree grows into a wall, blending with it and becoming part of it until without the tree the wall would collapse. His face was unchanging, neither young nor old, a face that might have been moulded from the stuff with which he worked, rough as plaster, enduring as concrete. Anthony was beautiful but unreal, as elusive as a recurring dream. Michael was reality, Michael was there, both the tree and the wall, past and future: the shadow that always lies behind the light. Waiting with the inexorability of time and the patience of stones . . . but for what?

"What are you thinking, Elsa my lovely?" A compliment, even an ironic one, was unlike him. "Elsa my . . . very . . . lovely . . ."

"I was thinking about you."

"Were you?" The memory of past kisses flickered between them, drawing his mouth towards hers. Deliberately, or so it seemed, he snapped the thread. "Unusual. Normally, you only think about yourself. You see other people simply as they affect you, in the moment when their existence touches yours. If you're thinking objectively about another human being, it must be a first."

"That's not true," Elsa said, adding, with unaccustomed hesitation: "Is it?"

"Have you ever wondered what your father did in the war? Do you know if Anthony was a failure at Eton—or whether Pa Stallibrass sent him in an attempt to make a blue-eyed boy out of his black-eyed gypsy son?" He opened the door to the flat and went in, leaving her to follow. "You probably don't even know if it *was* Eton, do you?"

"No," Elsa conceded, "I don't. Anthony doesn't talk about things like that. I know he was at Cambridge, though. It was while he was going out with Diana. He was a good student."

"He would be." Michael went into the kitchen, opened a cupboard. "How about some coffee?"

"Yes, please."

He shook ground coffee from a packet into the top of the percolator. "So what conclusions did you come to—about me?"

"I didn't. I know nothing about you. You tell me things when it suits you, but I still know nothing." She pulled out a chair and sat down, elbows on the table, propping her chin on her hands. "I asked you once what you wanted—do you remember? Not just from me but from life. What *do* you want? You didn't answer."

"Were you listening?"

"I . . . think so." Was she? She couldn't recall.

He sat down opposite her while the percolator began to splutter. His eyes looked straight into hers: eyes as grey as November, seeing too far into her soul. He said: "I've always been there for you, haven't I, Elsa? Yet you've never even been grateful." There was no acrimony in his tone: only a strange gentleness which she found somehow frightening.

"Would you like me to be grateful?" she asked, wondering.

"No. Only honest. You need me: you always have. You needed your father but he didn't care and now he's dead it's too late to change him. You probably needed your sister once, but that's history. You don't need Anthony no matter how pretty he may be. But you need me, Elsa, don't you? You *need* me. Say it."

I need you. It had been her own thought, some time quite recently, but she would not admit it.

She jerked her head in a brusque denial. His threat was warm as a caress, almost tender; but it was still a threat.

"What do you want of me?"

In the pause which followed, it was she who lowered her gaze. His expression held no disappointment; only understanding. Too much understanding.

"Truth. They found the body of a man on the Cable Star site last weekend. He must have died the day before your great-aunt. Fell from the scaffolding. Van Leer sites are supposed to be unlucky: did you know? Other people have fallen from Rupert's handiwork. Only this was one of mine—and I won't put up with ghosts."

"I know it was one of yours," Elsa said, remembering anger. "I could tell. I didn't like it."

"You wouldn't." Michael did not appear to mind. "So . . . you admit you've been there?"

"Of course I do."

"And the man?"

"You must know who he is. Why ask me?"

Michael's mouth twisted in the hint of a grimace. "Oh, I know, I thought—God help me—that running round in circles after Nicky would give you something to do. I found you a detective and the detective found you a crime. You could have stripped your stepmother of everything she has. But that wasn't enough for you, was it? Perhaps you'd like to tell me how her real husband wound up on a building site with his back broken and his head stove in. Did he fall, or—was he pushed? And if so, who pushed him?"

"It was an accident," Elsa said. "At least, it might have been. I'm not sure." She bit her lip. "I suppose it was my fault, but . . . I never imagined anything like that could happen."

"Why the hell did you meet him there?"

"*I* didn't meet him." She looked stung. "It was Nicky. I just hid and watched. I told Stephane what to say. I thought I could trap her into some sort of revelation—something that would incriminate her." She rifled through her bag for the tape. "I got this."

"Does it . . . incriminate her?"

Elsa did not answer: she might have been debating in her own mind. Her head was bent, her eyes fixed on the cassette. Michael found himself observing the way her eyebrows swept down to meet the straight line of her nose—the nose she had had so artfully remodelled. Its perfection jarred on him; he wished she did not look quite so beautiful.

He said: "Well, does it?"

"She confessed," Elsa said at last. "She practically confessed to murder. I heard her—it's there on the tape." She sounded almost incredulous. "Then—then they had a fight. I don't know how he came to fall; I couldn't see. She might have pushed him."

"*She confessed?*" Michael took the tape before Elsa had time to object. "Bullshit. Let me hear it myself."

"Stephane accused her," Elsa explained, "and she said, even

if it was true, nobody could prove it. That's a confession, isn't it?"

"Is it?" Michael had started to his feet but now he sat down again, turning the cassette in his fingers. "Have you played this to anyone yet?"

"No. I hadn't decided—what to do with it."

"Do nothing. Throw it away. As far as I am aware, tapes aren't admissible evidence in court. Nicky's a liar, anyhow; you've said so often enough. This isn't a confession, it's a boast. She's boasting to make herself interesting. Try to use this and you'll only make trouble—trouble for everyone, including you. Stick with bigamy: you've got legal documents for that. There'll still be questions asked, with Maglioli turning up dead, but that can't be helped. Just—get rid of this." He slammed the tape on the table with a gesture that was unexpectedly violent. "Get rid of it. Do you understand?"

The percolator had stopped long since but neither of them noticed. "Why should I? It's all I've got." There were tears in Elsa's voice though not on her cheek. She plunged again into the dreadful liturgy. "She killed him! Why should she get away with it? She killed him—"

Michael seized her by the arms, dragging her out of the chair, shaking her. Shaking her. "Stop it! Elsa—Elsa—"

"She killed him!" When she looked at him the fury was back in her face. Between reddened rims her eyes shone green as copper fire. "She took him away from me, she imprisoned him, she destroyed him—"

"Maybe." His tone held a savagery out of all proportion to the word. "Maybe she did destroy him: I don't know and you don't know and we never will. But she didn't kill him. You've got to accept it, Elsa."

"I *won't* accept it—"

"You've got to. Do I have to spell it out for you? I *know* she didn't kill him. I *know* she didn't give him an overdose of those fucking pills. So do you. So—do—you."

She sank back into the chair. Her tears dried and her white face became still whiter. After a long time she said: "How do you know?"

He was holding her hand, uncurling her fingers, one by one, tracing the lines of her palm. He might have been reading her fate. "No special reason. I must have realized from the beginning, but—I wouldn't let myself see it. I kept hoping the bastard would die naturally. People do! I know Nicky wouldn't have the guts to kill. As for her *petit ami*—there was a moment when I thought our friend Mowle would pin it on him, but it was no use. He isn't the type either. You: you have courage and daring and passion—all the qualities of a killer. All the things I love in you." Love: he didn't hear himself say it; nor did she. He had clasped her hand round his but she withdrew it. "Are you going to tell me about it?"

"Will you understand?"

"Will I? . . . I won't betray you: you know that. There's no evidence left. Nicky threw away the bottle of pills you refilled so carefully—presumably she suspected her Alexandre. There's no more proof, no more case to prove. Does it matter if I understand—or if I don't?"

"No."

Belatedly, he remembered the coffee. He made hers black, with a slug of brandy. She drank it without noticing.

"When I said Nicky killed him, I meant it," she averred. "She was morally responsible. You saw him. He couldn't draw, he couldn't write, he couldn't talk. The nurse told me he wet the bed. He couldn't go for a walk or—or even propel his wheelchair." The shiver crept back into her voice; her sight blurred. "I know you don't believe me, but he loved me. He *did* love me. I had to help him. I had to save him from her. Don't you see? I did it because there was nothing else I could do. I loved him"— she was crying in earnest now—"and that was all I ever did for him. That one thing . . . But it was enough, wasn't it? No one else could have done it. No one else loved him like that. No one else loved him—like me. Did they? . . . did they?"

"No, sweetheart. Oh no . . ."

She struggled to regain control; her mouth writhed and her eyelids squeezed at her eyes. After a minute or two, she blew her nose.

"Did he realize," Michael asked, "when you gave him the pills?"

"I think so." Her face was suddenly irradiated, as if at a beautiful memory. "I mashed them up and put them in a milk drink. Ovaltine. They were always giving him Ovaltine; he must have hated it. But he drank it that time. I kept stirring it, in case they wouldn't dissolve. I didn't know if they were soluble or not. Then I gave him some more just to swallow, and later some more. He was used to taking lots of pills but he must have known. He lay there holding my hand. He liked holding my hand . . ." She looked down on the hand she had withdrawn from Michael's as though she still expected to find the mark of Rupert's grip.

Michael thought of his former employer with a depth of loathing he had not known he could feel.

"Afterwards," he persisted, "all that business with Nicky—?"

"I told you. She was morally responsible. I wanted her to be punished."

"You didn't seriously believe you could get a court to convict her?"

"No—no, not that. I don't know what I believed. I wanted her to suffer the way she'd made him suffer. I wanted her to feel—trapped and helpless. I wanted her to be *afraid*." She clenched her coffee-mug between thin, strong fingers; her knuckles blanched. "Anthony was sorry for her. He's always sorry for people. I thought . . ." She broke off. "Anyway, it doesn't matter now."

"And your great-aunt?" His probing was reluctant, relentless, curiously tender. "Did she matter?"

"She was very old." Elsa looked pensive, lost in a recurrence of doubt. He saw her fall from one mood into the next with a strange swiftness, with no overlap, no graduation of temper. From rage to apathy, from conviction to regret. As if the normal processes that govern human reactions had disappeared, and emotion plucked her from one extreme to another without pause for reflection. She continued, trying to convince herself: "She wasn't really *alive* any more. Her brain was in a fog. She wasn't alive and she wasn't dead. She was just—in between. It must be terrible to be like that."

"She had a right to her fog."

"Yes . . . I suppose so. I didn't think about that. I thought— you see, she rambled on about things, all sorts of things. The night—Daddy—died, she got out. Your detective said so. She might have seen something. And I thought, what would Nicky do—if she was a killer? What would she do, if she was cornered, and scared, and she panicked? So—so I came back, when Nicky was in bed, and let Aunty Grizzle out of her room. I took her down to the road, and when a car came along fast I—did it. I hoped the driver would be drunk: then he'd be sure not to stop. Actually, he pulled over and got out to have a look, but when he saw she was dead he drove away again. He didn't see me. It was all too easy. Much too easy." She added, with a sort of horror: "She thought I was Diana. She often did. That's why she came with me. She kept saying: 'Diana' . . ."

"When you were a child," Michael said, "you hated her, didn't you?"

"She hated me," Elsa responded, bleakly. "I suppose she had reason—in the end."

There was a silence while Michael strove for the right words. If there were any right words. Elsa's voice fell into that silence like a raindrop into a still pool.

"Poor Aunty. Poor, stupid Aunty Grizzle. Do you know, when I was little she said I was a changeling? I think it was the colour of my eyes. Yellow-green eyes mark you for a witch's child: that's what she said. I used to feel that whatever I did, I would always be wicked—the wickedness was there inside me, part of me, like bones and flesh and skin. I couldn't get rid of it. As if I had, not an ordinary human heart, but the heart of some evil creature. A viper's heart. I could feel it in my chest sometimes, a great big lump of wickedness, weighing me down. Aunty Grizzle told me it was there and I believed her—and it is. It is."

Her hands shielded her face but the little Michael could see touched him like a physical pain. She did not cry much, not any more. There was only a slight shuddering in her body, a puckering between her brows.

He said: "Elsa."

When she didn't reply he got up and pulled her to her feet, gently this time. He held her against him and her head dropped on to his shoulder as if her neck was tired of supporting it. She was docile now, as though, with her final confession, all the demons had flown out of her.

Presently, he took her into the bedroom.

She was undressed and lying on the bed before she began to fight. She did not speak or protest, she simply fought him, not in play but with a viciousness that was new and dreadful, raking his cheek with her nails, trying to kick and punch, twisting her hips to avoid him. He pinioned her wrists and threw his weight on her to restrain her, and she bit his breast like an animal—like some small angry rodent, locked in combat with an enemy far stronger, more intent on hurting than getting away. He forced her legs open, jabbing his cock against her. She was dry but she seemed to moisten even as he entered her, as though she could no longer control her own body. It belonged to him in spite of her, because of her, and she was resisting not rape but surrender. He pushed hard, penetrating deep inside. The conflict tightened her muscles around him; pain and pleasure were intermingled, fury inseparable from desire. And then abruptly the fight was over, she was melting under him, her bites become love-nips, her thighs parting against his. He called her Elsa—*my darling*—*my love*—terms he had hardly used before. She licked the blood which ran down from the scratches on his face—his blood was in her mouth, he could feel her tongue on his skin, soft as a caress. A sensation too sweet to bear took him and filled him and went from him at last, ebbing in gasps and sighs and shivers, and he felt her sighing and shivering in response, felt the sweetness flowing out of her, and it was like a kind of dying.

It might have been one hour or many before Elsa became aware of the daylight fading and the shadows stretching across the ceiling. She lay like a leaf after a storm, fallen where the wind left her, limp and unmoving. Emotion and tumult seemed to have drained from her spirit, leaving her empty and temporarily at peace. She pictured herself as little more than a husk, light and transparent without her passions. Michael, in contrast, was real, solid, a vital, compact structure of physical matter, warm and breathing. Sometimes she thought he was the only real person she had ever known. Anthony, her father, Nicky—they were all phantoms of love and hate, drawn from dreams. Diana had been real once, but that was long ago. Michael was always real, always there. The living tree and the solid wall. A part of things. His touch woke a lust in her which obliterated all other feelings, and when he withdrew, sated, both lust and feeling were gone, as if the potence of his body had sucked her torments into himself. "All my sins," she murmured, and she imagined him, like a medieval scapegoat, running off into the desert pursued by the stones of the villagers, an outcast in a rag of goatskin whose back was bent with the burden of someone else's evil.

"What did you say?" He lifted his head from the pillow, looked at her from the corner of his eye.

"Nothing. Nothing important, anyway." She touched him with a tenderness born of her thought, a passionate pity for the weight of so many misdeeds.

"Hungry?"

"I suppose I must be."

He produced bread, cheese and pâté from the fridge, opened a bottle of wine. Elsa put her clothes on and sat down in the living-room.

"What shall we drink to?" she asked.

"Us."

She put her glass down. "Is there any *us*?"

"There is. There will be. Drink."

But she didn't drink. "What do you want of me?" The same question, the question he never answered.

"What do you think I want?"

"I'm not sure. I don't know if it's love—or just possession."

"Well then . . . nor do I. Maybe I want both. I have your love, whether you admit it or not. You can't help yourself. I can feel it in your body, a response you can't deny or resist. As for possession . . ."

"You know everything about me," Elsa said with quiet bitterness. "That's possession, isn't it? That's absolute, unquestioned ownership. I might as well be your slave."

"I don't want a slave." His tone grew very slightly sharper. "Try to look at things differently just this once—not for my sake but for your own. You've filled your life with a crazed obsession with your father and a self-indulgent vendetta against your stepmother. I want you to be free of all that. I want you to love and be loved like any other woman. I want you in my bed, in my home, in my boring daily routine. I want us to argue and make up and discuss politics and religion and where to go on holiday. You need a dose of reality to chase away the nightmares: ordinary, comfortable, mundane reality. I'm your reality, Elsa. Face it. Believe it. Me. Here. That's all I want." He placed the glass firmly in her hand. "Drink."

Michael equals reality. Reality equals Michael. There is no reality without Michael. She had always known it.

She drank.

"Socrates could not have swallowed his hemlock with more panache," Michael said.

She smiled. A warm, effortless smile without irony or pain. In that moment, he thought everything was as nearly perfect as it ever would or could be.

He put on a CD, Jacqueline de Pré playing Elgar, which he knew she liked. Beyond the French windows the clouds were breaking into separate layers, and the last of a winter sunset was melting into the depths behind them. The notes of the music seemed to be climbing up the clouds like a ladder, up and up to the top of the sky, and then plunging down to oblivion with the sun. Elsa watched until the final droplet of gold had dissolved, and although the afterglow still lingered it appeared to her that a curtain of darkness fell across the world. The darkness entered into her and lay coldly on her heart.

"There's something I have to tell you," Michael said.

She switched on a lamp: in the sudden light his face was full of an uncertainty which was new to her.

"Yes?"

"My turn for confession." The familiar shadow-smile flickered and faded, as though at a joke gone horribly wrong. "It'll leak out sooner or later: there's no way of preventing it, and . . . I'd rather you heard it from me. It won't be easy for you, Elsa. I'm sorry."

"What is it? What won't be easy?"

He sighed. "I encouraged you to investigate Nicky because I didn't want you hearing about this. It was unlikely, but you might have picked up something. You have a share in the practice—and there's Anthony. I thought, if you were preoccupied with Nicky, it would at least give me some time. I wanted to be sure of the facts, to check up if I could. I half hoped—I don't know—that it could all be hushed up. For your benefit, I suppose. Not your father's."

"My father?"

"It always comes back to your father, doesn't it?"

"You hated him," Elsa said slowly. "You never said so, but I knew. What have you done?"

"*I* haven't done anything. He has." Michael knew he sounded brutal, more brutal than he intended. He had meant to be tactful, even sympathetic. It was too late now. "I'm talking about Stallibrass House. His first great masterpiece. The springboard of his career. A glass-and-concrete temple to functionalism. Built, as you are no doubt aware, on a very tight budget for a millionaire who couldn't understand why it should cost more than the shoddy office blocks on which he had made his millions. Unfortunately, the budget was too tight. So Rupert . . . cut corners."

"He wouldn't."

"He would. He did. This was the quick way to fame—his big chance. The temptation must have been irresistible. Maybe he thought Miser Joe was asking for it—who knows? The contractor was used to making similar economies: he'd put up several of the office blocks. Stallibrass asked no questions as long as the bill stayed low. No one asked any questions until the place came on the market and someone sent a surveyor to have a look at it." He paused, but Elsa said nothing. The lamp was behind her and he could only guess at the fixity of her expression. "The surveyor came to me. He's an acquaintance of mine: he knew I would be honest with him. I went down to see over the house myself. I won't bore you with the list of defects: you've studied architecture, you'll know the sort of thing. Poorly insulated wiring, inadequate damp-proof courses, too much sand in the concrete. The main thing is the foundations. They're not deep enough. There's been some subsidence in recent years: you can hardly miss the cracks. The building will have to be pulled down."

"*No!*"

"Elsa . . . listen to me. There's not much likelihood of legal action—it's too long ago—but the house is *dangerous*. Your father—"

"My father would never have built anything unsafe. Never. It must have been the contractor. You said yourself he was a crook. How do you know it wasn't the contractor?"

"I know. I looked in the files. The actual drawings are all right but on a couple of them I found some notes scribbled in the corner. Rupert's handwriting. Notes to the builder. I've got them here." He nodded towards the desk in a recess across the room. "You can look if you like."

"No." It was barely a whisper. He moved a little to see her face, but she wasn't watching him. "What will happen," she asked at length, "when all this comes out?"

"To the house? I told you. They'll demolish it."

"To my father."

"He'll be ruined." Michael's voice was harsh, stone grinding on stone. All softness had been pared away. "Do you want me to say it's a tragedy? Even for you, Elsa, I can't perjure myself. He deserves it. He betrayed not only his own honour but the honour of his profession. He compromised on safety, and in so doing he gambled with human lives—not that human lives ever meant much to Rupert. A labourer died on that site. A local boy, not used to the ways of the contractor. Apparently he had complained that the work was substandard. *He fell from scaffolding.* An accident, they said. No doubt the scaffolding had been erected on the cheap as well. There have been too many such accidents. Too many people have fallen from Van Leer buildings."

Elsa tried to say: "I heard about that," but though her lips moved no sound emerged. In her mind, she seemed to see a figure falling from a building, over and over again, an interminable reply of the same fateful vision. The unknown workman. Diana. Stephane Maglioli. And herself, standing high above London, feeling the tug of the drop and the bewitchment of the scattered city lights.

> I shall live out my life in a moment;
> I shall soar in the wind like a swan . . .

We are all falling, she thought. From the moment of birth, we are falling. Down and down into the abyss . . .

A blackness filled her spirit, blotting out every last gleam of light. She said quietly: "You're glad, aren't you? This is what you've worked for, all these years. I always suspected it and when I saw the Cable Star building I was sure. Those curves . . . My father never used curves. You want to take it all away from him—all his greatness. Nicky wanted his money and his life, but you—you want his business, his reputation, the very ideals he created. And me. Yes—and me. Ever since you came to him as a student you've been waiting for this. Waiting and planning. *Haven't you?*"

He was silent. It wasn't the whole truth but he would not or could not deny it. He thought what a wretched paradox it was that his antipathy for Rupert had begun on the day he saw

Rupert's plain, overweight, unwanted daughter. Perhaps he had loved her from that moment, responding instinctively to her need, even as years before on the streets of Lübeck he had made a pet of a stray puppy which had bitten him. The puppy had been tamed in the end, following him everywhere in mute adoration, but Elsa . . .

"You've got the business," she said. "I can't change that. You've destroyed his ideals—now you'll take his reputation. But you shan't have me: do you hear? I'm *his daughter* and he loved me and I loved him and that's one thing you can't undo. I'd rather be *dead* than belong to you!"

"Elsa—"

He reached out for her but she tore herself away, blundering towards the French windows. Outside, there was a small balcony with a low iron rail. She pulled the window open and went out onto the balcony, leaning over the ironwork. Too far over. Michael started after her in sudden fear.

"Elsa . . . don't be melodramatic. Okay: he loved you and you loved him. It's a pretty story and if you want to tell yourself pretty stories—"

"Shut up! Shut up, shut up—"

"You're a grown woman. You don't need to stuff your head with garbage and dreams. You're beautiful and intelligent and talented. You can have *reality*."

"There is no reality."

"Don't say that." He was propped against the rail beside her, tilted back so he could see her averted profile. His finger under her chin forced her round to face him. "You drank to it: remember? You and me and reality."

"Don't *touch* me!"

Even his finger on her chin stirred a flicker of something deep inside her. She did not want it but it was there; his nearness drew her like a magnet. He had made himself a part of her, forced her to become a part of him, filled her with his treachery. She had sensed it when she saw the Cable Star building and now it was there before her, in his face, in her response. She was betraying Rupert with every second that she hesitated. Briefly she was aware of that alien heart—the viper's heart—pounding inexorably inside her, driving her like a machine. Stronger than desire, stronger than treachery, stronger than *her own will* . . .

She jerked backwards, thrusting Michael away. She had to move quickly—too quickly for thought or feeling. Any doubt, any vacillation and she would be lost. Her foot kicked against his ankles, sweeping him off balance. For a fatal instant he thought it was an accident. Then he felt the sudden hard shove in his chest—felt himself toppling back over the rail—

There was no time to struggle, no time for anything. Shock froze his last thought in a silent plea.

Dear God . . . Elsa—Elsa—

She heard the body crashing through a tree into the garden below. He had not cried out. Her breath was coming in gasps and a wave of sickness almost doubled her up. She clutched the rail for support but she didn't look down. She had an idea it was important, not to look down. She waited for lights to come on in the other flats, for voices and commotion. But everything was quiet.

She retreated inside, closing the window behind her. Shutting out the quiet, and the night, and the garden with its motionless occupant. She knew she had to act swiftly but she had only the vaguest notion of what to do. Her brain would not work properly; her thoughts seemed to be caught between narrowing walls, afraid to stray into areas which had suddenly become taboo. She went over to Michael's desk: there was a thick file on the top marked "Stallibrass." She picked it up, hugging it almost jealously against her. Underneath was a bunch of keys. The keys to Stallibrass House.

She stood for a few minutes with the keys in her hand. Within its narrow walls her brain whirled into action like a computer stuck on a single programme, obsessively calculating each variant of the equation to the millionth decimal place. She retrieved her coat and bag, ran to the door—halted, listening. There was still no sign of discovery from outside. She went back to the telephone, tapped out the number of Churston Grange.

Nicky answered.

In a bad imitation cockney which was the only disguise that occurred to her, Elsa said she was calling on behalf of Anthony Stallibrass. Would Nicky meet him at Stallibrass House at eleven o'clock? She rang off before Nicky could query the message. Eleven o'clock should give her enough time to make her arrangements. She did not doubt her stepmother would come. She had kept the appointment with Stephane; this appointment, too, would be kept. Even if she was suspicious, if she was uncertain, she would come. And, once again, she would come alone.

Elsa hurried out of the flat, banging the door behind her, and took the lift to the underground garage. She was halfway to Churston before she realized that she had left the tape in the kitchen.

She could not turn back now.

Nicky came, of course. She was suspicious, she was uncertain, but she came. She felt herself pulled this way and that by invisible threads, a puppet in the hands of a hidden puppeteer, responding in vain hope to every tug on the string. She did not really believe Anthony would be there but she wanted to believe it, wanted it badly enough to quell insidious doubts. When she paid off the taxi she told herself it would be all right, she could phone for another later from Stallibrass House. She stood in the road watching it drive away until the rear lights had vanished round a bend and the last of the engine noise had faded. There was no further traffic. The gates behind her appeared locked but they swung back at the touch of her hand; a barred pattern of moonlight slid across her coat. She began to walk up the drive towards the house. Shrubs which had not been pruned for years encroached on her path; they had grown to great bulbous shapes and where the moon fell on them their massed leaves looked as if they were made of black leather. Beyond, there were spaces of grass interspersed with trees whose knotted branches cast a mesh of shadow over the ground. The night was windless and Nicky missed the usual country sounds: there was no scutter of light paws, no rustlings and snufflings, not even the hoot of an owl. Only absolute quiet, absolute stillness. It seemed to her she was the only living thing in the park except for the strange half-life of plant and tree, and the idea reminded her uncomfortably of the site where she had met Stephane—the site which had appeared so bleak and empty. The Cable Star building had been unfinished; Stallibrass House was abandoned. Both tenantless . . . The shrubs

came to an end well before the house and it rose up from the
barren lawns in isolation as though no sapling would venture
near it. Wide black windows mirrored the moon. There were
no lights anywhere, no sign of Anthony. She knew a growing
urge to turn and run, an urge so strong it was almost panic—
but there was little chance of another taxi now and only a long
walk home. She had come this far: she might as well go on.
She mounted the steps to the front door, looking for the bell.
Then she saw the door was open. Like the gate, she thought.
She realized then that it had not been left unlocked out of
carelessness, but deliberately. For her, Fate pulling the strings.
She went in.

The click of the latch closing behind her coincided with a
sudden flood of light. Nicky blinked, turned.

Elsa was leaning against the door. The low-wattage bulb of
the type favoured by Miser Joe robbed her face of what little
colour it might have had and drew shadows under every jut of
bone. Nicky hadn't been expecting her but she wasn't really
surprised. Perhaps, in her subconscious, she had recognized the
voice over the phone, despite the unconvincing cockney, had
known, from the moment when Elsa spoke with Stephane's
words, that here was not only her enemy but her doom.

"I knew you'd come," Elsa said.

"I came to meet Anthony." But the statement held no real
conviction.

"You came to meet me," Elsa contended. "I sent for you."

A command, Nicky thought resentfully.

She said: "It was you, then. On the phone. It was you pre-
tending . . ."

"Of course it was. I wanted to see you. Alone. So I told you
to come here."

She walked down the hall and through a doorless opening
into what might have been a drawing-room. Nicky followed. A
sheer dark floor reflected a sheer pale ceiling; in between, heavy
curtains mantled the wall-length windows, and a huddle of
furniture was shrouded in dust-sheets. But there was no visible
dust, no cobwebs. The room was bare and untouched as if it
had been sealed in time; the long drapes of curtain and sheeting
hung as still as carvings. It was only when Nicky's roving gaze
focussed idly on a patch of wall that she saw the cracks in the
plaster and the discoloration around the skirting-board. She

thought: It all looks very new and modern but underneath it's crumbling away. The whole house seemed to her suddenly evil, a veneer of youth covering decay and corruption, like the picture of Dorian Gray. She was aware of a creeping smell, faint but definitely unpleasant: a smell at once familiar and unnatural. Not the kind of smell usually associated with an empty building. But as her senses grew accustomed it ceased to register.

She said: "Why here?"

Elsa did not answer. She pulled the dust-sheets aside and unveiled some chairs. "Take off your coat," she ordered. "Sit down."

Nicky took off her coat and sat. Opposite her, Elsa rested on the arm of a chair but did not take a seat. Both the position and her own height gave her the advantage; Nicky wanted to get up again but somehow she could not. She sat stiffly, fingers gripping the upholstery. "What is this all about?"

"You." There was a cold confidence in Elsa's voice. "You see, I know all about you. I had you investigated. I know about your activities in Paris—the man you drove to suicide—the boyfriend with whom you cheated on my father. I know you were once arrested for stealing. I know you married a French-Italian called Stephane Maglioli . . . and you never divorced him." Nicky started forward in her chair but Elsa gave her no chance to interrupt. "I know what you said to him before he fell to his death from the Cable Star building last week. I heard every word. I sent him to you. I found him and I sent him to you. I taped the whole conversation. You confessed to my father's murder—it's on the tape. *You confessed.*"

She was there, Nicky thought, somewhere in the holocaust of reaction. That's why Stephane was so nervous. She's been haunting me, manipulating me. Not Fate but Elsa.

She said: "I didn't mean—"

"Didn't you?" Elsa was on her feet, towering over her victim like a vengeful goddess. "It doesn't matter: don't you see? You struggled with Stephane, you pushed him off. No one will believe it was an accident. When they hear the tape they'll know you murdered him just as you murdered my father. I'll say you confronted me here and you tried to kill *me*. And they'll believe me—everyone will believe me."

"I tried to kill you—?"

"Of course." Her assurance was deadly. "Because of the tape. I told you about the tape, so you tried to kill me. It all fits."

"You're mad." Nicky stood up: she was trembling, but a measure of rationality had returned to her. Somehow, it made the situation simpler, knowing Elsa was mad. "I wouldn't kill you. I didn't kill anyone. I couldn't . . ."

"*You—killed—my—father!*" The more Elsa said it, the more she felt it was true. "You married him for his money and then you betrayed him. You tied him to a sickbed and mocked him with your saintly devotion—"

"I loved him!" Desperation lent the cry a genuine passion. "I tried so hard—I really did. He didn't love me—not even at the beginning. He didn't want a person: only a doll who looked and acted enough like Diana. In bed, he used to beat me. He was mad just as you're mad. The night we were married, he didn't make love to me, he raped me. He raped me and hit me and called me a whore. And do you know what name he used? Do you know? He said Diana—Diana—Diana—"

Elsa screamed. A scream with no words, only fury. Nicky saw her features distort; her hair seemed to writhe about her head. She shoved the chair in Elsa's path and ran.

In the hall, she made for the front door—hesitated—turned to the stairs. All reason had left her. Beyond the door lay the forsaken parkland, the lonely road. Upstairs, vacant rooms. She knew Elsa was close behind her but she did not look back. On the landing she glimpsed a bathroom. Bathrooms have locks. She flung herself inside, slammed the bolt home. She heard Elsa approaching, the clatter of her shoes on the uncarpeted floor. Then silence. On opposite sides of the door, both of them breathed and listened. Presently, Nicky heard the shoes walking away across the landing. She waited, her hand on the bolt, her heart hammering. A year or two seemed to crawl past. She would have to venture out some time soon. The house was deserted; even if she waited till dawn, no one would come. No help. She would have to help herself.

She sank to her knees on the tiles; her panting ceased; her pulse flagged. Her whole body was absorbed in listening. At last she expelled her breath in a sigh, rose slowly to her feet. Very carefully she began to coax back the bolt.

The landing was empty. A moonbeam slanted through a window and stretched towards the head of the stairs. Nicky tiptoed along, clinging to the wall. Below, the electric light had been switched off; the hall was a pit of darkness. There was not a footstep, not a rustle. Then she saw them on the top step, in a pool of silver. Elsa's shoes.

Nicky froze. So she was down there, down in the darkness, waiting for her. Shoeless and quiet as a cat. Cautiously Nicky inched her way back along the landing towards the refuge of the bathroom. Once again she was conscious of the smell, stealing up from below; her nostrils prickled. It was stronger now and she identified it easily: the smell of cars and garages. *Petrol.*

A locked bathroom was no refuge in a burning house.

Elsa's words returned to her with a new significance: "You tried to kill me." Past tense. Putting her in the past tense. "Everyone will believe me." Why? Because Nicky would not be there to contradict her . . .

She thought: I've got to get out. I've got to get out—

It was a big place: there must be other stairs, other exits. She crept round a corner and then took to her heels, forgetting all prudence. The passage appeared to run the length of the first floor, bending left and then left again. Nicky peered into the adjoining rooms but there was no way out, only pale mounds of sheeted furniture, curtains sagging from their rails, rolled carpets, stacked boxes. Through barren acres of glass the moon blinked and vanished, running with her, as close as her shadow. And then round another corner, at the end of the passage, she came at last on a second flight of stairs. She half ran, half fell down it, crossed a stretch of parquet, pushed back a sliding door. She was in a huge room where the windows had entirely swallowed up the walls; thin ribs of metal divided each vast pane from the next; through the ceiling she could see stars. The smell here was so strong that it had become a taste. It was a minute or two before she realized this must be a conservatory: scarcely any plants remained, only discarded pots piled one on top of another, an enormous spiny shape which might have been a species of palm, a hanging basket from which trailed a few brittle tendrils, like wisps of withered beard. The position of the moon might have told her she had come all the way round the central courtyard and was now almost back where she started: at the other end of the conservatory a second door led into the drawing-room where she had defied Elsa. But Nicky was past thinking of such things. She wanted only to get out.

She moved across the room to look for a way onto the terrace, knocking against an empty jardinière, halting in terror at the noise. Sap dripped from the dry plant onto the floor beside her. It smelt like paraffin. The fumes had begun to swim in her head. She found the door with difficulty and started to fumble with the spring lock. Thank God it didn't require a key . . .

The lights sprang up behind her without warning: three yellow orbs reflected again and again in the glass night on every side. Elsa was beyond her left shoulder, mirrored in the depths of the door. She seemed to be emerging from the darkness, approaching slowly and certainly; the light catching her hair formed a halo around her head. Nicky wrestled frantically with the lock but either it was jammed or haste made her clumsy. Elsa stopped, took something from her pocket. There was the *zzzip* of a match striking; a tiny flame sprang up in the glass. Nicky wheeled round.

"No—"

Elsa reached out: the flame curled round some shrunken leafy thing, dry as tinder. Nicky looked into her beautiful inhuman face and saw the eyes of Medusa.

"You're mad . . ."

The first trickle of paraffin ignited; a line of fire began to eat its way along the floors; sparks circled in the deadly air. Elsa seized Nicky's wrist, dragging her backwards. Nicky tried to wrench herself free—they collided with an earthenware jar, stumbled, crashed to the ground together. And then escape was forgotten and she was fighting as she had never fought in her life—as if all those times when fate had slapped her and she hadn't hit back were condensed into this one time, all those rages into one rage, and she kicked and clawed and pummelled in a frenzy beyond fear or thought. Elsa saw her enemy, her rival, the person she wanted to be—the antagonist who faced her at every turn, destroyed her every hope. She tore at hair and flesh and scarcely felt when her own hair and flesh were torn. Around them the flames leapt from wall to wall; the soaring panes began to splinter; the reflected inferno swallowed up the moon. Above their heads the hanging basket became a torch, dropping gobbets of fire. One landed on Elsa, turning her red curls into a living blaze. Nicky sprang back just in time. Scrambling to her feet, she saw a ring of flame closing around her, the door with its jammed lock in a narrowing gap. She

staggered towards it. The metal catch burned into her skin—
her foot drove through the glass just as the spring gave. Cold
air was sucked past her and somewhere in the background there
was an explosion. Then another. She stumbled out into the
night, glanced back—for a fraction of a second she saw the
room behind her all flame, and something on the floor that
reached out with blackened hands. She knew it was impossible
but she almost imagined it was moving, crawling through the
fire towards her . . . She fled across the terrace, blinded by the
sudden dark. She did not see the chasm of the empty swimming-pool waiting in front of her. The ground ceased: she
plunged forward, struck the bottom, rolled down the incline to
the deep end. She came to rest in the cleft of shadow beneath
the diving-board. A puddle of slimy rainwater licked her cheek;
last year's leaves clung damply to her hair.

EPILOGUE

She was in a small, bare room with no windows, sitting at a table. Her head ached and somehow she knew her mascara had run. Of course, that must have been the smoke from the fire. The smoke had stung her eyes and her mascara had run. She could feel the swollen lids pressing against her eyeballs. On the other side of the table, a policeman from long ago thrust his face towards her. "You common little sneak-thief," he was shouting, "do you really think you can fool *me?* It's on the tape. It's all on the tape—" His face grew huger and huger, distended veins empurpling his jowl. She struggled to escape but her fingers seemed to be glued to the arms of the chair. And then she saw the crack in the wall, and the flames creeping through the gap. She called for help but nobody heard. At last she managed to tear herself free of the chair, ripping the skin from her palms. She ran to the door and started to open it—but then she realized that Elsa must be just outside, Elsa with a box of matches setting fire to her own hair. A hand reached round the door towards her and it was black. Charred flesh flaked off the bones . . .

She jerked into waking, her heart thumping so hard she felt sick. Parts of the dream still clouded her brain. She registered the hospital room with its soothing cream-coloured walls, her bandaged hands on the coverlet. There was a nurse standing at the foot of the bed—not the nurse who had been there the previous night; another one. And looming over her, the face from her nightmare. Its complexion was no longer purple but turned to suet in the pallid light; its small eyes were fixed on her with unmistakable menace. Detective-Inspector Bullard. She sought to wake up, but the face remained, filling her vision, solid as fact.

"Lady Van Leer?"

She opened her mouth but only a kind of gasp came out. Elsa must have sent for him. Any moment now it would begin: the insults, the accusations, the dreaded interrogation technique. Any moment . . .

"Detective-Chief-Inspector Bullard." So he had been promoted. "I just wanted to ask you a few questions."

"I told you," the nurse interjected, "she may not remember what happened. Not for a while, anyway. She's suffering from shock as well as concussion."

"I'll be as brief as I can, miss. But it's a case of arson: I have to do my job."

It couldn't be just coincidence, Nicky thought, trying to hold on to an element of sanity. Even if it was—if the malignant gods had played this final trick on her—surely he must recognize her. Surely he could see—

"You went to meet your stepdaughter, Lady Van Leer: is that right?"

Nicky nodded, dumbly.

"The body was unidentifiable but when we found the car we were pretty sure it must be her. Wallet in the glove compartment—house plans on the passenger seat. Her boyfriend's place, wasn't it?"

"His family's," Nicky whispered.

"What was this meeting about? Anything special?" This was it. He must have discovered Elsa's tape. He must know everything.

"We'd had—there'd been some bad feeling." Nicky's lips shook; her usual glibness deserted her. "We wanted to straighten things out."

"Very sad." His sympathy was perfunctory. "No chance you saw anything of the arsonist, I suppose?"

"No . . ."

"Didn't think so. We'll be lucky to get this one. Probably local boys, high on dope and out for a lark. Big house like that, lying empty for years—it's God's gift to vandals. You didn't see them and I daresay they didn't see you. The Brigade say the fire started in the conservatory. Why couldn't you get out the front?"

Nicky took a glass of water clumsily in one bandaged hand. The nurse moved forward to assist her. When she had drunk, she said: "We—we didn't see the fire. Not till it was too late. I mean, we just walked into it."

Incredibly, impossibly, he was closing his notebook, heaving himself to his feet. "All right. I'll be sending someone to take a proper statement when you're feeling stronger. Sorry to trouble you, Lady Van Leer."

Lady Van Leer, rich widow of the great Sir Rupert: a far cry from a little blonde typist accused of pinching a diamond ring all those years ago . . .

When he had gone Nicky lay back on her pillows and eventually her racing pulse began to subside.

Her next visitor came two days later. Michael Kovacs. His right arm was in a sling and two black eyes did little to improve a face Nicky had never considered particularly attractive. She said, startled: "You too?"

"Me too." He sat down beside the bed. "A bruise on the forehead drops: hence the black eyes. I'm surprised you haven't got them."

"My bruise is round the side." She had a vague idea he had once been close to Elsa, but the exact nature of their relationship eluded her. She had never much liked him, rarely thought about him. She tried to think now but her mind was still functioning badly. "What happened to you?"

"I fell off a balcony."

"Not?" She had spoken before she could stop herself, the Cable Star building vivid in her memory. But Michael understood.

"Not a Van Leer balcony, not this time. One of more plebeian design. A tree broke my fall. They say I'm lucky to be alive." He paused. "So are you."

"I suppose so."

"Vandals, wasn't it? I gather that's the official theory."

"I . . . suppose so."

"Why didn't you tell them the truth?"

She said nothing, merely staring at him out of lustreless eyes. He noticed her hair straggled unevenly, maybe singed in the fire; against the fading auburn her small face was pale and shadow-lined.

He remarked thoughtfully: "Perhaps lying has become a matter of principle for you: is that it? Or—were you afraid of what else might come out?" He tugged something out of his pocket, tossed it on the bed. A tape. "You might like to have this."

Nicky picked it up.

"Did Elsa tell you about it?" Michael asked.

"Yes."

"Well, this is the only copy. Do what you like with it. I'm sick of the whole business." He sounded sick. Exhausted and sick. Not like a blackmailer.

Nicky said: "What do you want?"

Michael sighed. "The truth. Not for the police or the press or the public. Just for me. I want to know what actually happened, that night at Stallibrass House. I—*need* to know." He flipped the cassette with one finger. "Is it a bargain?"

She told him.

He sat there, fiddling with the sling, his head bent. She didn't try to see his expression. Even to Nicky, it would have seemed somehow indecent.

Finally, she asked: "Why did she do it?" Michael would know, she thought. He might not explain everything, but he would know.

"Oh . . . she wasn't only trying to kill you. In a way, that was incidental. She wanted to destroy the house. It was substandard—you wouldn't appreciate the details. She thought if she destroyed it, she could save her father's reputation. A wasted gesture. The foundations are still there . . ." For a moment, his mouth grew set. "She told me once, she loved that house. She talked about its originality, its innovative style. All bullshit. She loved it because it was his. She loved it and she destroyed it. Elsa destroyed everything she loved. And love—destroyed *her.*"

"It was quick," Nicky lied. "I'm sure it was quick."

She was a good liar. Michael believed her.

"Thanks," he said when he left. "You know whatever you decide to do, I won't interfere. It's up to you."

She thought about that later. She had a lot of time to think, in hospital. It was up to her. Here at the end, at the beginning, it was up to her. She had her inheritance, uncontested now. She had the incriminating tape. Chief-Inspector Bullard had not recognized her and her first marriage was buried with Stephane. *She had survived.* Of course, there was Alex: fortunately, she hadn't confided in him but as long as the money was there he would never let go. And perhaps Anthony was available—if he cared, if she cared, if the spectre of Elsa did not divide them. The past might be excluded but it could not be expunged. She could have it all.

It was up to her.

When she came out of hospital, Nicky went into the offices of Langley and Mayhew and signed away all claim to the Van Leer fortune.

She did it as quickly as the legal process would allow, giving herself no leisure for second thoughts. She didn't explain her motives and Mr. Mayhew was too stunned to inquire. She hadn't stopped to speculate on how she was going to manage. She could sell her jewellery: that would last her a fair while. Anyway, what did it matter?—she was used to being broke. Afterwards, when it was done, she felt light-headed and dizzy, elated and scared. She was free—free of all ghosts and all ties, free to go where she wished, to do what she wanted. A graceful exit—a new start. She would go to Australia or America: wasn't that what heroines did in books? She would get on a plane and soar up towards the sun, or stand in the stern of a ship, watching the wild waves and the white cliffs and the seagulls rolling away behind her, until they vanished into a blue mist over the edge of the world. She would have mountains and deserts and skyscrapers, shipboard romances, glamourous tycoons. Adventure. Her airy heart, light-winged as a butterfly, unburdened by love or hate, lifted easily in anticipation.

Alex arrived at the flat one afternoon when she was packing. Her singed hair was cut much shorter, no longer red but a streaky blonde. Her hands were blotched and puckered with burns, but she had been assured that these would disappear. Her emerald ring had gone.

"Have a drink," she said carelessly. "You know where it is."

He looked at the suitcases, frowning. "What is all this? You have no need to run away. Not now."

"I'm not running away."

"What, then?"

"I'm *leaving*."

"*Quelle merde*." Alex was scornful. "It's the same thing. Sit down, Nikki; talk to me. Stop panicking."

"I haven't panicked." She shook off his outstretched hand. "I mean it. I'm leaving. I've made too many mistakes. I just want to scrap everything and start again."

"A new life?" His smile was like a blight on her courage. "My poor Nikki! they all say that: didn't you know? No more lying, no more stealing—a fresh start. *T'es pas si bête*. The new life will be just like the old because the new Nikki will be just like the old. You cannot change yourself. You'll see. Besides, what about the money? The lawyers must still be squabbling over it. These things take time to sort out."

"It's sorted out. I'm leaving that too." Resolution or obstinacy tightened her lips, making her small mouth grow smaller.

He drew back, uncertain—tried a short laugh.

"It's a joke—isn't it? A stupid joke . . ."

"No joke." Her voice was hard, concealing inward doubts. "I gave it back."

"Back to whom?" For an instant, there was rage in his face. She thought he might strike her; but Alex was not naturally violent. He would always prefer to mock rather than to fight.

"I don't know. To whoever wants it. *I* don't. That money has brought me so much trouble, so much horror . . . I've had enough of it. I'm leaving here, I'm leaving the money, and I'm leaving you. That's all."

His rage had faded, to be replaced by a mixture of bewilderment and calculation. He was staring at her as if she were afflicted by some disfiguring disease.

At last he asked with a curious uncertainty: "Why are you really going, Nikki? What are you afraid of?"

"I'm not afraid. I'm not afraid of anything any more."

"I see . . ." What did he see? "I read about the inquest on Elsa Van Leer. They said the fire was started by vandals. And there was the old woman who was so much in the way—in *your* way. And Rupert . . .''

Nicky saw the same look in his eyes that she had seen in Stephane's when she had almost admitted to murder. A germ of fear, a grudging respect. She thought: Rupert died naturally, Mrs. Skerritt was killed in an accident, Elsa set the fire herself. She knew a sudden impulse to laugh hysterically.

Her mouth stayed tight, her expression inscrutable.

"I never thought . . ." He stopped, evidently reluctant to state his suspicions too clearly.

"You never thought what?" Nicky enquired with a new touch of coolness.

But Alex did not answer. Instead he murmured: "*La pauvre* Elsa. What did she know, I wonder? And why are you choosing to quit—*now?* Have you left a clue someone else could find?"

"Go and look," Nicky said, secure in her innocence, revelling in her deception.

He caught the sparkle in her eyes and thought he knew what it meant. Nicky, for her part, saw him for once nonplussed, taken at a disadvantage. She believed she had even shocked him. He might imagine her slipping Rupert an extra tablet or two in a moment of weakness, but it was something else to credit her with the planning and execution of no less than three successful murders. For the first time in their relationship, she sensed she was in command. If she told him to go now, he would go. For ever.

"Are you sure you won't have a drink?" she offered gracefully.

Alex seemed to flinch. Then he summoned up the glimmer of a smile, the flicker of a sneer. "Why not?"

His gaze followed her like that of a nervous animal while she unscrewed the cap on the bottle, splashed whisky into a glass.

"Join me," he suggested.

"No," Nicky said lightly. "I don't like whisky."

She remembered another occasion when he had joked about accepting her liquor. This time, he gazed into the glass for a long moment before he drank. Then he drained it to the dregs. It was a gesture of defiance, of bravado, a toast to the Devil. But there was doubt in his face.

"Goodbye, Nikki," he said. "I don't think we'll meet again."

"I don't think so," she affirmed softly. "Goodbye."

Adieu Alex. Goodbye for good.

He put down the glass rather quickly, as though it burnt him.
She saw him to the door. When he had gone she poured herself
a gin and sat down amidst her new luggage. Then she began
to laugh.

Michael heard of Nicky's action with little interest. He had
been to Elsa's funeral, in the village church near Churston
Grange, had stood at the back in his old flying-jacket, unre-
markable and unremarked. It was the first real spring day:
there was a clump of daffodils by the lych-gate, a softness in
the air, a green shimmer in the trees where the leaf-buds were
thinking of unfolding. Unlike the chill ceremony for Rupert,
this was well attended: acquaintances from London, locals, the
inevitable flock of journalists. A funeral, Michael reflected
wryly, is the only social occasion where the host cannot object
to gatecrashers. And here they all were, come to enjoy the tragedy. Elsa had been young, beautiful and potentially brilliant,
and the vicar could not fail to dwell on it. Handkerchiefs were
out among the congregation, pencils among the press. Recent
headlines had suggested a scenario reminiscent of *The Fall of
the House of Usher*. Michael was not sorry to note that Anthony
Stallibrass attracted most of the attention: the expression of
suffering induced by grief and publicity gave him the look of
an unflinching Romeo, whose stiff upper lip preluded either
self-dramatization or suicide. He was supported by a half-caste
girl, not pretty but with a kind of serenity in her dusky face
and thick fall of dark hair. He must have had enough of redheads by now, Michael thought. A wave of loathing rushed over
him for what he saw as the hypocrisy of Anthony's lifestyle, his
affectation of martyrdom. Michael's contempt was so strong it
was almost hatred. He looked round at the mourners, both
friends and strangers, and they appeared to him like the audience at a play, wallowing in the luxury of a secondhand sorrow. None of them had known Elsa as he did. None of them
ever would. He would take her secrets to his own grave. His
eyes were dry and his heart was dry and his spirit was as empty
as a desert.

In the weeks that followed he found it hard to work, harder
to sleep. He called the solicitors and offered to help sort out
Elsa's things: Mr. Mayhew, with a vast fortune on his hands

and the remaining Van Leers scattered throughout the remoter parts of Southern Africa, was only too glad to accept. Michael went to her flat and rifled through old letters, mostly from Barbara Heydon, forms and bank statements and the assorted garbage of modern life. There was even a bundle of Diana's letters from school, written in a rounded childish script and betraying, at times, a tell-tale anxiety. "You mustn't listen to Aunty Grizzle, you know what she is. You're *not* fat, just a little plump, and Matron says it's natural for some adolescents and you'll grow out of it soon. Anyway, there's a girl here called Sapphira Cavendish who's much fatter than you . . ."

At the back of a drawer he found an envelope containing a sheaf of sketches. On the top was a drawing of a head, the lineaments distorted as though to express some concept of Elsa's rather than to conform to the standard rules of portraiture. Presumably it was an idea for a sculpture: even on paper it appeared three-dimensional, solid, with a suggestion of pain in the impress of every line—not the pain of the subject but the pain of the artist. Bone and feature seemed to have been twisted from iron wire, pummelled into clay, hammered into rock. The expression was wry and somehow sad but behind it was a core of hardness, a steadfast quality which, he was sure, would have been conveyed far more clearly by the actual sculpture. He looked at it for several minutes before he realized it was himself.

Elsa had never done portraits, he reflected. Only that blank mask of Nicky which he thought she had later destroyed. She must have done this from memory: he had not sat for her and she had no photograph. This was her inner vision of him, the image of feeling rather than sight. Across the bottom she had scrawled a single word: *Reality* . . .

He laid the paper in his lap and buried his face in the crook of his arm, so the light should not fall on his tears.

UNPROFESSIONAL
ACKNOWLEDGEMENTS

I should like to thank my mother for the typing, my father for the architectural background, Graham Midmer, of Lloyd's Bank, Lewes, for financing me, Twinings for their Rose Pouchong and Earl Grey teas on which I subsisted, and Channel IV News for keeping me in touch with the world.